D1315490

ZULU

Caryl Férey

ZULU

*Translated from the French
by Howard Curtis*

Europa
editions

East Baton Rouge Parish Library
Baton Rouge, Louisiana

35127956

Europa Editions
116 East 16th Street
New York, N.Y. 10003
www.europaeditions.com
info@europaeditions.com

This book is a work of fiction. Any references to historical events,
real people, or real locales are used fictitiously.

Copyright © 2008 by Éditions Gallimard, Paris
First Publication 2010 by Europa Editions

Translation by Howard Curtis
Original title: *Zulu*
Translation copyright © 2010 by Europa Editions

All rights reserved, including the right of reproduction
in whole or in part in any form.

Library of Congress Cataloging in Publication Data is available
ISBN 978-1-933372-88-4

Férey, Caryl
Zulu

Book design by Emanuele Ragnisco
www.mekkanografici.com
Cover photo © by Marco Morosini

Prepress by Plan.ed – Rome

Printed in Canada

CONTENTS

ZULU

Be the tiny blade upon the grass:
greater than the spindle of the whole world's mass . . .

—Attila József
(translated by Zsuzsanna Ozsváth and Frederick Turner)

*To my friend Fred Couderc
whose giant's wings taught me to fly
and his wife, Laurence,
a nervous glider.*

*Zone Libre,
for the sound—full volume.*

PART ONE
THE HOT HAND

1.

*A*re you scared, little man? . . . Tell me, are you scared?"
Ali said nothing—too many vipers in his mouth. " You
see what happens, little Zulu? You see?"

*No, he didn't see anything. They'd grabbed him by the roots
of his hair and dragged him out to the tree in the garden to make
him look, but Ali stubbornly kept his head down between his
shoulders. The words of the giant in the ski mask hit the back of
his neck. He didn't want to look up. Or scream. The noise of the
torches crackled in his ears. The man gripped his scalp tight in
his callous hand.*

"You see, little Zulu?"

*The body was swaying like a damp rag from the branch of the
jacaranda tree. The torso glistened dimly in the moonlight, but
Ali didn't recognize the face. This man hanging by his feet, this
bloodstained smile over him, wasn't his father. No, it wasn't him.*

Not really.

Not anymore.

The sjambok[1] *cracked again.*

*They were all here, they'd all gathered for the kill, the "Green
Beans" who'd been formed to keep order in the townships, these
blacks in the pay of the mayors who'd sold out to the authorities,
and the warlords, and the others, too, the ones who broke the boycott and got their ears cut off. Ali wanted to beg them, to tell them
there was no point, they were wrong, but in his throat there was
emptiness. The giant was still holding him.*

[1] Whip.

"Look, little man. Look!"

His breath stank of beer and the poverty of the Bantustan.[2]
*He struck again, twice, great stinging blows that tore his father's
flesh, but the man hanging from the tree no longer reacted. Too
much blood lost. Skin hanging off him. Unrecognizable. The real
world cracked open. Ali floating weightless to the other end of
the sky. This wasn't his father. No.*

*They twisted his skull like a screw and flung him to the
ground. Ali fell on the dry grass. He didn't recognize the men
around him, the giants were wearing stockings and ski masks,
and all he could see was the rage in their eyes, their vessels bursting like rivers of blood. He hid his head in his hands, trying to
bury himself in them, to curl up and disintegrate, become amni-
otic fluid again. A few feet away, Andy was weakening by the
minute. He was still wearing the red shorts he wore at night, all
soaked in urine, and his knees were knocking together. His
hands had been tied behind his back and a tire placed around his
neck. The ogres were shoving him, spitting in his face, shouting
abuse, vying with each other to find the right formula, the best
reason to justify killing him. Andy was looking at them, his eyes
popping out of their sockets.*

*Ali had never before seen Andy lose his nerve—Andy was fif-
teen, his big brother. Of course they often fought, much to their
mother's displeasure, but Ali was just a kid and couldn't defend
himself. They preferred to go fishing, or play with the little cars
they made out of barbed wire. Peugeot, Mercedes, Ford, Andy
was an expert. They'd even put together a Jaguar, an English car
they'd seen in a magazine that fired their imagination. Now his
knock-knees were shivering in the torchlight, the garden where
they had dragged him stank of gasoline, and the giants were
arguing around the cans. In the distance, out on the street, people were shouting,* Amagoduka[3] *from the country who didn't*

[2] Blacks-only enclave during the apartheid period.
[3] Migrant workers.

know what was being done to their neighbors, didn't know that a necklacing was in progress.

Andy was weeping, his tears black on his ebony skin, his red shorts damp with fear . . . Ali saw his brother stagger when they threw a match on the gasoline-soaked tire.

"You see what happens, little man! You see!"

A scream, the gasoline running down his cheeks, the twisted figure of his brother fading, melting like a rubber soldier, and that horrible smell of burned flesh . . .

The birds were describing impossible diagonals between the edges of the cliff, swooping down suicidally toward the ocean, then coming back up again in a flurry of feathers.

From his vantage point on the platform, Ali Neuman watched the freighters passing on the horizon. Dawn was coming up over the Cape of Good Hope, orange and blue in the Indian Ocean's spectrum. He only came to see the whales when he couldn't sleep—humpback whales, which came from September onward to frolic at the tip of Africa. Ali had once seen a couple of them after mating, going under for a long, amorous dive, and coming back to the surface covered in foam. The presence of the whales brought him a kind of peace, as if their strength was somehow transmitted to him. But the mating season was over—forever. Daylight was breaking through the sea mist, and they wouldn't come, not this morning, not tomorrow.

The whales were hiding from him.

The whales had vanished into the icy seas—they, too, were afraid of the Zulu.

The abyss beckoned, but Neuman turned away and walked back down the path. The Cape of Good Hope was deserted at this hour—no buses, no Chinese tourists posing politely in front of the legendary signpost. There was only the wind from the Atlantic blowing over the bare heath, and the familiar ghosts chasing one another in the dawn, and the desire to do battle with the whole world. A deep rage. Even the baboons in the park were keeping their distance.

Neuman walked across the heath as far as the entrance to Table Mountain National Park. The car was waiting on the other side of the barrier, dusty and insignificant. The sea air had soothed him a little. But it wouldn't last. Nothing ever lasted. He stopped thinking, and switched on the ignition.

The important thing was to keep going.

2.

B *ass! Bass!*"[1]
The blacks in their torn espadrilles clinging to the guardrail were waiting for the traffic to slow down to sell their wares.

The N2 linked Cape Town proper with Khayelitsha, its largest township. Beyond Mitchell's Plain, built by the coloreds expelled from the white zones, stretched an area of dunes, and it was on this sandy plain that the apartheid government had decided to build Khayelitsha, "new house," a model of social planning, South African style—in other words, as far from the center of the city as possible.

In spite of the chronic overcrowding, Josephina refused to move, not even to the well-equipped settlement of Mandela Park, south of the township, which had been built for the emerging black middle class—beneath her blind smiles and her unfailing kindness, Neuman's mother was as stubborn as a mule. It was here they had both found refuge, twenty years before, in the old neighborhoods that made up the heart of Khayelitsha.

Josephina lived in one of the core houses[2] on Lindela, the township's main thoroughfare, and didn't complain, even though there were often five or six people sharing the same space, which consisted of a bedroom, a kitchen, and a cramped bathroom that she had agreed to have enlarged now that she was older. Josephi-

---

[1] Boss.
[2] Small, solidly built houses intended to be enlarged.

na was happy in her way. She had running water, electricity, and, thanks to her son, "all the comforts a seventy-year-old blind woman could dream of." Josephina wouldn't budge from Khayelitsha, and it had nothing to do with her huge size.

In the end, Neuman had stopped insisting. They needed her experience—Josephina was a qualified nurse—her advice, her faith. The team at the dispensary where she worked as a volunteer did what it could to tend the sick, and, whatever she said, Josephina wasn't completely blind—even though she couldn't see faces clearly anymore, she could still make out shapes, she called them her "shadows." Was it her way of saying she was slowly leaving the surface of this world? Neuman found that hard to accept. They were the only survivors of the family, and there wouldn't be any others. The props had been blown away from under him, and his mother was all he had left.

Neuman worked too hard, but he always came to see Josephina on Sundays. He'd help her fill out papers, and then stroke her hand and take her to task about how they were going to find her lying dead on the street if she kept running around the township from morning to night. She would laugh, and say through her sputtering that she was getting old and had let herself go so much that they'd soon need a crane to move her around, and he, too, would end up laughing. To humor her.

A hot wind was blowing through the windows of the car as Neuman passed the Sanlam Center bus terminal and turned onto Lansdowne Street. Corrugated iron, wooden planks, old doors turned upside down, bricks, scrap iron—they built with whatever was around, whatever they could pick up, steal, exchange. The slums seemed to be heaped one on top of the other, the tangled aerials on their roofs engaged in a battle to the death under a leaden sun. Neuman drove along the asphalt road leading to the old part of Khayelitsha.

He was thinking about the women he had never brought home to his mother, and about Maia, who he'd go to see after Sunday lunch, when something he glimpsed out of the corner of his eye jolted him out of his thoughts. He braked, just in front of a cigarette vendor, who had no time to approach him before Neuman reversed some twenty yards as far as the waste ground.

Behind the row of multicolored ribbons that marked off the site of the future gymnasium, two young guys were roughing up a kid, a filthy, emaciated little kid who could barely stand. Neuman sighed—he was early, they wouldn't be coming out of church yet—and opened the door.

They'd thrown the kid to the ground, and were kicking him and trying to drag him over to the foundations. Neuman walked toward them, hoping he'd scare them away, but they kept right on going—two tattooed guys in bandanas who looked like *tsotsis*.[3] The kid had his face in the dust, there was blood trickling from his mouth, and his scrawny arms certainly couldn't protect him from the kicks.

The older of the two guys looked up and saw Neuman coming onto the waste ground.

"What do you want?"

"You two, get out of here."

Neuman was bigger than the two *tsotsis* combined, but the older one had a gun under his yellow Brazil T-shirt.

"No, you get out of here," he hissed, "pronto!"

The young black aimed his revolver at his face, a Beretta M92 semiautomatic, similar to the ones the police used.

"Where did you get that gun?"

The *tsotsi*'s hand was shaking, his eyes translucent. High as a kite, probably.

"Where did you get that gun?" Neuman repeated.

"I told you to get out of here, or I'll put a bullet in you!"

"Yeah," his associate said. "Leave it alone, O.K.?"

[3] Township gangsters.

On the ground, the boy was holding his mouth, making sure he had all his teeth.

"I'm a police officer. Give me that gun now and I won't come down on you hard."

The two guys exchanged evil glances and a few words in Dashiki, the Nigerian dialect.

"You know what, I'm going to blow your head off!" the older one said.

"And spend the rest of your life in jail playing wife to the big shots," Neuman went on. "With that pretty face of yours, there'll be plenty of cocks for you to suck."

That hit home. They both bared their teeth, dirty rows that looked more like trenches.

"Asshole!" the leader said, before turning and walking off.

His associate followed him, limping badly. Clearly both junkies. Neuman turned to their victim, but there was just a pulpy mess on the ground. The boy had taken advantage of the altercation to crawl as far as the foundations of the gymnasium. Now he was moving away as fast as he could, his nose running with blood.

"Wait! Don't be afraid!"

At these words, the boy threw a terrified glance at Neuman, stumbled over the rubble in his tire-rubber sandals, plunged into a length of concrete piping, and disappeared. Neuman approached and took a look at the circumference of the pipe. The opening was too narrow for an adult as big as he was to squeeze in. Did it lead anywhere? He called into the darkness, but there was no response.

He stood up, dispelling the smell of cold piss. Apart from a mangy dog sniffing the stagnant water in the foundations, the site was deserted. There was only the sun and that trail of blood in the dust.

The township of Khayelitsha had changed since Mandela

had come to power. Apart from water, electricity, and tarred roads, little brick houses had sprung up alongside administrative buildings, and you could now go to the center of the city from here by public transportation. Many people criticized the "one step at a time" policy instituted by the nation's icon, hundreds of thousands of households still lived in poverty, but that was the price to pay for the "South African miracle"—the peaceful transition to democracy of a country on the verge of chaos.

Neuman parked his car in front of the area of parched earth that constituted his mother's garden. The local women were coming back from Mass, nicely dressed in the colors of their congregation. He looked for Josephina amid all the frills, but saw only kids under the sunshades. He knocked, and opened the door. The first thing he saw was the torn blouse on a chair.

"Come in!" she called, hearing his steps in the hall. "Come in, son!"

Neuman found his mother in the bedroom, lying in the rumpled bed with a nurse bending over her. Josephina's forehead was bathed in sweat, but she smiled when she saw him in the doorway.

"There you are."

He took the hand she held out to him, and sat down on the edge of the bed. "What happened?" he asked anxiously.

His mother's eyes widened, as if he was everywhere. "Don't make that face," she said softly. "You're not so handsome when you're angry."

"I thought you were blind. Well?"

"Your mother blacked out," the nurse said from the other side of the bed. "Her blood pressure's fine, but please don't upset her: she's still in shock."

Miriam was a beautiful twenty-year-old Xhosa with eyes the color of cedar. Neuman barely noticed her.

"Are you going to tell me what happened, yes or no?"

Josephina had swapped her nice dress for an old housecoat, not exactly her Sunday best.

"Did someone attack you?"

"Pooh!" She made a disgusted gesture, as if chasing away flies.

"Your mother was attacked this morning on her way to church," Miriam said. "The attacker knocked her to the ground and took her bag. They found her unconscious in the middle of the street."

"It was more of a surprise than anything else," his mother said, patting his hand. "But don't worry: I was more scared than hurt! Miriam took care of everything."

Neuman sighed. Among her many activities, Josephina was a member of a street committee whose job it was to settle family problems, arbitrate disputes, and liaise with the local authorities. Everyone knew her son was the head of Cape Town's Crime Unit—attacking her was like putting your head in the lion's mouth.

Josephina lay there on the white sheets of the four-poster bed—a crazy idea of hers, as if she was a Zulu princess—her face drained of color and covered in sweat. Neuman wasn't convinced by her attempts to smile.

"The idiot could have broken your bones," he said.

"I may be fat, but I'm solid."

"A force of nature, specializing in blackouts," he said. "Where does it hurt?"

"It doesn't . . . No, it's true!" She moved her hands like an old tree waving its branches in the wind.

"Your son's right," Miriam said, putting away her instruments. "Now, you really need to rest."

"Pooh . . ."

"How many attackers were there?" he asked. "One or two?"

"Oh, just one. One was enough!"

"What did he steal?"

"Just my bag. He also tore my blouse, but that doesn't matter, it was an old one!"

"You were lucky."

Through the window, the local kids were checking out Neuman's car and laughing. Miriam pulled on the curtains, plunging the little room into semi-darkness.

"What time did it happen?" Neuman went on.

"About eight," Josephina replied.

"That's a bit early to go to church."

"The thing is . . . I was going to the Sussilus first, for our monthly meeting . . . I was in charge of the tontine . . . Sixty-five rand."

His mother also belonged to several associations—savings clubs, burial societies, the association of parish mothers—so many, he couldn't keep up with them. Neuman frowned—it was already after ten.

"Why wasn't I informed about this?"

"Your mother wouldn't hear of it," the nurse replied.

"I didn't want to worry you over nothing," Josephina said by way of justification.

"I've never heard anything more stupid. Did you tell the township police?"

"No . . . No, it all happened so quickly, you see. The attacker came up behind me, grabbed hold of my bag, and I fell and fainted. A neighbor found me. But whoever it was had long gone."

"That doesn't explain why the police haven't sent anyone to talk to you."

"I didn't report it."

"What!"

"She never listens to anyone," Miriam said. "You should know all about that, right?"

In fact, it was Neuman who wasn't listening. "And why exactly didn't you report it?"

"Look at me. I'm fine!"

Josephina's laughter shook the bed and made her big breasts quiver. The attack, the fall, the blackout—it all seemed to her like another continent.

"There may be witnesses," Neuman went on. "They need to take a statement from you."

"What could a blind old woman tell the police? And anyway, sixty-five rand is so little, there's no point getting worked up over it!"

"That's not Christian charity, it's foolishness."

"My boy," his mother said, affectionately, "my darling boy—"

He cut her off. "Just because you're blind doesn't mean I can't see what you're playing at."

His mother had radar in her fingertips, sensors in her ears, and eyes in the back of her head. She had been living in the neighborhood for more than twenty years, she knew its people, its streets, its dead ends. She must have some idea of her attacker's identity, and the way she was trying to downplay the attack made him think there was a reason she wasn't saying anything.

"Well?"

"I don't like to insist, Mr. Neuman," the nurse said, "but your mother has just had a sedative, and it's going to start to take effect."

"I'll see you outside," he said, anxious to get her out of the house.

Miriam raised her eyebrows, two impeccable arabesques, and picked up her bag. "I'll be back this evening," she said to Josephina. "In the meantime, you rest, O.K.?"

"Thank you, sweetheart," the old woman nodded from the four-poster.

It was the first time Miriam had met Josephina's beloved son. A slim, powerful body, fine, regular features, closely cropped hair, elegant, dark, piercing eyes, the kind of lips you might dream about—exactly the way his mother had described him. Neuman waited until the young Xhosa had left, then stroked the hand of this stubborn woman he loved so much.

"The person who attacked you," he said, following the line of her veins. "You know him, don't you?"

Josephina closed her eyes, still smiling. She wanted to lie, but his hand felt so warm in hers.

"You know him, don't you?" he insisted.

She sighed from the depths of the bed, as if the past were present—Ali had the same hands as his father.

"It's his mother I knew," she admitted at last. "Nora Mceli. A friend of Mary's."

Mary was the cousin who had taken them in when they had fled to Khayelitsha from the Bantustan of KwaZulu. As for her friend Nora Mceli, she was a *sangoma*, a healer, who had treated him once for a terrible sore throat. Neuman remembered a woman with eyes like an angry ox who, with the aid of a great many concoctions, had finally managed to tear out the ball of fire burning his throat.

"We lost touch after Mary died, but Nora had a son," Josephina went on. "He was with her at the funeral. Simon. Don't you remember?"

"No. Is that who attacked you—Simon?"

Josephine nodded, almost shamefacedly.

"Does his mother still practice?"

"I don't know," she said. "Nora and Simon left the township a few months ago, from what I heard. The last time I saw them was at Mary's funeral. Simon must have been nine at the time. A sweet kid, but not in good health. I treated him once at the dispensary. The poor boy had a heart murmur, and suffered from asthma attacks. Not even Nora could do anything. Maybe that's why they left the township. Ali"—here she squeezed his big male hand—"Nora helped us when we needed help. I can't report her son. You do understand that? And besides, to attack an old woman like me, you really must be in a bad way, don't you think?"

"Or a complete coward," he said, through clenched teeth.

Josephina always had excuses for everyone. She'd been listening to too many sermons.

"I'm sure Simon doesn't remember me," she said gallantly.

"That would surprise me."

With her rustling white dresses, her size, and her walking stick, Josephina was about as inconspicuous as the northern lights. He saw her cheap trinkets on the night table, her photos of him—she was all he had in this charnel house of a world.

"Was Simon alone when he attacked you?"

"Yes."

"Does he belong to a gang?"

"So I heard."

"What did you hear exactly?"

"Just that he was hanging out with other street kids."

"Where?"

"I don't know. But if he's wandering the streets like they say, something must have happened to his mother."

He nodded gently. Josephina yawned despite herself, revealing the few good teeth she still had left. The sedatives were taking effect.

"O.K., I'll see what I can do." He kissed her on her forehead. "Now sleep. I'll be back this evening, to see how you're doing."

The old woman chuckled, at once sorry and delighted to be the center of attention.

Nicolas adjusted the curtains, to make the room completely dark.

"By the way," she whispered behind him. "What do you think of Miriam?"

The young nurse was waiting outside the house, her slender figure standing out against the painted sky.

"A real tub of lard," he said.

3

Oscar and Josephina had their second child the day after the historic fight in Kinshasa in November 1973. That night, amid scenes of indescribable chaos, Muhammad Ali, the boxer who'd converted to Islam, had confronted George Foreman, who everyone thought was unbeatable. It wasn't so much the world heavyweight championship that had been at stake in the fight as the assertion of black identity, and the proof, through fists, that the struggle for black rights was not in vain. That night, Muhammad Ali, who hadn't boxed much since his trouble with the draft board, had defeated the brute strength of Foreman, the champion of white America, demonstrating that power could be overturned, as long as you fought with intelligence and determination.

The message, coming as it did during the worst days of apartheid, had galvanized Oscar. The child would have the same name as the champion—Ali. Josephina thought it was a nice name, Oscar saw it as a premonition.

Oscar was an educated man, and didn't have much truck with old wives' tales, but the *amaDlozi*, the venerable ancestors, had surely leaned over their new son's cradle. Like the boxer who had defended the black cause, their son would be a champion—in everything he did.

And in fact, Ali Neuman had risen to be head of the Crime Unit of the Cape Town police not through positive discrimination but simply because he'd been better than anyone else. More gifted. Quicker on his feet. Even the old redneck cops, the ones who'd followed orders, the lechers, the permanent drunks, thought he was pretty smart—for a *kaffir*.[1] The others, those who knew him only by reputation, saw him as a tough customer, the descendant of some Zulu chief, not someone you'd want to provoke over anything racial. The blacks had suffered most from a third-rate education[2] and remained a minority among the intellectual elite. Neuman had shown them that he was descended not from the monkey but from the tree, just like them—which didn't mean he was a pussycat.

Walter Sanogo, the captain in charge of the Harare police station, knew who Ali Neuman was. The white man's pet. You just had to see the cut of his suit—no one here could afford clothes like that. It wasn't that Sanogo felt jealous, they simply lived in different worlds.

Designed to accommodate two hundred thousand people, Khayelitsha now had a million, maybe two—or three. After the squatters, the homeless from the other overcrowded townships, and the migrant workers, Khayelitsha was now absorbing refugees from all over Africa.

"If your mother doesn't report her attacker," he said, "I don't see how I can bring anyone in for questioning. I understand how angry you are after what happened to her, but gangs of street kids are as common as crickets these days."

The fan was humming in the captain's office. Sanogo was about fifty, with a nasty scar at the side of his nose, his shoulders sagging wearily beneath his uniform. Half of the wanted notices above his head were a year or two old.

"Simon Mceli's mother was a *sangoma*," Neuman said. "She seems to have left the township, but not her son. If Simon is part of a street gang now, we should be able to track him down."

The captain sighed regretfully. It wasn't that he didn't want

[1] A black.
[2] In 1983, President Botha extended the civil rights of coloreds (persons of mixed race) and Indians, but not those of blacks, who saw this as an insult.

to help, but there was nothing he could do. Every day, more or less, in groups or alone, people in flight from somewhere else arrived in the township, people who had seen their fields burned, their houses pillaged, their friends killed, their wives raped in front of their families, people who had been driven from their homes by petroleum, epidemics, droughts, violent coups, and genocides, people with misfortune snapping at their heels, terrified people who, out of some instinct for survival, converged on the peaceful Cape province. Khayelitsha had become a buffer between Cape Town, "the most beautiful city in the world," and the rest of sub-Saharan Africa. A hundred? A thousand? Two thousand? Walter Sanogo didn't know how many arrived each day, but Khayelitsha was going to explode with all these refugees.

"I've got two hundred men here," he said. "And hundreds of thousands of inhabitants. Frankly, if your mother doesn't have any medical complications, let it go. I'll tell my men to give some of these kids a talking-to, and they'll get the word out."

"A gang of kids that's attacking old ladies isn't going to be scared off by that," Neuman said. "And if they're hanging out in the area, someone must have seen them."

"Don't count on it," Sanogo retorted. "People demand greater security, they demonstrate against crime and drugs, but the last time we blitzed the township, they threw stones at us. Mothers protect their sons, what can we do? People tell themselves that poverty and unemployment are the cause of all their ills, and crime a way of surviving like any other. The Casspirs[3] have left an indelible mark on everyone's mind," he said fatalistically. "And most people are afraid of reprisals. Even when there have been murders in broad daylight, no one has ever seen anything."

"Couldn't you at least have a look on your computer?" Neuman asked, pointing to the cube on top of the desk.

[3] Armoured vehicles used during the apartheid period.

The captain didn't move an inch. "Are you asking me to start an investigation into an attack that, legally at least, didn't even happen?"

"No, I'm asking you to tell me if Simon Mceli is associated with any known delinquents, or if he's part of a gang," Neuman replied.

"At the age of ten?"

"All these gangs have their little minions to help them. Don't tell me you didn't know that."

The tone of the conversation, friendly until then, had suddenly cooled. Sanogo shook his head as if warming his spinal cord. "It won't get you anywhere," he said.

Neuman looked at him with his snakelike eyes. "Do it for me."

Sanogo gave a pained grin, and swiveled around to face his computer with all the speed of a barge. "You're not actually going to investigate this? Khayelitsha isn't within your jurisdiction."

"I'd just like to set my mother's mind at rest."

Sanogo nodded, heavy-lidded. After a while, lists of names began appearing on the screen. Simon Mceli wasn't on any of them.

"We don't have any records on your boy," he said, sitting back in his chair. "We close about twenty per cent of our cases. With statistics like that, if he's part of a gang, you've probably got a better chance of finding him in a mass grave."

"I'm interested in him alive. Are there any new gangs in the township?"

"Well . . . The younger brothers often take the place of the older ones. There's no shortage of black sheep."

"Talking of which," Neuman said, "I had a word this morning with two guys on the gymnasium site. *Tsotsis*, not much more than twenty, speaking Dashiki."

"The Nigerian Mafia, maybe," the captain suggested. "They control the main drug networks."

"One of them had a Beretta similar to a police gun."

"No shortage of weapons, either." Walter clicked on an icon to shut down his computer, and stood up. "Listen, I can't start an investigation into a street robbery when I have twelve rapes, one homicide, and dozens of assaults reported last night alone. But tell your mother not to worry. Usually, anyone who attacks an old lady doesn't have long to live."

*

The annex of the Red Cross Hospital had been created as part of a large-scale program intended to slow down the endemic spread of AIDS. Miriam had been working in the dispensary for a year. It was her first job, but she felt as though she had spent her whole life relieving other people's distress.

Her mother had contracted the virus in the most common way possible—her lover at the time beat her and accused her of cheating on him whenever she asked him to wear a condom. Her sisters, terrified by the disease, had run away, but Miriam had taken care of her mother to the end. She hadn't wanted to die in the hospital—they beat women with AIDS in the hospital, she said, they accused them of sleeping around, of asking for it. Her mother had died like a plague victim, in her arms, seventy-five pounds of little more than tears. After that, Miriam could have treated the whole world. The whole world was sick. Especially Africa.

Children were playing a game of *morabaraba* with little stones in the packed lobby of the dispensary. Neuman spotted the young nurse surrounded by patients, her hair carefully braided and her white blouse clinging nicely to her breasts. Miriam waited while he walked toward her. A dream that faded as soon as he spoke.

"I didn't see you go," he said by way of apology.

"I got tired of waiting for you. I have work." She pointed to the syringes rolling on the tray.

She was sulking. Or pretending to.

"I wanted to thank you for taking care of my mother," he said.

"It's my job." Her coppery eyes sparkled like fireworks.

"I didn't even pay your fare," he said, holding out a fifty-rand bill.

Miriam pocketed the money without batting an eyelid. It was three times what the ride had cost, but that would teach him to be so unpleasant, handsome as he was.

"You know I would have done it for nothing," she said all the same. "Your mother helped me a lot when I started at the dispensary."

"She'd help stones to get on their feet."

"Are you comparing me to a stone?" she said, sweetly.

"A precious stone—at least for her," he hastened to add. "Thanks again."

She looked him up and down. Zulus sometimes went on and on when trying to be polite, but this strange specimen had an ulterior motive, and his beautiful eyes wouldn't make the slightest difference.

"I'm looking for a boy," he said. "Simon Mceli. He was treated here some time ago. About ten years old. His mother was a *sangoma* in the township."

"I don't know," she said, a faraway look in her eyes. "But it must be written down somewhere."

Miriam seemed much more intrigued by the scar on his forehead, which she had only just noticed.

"Can you show me?" he insisted.

She nodded, breathing heavily—at least he had thanked her—and went into the adjoining office to consult the medical records. Miriam pulled out a metal drawer and looked through the patient files. The room was small, hot and damp, and she could feel his breath on her shoulder. She was slightly uncomfortable, the two of them in here together.

"Yes," she said after a moment, pulling a file from the sliding drawer. "Simon Mceli. He was here in January 2006."

"What was wrong with him? Asthma?"

"I can't tell you that," she replied, impishly. "I'm not even sure I should be doing this at all."

He thought she was acting strangely. "Can you at least tell me his last known address?"

"124 Biko Street, Block C."

It was a five-minute drive from there.

"Thanks," he said.

Miriam felt hot in her white blouse. No ventilation. She tried to find something witty to say to keep him, but it was as if the walls didn't want them here anymore. In a flash, he was gone.

Block C was a poor area filled with corrugated iron houses, often with backyard shacks attached, where neighbors gathered to watch television. The place was like an accident waiting to happen. Since the last tourist bus carrying whites looking to salve their conscience in the post-apartheid period had fallen victim to a gang of robbers, whites had stopped coming here, apart from members of the NGOs that operated in the township. The tour operators had fallen back on minibuses, which were less ostentatious, for carefully targeted visits—schools, handicraft stalls, charities.

Biko Street. Neuman parked beside the electricity meter, from which a spider's web of wires spread out toward the houses. The number 124 was painted on a tin can stuck to the front of the door. No name, no letter box—no one in the township ever received mail. He knocked at the plywood door, which almost fell on his feet as it opened.

A woman appeared in the doorway of the shack, wearing a satiny acrylic dress most notable for how little of her body it covered. The lines at the corners of her eyes spoke of constant misfortune and lots of sleepless nights. She had clearly just gotten out of bed.

"Who is it?" a man's voice called from behind her.

"Let it go, King Kong. You wouldn't measure up." She had a smile that went well with her skimpy dress.

"I'm looking for a woman," Neuman said. "Nora Mceli."

"Nope, not me. Pity, isn't it?"

"That depends on what's happened to her. Nora was still living here in 2006 with her son Simon. It seems she left the township a few months ago."

"Could be."

"Nora Mceli," he repeated. "A local *sangoma*."

The woman, standing there on the earth floor, wiggled her hips.

"Who the hell is that?" the voice behind her called.

"Take no notice," the woman said, with a confidential air. "He's always in a bad mood when he's been drinking the night before."

"Stop wiggling your ass and answer me!" the man shouted. "This is my house!"

Neuman walked past the woman, her eyes now like cold embers. She made no attempt to stop him. A black of about thirty, wearing nothing but a pair of shapeless shorts, lay on a straw mattress that took up half the room, drinking a beer. The floor was strewn with cigarette butts, underpants, and beer cans. Part of an engine stood in the kitchen sink. The woman was only passing through.

"I'm looking for Nora Mceli. The *sangoma* who used to live here."

"She's not here anymore," the man replied. "What are you doing in my house? This is private property!"

Neuman flashed his badge at the man's crumpled face. "Tell me what you know, or I might decide to take a look around."

The man shrank in his soccer shorts—the place stank of *dagga*, the locally grown weed.

"I told you I don't know her. I took over the house from my cousin, Sam." He made a gesture with his head. "You'll have to ask him. I don't know anything. I'm not even sure when I was born!"

The woman chuckled, and the man followed suit.

"He's telling the truth!" she assured Neuman, calmly.

She was still swaying in the doorway. Pepper and honey—that was what her skin smelled of. He remembered that he hadn't told Maia he was coming.

Fortunately, Cousin Sam was more forthcoming. Nora and Simon had left about a year earlier. The *sangoma* wasn't well liked in the neighborhood. She was accused of making *muti*, magic potions, and casting spells. People even said that was why she had fallen ill, her powers had turned against her. As for her son Simon, he remembered a taciturn, sickly boy distrusted by everyone for reasons of superstition.

"They've never been back," Sam assured him.

"Didn't Nora have any family?"

Sam shrugged. "She sometimes mentioned a cousin on the other side of the railroad tracks."

The squatter camps.

The sun was chasing away the noon shade. Neuman was walking to his car when he got the call from Dan Fletcher.

"Ali. Ali, you'd better get over here."

*

The clouds were flowing like liquid nitrogen from the top of Table Mountain down to Kirstenbosch Botanical Gardens. Neuman walked along the path without a glance at the bright yellow and white flowers in the borders. Dan Fletcher was waiting under the trees, his hands in his pockets, the only thing about him that gave an impression of calm. They exchanged friendly nods.

The breeze was cooler in the shade of the Fragrance Garden. *Wilde Iris* (*Dietes grandiflora*), said the sign. Neuman kneeled. There was a smell of pine and wet grass and other plants with learned names. The girl lay among the flowers. A white girl, almost hidden behind the grove of acacias. Quite a young girl, to judge by the morphology and skin texture.

"One of the municipal employees found her," Dan said, standing over him. "Around ten-thirty. The gates open at nine, but this part is quite isolated. We've cleared the park of visitors."

Her summer dress had been pulled up to her waist, revealing legs flecked with blood. A little cloud of insects was buzzing around her face. The poor girl had been hit so many times, you couldn't make out the bridge of the nose, or the arch of the eyebrows. The cheekbones and eyes, too, had disappeared in a mess of flesh, bone and cartilage. The mouth had been smashed in, the teeth driven down her throat, the forehead shattered in several places. She had been killed in such a way as to wipe out her features, eliminate her identity.

Dan couldn't look at the body. He was barely thirty, but had a fair amount of experience—he'd already been with Neuman for four years, which, according to him, counted double. He had seen drowned people, people who'd been burned alive, people riddled with shotgun shells. But this girl was going to give him sleepless nights.

"Any idea who she is?" Neuman asked.

"We found a video club membership card in the pocket of her cardigan," he replied. "The name on it is Judith Botha, and there's an address in Observatory."

The city's student district.

"No purse?"

"We're still searching the bushes."

Deaf to the bustle of the crickets, Neuman seemed mesmerized by a bright red petal that had gotten stuck to the victim's hair. The sight of those fingers, retracted like newly squashed spiders, made his breath come in little gulps. He thought about the last moments of her life, the terror she must have felt, the fate that had led her here, to die surrounded by Wilde irises. A girl who wasn't yet twenty.

Dan still stood silently in the shade of the acacias. He'd wanted to tidy the house a little before Claire got back, but hadn't had time, four days without her had seemed an eternity, now the squad was in action and all these smells were making him feel dizzy—the only scent he liked was his wife's.

Neuman finally stood up.

"What do you think?" Dan asked.

"Where's Brian?"

"I called him on his cell phone, but there's no answer."

The scents were becoming headier than ever. Neuman looked with a grimace at the girl's twisted body. "Call him again."

4.

The world capsized into the ocean of night and Brian Epkeen fell deep into an abyss, then woke with a start. The noise of the sliding door had made a kind of click in his head. The noise came from downstairs, not loud but perfectly audible. After a while it stopped.

Brian rolled over in bed, narrowly avoiding the head on the pillow next to his, and retreated to take stock. The birds were chattering beyond the bedroom window, curly red hair peeped out from beneath the sheets, and someone had just entered the house.

Brian reached for his revolver, but it wasn't on the desk. He saw the head turned away from him, the tousled hair, but no clothes on the floor. He slid out of the sheets without a sound, grabbed the .38 from under the bed, walked naked across the carpet to the door, and softly opened it.

He felt woozy, he still didn't know where his clothes were, but there was definitely someone downstairs. He could hear footsteps heading out of the living room. The person was rummaging in the hall now. He crept down the stairs, rubbing his eyes, which were taking their time to focus. When he got to the foot of the stairs, he flattened himself against the wall. The intruder hadn't had to climb over the railings to get in—the gate had been left open.

Now completely awake, Brian gripped the handle of his gun. He didn't know why he had left everything open, but he had a good idea—the redhead upstairs. In any case, the house was too big for him, it wasn't just a matter of the security system anymore. He advanced toward the hall, gripped by contradictory feelings. Silence seemed to have seeped into the walls of the house, the birdsong had stopped. Brian crept around the corner and stopped for a moment in surprise. There was the thief, rifling through the pockets of his jacket, which by some miracle was actually hanging on the coat stand.

The intruder had just found two hundred-rand bills in the wallet when he sensed a presence behind him.

"Drop the money," Brian said, in a hoarse voice.

Even though caught in the act, the other man didn't flinch. He was a young white, about twenty, dressed in the latest fashion—Gothic boots, baggy jeans, an extra-large T-shirt with a picture of a hardcore band on it—and with long light chestnut hair like his mother's.

"What are you doing here?" David retorted, staring at his father, the bills still clutched in his hand.

"I could ask you the same question," Brian said. "This is my house."

David did not reply. He put the wallet back in the jacket, but not the bills. There was no trace of remorse or shame on his corn-fed Brad Pitt face. The prodigal son seemed to be in a hurry.

"Is this all you have?" he asked, indicating the bills.

"I stashed the rest in the Bahamas."

Brian hadn't moved, hoping that the revolver would hide his nudity, but David was looking with an air of disgust at his father's big dangling cock.

David was studying journalism. He smoked grass, was always broke, an idler. His mother's beloved son, their only son, their star, arrogant as could be and clever enough to have set up house at the home of his girlfriend's parents. He was a new-generation white who considered himself a leftist liberal, and not only spoke about the SAP[1] in insulting terms but

[1] South African Police.

called his father a fascist and a reactionary. It really hurt him to hear that, like a blow to the gut, but all the same, Brian loved his son—he'd been the same at his age.

This wasn't the first time David had come here to steal from him while he was asleep. The last time, he'd not only gone through his pockets but also the pockets of the girl who'd been sleeping upstairs.

"I need money," he said.

"You're twenty years old, look after yourself."

Brian tried to grab the bills, but David stuffed them in the extra-large pocket of his jeans and looked around for whatever else he could swipe.

"Did your mother send you?" Brian asked.

"You didn't pay her this month."

"It's only the second, damn it."

"It wouldn't make any difference if it was the tenth. How do you think she gets by?"

David had more than one insult in his armory. Brian grinned bitterly. He had borrowed money to keep the house, hoping that David would come and live here, with his girlfriend if he wanted, or his boyfriend, he really didn't care. But not only had his son not wanted to come, Ruby had continued to fill his head with lies.

"I hear your mother drives around in a BM coupé with that dentist of hers," he said. "She should be able to survive till the end of the month, don't you think?"

"What about me?"

"Your school fees, the two thousand rand I send you every month, isn't that enough?"

Behind his grunge rebel hair, David was sulking. "Marjorie's parents have thrown us out," he said.

Marjorie was his girlfriend, a Goth with piercings everywhere—he'd seen her seen once or twice coming out of David's school.

"I thought her parents really liked you."

"Not anymore."

"You could come and live here."

"Very funny."

"Why don't you go to your mother's?"

"She has her new life now, I don't want to piss her off. No, what we need is an apartment in town, not too far from the faculty. We'd like to rent in the Malayan quarter, but you have to pay the first two months in advance, then there's food, and bills."

"Don't forget taxis. Best way to get to the faculty, don't you think?"

"So what about it?" David said, impatiently.

Brian sighed again, touched by so much love.

It was then that David noticed the woman's dress hanging on the chair in the hall. "I see you're entertaining," he said. "Do you know this one's name?"

"Didn't have time to ask. Now get the hell out of here."

"And you, go wash your dick."

David brushed past him, walked across the living room without a word, and slammed the door, leaving a deafening silence in his wake.

Brian wondered how the little boy who used to run after penguins on the beach could have become this skinny stranger who acted like some kind of mother superior, and was cynical about everything. What saddened him wasn't so much the fact that he'd found him rifling his pockets while he was asleep as the way he had of leaving without a word, just giving him that horrible look, always the same one, a mixture of contempt and bitterness, as if he was seeing him for the last time. Brian put down the revolver he was still holding—it wasn't loaded anyway—saw his crumpled clothes on the kitchen table, the purple blouse on the floor, the matching bra, and went glumly back upstairs.

It was hot in the bedroom. The woman with the curly red hair was still lying on the bed, the sheets now down below her buttocks. They were diaphanous, curvy, as fine and soft as wax. Tracy, the barmaid from the Vera Cruz. A thirty-five-year-old redhead with bleached bunches he'd been seeing for a while, small but hot stuff.

Sensing his presence, Tracy opened her apple-green eyes, and smiled when she saw him. "Hi."

Her rumpled face still bore the marks of the pillow. He wanted to kiss her, to erase what had just happened.

"What time is it?" she asked, making no attempt to cover herself.

"I don't know. About eleven."

"Oh, no!" she simpered, as if they had only just fallen asleep.

Brian sat down next to her, with one leg still out of the bed. The confrontation with his son had laid him low, he felt like some kind of creature washed ashore, being pecked at by sea-gulls and crows.

"What's the matter?" she asked, stroking his thigh. "You seem worried."

"No, I'm fine."

"In that case, get back in bed. We have plenty of time, before we go to your friend Jim's."

"Who?"

Tracy's eyelids performed an arabesque. "Your friend. Jim. You told me we were going to spend Sunday by the sea. He gave you the keys to his villa."

Brian did a double take—oh, God, he really should stop using the famous Jim. The last time he'd raved about this so-called friend, it had been to invite a young woman lawyer to come and play golf in his private club in Betty's Bay. What on earth possessed him to talk about the guy? He must have a sick mind.

Tracy pulled back the sheets, revealing two creamy breasts, which, if his memory served him well, were very sensitive. She smiled. "Come here, you."

Brian let himself be drawn in by what her fingers were doing. They stimulated each other's senses for a while, worked themselves up into a frenzy, both came, although not at the same time, exchanged a few exhausted caresses, and finished it all off with a kiss.

A few moments later he disappeared into the bathroom and took a shower, wondering what he could say to sweet-talk Tracy, then looked at his image in the mirror and decided not to bother.

Brian Epkeen had been handsome, but that was in the past. There had been too many fuck-ups, too many missed opportunities. Sometimes he hadn't given enough love, sometimes he'd loved too much, or else gotten it all wrong. For forty-three years he'd been scuttling about like a crab, sometimes wandering far off course, sometimes making sudden sideward leaps.

He grabbed an unironed shirt, which, in the mirror, vaguely reminded him of himself, put on a pair of black pants, and strolled across the bedroom. Tracy, still lying on the bed, was asking him to tell her more about their Sunday by the sea when Brian switched on his cell phone.

He had twelve messages.

*

Cape Town lay at the foot of Table Mountain, the magnificent massif that towered three thousand five hundred feet above the South Atlantic. The Mother City, it was called. Brian Epkeen lived in Somerset, a gay area full of trendy bars and clubs, some open to everyone, without restrictions. European colonists, Xhosa tribesmen, Indian and Malayan coolies—Cape Town had had a mixed population for centuries. It was the country's flagship city, a little New York by the sea, but also the place where Parliament was located, which meant that it was here that the apartheid policy was first applied. Brian knew the city by heart. It had both inspired strong emotions in him and just as often made him nauseous.

His great-great-grandfather had come here as a ragged, illiterate farmer who spoke the kind of degenerate Dutch that would become Afrikaans, believed in an eye for an eye, and wielded the Old Testament in one hand and a rifle in the other. He and the Boer pioneers with him had found a barren land peopled by Bushmen with prehistoric customs, nomads who couldn't tell the difference between a game animal and a domestic one, who pulled the legs off cows and ate them raw while they mooed to death, Bushmen they had driven out like wolves. The old man didn't spare anyone—if he had, there was a good chance his family would have been slaughtered. He refused to pay taxes to the English colonial governor who left them alone to face the hostile natives, clear the land and survive as best they could. The Afrikaners had never depended on anyone or anything. That was the blood that Brian had in his veins, the blood of dust and death—the blood of the bush.

Whether out of some ancestral memory, or some sense of being a dying race, the Boers were the eternal losers of history—following the war that took their name when British conquerors burned their houses and their land, twenty thousand of them, including women and children, had died of hunger and disease in the English concentration camps into which they had been herded—and the establishment of apartheid had been their greatest defeat[2].

In Brian's opinion, the reason his ancestors had established apartheid was because they were shit scared. Fear of the black man had taken over their bodies and minds with an animal

[2] The Natives' Land Act, granting 7.5 percent of the land to the native population, was the beginning of apartheid.

force that recalled the old reptilian fears—fear of the wolf, the lion, the eaters of white men. That wasn't the basis on which to build anything. Phobia of the other had destroyed their powers of reason, and although the end of the despised regime may have restored some dignity to the Afrikaners, fifteen years weren't enough to wipe out their contribution to history.

Brian drove past the quaint old buildings in the city center, then the colorful facades of the colonnaded houses on Long Street. The avenues were largely free of traffic, most people had gone to the beach. He climbed toward Lions Head, managing to get a little coolness by putting his hand through the open window—the air-conditioning in his Mercedes had long since given up the ghost. A collector's item, just like him— Tracy had said that, and he had taken it as a compliment. He wasn't thinking about her as he drove, or about the weekend with "Jim."

David's intrusion had left a bitter taste in his mouth. They had hardly spoken for six years, and when they had it had been so unpleasant it would have been better to keep quiet. Brian hoped that things would work out, but David and his mother still bore him a grudge. He had cheated on her—that was true—mostly with black women. Brian was faithful only to his beliefs, but when you came down to it, it was all his fault. Ruby had always been a tragic, deeply wounded fury, and he'd been a complete idiot—it was plain as could be that the woman was a force-ten storm warning. They had met at a Nine Inch Nails concert during a festival in support of the release of Mandela, and the way she had been exploding in the middle of that electronic din should have made him sensitive to the cyclones to come—a girl who bounced up and down to the riffs of Nine Inch Nails was obviously pure dynamite. Brian had fallen in love, an encounter of two parallel lines suddenly converging, a hot beam of love making straight for her crazy eyes.

In Constantia, Epkeen narrowly missed the colored with the bandaged head zigzagging in the middle of the road, and stopped at the red light. The man, his shirt torn and blood-stained, walked on a little way, then collapsed, and lay there in the sun with his arms out. Other down-and-outs were sleeping it off on the sidewalks, too befuddled with alcohol to hold out their hands to the few passersby.

Brian turned at the corner of the avenue and took the M3 in the direction of Kirstenbosch.

Two police vehicles were blocking access to the Botanical Gardens. Brian saw the forensics van in the parking lot, Neuman's car parked close to the souvenir shops, and groups of tourists disconcerted by the irritability with which they were being turned away. The clouds were tumbling from the top of the mountain like frightened sheep. Brian showed his badge to the constable manning the barrier, passed under the arch of the big banana tree at the entrance, and, pursued by swarms of insects, followed the birdsong to the main path.

Kirstenbosch was a living museum, a multicolored tide of plants, trees, and flowers stretching to the foot of the mountain. On the English-style lawn, a pheasant flew off as he passed, making a mocking sound as it did so. Brian reached the acacia grove.

A little farther on, he saw His Majesty, his tall frame stooped beneath the branches, talking in a low voice with Tembo, the medical examiner. An old black in green overalls was standing behind them, cut in half by the shade and his overlarge cap. One lab team was taking prints from the ground, another had nearly finished taking photographs. Brian nodded to Tembo in his jazzy felt hat—he was just leaving—and the old man in his municipal overalls. Neuman was waiting for him before he himself left.

"You're not looking too good," he said when he saw him.

"In ten years, my friend, just you wait."

At that moment, Brian saw the body in the middle of the flowers, and the front he had been keeping up since the minute he woke up this morning, already somewhat undermined, now crumbled a little more.

"It was this gentleman who found her this morning," Neuman said, indicating the gardener.

The old black said nothing. It was obvious he didn't want to be there. Brian bent over the irises, taking deep breaths to steady his nerves. The girl was lying on her back, but it was the sight of the head that made him recoil. You couldn't see her eyes, or her features. She'd been wiped off the map, and her tensed hands, which seemed to be reaching toward an attacker both unseen and omnipresent, made her look as if she was petrified with fear.

"The murder took place about two o'clock last night," Neuman said, in a mechanical voice. "The ground's dry, but the flowers are trampled and stained with blood. Probably the victim's. There are no bullet holes. All the blows are concentrated on the face and the top of the skull. Tembo thinks it was a hammer, or something similar."

Brian was looking at the white, blood-spattered thighs, the slightly plump legs—a girl David's age. Chasing away these visions of horror, he saw that she was naked under her dress.

"Rape?"

"Hard to say," Neuman replied. "We found her panties beside her, but the elastic is intact. We know she had sexual intercourse. What we still have to establish is if it was consensual or not."

Brian moved a finger over the girl's bare shoulder and lifted it to his lips. The skin had a slightly salty taste. He put on the latex gloves Neuman handed him, examined the victim's hands, her bizarrely retracted fingers—there was a little earth under the nails—and the marks on her arms: small grazes, in almost straight lines. The dress was torn in places, leaving big holes.

"Two fingers broken?"

"Yes, on the right hand. She must have been trying to defend herself."

Two male nurses were waiting on the path, their stretcher on the ground. Standing in the sun all this time was starting to get on their nerves. Brian straightened up, his legs like mercury.

"I wanted you to see her before they took her away," Neuman said.

"Thanks a lot. Do we know who she is?"

"We found a video club membership card in the pocket of her cardigan, registered to Judith Botha. A student. Dan's gone to check it out."

Dan Fletcher, their protégé.

The insects were buzzing under the acacias. Brian swayed for a moment to avoid them. Neuman's eyes were like two black suns—the sense of foreboding that had been with him since dawn hadn't left.

*

Outside the 7-Eleven in the working-class district of Woodstock, the wailing siren of an ambulance had attracted a crowd. There was a body on the sidewalk, people were holding their heads in alarm, the men from the Explosives Unit had arrived in their bulletproof vests. Dan Fletcher drove along the seedy avenue before turning onto the M3. Although up until now Cape Town had largely avoided *brinks*, those everyday acts of terror of which Johannesburg was the epicenter, this kind of scene was becoming increasingly frequent, even in the center of the city. It was a worrying development, and the press were having a field day with it.

Dan had searched Judith Botha's studio apartment without finding any vital clues as to her disappearance. The neighbors hadn't seen her over the weekend, and the apartment seemed to be a typical student pad—law books, paperwork from college, stupid postcards, DVDs, slices of pizza, a photo of a blonde who fit the description of the victim smiling at the camera. Dan had found a number for her parents, Nils and Flora Botha. The servant who had finally answered the phone didn't have any idea where Mrs. Botha was, but her husband, Nils, must be "at rugby."

Fletcher didn't know Nils Botha, and didn't know anything about rugby, but Janet Helms, who was steering the investigation from headquarters, brought him up to speed. A former selector for the national team, the Springboks, and himself a player at the time of the embargo and the sporting boycott, Nils Botha had for the last twenty years been the celebrity coach for the Western Cape team, the Stormers. He and his wife, Flora, had two children: a son, Pretorius, who lived in Port Elizabeth, and Judith, who had just started university at Observatory.

Dan remembered the disfigured face surrounded by flowers, the viscous lianas of her blonde hair, the lumps of brain escaping from the skull. He thought he had hidden his squeamishness from Neuman but he didn't fool anyone, especially not the old cops at headquarters, who had been there and done that. "Hot Lips" was the nickname given him by Sergeant Van Vlit, the shooting instructor, terror of the young recruits. The name had made the rounds of the force, and Dan had even found gay magazines in the drawer of his office, the pages stuck together, but then it had calmed down. Dan had assumed the hazing was over, but he was wrong. Neuman had recruited him for his talents as a sociologist, and had no intention of putting up with the homophobic remarks of the rednecks at headquarters. He had knocked out Sergeant Van Vlit with a blow to the back of the neck, pulled down his pants in front of everyone, grabbed his famous chromium-plated Colt, of which he was so proud, stuck the barrel of it into his big pimply ass, and left him there. His cold fury said it all—no need for warnings. That was the end of the nicknames, and the beginning of their collaboration.

Dan extricated himself from the M3 overlooking the city, drove onto the other side of the mountain, and reached the sports complex.

The Stormers were preparing for the Super 14, the southern hemisphere championship. They were still in the early stages of training, and had a lot of catching up to do if they were going to beat the New Zealanders. Fletcher found Botha on the touchline, hurling abuse at his big sweaty babies as they practiced their maul. Every time the ball was dropped he flew into a rage. Only the waving of Dan's police badge persuaded the coach to shift his attention to this runt with eyes like a woman's who had just appeared. He left his assistant to continue training the forwards on the yoke until they dropped.

Botha was sixty years old, stocky, with graying hair, his trapezius muscles bulging from his T-shirt. He sported a cap with the club colors and lots of hair on his forearms.

"What's up?" he asked, alerted by the expression on Dan's face.

"We're looking for your daughter, Judith. Do you know where she is?"

Botha's face turned red. "At home! Why?"

"I've been to her apartment in Observatory, there's no one there," Dan replied, calmly. "And there's no answer from her cell phone."

Botha sensed immediately that something serious had happened. "What do you mean, there's no answer on her cell phone?" He felt in the pockets of his beige shorts for his phone, as if that was a solution to the problem.

"Could you describe Judith for me?" Dan asked. "Physically, I mean."

"Well, she's blonde, she has blue eyes, she's five and a half feet. Why are you looking for my daughter? Has she done something wrong?" Botha was looking at him incredulously.

Dan's pulse beat faster. "We found the body of a young woman this morning," he said, "in Kirstenbosch Botanical Gardens. The body hasn't been identified yet, but there was a video membership card in her cardigan, with Judith's name on it. The description of the victim fits your daughter, but we're not sure of anything yet. Do you know how your daughter spends her time—what she was planning to do last night, for example?"

The coach's red face slowly fell. Botha was known for his halftime rants and his liking for a rough game, but this effeminate little cop had knocked him for six.

"Judith . . . Judith was supposed to be revising for her midterm exams with her friend Nicole. In Nicole's apartment. It had all been arranged."

"Nicole who?"

"Wiese. Nicole Wiese. They're at university together."

The forwards were dropping like flies in the sun.

"Do you have her cell number?" Dan asked.

"Nicole's? No. But I have her father's number. The girls have known each other since they were little."

"Any idea where they might have gone?"

"No."

"Does Judith have a boyfriend?"

"Deblink. Peter Deblink. He lives in Camps Bay." He made Deblink's address sound like a guarantee of moral rectitude. "His parents have a restaurant. My wife and I often eat there."

"Were they together last night?"

"I told you, Judith was revising for her exams with her friend from university."

"Your daughter lied to you," Dan replied.

The players were still laboring under the yoke, but Botha had stopped watching them. The body they'd found was his daughter . . . He could feel his thighs harden, his hair stand on end. At that point, Dan's cell phone vibrated in his jacket pocket. He apologized to the coach, whose face had by now turned white, and took the call. It was his colleague Janet Helms.

"I just got through to Judith Botha," she said immediately. "She's in Strand with her boyfriend and only just switched on her cell phone."

Dan's insides relaxed. "Did you put her in the picture?"

"No. I thought you'd prefer to question her yourself."

"Well done. Tell her I'll see her at her parents' house."

On the touchline, Botha had pricked up his ears, and was trying to read Dan's lips, looking for a clue, anything that would tell him she was alive.

"Your daughter's at the beach," Dan said.

Botha's shoulders sagged. The relief was short-lived—Dan called Neuman, who picked up immediately.

"Ali, it's me. I think I have the dead girl's name. Nicole Wiese."

5.

It's her."

Stewart Wiese's fingers were twisting like boa constructors as he stood by the gray marble slab. The room smelled of antiseptic, and the medical examiner's efforts to make his daughter presentable certainly weren't going to lessen his anger—as for his sadness, he'd save that for his wife.

Stewart Wiese was a former second row player for the Springboks—world champion in '95, selected about fifty times for the national team, with thighs like buffaloes and a skull that could break stones. The rugby fields had accustomed him to blows, he had taken plenty himself and had given out more than his fair share, but he was in a good position to know that those you didn't see coming were the worst of all. Now the apple of his eye no longer had any eyes, or anything that reminded him of his daughter.

"Would you like to sit down?"

"No."

Wiese must have put on more than thirty pounds since his days as a prop forward, but he hadn't lost his readiness for a fight. He refused the glass of water that the medical examiner's assistant offered him, and glared at Neuman. He thought about his wife, mad with grief even before the death had been confirmed, and the chasm opening beneath his feet.

"Any idea of the bastard that did this?"

It wasn't so much a question as a threat.

Neuman looked at the photograph of the young blonde

woman, just turned eighteen, residing at 114 Victoria in the chic suburb of Camps Bay. Nicole Wiese, a nicely dressed little doll—you wanted to buy her an ice cream, not bash her head in with a hammer.

"I don't suppose your daughter had any enemies," he said.

"Not like that."

"Did she have a driver's license?"

"No."

"She didn't get to Kirstenbosch on foot. Any idea who might have driven her?"

Wiese was kneading his big hands to stop them shaking. "Nicole would never have been out at night with strangers," he said.

He was looking at his daughter's mashed-up face as if it were someone else's. He didn't want to believe that the world was nothing but an illusion. A house of cards.

"You think she was in the wrong place at the wrong time?" Neuman asked.

The rage Wiese had been containing exploded suddenly. "No, I think a savage did this! A savage slaughtered my daughter!" His voice boomed in the cold air. "Who else could have done something like this? Who else? Can you tell me that?"

"I'm sorry."

"Not as sorry as I am," Wiese retorted, his jaws still clenched. "But I won't let this happen. No, not like this."

The color had drained from his face, and his temples were throbbing with anger. He had thought his daughter was with Judith Botha, the two of them were supposed to be spending the evening studying for their midterm exams over a pizza. Instead, she'd been found dead miles away from there, murdered in the botanical gardens at Kirstenbosch in the middle of the night.

"Was Nicole . . . was she raped?"

"We don't know yet. The postmortem will tell us."

Wiese rose to his full height—he was slightly taller than Neuman. "You ought to know," he bellowed. "What the hell's your medical examiner doing?"

"His job," Neuman replied. "Your daughter had sexual intercourse last night, but there's nothing to show that she was raped."

Wiese went red, as if stunned. "I want to see the chief of police," he said, in a toneless voice. "I want him to deal with this personally."

"I'm the head of the Crime Unit," Neuman said, "and that's precisely what I'm going to do."

Thrown by this, Wiese hesitated. The medical examiner's assistant had put the sheet back over the corpse, but he continued to stare at it, a faraway look in his eyes.

"Can you tell me when you last saw Nicole?"

"About four in the afternoon. Saturday. Nicole was supposed to be going out shopping with that little bitch Judith Botha, and then revising for her exams."

"Do you know if she had a boyfriend?"

"Nicole broke up with the last one before the summer," he said. "Ben Durandt. Nobody since then."

"When you're nineteen, you don't necessarily tell your father everything," Neuman said.

"My wife would have told me. What are you implying? That I don't know how to keep my daughter under control?"

His metallic eyes misted over with anger—he'd find the man who'd slaughtered his daughter and bring him down, tear the bones from his body, destroy him.

"My daughter was raped and murdered by an animal," he said, categorically. "A monster of the worst kind. He's out there somewhere, thinking he's gotten away with it, and that's something I can't accept. If you don't know who I am, you're going to find out. I don't give up easily, captain. I'll move heaven and earth till the bastard is caught. I want every department in your fucking police force involved, I want your bloody inspectors to move their asses, and I want them to get results, fast. Is that clear?"

"The law's the same for everyone," Neuman said, with an emphasis that Wiese took for arrogance. "I'll find your daughter's killer."

"I hope so, for your sake," Wiese said, between clenched teeth. His bare neck was streaming with sweat. He threw a last glance at the sheet covering his daughter.

Neuman was starting to realize what had been bothering him in this interview. "An officer will be over to see you tomorrow morning," he said before letting him leave.

A white officer.

*

The hills and secluded inlets of Clifton, with their dense vegetation, had given way to luxury residences, villas with rooftop parking, security guards, and direct access to the beach. The area was now firmly part of the urban spread, and they were building ever higher up the side of the hill—it was already too late to save the landscape.

25 West Point. With its gilt and lacquer and profusion of mirrors, the Botha family apartment was as heavily made up as a Sydney drag queen, a monument to eighties glitz. In a living room with a panoramic view, Flora, her face drawn by the sun and foundation cream, was sitting on the couch waiting for Judith to return. Her husband, pacing restlessly around the coffee table, was talking for the two of them. In lying to everyone, the stupid girl had created a deep rift between the two families. Stewart Wiese had called a little earlier, and they'd had a heated argument that had solved nothing. The Springbok had finished his career in Nils Botha's Stormers, and the two men had remained friends. Their daughters had been at

school together, had the same circle of friends, went out to the same places, they had never wanted for anything or ever caused the slightest concern. They were supposed to be revising for their exams, not spending the night on the streets, or going for weekends to the coast. Botha was boiling with anger, incomprehension, and a sense of betrayal. Dan Fletcher let him stew, while his wife sat on the flowered couch, twisting her fingers.

Dan was thinking about his wife, Claire—he'd be picking her up from the hospital in a while—when there was a ring from the entry phone. Flora jumped up like a spring, and trotted across the marble floor in her high heels, but Nils got there first. It was the doorman, announcing that their daughter had arrived.

After a few moments, the door of the private elevator opened and Judith appeared, together with her friend Peter, a local boy who had swapped his Ray-Bans for blond streaks.

"What's going on?" Judith asked when she saw her mother's distraught face. "Has something happened?"

Botha pushed his wife aside, swooped on his daughter, and slapped her across the face. Flora let out a stunned cry. With a whine, Judith collapsed on the floor.

"Nils!" Flora said. "You—"

"Shut up! And you, listen to me," he roared at his daughter. "Yes, something's happened. Nicole has been murdered! Do you hear! Someone killed Nicole!"

The maid, who had been hiding at the end of the corridor, ran to the kitchen. Judith burst into tears. Peter retreated toward the elevator. Botha glared at him, then bent over Judith and grabbed her by the arm as if pulling a weed from the ground.

"Do you think this is quite appropriate?" Dan Fletcher said.

"I'll treat my daughter as I see fit!"

"Can't you see, she can hardly stand."

Botha didn't give a damn. He had beaten men to the ground before. If you could do it in rugby, why not in life? All he could see was the lying, the deception, the rift with Stewart Wiese, the loss of business contacts, and all the other trouble that would ensue. All because of this young fool, his daughter.

Judith was still on the floor, her hands over her face. Flora went to her, ill at ease, not knowing how to deal with her.

"I'd like to speak to Judith alone," Dan said.

"I have a right to know why my daughter lied to us!"

"Please, Mr. Botha, let me do my job."

Botha made a sour face. The little cop was talking in a low voice and looking at Judith with a compassion that set his nerves on edge. She huddled pitifully against the elevator door, while her mother tried awkwardly, and inaudibly, to console her.

Now Dan kneeled and looked at her, noticing the freckles behind her disheveled hair. He took her hand and helped her to her feet. Her mascara had run, staining her fingers. Peter Deblink stood with his back to the elevator and his eyes on the floor, as if counting the marble tiles.

"You too," Dan said.

Swerving past Nils Botha, the young couple followed Dan out onto the terrace.

A cool wind was blowing, birds soared, turquoise waves crashed on the immaculate beach below, a little corner of paradise that had ended up in the wrong place. Judith, still in shock, collapsed onto a folding chair, where she could cry more freely.

There was a moment's silence, broken only by the sound of the rollers. Dan was as delicate-looking as Montgomery Clift, with a gleam in his eye that was only for his wife. He peered down at Judith. She was pretty, he thought, no more than that.

"You have to help me," he said. "O.K.?"

Judith did not reply. She was gathering her tears. "What happened?" she sniffed.

"We don't know yet," Dan replied. "Nicole's body was found in Kirstenbosch Gardens this morning."

Judith looked up, incredulous. Her father's fingers had left Paleolithic marks on her cheeks.

"You were Nicole's best friend, from what I've been told."

"We've known each other since we were kids," Judith said, her throat tight with emotion. "Nicole lives in Camps Bay, on the other side of the hill."

She made a movement with her head, which went no farther than the green plants on the terrace.

"Did you often cover for her?"

"No . . . No."

Dan looked into her moist eyes, saw only shame and sadness. "Tell me the truth."

"I . . . I have a studio apartment in Observatory, near the university. Nicole used to tell her parents that she was going to sleep over at my place so we could go through our course together."

"And that wasn't true?"

"It was just an excuse to get out of the house. I don't like lying, but I did it for her, as a friend. I tried to tell her our parents would find out in the end, but Nicole begged me and . . . Anyway, I didn't have the heart to refuse. I feel terrible about it. It's awful." She hid her face in her hands.

Dan turned to Deblink. "Were the two of you with her last night?" he asked.

"No," the blond boy said. "We were at Strand diving in a cage with the white sharks. The excursion was due to start at seven this morning, so we spent the night in the guest house that organized it."

That would be easy to check.

"And Nicole?"

"She had a duplicate key," Judith said. "That way we were freer."

"Did she tell you where was going, and who with?"

"No."

"I thought you were friends."

Her expression changed. "To be honest, we haven't seen much of each other lately."

"You're in the same faculty."

"Nicole hardly ever attended anymore."

"I see."

"She wasn't that crazy about law."

"She preferred boys."

"Don't put words in my mouth."

"But she slept with boys."

"Nicole wasn't a tramp!" her friend protested.

"I don't see anything wrong in her liking boys," Dan said. "Was Nicole seeing someone?"

Disarmed, Judith shrugged. "I think so."

"You think so?"

"She didn't tell me in so many words, but . . . I don't know. Nicole had changed. She'd become evasive."

"How do you mean?"

"I don't know," she said softly. "It's just a feeling. We've known each other a long time but something had changed in her. I couldn't say why, but Nicole wasn't the same anymore, especially lately. That's why I think she was seeing someone."

"Strange she didn't talk to you. You were her best friend."

"Yes, I was."

A wind of sadness swept the terrace.

"Did Nicole often change boyfriends?"

"Oh, no. She wasn't a collector, I told you. She liked boys but like everyone, you know—in moderation."

Deblink didn't bat an eyelid.

"Ben Durandt," Fletcher said. "Know him?"

"A friend from Camps Bay," she said, sullenly. "They were together for six months."

"How was he with Nicole?"

"Good for driving a convertible."

"The jealous type?"

"No." She shook her head. "Durandt is too fascinated by himself to be interested in anyone else. Anyway, it was just a casual thing. Nicole was pissed off with him." She was starting to relax a little.

"Do you know if they slept together?"

"No. Why do you ask that?"

"I'm trying to find out if Nicole slept with boys, if the sexual relations she had on the night of the murder were consensual or not."

Judith lowered her eyes.

"What about you?" he asked Deblink. "What do you think?"

"We hardly knew each other," he replied, pulling a face.

"I thought you were both regulars at Camps Bay?"

The beaches at Camps Bay were popular at weekends with the city's gilded youth.

"I did meet her there, with Judith. But only once, and then only in passing."

"You mean Nicole didn't hang out at Camps Bay anymore?"

"That's right."

"She'd changed, like I said," Judith cut in.

A gull hovering near the terrace squawked. Dan turned back to Judith. "What was the agreement between the two of you last night?"

"Nicole phoned to say she was going out. I'd already arranged to see the sharks with Peter, so she had the apartment to herself for the evening."

"Why did the two of you lie to your parents?"

"My dad's not too bad," Judith replied, biting her lips. "He let me take a flat near the faculty. But Judith's father is very . . .

you know, conservative. He didn't like her going out. Or only with boys he knew. He was afraid of assaults, rapes."

One every five minutes, according to the national statistics.

"Is that why you covered for her?"

"Yes."

"Did Nicole go to the local bars?"

"That's what she told me."

"Did she have new friends?"

"I guess so."

Dan nodded in the evening breeze. "We found a video club card in her cardigan, with your name on it," he said.

"Yes, I lent it to her, in case she wanted to rent films."

"Is that what happened yesterday?"

"I don't know. Nicole had the keys and came back when she wanted. I didn't ask her questions. We only saw a bit of each other in the mornings, when she came back to sleep."

"Did she sometimes not come back to sleep?"

"Yes, once, this week. Wednesday. Yes, Wednesday," she repeated. "I woke up in the morning, and there was no one on the couch."

"Didn't Nicole tell you where she had slept?"

"No. I just told her it couldn't carry on like that. That her parents would catch us in the end. But I gave in again when she asked me about Saturday. Like an idiot."

Childhood memories caught her by the throat: changing their dolls' clothes, giggling, secrets. Judith tried to hold back her sobs, but the wave overwhelmed her. She put her hands over her face.

Evening was falling gently over the ocean. Fletcher looked at his watch. Claire was coming out in less than an hour.

A few feet away, his hair being given a rough time by the wind, Peter Deblink stood like a block of wood. He hadn't made any move to comfort his girlfriend. Dan squeezed her shoulder, and left for the hospital.

*

From tomorrow (not long now), the journey into you. A slow journey, like a horse-drawn carriage. How does your sex taste? Do you know it changes depending on the season, the angle of the sun, the mood of the moon? Is your mouth still a virtuoso of the "agonic orgasm"? Will I still be the pilot fish that swims ahead? I think about it, so I'm already there—imagining, from a distance, the delights of immersion. Very soon to be yours, my darling!

For the twelfth time, Claire read the note that Dan had slipped in with the flowers. She kept the note and gave the roses to the Xhosa nurse who had been pampering her for the last three nights.

When you're thirty, you worry about your choices, mostly crucial ones, you worry about your marriage, car accidents, but not cancer—cancer of the breast, which had been detected three months earlier, and had metastasized. The ground had given way beneath them, Dan had seen only an abyss, but Claire seemed to be bearing the chemotherapy and the loss of her hair. The latest series of tests had turned out well, by and large. They just had to wait and see how things developed. Of course the kids didn't know anything about it. Tom, who was four and a half, was convinced that his mother had "caught the autumn" and her hair would soon grown back again, while Eve quite simply hadn't noticed anything.

Dan picked up his wife from the lobby of Somerset Hospital. Claire was wearing a black beret on her bald head and a short skirt that revealed her thin knees. She smiled as he walked toward her through the crowd, took him by the shoulders, and kissed him hard on the mouth by way of welcome. A long, languorous kiss, just like their first dates. You had to kiss your misfortune, that was what she said. She might be an angel knocked off her pedestal, but the disease wouldn't have her skin—that was his exclusive preserve.

People passed them, as their reunion showed no sign of ending.

"Have you been waiting long?" he whispered in her ear.

"Twenty-six years in two months," Claire replied.

Dan freed himself from her loving embrace. "Then let's get out of here."

He took her delicate hand and her overnight bag, and led her to the exit. The air in the parking lot suddenly felt new, the sky almost as luminous as her swallow-blue eyes.

"The children are waiting for you so we can have a little party," Dan announced. "The house is in a bit of a mess, I didn't have time to tidy up, but the nanny's made some cakes."

"Cool!"

"I told them we wouldn't be back before eight," he added, casually.

It was only just six-fifteen.

"Where are you taking me, Casanova?"

"Llandudno."

Claire smiled. There was a little inlet they knew along the peninsula, a quiet spot where they could safely bathe naked. Snuggling up to him, she saw the unmarked police car in the parking lot.

"Are you on duty?"

"Yes. Bad timing, I know. They found a girl in Kirstenbosch this morning."

"The rugby player's daughter?"

"You know about it?"

"They mentioned it on the radio. Are the guys coming to dinner?"

She meant Ali and Brian, their dearest friends, and their little ritual of inviting each other to make up for the unpredictable hours, the stress, the rotten work.

"We were thinking tomorrow night. If you feel up to it, of course," he hastened to add.

"We already talked about that," Claire said, firmly. "Let's not change anything, O.K.?"

She didn't want to be treated like a patient, but like someone in recovery. Ali and Brian both agreed. Dan kissed her again.

"Did you find what I asked for?" she asked as she got in the car.

"Yes, it's on the back seat."

Claire twisted in the front seat, took hold of the hat box, and put it on her knees.

"Close your eyes," she said.

"They're closed."

Claire gave him a sideways glance, quickly removed her beret, took the wig out of the box and adjusted it in the rear-view mirror. A platinum-blonde bob, with two sixties streaks below the ears. Mmm, not too bad. She patted her husband's arm.

"How do I look in acrylic?"

Dan shuddered, despite himself. There was a cruel, avid smile on her lips, the smile of a mistreated doll, and those blue eyes in which her own death gleamed.

"Terrific," he said, switching on the ignition.

They had two hours in front of them—a whole lifetime.

*

The evening papers led with the murder of Nicole Wiese. Her father had been world champion just after the first democratic elections, when Mandela had put on a Springboks shirt and stood listening to the new South African anthem and shaking the hand of the captain, Pienaar, an Afrikaner. That day, Stewart Wiese had become one of the ambassadors of the new

South Africa—and what did it matter if the invincible All Blacks had caught gastroenteritis on the eve of the final?

As the eye of the storm, Stewart Wiese had announced that he would be giving a press conference, which was not a good omen in a country in the grip of violent crime. The figures would get a going over—more than fifty murders a day—the inadequacies of a police force that couldn't protect the citizens, and then, probably, the importance of reintroducing the death penalty.

Night was falling on the township. Ali Neuman switched off the radio and served the meal in the kitchen. He had made a dish of lentils with coriander and a cocktail of fruit juices. Woozy with medication, his mother had slept part of the afternoon, but seemed to be regaining strength. This morning's attack? What attack? Josephina claimed she was as fit as a fiddle, better almost than she'd ever felt in her life. Whereas he, although as handsome, strong, etc., as ever, was looking tired. The usual palaver.

Neuman did not tell her about his day, or what he had seen. He left her favorite chocolates on the kitchen table—they were her only pleasure—and kissed her on the forehead before leaving, promising that yes, yes, one day he'd introduce her to his "girlfriend."

All a sham.

Without street lighting, and fragmented into a multitude of mini-territories, the townships were particularly dangerous in the evening. Manenberg was no exception. The Rastafarians had organized marches against crime and drugs, but the organized gangs continued to lay down the law. Even the schools in Bonteheuwel had been closed by decree of the gangs, and the authorities remained powerless to ensure the safety of the pupils. In Manenberg, three quarters of them took drugs and were involved with the *tsotsis*.

Neuman parked his car outside Maia's house, one of the few permanent structures in the area. High-flying planes blinked in the mauve sky. He glanced at the unpaved streets receding into the distance and closed the car door. A ray of light was filtering through the skylight of her bedroom. He knocked gently at the door, in order not to scare her—four times, it was one of their codes. Muffled steps approached.

Maia smiled when she saw him, her demi-god looming out of the darkness. "I've been waiting for you all day," she said, with no reproach in her voice.

She was wearing only a short, shimmery nightdress and the pair of slippers he had bought her. She kissed his hand and drew him inside. The decoration of the living room area had changed since last week. Maia had torn down the ill-assorted pieces of wallpaper and put up paintings, her own paintings, done on boards or salvaged wood. Maia was happy to see him but said nothing—code number four. You just had to remember them.

Without a word, she drew him toward the bedroom, lit the candle next to the mattress and lay down on her stomach. Her golden thighs gleamed in the dim light, her legs—he knew every muscle, every fold of them, he had caressed them a thousand times. Maia closed her eyes, letting herself be looked at, her arms hanging loose from her body, as if she was about to fly away. A dog barked outside.

Another plane passed. The candle wax dripped on the carpet. Still as a sculpture, Maia waited, her eyes closed, as if dead. At last, he ran his hand through her carefully braided hair and gently stroked the curve of her neck. She smiled. There was no need to open her eyes. "I'd know your hand three yards away."

Her body was as warm and soft as her lips. He stroked her shoulders, her back, slightly rough to the touch. One, two, three, he counted five scars. Maia began writhing and whimpering. Maybe she was faking it. It didn't matter. He lifted her nightdress, revealing the small of her back, her round buttocks, which she stretched toward him, like an offering. Neuman had stopped thinking. His fingertips made powder trails on her ransacked body, an invisible thread that drew a thousand delighted little squeals from her.

He looked up and saw, in the candlelight, the photographs on the walls. Photographs out of magazines that Maia had put up to brighten the room, advertisements showing women in tropical paradises, with beaches and isolated atolls in the background, half-crumpled photographs, some of them damp from being picked up out of the garbage on the streets. You almost wanted to throw up with the pity of it.

Neuman left without even glancing at her paintings, leaving a handful of banknotes on the fridge.

*

The botanical gardens were empty at this hour, the dawn still a memory. Neuman walked across the English lawn, holding his shoes in his hand. The grass felt soft and cool beneath his feet. The foliage of the acacias trembled in the darkness. Neuman folded back the ends of his jacket and kneeled by the flowers.

Wilde iris (*Dietes grandiflora*), read the notice. The police tapes were still there, waving in the breeze.

They hadn't found Nicole's purse at the scene of the crime. The killer had taken it. Why? For the money? How much money could a student have in her purse? He looked up at the clouds scurrying wildly beneath the moon. The presentiment was still there, omnipresent, like a tightness in his chest.

He wouldn't sleep. Not tonight, not tomorrow. The pills had no effect, except to leave a taste like soft dough in his mouth. Chronic insomnia, despair, compensatory phenomena, despair—his brain was going around in circles. Not just since this morning. Taking one of his walks along the Cape of Good Hope wouldn't make any difference. There was this cold monster inside him, this beast that was impossible to spit out. However hard he fought, however much he denied it, tried to make each morning the first rather than the last, he was waging a war he had lost in advance. Maia—just a front. Tears welled in his eyes. He could invent activities for himself, erotic codes, lists of passionate attractions like so many phantom loves, the glue simply didn't hold. Before long, his masks would fall in a rain of plaster, walls that would carry everything away in their collapse, like old scenery sent for scrap. Reality would explode one day, it would take him by the throat and make him bite the dust, as he had in that garden as a child. His Zulu skin was hanging by a thread. He could try to dent reality as much as he wanted, make plans, forenames with female lines, he would fall, engine in flames, on the same no man's land. A land without man—without a man worthy of the name.

Neuman wasn't a man anymore. He had never been a man.

Maia could writhe on the mattress all she liked, split the atoms of desire that separated them. Neuman's sexual organ was dead. He had died with it.

6.

Ruby didn't much trust particular men, and some men not at all. Her father had left suddenly, without leaving an address, abandoning his wife and children.

Ruby, the youngest, was thirteen at the time. No explanation. Her father had left a void behind him and built a new life for himself, with other people.

The years had passed, but Ruby had never tried to track him down. Her sister had become anorexic, her brother was a divorcé hardened by two marriages as pathetic as they were hasty, and their mother had never remarried. The bastard had wrecked their lives, he could die incognito.

The emotional emptiness that had eaten away at them had turned to anger. Ruby had loved her father. She had believed everything he had said to her, all the hopes he had instilled in her when he took her on his knees and played card tricks for her, or drew the tarot for her—"You're going to be a great reporter!" He had seemed so proud of her, so sure of himself and the time they would have. Ruby hadn't suspected a thing. Her father and all the men in the world were traitors. Especially Brian. Brian Epkeen, the love she had never dared to dream of, her battered prince whom she would collect from the gutters, his face swollen, Brian who she had sponged and bandaged and put back on his feet, the bastard had ruined everything. Ruby had given him everything, her love, her ass, her time, and he had rejected all of it.

They had been separated for six years. Ruby'd had a few

disappointments since then, but she couldn't resign herself to the idea of growing old without love. Impossible. Love was her drug, her greatest addiction, her only way of mourning her father. But now, fortunately, there was Rick.

Fifty-three years old, but still looking good, Rick van der Verskuizen had the most fashionable dental practice in the city, a house in the middle of the wine country—she'd just moved in—and children grown up enough not to bother them. A considerate man, someone who offered prospects, not someone who came home at all hours in a state of shock, high on adrenaline or speed, and despite his fine egalitarian words took it out on her.

To bring you my love
to bring you my love
to bring you my love!

Ruby was wandering around the bedroom, the music at full volume. She hadn't yet put on her makeup, and was barely dressed, going back and forth from the bed to the bathroom, singing at the top of her voice.

Her record label hadn't withstood the era of downloading. Twelve years of passion and hard work, risk-taking and crazy nights had gone up in smoke. With a heavy heart, she'd closed up shop. She could have changed professions, like most of the artists she produced, but Ruby didn't know anything about other professions, and didn't give a fuck about any of them anyway.

That mindset hadn't helped her to find a job. None of the majors wanted to work with a hothead like her, the others had seen her too often backstage, drunk, clinging to whatever man was around, taking whatever was offered. Three years of hell, thinking it would never end, but things had been looking up since she had gotten this job as a production assistant. No more casting sessions for reality shows, no more shoots for hip magazines that paid you in clothes, no more humiliating apologies to her bank president for unpaid checks, no more temporary contracts, no more periods of unemployment. Once again, she would have a recognized social activity, a little money, independence. Of course, it wasn't the job she'd dreamed of. Rick had used his contacts. Having never had to depend on anyone, she'd had to smile at people. Shut her big vinyl suffragette mouth. Swallow her forty-two years and act as if she was living for the first time. But what of it? The job had gotten her out of the rut, and besides, she didn't exactly have a lot of choice these days. Forty-two. She would soon be past childbearing age. In a few years she wouldn't be able to flash her ass anymore and get a man to do anything she wanted, go anywhere she wanted. A few more years, she thought, and it would all be over—the unrelenting kisses, the sweet talk that led to the altar. What would become of her if Rick threw her out, too?

Her cell phone rang on the chest of drawers in the bedroom. Ruby turned down the volume of the music, wedged the cell phone against her ear, and pulled up the zipper of her dress.

"Hi."

"Shit."

"Yes, it's me."

Brian. For a moment, there was silence in the chaos of sound waves.

"I'm busy right now," Ruby said. "What is it?"

"Was it you who sent David to go through my pockets?"

"I have nothing to say to you."

"Admit it."

"I told you, you can just fuck off."

"David, too, it seems. What happened with Marjorie's parents? Apparently he got thrown out, and now he's looking for an apartment."

"I don't know anything about that."

"If I know him, he was probably smoking joints in their living room."

"You don't know your son, Brian. You've only ever been interested in your own dick. Don't be surprised if he hates your guts."

"I think you're exaggerating."

"I assure you I'm not."

He laughed dismissively, but Ruby's voice was hard as stone.

"David told me you've moved in with your new boyfriend."

"That's none of your business."

"We could come to an arrangement about the rent for the apartment," Brian went on. "Fifty-fifty, do you agree?"

"No."

"Your dentist is rolling in it, so I think you could make an effort."

"I don't see why he should pay for your son."

"He's your son, too."

"What happened between us has nothing to do with Rick. Leave us alone."

"Since when have you been interested in teeth?"

"Since I stopped seeing yours."

"Ha ha!" His laugh was so forced it was painful.

"You never made me laugh, Brian," she said, icily. "Never. Now leave me alone, O.K.?"

Ruby threw her cell phone on the bed, turned up the volume, and went into the bathroom to put on her makeup, with the music at full blast. Light mascara, eyeliner. Her hand was shaking slightly. Brian. She cursed herself in the mirror. Brian had deceived her, like her father. Ruby could never forgive him for that. She had thought it would pass, but it hadn't.

The guitars suddenly stopped screaming from the bedroom.

"What kind of wild music is this?"

P. J. Harvey. Five feet of dynamite, a voice like flint, riffs that could break stones. Rick appeared in the doorway, his hair still wet from his session in the pool. He was wearing a toweling bathrobe and a watch shaped like a TV set. Ruby was finishing her makeup. He moved his hand over her ample buttocks.

"Are you going out?"

"Yes," she replied, "and I'm already late."

"Pity."

Ruby could feel his erection against her back, getting harder as he snuggled up to her. He was smiling in the bathroom mirror with his thirty-two impeccable teeth. He slid his hand under her dress, moved it to the front of her panties and down onto her pubis.

"We'll have to hurry," he breathed in her ear.

Ruby arched as he started to masturbate her. "I don't have time," she whimpered.

"Two minutes," he said, breathing harder.

"I'm going to be late."

"Yes. It'll be good."

"Rick."

She was writhing, trying to get away, but he held her firmly, kneading her clitoris. He lifted her dress and pressed his cock between her buttocks.

"Rick. No, Rick."

But he had already lowered her panties.

It was a lovely summer's day, the insects were dancing in the shady garden, chased by birds. Ruby went out via the terrace, carrying her bag—she was going to be late after all. Rick readjusted his bathrobe and grabbed the newspaper lying on the deckchair.

"See you tonight, darling!" he said.

"I'll call you after the production meeting!"

"O.K.!"

She smiled to hide her embarrassment. He had hurt her earlier.

The bull mastiff that guarded the property came up to her to be stroked, but quickly turned away. Ruby got in the BMW coupé parked in the forecourt, avoided looking at herself in the rear-view mirror, narrowly missed the dog, and drove out onto the vineyard road, with P. J. Harvey playing in the background to drown out her tears.

*

As swanky as its sister, Clifton, Camps Bay had a view over the Atlantic and the foothills of Table Mountain, which protected it from the polar winds. A few gossamer clouds on the hilltops, freighters on the sky-blue horizon, the indolent palm trees along Victoria road, the whole suburb was like an El Dorado within easy reach.

"Everything O.K.?" the barman said. "You don't look too good."

Brian was drinking a coffee and looking out to sea. He'd just been talking to Ruby on the phone, and didn't know whether to laugh or cry.

"Just shut up and give me another espresso."

The terrace of the Café Caprice was almost empty at this time of day. Tattooed guys who were into bodybuilding, sports cars with their tops down, mass-produced bimbos, flat-screen sunglasses—the hip young people of Camps Bay wouldn't be out on parade before eleven.

"How about a pastry?" the barman said, wiping the next table with a sponge.

"No."

"If you like, I have some great saus—"

"I said no!"

Brian hated *boerewors*, the sausages he was given in the morning as a child simply because he was an Afrikaner—to him, they tasted like unwashed feet. He closed the *Cape Times* and sighed into the air. Stewart Wiese had issued a press release that was particularly scathing about the law and order situation in the country, with an all-out attack on the police for being unable to prevent the murders and rapes of which his daughter had been just one more victim—one too many. The statement had immediately been picked up by the national media. Brian had done the rounds of the barmen who worked along Victoria with a photo of Nicole, but none of them remembered seeing her recently, which corroborated Judith Botha's testimony. Taking over from Dan Fletcher, he had questioned Ben Durandt. "O.K. for driving a convertible." Nicole's only (known) boyfriend fit the picture painted by her friend Judith. He paid the check and, his mind somewhat soothed by the sound of the sea, climbed the little coast road that led to Stewart Wiese's house.

Despite the worries about safety and the high demand for property, Camps Bay was still the flagship suburb of Cape Town, a seaside and residential resort protected by Chapman's Peak, one of the most beautiful roads in the world, which you now had to pay a toll to use. The only blacks you saw here parked the cars or helped in the kitchens. You had to go down as far as Hout Bay to see the first townships, which were nothing more than collections of huts clustered around the villages on the coast.

Fear of criminals had replaced fear of blacks in most well-to-do whites, who had retreated to their *laager*.[1] Armed response, surveillance cameras, walls protected by barbed wire and electrification—the facilities of the house where

---

[1] Entrenched camp, a key concept in the Afrikaner mentality.

Nicole had grown up were the very least to be expected in a residence of this caliber.

The teak terrace overlooked the villa of a film director who was absent half of the year. Brian stood at the guardrail, smoking a cigarette and looking out over the bay. The maid, an old-fashioned Xhosa who spoke pidgin English, had asked him to wait near the swimming pool. Stewart Wiese was in the living room talking to the funeral director.

The former Springbok had gone into the wine trade, and had shares in several local companies, including some of the best vineyards in the region. Brian peered in through the plate-glass window into the study, and saw trophies on the shelves, club pennants, the flag of the National Party, until recently still the majority party in the Western Cape.[2]

Heavy footsteps shook the boards of the terrace.

Brian had forgotten what he looked like, but now recognized him immediately. Stewart Wiese was a massive six and a half feet, with a battered face, cauliflower ears from thousands of scrums, and steel-gray eyes still red with tears.

"Are you in charge of the investigation?" he asked the cop who'd just shown up in his black fatigues.

"Lieutenant Epkeen," Brian said, his hand disappearing into Wiese's.

After his rough Saturday night, he had left his suit at the dry-cleaners. Wiese snarled dubiously at his T-shirt. His two little girls, aged four and six, were staying with their grandparents until their sister's funeral; his wife was asleep in the bedroom, under sedation, and couldn't talk to anyone. He quickly went over everything as if it was a formality: Nicole was in her first year of law at the faculty in Observatory, if you were studying law you had to work hard, not go out all the time, the streets

[2] During apartheid, the ruling National Party had passed a number of laws favoring coloreds over blacks, and most coloreds had continued to vote for them rather than the ANC, for fear of becoming the subject of discrimination.

weren't safe, the customers of the hottest restaurant in the city had been robbed by an armed gang as recently as last week, on a Saturday night, young white girls were particularly at risk, which was why he had kept a close watch on when Nicole went out and who she went out with. He had never doubted Judith Botha, or her loyalty. He and his wife couldn't understand what could have happened—it was beyond them.

Brian could understand this father's aggressive mood—even the death of an idler like David would destroy him—but something in the way Wiese put forward his arguments bothered him.

"Your daughter hadn't been seen in any of the bars in Camps Bay for a while," he said. "Did Nicole mention a new place she liked to go?"

"My daughter's not in the habit of hanging out in bars," Wiese said, looking hard at him.

"Precisely. Someone may have forced her to go there, gotten her drunk."

"We're strict Adventists," Wiese stated.

"You also used to be a top sportsman. With all the touring and the training, I don't suppose you saw much of your daughter as she was growing up."

"I had her young, I agree, and I was very busy with my career, but since I retired from sport we've had time to get to know each other."

"Your daughter must have had a close relationship with her mother," Brian went on.

"She spoke to her more than to me, yes."

That seemed straightforward enough.

"Nicole went out several times last week."

"As I've said before, she was supposed to be revising with Judith."

"If Nicole thought she needed an alibi to go out, I suppose it was because she knew what your reaction would be?"

"What reaction?"

"What would have happened, for instance, if she'd met young people from outside your social circle, coloreds, even blacks?"

Stewart Wiese was back on the rugby field, ready for a scrum. "Have you come here to call me a racist, or to find the bastard who killed my daughter?"

"Nicole had sexual intercourse on the night of the murder," Brian said. "I'm trying to find out who with."

"My daughter was raped and murdered."

"We don't know yet if she was raped." Brian lit another cigarette. "I'm sorry to go into detail, Mr. Wiese, but it sometimes happens that a woman's vagina becomes lubricated as a defense against the violence of rape. That doesn't make her a consenting victim."

"Impossible."

"Why do you say that?"

"My daughter was a virgin," he said.

"I've been told there was a boy named Durandt."

"That was just a flirtation. My wife and I talked about him last night. Nicole didn't love him. At least not enough to go on the pill."

There were other kinds of contraception, especially with AIDS ravaging the country, but this was a slippery slope to go down, and Durandt had confirmed that they had never slept together.

"Did Nicole ever confide in your wife?" Brian resumed.

"Not about that."

"About anything else?"

"We're a close family, lieutenant. What are you getting at?" His eyes were like chrome-plated marbles in the sun.

"We found a membership card for a video club in Nicole's cardigan," Brian said. "According to the records, several pornographic films were rented using that card in the last few weeks."

"The card belonged to Judith Botha, or so I heard!" He was becoming heated.

"Nicole used it."

"Is that what Judith told you?"

"It wasn't Judith who put that card in Nicole's cardigan."

Wiese was disconcerted. He didn't like the turn the conversation was taking, or the attitude of the cop who'd come to question him. "That doesn't mean my daughter rented that kind of film," he said. "That's a horrible thing to say!"

"I spoke to Judith on the phone earlier. She claims she never rented any porn films."

"She's lying!" Wiese yelled. "She's lying like she always lied, to Nils Botha and to me!"

Brian nodded—he'd check later with the assistants at the video club.

"Did your daughter keep a diary or anything like that?" he asked.

"Not as far as I know."

"Can I see her bedroom?"

Wiese had folded his trunk-like arms, as if mounting guard. "This way," he said, opening the plate-glass window.

The rooms of the house were vast and filled with light. They climbed to the upper floor. Wiese walked noiselessly past the room where his wife was sleeping off their grief and pointed to the door at the end of the corridor. Nicole's room was that of a studious post-adolescent. A few photos of film stars above the desk, a computer, a stereo, a series of photo-booth pictures of her and her friend Judith in their school days, laughing and pulling faces, a bed covered with a neat quilt, shelves filled with books, Mandela's autobiography *A Long Way to Freedom*, a few South African and American detective novels, boxes, candlesticks, knickknacks. Brian opened the night table, found a jumble of letters, looked through them. Adolescent letters, dreams of love for the future. No name mentioned, except a certain Ben (Durandt), described as superficial, and more interested in Formula One than in finding a kindred soul. She had found someone else. Someone she had hidden from everyone.

Nicole's father was standing in the doorway, a silent sentinel. Apart from the blouse on the back of a rattan chair, everything had been carefully put away. The bathroom too was tidy, with makeup and beauty products stacked in front of the mirror. Brian searched the medicine cabinet: cotton wool, antiseptic, various oils. He opened the little locally made boxes on the shelf, the drawers in the chest, the shoe closet, all he found were expensive garments with empty pockets or female accessories whose use was a mystery. Nor was there anything under the mattress, the pillow, the cushions. Nicole didn't keep a diary. He switched on the computer on the desk, clicked on some of the icons.

"What are you looking for?" Wiese asked, standing behind him.

"A lead, believe it or not."

Brian checked the e-mails, the messages sent, messages received, noted down the names and addresses, but didn't find anything specific. Nicole's life was hazy. He cleared his throat, closed his eyes to sweep away what he had seen, and opened them again after a while, as if new. He thought for a moment, then bent and looked at the computer tower. There was a thick layer of dust on the top. Finger marks were clearly visible.

He kneeled, took out his Swiss army knife, unscrewed the left side of the tower, and removed the metal panel. There was a little plastic bag next to the hard drive, containing a number of unusual objects: geisha balls, a mini-vibrator with rabbit ears to be connected to an iPod, condoms, edible body foam, a vibrating ring with a clitoris stimulator, women's power capsules, anal lubricating and anesthetizing spray, a whole array of state-of-the-art sex toys, all neatly wrapped.

Leaning over him like a dead tree, Wiese did not react immediately. He turned away his face and looked out at the swimming pool shimmering beyond the window. It was no use—his shoulders started shaking, faster and faster.

7.

Cape Town was South Africa's showcase. Shaken by the murder of a well-known historian the year before, and shocked by the death of the reggae singer Lucky Duke, a living legend who had been involved in the anti-apartheid struggle, shot down by thugs in front of his children as he was taking them to see their uncle, the First National Bank had launched a huge anti-crime campaign, bringing together the private sector and the main opposition bodies.

This was a clear challenge to the government's passive attitude in the face of the country's chronic security situation. The argument that crime = poverty + unemployment didn't hold water anymore. In spite of what the president had said, crime wasn't "under control." You just had to switch on the TV or open a newspaper to be aware of how widespread the problem was. The number of homicides may have dropped thirty percent since the ANC had come to power, but that was because the statistics took into account the inter-ethnic violence that had preceded the democratic elections, which had claimed thousands of lives. What was at stake now was quite different: how could the leading democracy in Africa be the most dangerous country in the world?

The potential economic gains were enormous—there was talk of creating 125,000 jobs, if the homicide rate could be reduced by fifty per cent—and the country, which at a time of globalization was experiencing the biggest growth in its history, needed foreign investors. Especially now, when South Africa was getting ready for the biggest media event on earth, the World Cup, due to take place in 2010—four billion viewers for the final matches, a million supporters who had to be kept safe, all the TV coverage, the interviews. The whole world would be watching, and South Africa simply *could not* afford the terrible image it had. Who wanted to invest in a country branded the world's most dangerous place? The financial backers had to be reassured at all costs. That was why the FNB had committed twenty-five million rand, raised from those who had signed its petition, to protest against the government's inaction and to mobilize opinion over what was happening to the very symbols of the country.

It wasn't the poor who attacked security guards with bazookas, it wasn't the unemployed who had killed the director of Business Against Crime the previous year. They were dealing with a wave of organized crime, gangs, small or large, linked to Mafias, gangs with sophisticated infrastructures similar to those of the Mob in the USA in the thirties. The police were corrupt, or even in collusion with the criminals, the justice system was ineffective, the government was doing nothing. Through the anti-crime campaign, the private sector wasn't attacking democracy but the men who were sitting on top of the powder keg—especially the ANC.

Superintendent Karl Krüge was sweating in his big leather armchair. He'd put on too much weight in the last few years. Krüge had been running the SAP in Cape Town since the 1994 elections. It was his ambition and his duty to be remembered as the man who had been in place during the democratic transition. He would be retiring in two years and was pushing behind the scenes for Ali Neuman to succeed him. A young Zulu officer in charge of the police in a Xhosa province where the blacks were in the minority would demonstrate that there had been a small palace revolution, and would send a strong message in a country that was finding it hard to keep its prom-

ises. Krüge knew Neuman, knew his history, his almost aristocratic disgust at the widespread corruption. His successor as
the head of the SAP would be a highly competent black, not
an unqualified Zulu. But media coverage of the murder wasn't
helping things.

"Have you read the newspapers?"

"Some," Neuman replied.

"They're all saying the same thing."

"They all belong to the same people."

"We're not here to discuss the concentration of power in
the media," Krüge replied. "The whole lot of them will be
coming down on our heads."

The office looked out on Long Street and the African market. Neuman shrugged. "I'm not afraid of the storm."

"Well, I am. I've just had the Attorney General on the
phone. They need to be thrown a bone, and soon. Stewart
Wiese has a lot of influence, and he's moving heaven and earth
to get everyone on his side. The message is getting through, the
public is in shock. You know how powerful symbols can be."

Neuman, sitting there in his dark suit, nodded. The FNB
was also one of the main sponsors of the Springboks, which
explained the speed and virulence of the media campaign. Of
course it was a paradox to see banks waging war on crime,
when these same banks sustained tax havens and laundered
dirty money, but Neuman knew that was an argument that carried no weight in an era of globalization.

"I'll be meeting the medical examiner in a while," he said.
"He should have the first results of the postmortem. Contrary
to what Wiese said in his press conference, we're not sure his
daughter was raped. What seems more likely is that she was
trying to break free of what she felt were, let's say, the restrictions of her social class. Nicole went out without her parents
knowing, and sometimes stayed out all night. Our prime suspect right now is a boy she'd been seeing for a while, and we're

trying to track him down. I've put Epkeen and Fletcher on the case."

"Fletcher's good," Krüge said. "But Epkeen. I'm really not sure about him."

"He's my best detective."

"He never comes in before eleven," Krüge remarked.

"He sometimes doesn't come in after eleven either," Neuman said sarcastically.

"I don't like loose cannons like that."

"I admit he's not very disciplined, but I have total confidence in him."

"I don't."

Brian Epkeen had been "on the other side" during apartheid, he'd been in trouble with the police, and hadn't joined the force to follow procedure. He had come on board only because Neuman had gone looking for him. One day, he would blow up in their faces.

Krüge sighed and massaged the back of his log-like neck. "On your head be it, captain," he said by way of conclusion. "But I have no intention of ending my police career with a failure. Find me the suspect. Better than that, find me the killer."

Neuman stood up and left.

Tembo was waiting for him at the Durham Road morgue.

*

Brian Epkeen had never dreamed of joining the police, even after Mandela was elected. It was meeting Neuman that had changed everything.

Like the ANC leader, Neuman had become a lawyer—defending the rights of those who didn't have any—before joining the SAP in Cape Town. The new South Africa was hungry for justice, and Neuman knew Epkeen by reputation—not many whites would have taken on the task of tracing militants who had disappeared. One of the two men had changed his name to escape the militias in the Bantustans, the other to escape a historical principle that had its roots in colonialism. Neuman believed in his destiny, and he could be persuasive. They were cut from the same cloth. Wanted the same country. In every other way, Brian was more or less the opposite of Neuman. He had no ambition, liked living it up, had broken a thousand times over with the world he'd grown up in. Neuman liked his energy, his strangely innocent despair, and above all the impetus that threw him into the arms of women, as if he only had to exist to be loved. Detached as he seemed, Brian was the rope above his void, his last bullet, the only man he could have talked to.

He never had.

They arrived at Dan's with flowers for Claire.

The couple lived in a little house in Kloof Nek, overlooking the city. Dan Fletcher shared their ideas on South African society, the way to improve it, the nature of the ties that bound them. The calamity that had struck his wife had set the seal on their pact.

Claire greeted them at the gate with a hug and a brave smile.

"How are you?" Neuman asked.

"Better than you two. You look like you've just come from a funeral!"

She had grown thinner, her peaches and cream complexion had grown paler with the chemo, but she was as pretty as ever. Her blonde wig suited her. They clung to her arm, joking as they asked about her health—they liked to keep things lively—and followed her down the drive. Dan was waiting under the hollyhocks in the arbor, conforming to the ritual of a barbecue in the garden. The children greeted them excitedly.

They dined all together on the terrace, forgetting all about the possibility of a relapse, which would be shattering.

The glass of Pinot Claire had allowed herself was making her tipsy.

Brian opened another bottle. "I'm with a barmaid at the moment," he said, by way of explanation.

"That's original. What's she like?"

"No idea."

"Come on!" Claire laughed. "Do you at least know her name?"

"Listen," he cried, "it's difficult enough remembering my own!"

She laughed even more loudly, which was of course the intention. "But for the moment," she said, "what with you, and Ali hiding his lady-love from us, I'm still the only girl here."

"Yes," Brian said. "That's what Ruby used to say when we went to a restaurant."

Ali Neuman smiled along with them, putting on a good show, but the cracks in his fortifications were getting wider. He had never introduced Maia to his friends. No white ever entered the townships—that was why he had chosen her. What would he have told them anyway? That he had picked up this poor girl on the street, like a garbage bag torn open by dogs, that she couldn't read or write, just paint a little on pieces of wood, that he kept a woman so that he could caress her whenever he liked, to satisfy his urges as a man or what remained of them, that Maia was a useful front, a social cover, a picture postcard? He would never introduce her to them—never.

A shadow loomed in the twilight. Neuman stood up to clear the table and stood for a moment under the trees, waiting for it to pass.

Brian was watching him from a distance, joking to distract attention, but he wasn't deceived—lately, Ali had been acting very strangely.

In the garden, it was the hour of the cat—two bastard tabbies that were pretending to tear each other to pieces. The children had put on their pajamas, and were watching the cats and stamping the ground with joy. At last the table was cleared, indicating that it was bedtime, but the kids wanted to stay up.

"Uncle Brian! Shall we fight? Come on! Uncle Brian!"

"I don't fight with gargoyles."

"I'm Darth Vader!" Tom cried, flourishing a length of plastic. Eve was also waving her arms ecstatically.

"You should stop sniffing the glue," he advised them.

The kids didn't understand half of what he said to them, what mattered was the tone. After a while, they gave everyone a hug in turn, then followed their mother upstairs. As darkness fell, the garden was suddenly calm. Dan lit the candles in the storm lamps, and Neuman opened the file in progress. They soon forgot all about the balmy evening.

Nicole Wiese had been trying to escape, and they could understand her—at eighteen, she had wanted to see life, not its wrapping, however gilded. Judith Botha had acted as her cover, and had occasionally let her use her apartment. The forensics team had gone over that apartment with a fine-toothed comb, but the only prints they had found belonged to the two girls and young Deblink. Inquiries in the area hadn't turned up anything, nor had checking out the university in Observatory. Nicole only ever went there to fill in forms, confirming what her friend Judith had said.

Brian had followed up the sex-toy lead. Having found no trace of an Internet purchase on her computer—in any case, Nicole wouldn't have risked having such things delivered to her home—he had been all over the city's sex shops, until he had found the shop that had sold them to her—several purchases in the last three weeks. The assistant he had questioned, dressed in skintight latex, had a good memory for faces: there was no boy with Nicole. Brian had then paid a visit to the video club. *In Your Ass, Appointment with My Pussy, Fist Fucking in the Rain.* Nicole hadn't rented a film on Saturday night, but several in the last few weeks. The assistant remembered the girl (he had asked her for her identity card), but she had been alone.

Fortunately, Fletcher had had better luck.

"I went through Nicole's phone bills and bank account," he said, consulting his notebook. "I have a list of phone numbers, but they haven't turned up anything yet. Her bank account shows she had regular expenses that more than covered her lifestyle, which was quite modest considering her family's standing. The card purchases were for clothes from downtown stores, student stationery, drinks at various bars in Observatory, that kind of thing. The last time she used her card was on Wednesday evening, at the Sundance. Sixty rand."

"A club popular with students," Brian said.

"Wednesday," Dan went on. "The night Nicole didn't come back to Judith's to sleep. I checked the hotel registers, no trace of her name. So we don't know where she slept that night, or who with, but we do know she withdrew cash on the day of the murder, at eight in the evening. A thousand rand, from an ATM in Muizenberg, on the south coast of the peninsula. A thousand rand, that's quite a bit of money for a girl her age, especially as she usually only took out small amounts."

"Is there much drug dealing at the Sundance?" Neuman asked.

"Not even coke," Dan replied.

"Strange."

"Why?"

"Nicole was completely high when she was killed," Neuman said.

He had just had the first postmortem report from Tembo. Nicole Wiese had died about one in the morning, in the botanical gardens, killed by blows from a hammer or similar object—a club, an iron bar. Thirty-two points of impact, mostly concentrated on the face and skull. Lesions, hematomas, and multiple fractures, including the right humerus and three fingers. A fractured cranium. No fragments of skin under the nails, no sperm in the vagina. Contrary to her father's hasty statements, rape had not been established—nor had there been anal relations. The only thing certain was that the girl was not a virgin at the time of her death. They had also found sea salt on her skin, grains of sand in her hair, and some unusual scratches on her arms and thorax, caused by barbed wire. The marks were recent.

"She may have scratched herself climbing over a fence," Brian suggested.

"Entrance to the gardens is free," Neuman replied.

But the most surprising item came from the toxicological analysis, which had revealed the presence of a mixture of plants absorbed several days earlier—the precise date had still to be established—as well as a cocktail composed of marijuana, a methamphetamine base, and another chemical substance, not yet identified.

"Methamphetamine," Brian repeated.

"The basis of *tik*," Neuman said.

The new drug that was ravaging the youth of Cape Town.

"According to Tembo," Neuman went on, "the product was inhaled not long before the murder. Nicole was probably completely out of it when she was attacked. The killer may have used the drug to take advantage of her, or to get her to the gardens without her resisting."

The news left them puzzled for a moment. Manufactured from ephedrine, methamphetamine could be smoked, inhaled or injected intravenously. In the form of crystals (crystal meth), *tik* cost a sixth of the price of cocaine, for an effect that was ten times more powerful. Smoking or injecting methamphetamine produced a quick rush: physical stimulation, an illusion of invincibility, a feeling of power, self-control, energy, excessive volubility, sexual euphoria. In the medium term, the effects were reversed: intense tiredness, uncoordinated movements, uncontrollable nervousness, paranoia, visual and auditory hallucinations, irritation of the skin, delirium (a feeling like insects swarming on the skin), unavoidable bouts of sleep, nausea, vomiting, diarrhea, blurred vision, dizzy spells, pains in the chest. Highly addictive, *tik* led to depression or to psychoses similar to schizophrenia, with irreversible damage of the brain cells. The paranoia could also induce thoughts of murder or suicide, and psychotic symptoms persisted for months after withdrawal.

Either the girl had been completely reckless, or she had been deceived about the nature of the merchandise.

"Nicole's boyfriend still hasn't showed up," Neuman said. "So there's a strong likelihood he's connected to the drugs. *Tik* has spread through the townships, but much less on the coast or among whites. Something doesn't feel right about this."

"Do you think she was planning to buy drugs with the money she withdrew in Muizenberg?"

"Uh-huh."

"Anything from our informants?"

"We're sounding them out, but nothing yet. If anyone's dealing on the coast, or there's a new drug on the market, no one seems to know."

"Strange."

"It may have something to do with the unidentified substance," Brian suggested.

"Possibly."

Methamphetamine was the basis of *tik*, but you could find all kinds of things in it: ephedrine, ammoniac, industrial solvent, Drano, battery lithium, hydrochloric acid.

Claire appeared on the lawn. It was cooler now that night had fallen, she had put the children to bed, and she was holding her bare arms as if they were about to crumble.

The three men fell silent, waiting for her to speak.

"Can I join you?"

Her jeans hung slightly loosely on her, but she had lost

nothing of her gracefulness. She was like a bird of paradise, brought down in mid-flight.

*

The Observatory district was home to part of the student population, but was mainly concentrated on Lower Main Street, where the alternative bars and restaurants were to be found. Neuman parked outside a Tex-Mex restaurant with a blinking sign, and made his way through the groups of young people strolling on the sidewalks.

There was a mixed crowd trying to get into the Sundance. A Xhosa as fat as a walrus was lazily letting them through. Neuman spotted the surveillance camera above the barrier, and stuck his badge and Nicole's photo under the big guy's nose.

"Have you ever seen this girl?"

"Hmm." He stepped back to take a better look. "I think so."

"Do you have a good memory for faces, or what?"

"Well—"

"Nicole Wiese, the girl the newspapers are talking about. She was here last week."

"Yes. Yes."

The walrus searched in his memories, but apparently they were a mess.

"Wednesday?"

"Could be, yes."

"How about Saturday?"

He chewed that over. "Hmm."

"Alone or with someone?" Neuman asked impatiently.

"That I couldn't tell you," he said, admitting his helplessness. "There's a festival on at the moment, and after midnight anyone can get in. Hard to say who's with who."

He would have said the same thing about the Middle East conflict.

Neuman pointed to the straw huts beyond the outside wall. "What barman was working here on Saturday night?"

"Cissy," the man replied. "A colored girl, with big tits."

So he had a memory for some things after all.

Neuman walked across the sandy garden where young people were drinking beer and shouting as if they were on the beach. The pimply guy with long hair shaking cocktails behind the outside bar seemed as drunk as his customers.

"Where can I find Cissy?"

"Inside!" he cried.

Following the direction of his bloodshot eyes, Neuman opened the wooden door that led into the club. The latest Red Hot Chili Peppers was bouncing off the walls, the room was packed, the light dim beneath the spotlights. There was a smell of grass in spite of the warnings on display, but also a strange smell of something burning. Neuman pushed his way through to the bar. Few of the customers were over thirty. They were knocking back oddly colored cocktails, which would probably end up in the toilets or the gutters, if they could reach them in time. Cissy, the barmaid, had brown skin, and her breasts were squeezed into an unusually flexible leotard. She was being ogled by a bunch of tipsy youngsters. Neuman leaned over the umbrellas sticking out of the greenish cocktails she was making.

"Have you ever seen this girl before?"

From the chewing-gum grimace she threw at the photograph, it was obvious Cissy was more preoccupied by her cleavage than the melting of ice cubes.

"Dunno."

"Take a closer look."

She gave a pout that went down well with the school of pilot fish clinging to the bar. "Maybe. Yes, looks familiar."

"Nicole Wiese, a student," Neuman said. "Maybe you saw her face in the newspapers?"

"Er . . . no."

Cissy didn't even know what she was saying, she was thinking of her cocktails and the piranhas waiting for her.

"They won't get cold," said Neuman, moving aside the glasses on the bar. "A pretty blonde like this," he insisted, "isn't so easy to forget. Try to remember." He had taken hold of her wrist—gently, but he wouldn't let go. "Nicole was here on Wednesday night," he said, "and possibly Saturday, too."

The lights began to dim.

"Saturday, I don't know," the barmaid finally said, "but I saw her on Wednesday night. Yes, Wednesday. She talked for a while to the girl who's performing."

The lights went out suddenly, plunging the room into darkness. Neuman let go of the barmaid's wrist. Everyone had turned to look at the stage. He walked away from the bar. It was hot and the smell was sharper now. Coal. There were coals in the middle of the stage, a red-hot bed of coals he could see through the anonymous heads. Suddenly, the floor began to vibrate with the beating of drums. *Boom boom boom.* A thin line of smoke rose along the proscenium, every beat of the drums was accompanied by a flash of light directed at the audience, but Neuman was somewhere else. Those drums, that hypnotic rhythm from the depths of time, was the *indlamu*, the Zulu war dance. For a moment, he saw his father dancing, without weapons, in the dust of KwaZulu. The rhythm became more and more sustained. The four blacks beating the drums began to sing, and the stage rose. The intensity of the drums, those grave, sad voices coming from the earth before battle, his father's hand on his head when he left to demonstrate with his students, his voice telling him he was still too young to go with him but one day, yes, one day they would go together, his hot, reassuring hand, his smile, a father already proud of his son— everything came back to him like a boomerang that had traced an arc reaching to the other end of the world.

A woman appeared, dressed in a *kaross*[1] descending to mid-thigh. A steaming vessel, perfumed with oils and spices, she began to dance to the muffled drumbeats. Her skin gleamed like the eyes of cats at night, *boom boom boom*, she was dancing in the very heart of the beast, she was the bush, the Zulu dust, and the high grass where the *tokloshe*, the spirits of the ancestors, roamed—Neuman could see them emerging from the shadows to which history had consigned them, the members of the tribe, those he had loved and had lost contact with, those he had not had a chance to know and had been killed in his place, all the tormented and injured members of a people dead inside him. The sound of the drums cracked through his skin, the air was saturated with it, and there he stood, in front of the stage, like a tree waiting for the lightning.

The people in the front row held their breath when the dancer leaped onto the coals. Her bare feet hammered the glowing carpet of fire, jumping up and down, constantly seeking a new burn, to the rhythm of the drums and the chorus tearing through space and time. She danced with her eyes half-closed, raising her knees over her head, stamping the ground, sending coals spurting out toward the front rows, which moved back. Anger was being turned into art. Deep within the trance, there was only her, five foot nine of muscle firmly planted on the hot carpet, a hypnotized crowd in front of the stage, and her flaming beauty above the chaos.

Neuman shuddered when the others applauded. Good God, where had this creature come from?

*

Zina was wearing a little crimson dress and, clearly, nothing else. She was showing more than enough. Neuman had found

---

[1] A cloak made of animal hide.

her in her dressing room, between a bag of cotton wool and her stage costumes lying on the imitation leather couch.

There was a smell of burning in the room. Thin braids hung down the back of her neck, with two skillfully curled wisps against her cheeks. The lines in the corners of her eyes betrayed the fact that she was about forty, but her finely honed body was that of an athlete. Her features seemed carved out of clay, a hard, handsome face that gave an impression of diffuse anger and almost haughty nobility. Zina barely glanced at the photograph Neuman showed her, busy as she was rubbing the hard skin of her feet with *intizi*, a traditional ointment made from animal fat, which would soothe the burns.

"You know what happened to this young woman, don't you?"

"Hard to avoid the news," she replied.

Masks, tubes of paint, pigments, musical instruments—the dressing room was a complete mess. He saw her leopard skins, the Zulu clubs against the wall, and the traditional shields Inkatha had used on their marches.

"Did you know Nicole Wiese?"

"The fact that you're here," she retorted, "tells me you already know the answer to that question."

"You were seen together on Wednesday night."

"Is that so?"

Sitting on the stool by the dressing table, Zina continued massaging her feet—walking on fire wasn't so difficult, but dancing on it was another matter.

"Is that all you can say?" Neuman went on.

"We're playing here for the duration of the festival. Nicole came up to me at the bar after the show. We had a drink. That's pretty much it."

"Was Nicole on her own when she approached you?"

"I think so. I didn't notice."

"What did she say to you?"

"That I was great."

"Does that happen often?"

She looked up and gave a wicked smile. "You're a cop. You can't imagine the kind of aura a person can have onstage."

Whether this was irony or venom, she was in her element. He was still trying to figure her out.

"Why are you looking at me like that?" she asked.

"Nicole didn't go home that night."

"I'm not her mother."

"No one knows where Nicole slept that night. What did you and she talk about?"

"The show, obviously."

"What happened after that?"

"We had a drink, and then I went home and went to bed."

"Did Nicole tell you where she was going? Who she was meeting?"

"No."

"She doesn't seem to have made much of an impression on you."

"We didn't have all that much to say to each other. Nicole was a nice girl, but she looked at me as if I was made of gold. I'm used to groupies like that, it comes with the job," she added in a neutral tone.

"But you took the time to have a drink with her."

"I wasn't going to throw it back in her face. Are you cops always like this?"

"There are some dead bodies it's hard to get out of your mind. Nicole's, for example. Did you see her on Saturday night?"

"We met briefly, after the show."

"What time was that?"

"About eleven-thirty."

That was what the stage manager who let him backstage had told him.

"Was Nicole on her own?"

"When I saw her, yes. But the club was packed." Zina crossed her legs to get off the last fragments of incrusted coal.

"Did she seem to be in her normal state?"

"If you mean with stars in her eyes, yes."

She didn't know the half of it.

"We discovered a *tik*-based drug in her body," Neuman said. "A hard drug mostly found in the townships."

"I'm too old for crap like that, if that's what you're thinking," she replied immediately.

"Nicole lied to everyone: she'd stopped hanging out with young people from her social set, she'd dropped out of her classes, she went out on the sly, her parents thought she was a virgin but she was collecting sex toys, and she had intercourse with one or more unknown men."

Zina wasn't the kind of person to be taken aback by any of that. "She was of age, wasn't she?"

There was a knock at the door, and one of the musicians came in—Joey, a thickset Zulu with a Che Guevara T-shirt and a joint in his mouth.

"I didn't tell you to come in," Zina said.

"This show is making me deaf! Are you joining us? We're eating in the restaurant down the street."

"I'm coming."

The musician glanced cautiously at the big black man leaning against the wall, and disappeared in a cloud of acrid smoke.

"Any more pathetic questions to ask me?" Zina said bluntly. "I'm starving."

He shook his head. "No. Not for the moment."

"You mean you're planning to come back?"

"*Sinjalo thina maZulu.*"[2]

She smiled with a knowing air. "I didn't think you looked much like a cop."

---

[2] "We Zulus are like that."

With these words, Zina grabbed her linen bag from next to the dressing table and stood up. Her body was supple, her muscles a thousand little animals rumbling inside the material of her dress.

Neuman looked down at her bare feet. "Do you go outside like that?"

"What did you think—that I can dance on fire because of my supernatural powers?"

A tropical downpour was beating on the sidewalk of Lower Main Street. The night owls had deserted the terraces like a flock of sparrows and packed into the bars. Zina measured the distance separating her from the restaurant where the musicians were waiting for her, and looked one last time at Neuman, who seemed indifferent to the rain.

"How much longer will you be performing here?" he asked.

"This was our last show at the Sundance," she said. "Next weekend we're opening at the Armchair, down the street."

The rain had made new patterns on her dress. It was time to say goodbye.

"I'm sorry if I annoyed you," he said.

"It's not you, it's what brought you."

"I'm looking for the person who killed that girl, that's all."

"Should I wish you luck?"

The rain clung to her hips. Or vice versa. Neuman looked at it streaming down her ankles onto the asphalt. He and she were both soaked by now.

"Right, I'll say goodnight," she said, "or my feet will drown."

Zina extricated herself from the gutter, now overflowing with rain, and left to join the rest of her group. Neuman watched her walk away down the deserted street, in an even more somber mood than before—a cloak of rain had descended over his life.

8

As the police forces and the intelligence services were constantly stepping on one another's feet, the ANC had had to create the Presidential Intelligence Unit, a special unit to keep an eye open for their disagreements as well as to collect information both inside the country and abroad. Janet Helms had been working for this unit when Dan Fletcher had headhunted her—this young colored woman was a genius with computers, a hacker without equal, who might look like a kindly seal but was nobody's fool. At Fletcher's insistence, and with Superintendent Krüge's help, Neuman had obtained her transfer.

The Fletcher/Helms team had soon proved its efficiency. His tortured eyes, his fragile elegance, his almost feminine ways. Janet had quickly fallen in love with the young sergeant. Yet another blind alley for her: Dan Fletcher had children, and a wife he was apparently madly in love with. Janet had seen her photo on his desk, a pretty girl, you had to hand her that. One more prospect blocked off, as if her size wasn't enough.

Janet Helms had always thought of herself as fat. There was nothing she could do about it. Whatever she had tried—food supplements, psychiatrists, women's magazines, TV shows, the advice of experts—her outward appearance remained far too big for her liking. Janet had drawn the wrong costume in the wrong size. She would always be a colored girl with a rather ordinary face, with hips she'd inherited from her mother and a big posterior that no trick could reshape. She'd have to make do with this model. Disappointment—size XXL.

The rumors about his wife's cancer had struck her to the heart. Commiseration, hope, shame, Janet hated her thoughts—let her die!—but her imagination had started running away with her. She'd been twenty-five years without a boyfriend, she could wait a little longer. One day, she would be the only one able to console him. Janet would take it all on: her share of mourning, the children, his hands on her body, all the rest. The love she felt was beyond shame. Dan smelled so good, leaning over her shoulder.

"Looks like we've caught ourselves a fish," he said, staring at the screen.

"Yes."

They were viewing the tapes from the Sundance. There was Nicole, a few hours before the murder, in the company of a man, a young black who hadn't come forward as a witness.

"I'll start looking in the headquarter records," Janet said, sliding her chair over to her computer.

She had drawn up a Photofit of the suspect and was beginning her search when Neuman came into the office. She nodded to him—she barely knew him—and got on with her work. She was a little in awe of him. He peered at the screen. Through the gray stripes on the video image, he recognized Nicole Wiese outside the Sundance, in the company of a tall, well-built young black, wearing gangster-style clothes and jewelry. He muttered to himself—her father was not going to be happy.

"This video was taken on Saturday night," Dan said, "at 9:50, when they arrived. The next time we see them is two hours later, just before midnight, coming out of the club. We don't yet know who this guy is, but we know he was with Nicole on Tuesday evening."

"Tuesday?"

"Yes, I know it was Wednesday that Nicole didn't come back to Judith's. Anyway, these two were together an hour before the murder."

Neuman paused the image on the slender figure of the young black.

"If he's in our records, Janet should find him soon enough," Dan said.

Janet, who was still tapping away in a corner of the office, did not react, absorbed as she was by the play of her fingers on the keyboard.

Neuman let the tape run on. Nicole did not seem to be behaving unusually. She and the man just looked like two young people coming out of a club.

"Have you looked at the Wednesday tapes?"

"Yes," Dan replied. "Nicole arrived at nine-thirty, and left around midnight. But she was alone that evening. No boyfriend or girlfriend."

While waiting, the two men put together a first scenario with the information they had at their disposal. Nicole leaves the family home on Saturday afternoon, supposedly to go shopping with her friend Judith, instead of which she meets her black boyfriend on one of the beaches on the peninsula, probably Muizenberg. Nicole withdraws a thousand rand from an ATM at eight o'clock, they eat somewhere on the way, and get back to Cape Town without even stopping at Judith's apartment to freshen up. They spend the evening at the Sundance, watch the show by the Zulu group that Nicole saw three days earlier, and leave the club just before midnight. Nicole dies an hour later, in Kirstenbosch.

The park was half an hour's drive from Observatory. That left about forty minutes unaccounted for. What had they done during that time? Made love under the stars, after Nicole had been initiated into the joys of methamphetamine? Or had she been drugged in order to be taken advantage of? Why bother, if she was willing? *Tik* led its users to neglect the elementary rules of safe sex, but GHB was easy to obtain and a surer way to rape girls without their knowing. A third party might have followed them, or come across them by chance in the gardens. In that case, what had become of the young black?

Officer Helms, pounding her keyboard a few feet away, suddenly stopped.

"I've got him," she said. "Stanley Ramphele. A small-time marijuana dealer, currently on a suspended sentence. We have an address for him. A mobile home in Noordhoek."

A village on the coast of the peninsula.

Brian Epkeen arrived as they were leaving. Neuman decided to take him along—he looked as if he could do with some fresh air.

*

"I see your car's still as much of a dump as ever," Dan commented, opening the glove compartment of the Mercedes, where ants were sharing some old pieces of cake.

"It's my son's last snack," Brian lied.

There was a bit of everything in the glove compartment: cassettes with cracked cases, pencils, pre-stamped envelopes, a flashlight, a toothbrush, condoms, a book with its pages ruined by sand, even a *knout*—a thong of hippopotamus hide attached to a copper loop, which his ancestors had used for whipping cattle. Dan extracted the Colt .45 from the mess, wiped off the cake crumbs stuck to the barrel, and noted that the cylinder was empty. Brian never loaded it. But he could kill people if he had to. He already had, and he didn't regret it—but he had enough memories weighing him down as it was.

In the back seat, blind to the imposing view of Chapman's Peak, Neuman was collating the information from headquarters. Stanley Ramphele, twenty-one, was the younger brother of

Sonny, a dealer with a record as long as your arm who was currently serving a two-year sentence in Pollsmoor Prison in the Western Cape. Stanley was also selling dope, that was what he'd been given the suspended sentence for. He had no qualifications, and wasn't involved with social services, but he seemed to have kept his head down since his arrest six months earlier. A government allowance paid the rent for the mobile home he shared with his brother in Nordhoek, an isolated village on the wildest bay of the peninsula. According to the local police, the brothers limited themselves to dealing the local grass.

"They may have graduated to meth," Fletcher commented.

"The surfers on the coast are more into ecstasy or coke."

"Unless they're being sold *tik* under another name."

The Mercedes had to slow down behind a tourist bus. They passed the bronze statue of the last leopard killed in the region a century earlier, and reached the coast road. Sandstone cliffs plunged into the raging sea, which could be heard roaring below. A dusty road ran alongside the ocean, cutting across the immaculately white dunes.

Dan bent over the map. "It must be this way," he said. "After the stud farm."

Noordhoek Bay was a dangerous place that didn't attract many visitors. The rollers and the sharks made bathing impossible, and, as a number of crimes had been committed on the beach, a sign advised walkers not to stray too far from the parking lot. The Mercedes passed the village and bounced over the worn trail that ran parallel to the sea. A few houses nestled in the hollow of the dunes, some of them just dilapidated shacks. Brian finally pulled up next to an old pickup truck parked a few yards from a run-down mobile home half eroded by salt. Ramphele's house, according to their information. The curtains, yellow with nicotine, were drawn. They got out of the car. Neuman made a sign to Brian, who walked around to the other side of the makeshift dwelling.

A motorbike stood sheltered from the wind, under a tarp. Neuman and Dan walked up to the battered door. In a few strides, Brian had reached the back of the mobile home. He glanced in at the window and made out a form through the filthy curtains. He placed his hands on the window. There was someone on the other side, a few inches away. A black, his head tilted against the back of the window seat, not sleeping. Flies were galloping over his skull.

Neuman did not have to force the lock, the door was open. A swarm of insects was buzzing inside. The young black sat at the plastic-coated table in the living room area, his half-closed eyes staring up at a particular point on the ceiling. Stanley Ramphele—he looked like his mugshot. A used syringe lay on the cushion, and some whitish powder in a plastic sachet. Holding his breath—the smell of shit was overpowering—Dan went over and took his pulse, and indicated with a sign that he was dead.

"I'll call it in," he breathed, retreating to the door.

Neuman forgot the smell of shit and the flies. The young Xhosa's eyes were empty, as if drawn with a lead pencil, his body as cold as stone. He'd been dead for several days—the sphincters had relaxed and the excrement that had soiled his pants had seeped through to the window seat and dried. Neuman looked closely at the body. No sign of struggle, no bruises, no apparent wounds. A needle mark on the left arm. A tourniquet lay beside him. Neuman put on plastic gloves and examined the powder on the table. Presumably methamphetamine. He searched the mobile home.

A laptop, brand-name clothes on the unmade bed, a pair of Italian sunglasses, a few jewels—pure paste—a motorcycle helmet. Neuman found a little marijuana under the mattress, but no powder. He peered under the bed, and pulled out a dust-covered object. A woman's purse. There was a cell phone inside, a few Kleenex, three condoms in their wrappers, several small flasks, and some papers with the name Nicole Wiese on them.

There was also a coin purse, containing barely a hundred rand. He took the stopper from one of the flasks. The liquid was greenish, the smell difficult to identify. There were no labels on the flasks, but one of them had been emptied.

The roar of the sea could be heard through the open door of the mobile home. Neuman stood up, saw Brian inspecting the dusty ground, and headed for the toilet. He recoiled as soon as he stepped inside. A dark, furry trap door spider was looking at him from the cistern pipe. The spider was the size of his hand, the operculum open as if either ready to beat a retreat or to bite. Two little brown eyes staring at him, legs moving. The lid of the toilet bowl was down, the skylight closed with a latch. How had it gotten in here? Neuman closed the toilet door, cold sweat down his spine.

Brian was standing in the doorway of the mobile home, silhouetted in the noon sun. "The motorbike outside has two hundred and fifty miles on the meter," he said. "A Yamaha that must be worth about thirty thousand rand. Not bad for an unemployed kid, eh?"

Neuman was looking distinctly odd.

"What's the matter?"

"I found Nicole's bag under the bed, and some dope," he said. "There's also a spider in the toilet."

"A spider?"

"A hairy one."

Dan arrived, his cell phone in his hand. "The forensics team will be here in twenty minutes," he said.

Outside, a warm wind was stirring the sand. Neuman searched the pickup parked outside the mobile home. The papers in the glove compartment were still in the name of Sonny Ramphele. Chocolate bar wrappers lay on the seats, along with ice cream sticks and soda cans. The sand on the flooring was darker than in Noordhoek, where it was too cold to bathe anyway. Stanley hadn't been wearing a helmet when he arrived at the club on Saturday night, they must have taken this vehicle and gone to the east of the peninsula, where the coast was more hospitable.

His cell phone vibrated in his pocket. It was Miriam, the nurse from the dispensary. He took the call.

*

Overcrowded minibuses were trying to push their way through by hooting their horns, but it was noon and the N2 was quite congested. Neuman was fuming at being stuck behind a brand-new tank truck—his mother having gotten into trouble again, he had left Brian to deal with things in Noordhoek—when he received a call from Tembo. He had finished the supplementary analyses of Nicole Wiese's postmortem.

"I've found the name of the plant she ingested a few days before the murder," he said. "It's *iboga*, a plant from West Africa used in shamanic ceremonies. But we still don't know the name of the substance inhaled with the *tik*."

"What do you mean, you don't know?"

"There's certainly a chemical molecule, but its composition isn't listed anywhere."

"Some crap that was added to cut the drug?" Neuman suggested.

"It's possible," Tembo replied. "Or else it's a new combination of products, a new drug."

The traffic had slowed again. Neuman was brooding. The far right of the AWB[1] and the sectarian factions that had trafficked pills during apartheid to fuddle the brains of progressive-minded white kids didn't have the clout they had once had. Besides, Nicole Wiese came from the Afrikaner elite and

[1] The Afrikaner Weerstandsbeweging (Afrikaner Resistance Movement).

her father was a major financial supporter of the National Party. It wasn't in the interest of these wolves to tear each other to pieces.

"The ideal thing would be to have a sample of the product," Tembo resumed. "We could make tests, dig a bit deeper."

An arrow indicated the turnoff for Khayelitsha. Neuman remembered the sachet of powder found next to Ramphele.

"Don't worry," he said, as he took the exit. "I think I may have found something to keep you busy."

The Red Cross Hospital annex was at the corner of the Community Center, which was divided into four "villages." Boys in shorts were playing outside the painted wooden building, others were coming out clinging to their mothers' already over-laden arms. Miriam was sitting on the steps, smoking a cigarette and making circles in the dust with her foot—drawing aboriginal dreams that vaguely resembled Ali Neuman. His car pulled up in the forecourt of the dispensary. She just had time to wipe out her drawings, and there he was, looming over her, with his halo of black hair and his thorn-sharp eyes.

"Thanks for calling me," he said, by way of preamble.

"It's what you asked me to do, isn't it?"

"Not everyone would have done the same."

Her hand in the air to shield her from the sun, Miriam let him stew in his traditional polite formulas—at least he was looking at her.

"How is she?"

"We had to rehydrate her," she replied. "Your mother is acting in a very foolish way, if you don't mind me saying so."

"I agree."

Josephine had left Khayelitsha at about nine o'clock in the morning, and had been found three hours later wandering in a squatter camp near Mitchell's Plain, a buffer zone between the township and the N2. Taking the bus, getting off along the highway, walking on the uneven ground leading to the squatter camps—her behavior was close to recklessness.

"What was she doing there?"

"You'll have to ask her that," she said, without concealing her exasperation. "Some kind people called the dispensary, but next time things could turn nasty. It's time you gave her a good telling off, captain. Your mother isn't a young woman anymore, and walking for hours in the sun like that really tired her out. I don't know what the two of you are made of, but after the blackout she had at the weekend, this is becoming suicidal."

Her brown eyes gleamed with righteous rebellion.

Neuman held out his hand and helped her to her feet. "Where is she?"

"In the little ward," Miriam replied, squeezing his palm, "on the right."

But all she could think of at the moment were his bear-like paws, which could so easily lift her to heaven. She was going crazy, too. She led him inside.

A small, colorful crowd was trying to contain its impatience beneath the blades of the ceiling fan. There was no air conditioning, but bottles of water were being distributed to the resigned patients. Josephina was lying on a gurney that, given her size, was more like a shopping cart. At the sound of his steps, she turned her blurred eyes to him and smiled.

"There you are, son! I told Miriam a hundred times that you had other things to do, but the girl won't take no for an answer!"

"A fine way to talk about your friends!" he said, kissing her.

"Hee hee hee!"

It didn't bother her anymore that she was stuck here like a beached whale, now that she had God in front of her in her own black-and-white film.

"Tell me, Ma, don't you think you're a bit old to be running away from home?"

She took his hand, and didn't seem too ready to give it up to anyone. "I didn't think I'd get lost, but obviously, as I don't go there often . . ."

"What on earth were you doing there?"

"Oh . . ."

"Answer me."

Josephina sighed, which almost knocked her off the gurney. "They told me Nora Mceli was dead," she said. "You know, Simon's mother. I don't know if it's true, but someone gave me the name of a cousin of Nora's, Winnie Got, who apparently looked after the boy when she was sick. They told me she was living in a squatter camp between Mandalay and Mitchell's Plain. I wanted to see if she knew anything about Simon."

"You're stubborn as a mule."

"The child is lost, Ali. If we don't do anything for him, he'll die, I know it."

Accidents, illness, stray bullets—the life expectancy of street kids was fairly limited.

"I'd like to do something," he said. "But we can't save them all."

Josephina assumed a solemn air. "I've been having bad dreams," she said, looking at him with empty eyes. "The ancestors wouldn't be happy if we left Simon to his fate. No, they wouldn't be proud of us."

Immemorial ties united them one with another—to defend the ideal of the *ubuntu*, to welcome several generations under the same roof, the sense of the extended family, so essential to South African society and still seen as such in spite of decades of separatist policies. Without this solidarity, they, too, would have been lost. Simon was part of the inner circle.

"Why didn't you tell me?" he said. "We could have gone together."

"I saw your name in the paper," his mother replied. "That poor girl who was murdered. I didn't want to—"

"You didn't want to bother me. Right." His tone changed. "Can you get up or would you prefer to be carried to the car? I'm parked outside."

"Oh, if you help me, I can try and get up! I haven't dared move from this thing for two hours. I feel like an ocean stuck on a cockleshell, hee hee hee!"

Nothing seemed to bother her at all.

*

The main thoroughfare crossing the township of Khayelit-sha started at Mandalay Station and crossed Cape Flats, a sandy windswept plain where dilapidated houses, "matchboxes," and cobbled-together shacks co-existed, barely visible from the highway. It was in this gray zone that the squatters had settled, a camp that kept growing, where the police rarely set foot. Wooden signs, barbed wire, pickets, corrugated iron, advertising hoardings, old newspapers—shacks were built with whatever was lying around, fetuses that blew away at the first storm warning. The luckiest lived in containers. Everyone washed outside, because of lack of space and running water. Among the few signs that the camp was becoming permanent were the fact that the barriers marking the boundaries between plots had been replaced here and there with cut sheets of concrete, and the fact that there was now even the odd hedge, a real achievement in the sands of Cape Flats.

According to the information Josephina had gleaned, Winnie Got lived in a spaza shop, a little unlicensed grocery selling staple goods—matches, candles, alcohol for fuel, flour, batteries, milk, and a few cold drinks. Neuman drove around, watched with a mixture of hostility and curiosity by the people on the streets. An electricity line ran across the area, connected to wires that straggled wildly like lethal creepers and seemed to lead nowhere. The camp was changing so quickly and so anarchically that it was difficult to find your way around. At last, after a tiresome treasure hunt, he found Simon's guardian in her shop.

Winnie was wearing a *kikoi*, an East African dress, and soft, garishly pink pumps. Neuman introduced himself as Josephina's son. The heat in the shop was stifling. A shelf of Duralex glasses stood proudly next to a battered refrigerator. Neuman bought two acidulated sodas. They sat down on the window seat to talk, on a flowered mattress that had seen too much sun.

Winnie Got spoke a mixture of English and township slang. She was thirty-eight and had had three children by three different fathers, who had never known their grandmother—if they had, then, according to tradition, she would have taken care of them. Her cousin Nora had showed up at her house a year earlier, with her kid and her illness. Winnie didn't know what kind of illness it was, rumor said it was the evil eye, the spells she had cast had come back on her like a boomerang. In any case, the poor woman was already very weak when she arrived, and had died two months later. Winnie had kept Simon, who, having no father, would otherwise have found himself out on the street. The boy had stayed with her for a while, then one day he had disappeared, without leaving an address.

"I never saw him again," Winnie said in conclusion.

There was no tenderness in her expression as she said this. Her cousin had died and had left behind nothing but rumors and an orphan who was nothing to do with her.

"What happened with Simon?" Neuman asked. "Why did he run away?"

"I don't know," she said, with a shrug. "I tried to talk to him, but he was acting tough with his little gang."

"What gang?"

"Street kids," Winnie replied. "Plenty of them in the area.

Simon would go to the beach to play soccer with them. One day he didn't come back."

"When was that?"

Winnie fanned herself with a year-old women's magazine. "Three months ago, I'd say."

"And you haven't seen him since?"

"I saw him wandering around once on the edge of the area, but it was almost impossible to approach them."

"Why?"

"He'd turned wild." Winnie gave a bitter grin. "He'd become like the others."

"Can you describe these kids?"

"There were half a dozen of them. Simon, some others his age, and an older boy, in green shorts."

There must have been thousands of boys wearing green shorts in the township.

"Any idea where I could find them?"

"Why are you asking me all this?"

"Simon was seen in Khayelitsha last week," Neuman said.

"He has to hang out somewhere."

"He attacked a blind old lady who happens to be my mother. She's a pain in the ass, but she's mine. So, where can I find this gang?"

"Don't know," Winnie said. "I told you, I haven't seen them for a while."

Neuman finished his soda. According to Josephina, Simon had been alone when he had attacked her. Their strength lay in the group. Alone, they were nothing.

"Did Simon leave anything here?" he asked.

"Not much."

"Can I see?"

Everything she possessed was stored in suitcases in the adjoining bedroom. Winnie soon returned, carrying a tin can with a bashed-in lid.

"This is all I've kept."

There was a birth certificate (Simon had turned eleven the previous month), a record of the vaccinations given at the dispensary in Khayelitsha, a school book and a photograph, stapled at the edge. In spite of his round cheeks, the boy had had difficulty smiling.

"As you see, there's not much."

Neuman looked at the photograph. That face.

"Would you like a beer?" Winnie asked. "On the house."

"No," he said, his mind elsewhere. "No, thanks."

The photograph was barely a year old, but it took Neuman a while to recognize him. The other day, on the construction site, the sickly boy with the necrotized face he had saved from the *tsotsis*, the boy who had escaped through the pipe. That was Simon.

9.

Ruby didn't know. The only one who knew about it was Ali, one evening when they'd lowered their guard. Brian was seventeen at the time, Maria twenty.

Maria hadn't read *Ada or Ardor*, and wouldn't have understood it if she had. Where she came from, you didn't frolic in the grass around the castle with your cousin. The walls of her house hadn't been built by the first white farmers in southern Africa, her father hadn't been an important official or a lover of race-horses, her mother didn't make *boerewers* in the morning while wondering what the weather was going to be like today, the window of the kitchen didn't look out on a meadow, or the bedroom window on a little wood that made you forget the electrified gates around the property. Maria didn't have stables, or horses, or a hi-fi, or LPs, the Clash, Led Zeppelin, the Plimsouls, she didn't know anything about rock bands who encouraged a sense of rebellion, or about the broken hearts to be found in books, or subtle desires, or transgression, she had never heard of Nabokov, or the ardor of love. Maria couldn't read.

She would have liked to become a social worker, but she hadn't been given the chance. Maria was black. She had two dresses, one red and one sky blue, and the sky blue one was the nicer of the two. Brian had told her that, one day when she was coming back from the stables, with her pails full of shit, her rubber boots and her dirty apron. Maria had been afraid at first—this smiling white boy was the *bass*'s son—but his sea-green eyes gleamed so brightly that she had forgotten her mother's warnings. No white had ever told her she was pretty. It had taken two months for them to feel at ease with each other, for Maria to replace the Ada of his dreams. Brian and Maria made love for the first time hidden in the little wood behind the family home, while the electricity wires surrounding the estate crackled above them. Brian was jubilant—if only his asshole of a father knew.

"I'll teach you to read," he had declared, lying with her in the bracken.

She laughed.

He didn't know anyone could laugh like that. So wonderfully. As if, when he was in her arms, apartheid didn't exist. It was the end of childhood, the beginning of romance. Before long, Brian was doing everything he could to eat his forbidden fruit, taking the most outrageous risks, skipping classes, friends, sports, to take her into the woods. Maria would laugh, and he would take it for love.

Two years passed without any problems, or any change in their carnal appetites. Maria would decipher the words of the books he brought with him into the bracken, and Brian the instruction manual of the female body she offered in exchange. Maria smelled of musk and spice and fruits of the forest.

"Will you ever leave me?"

"You're crazy!"

She would laugh.

And of course he would take that for love.

One day, Brian had come home at noon, when Maria was working, to surprise her. The house was empty, his mother had gone into town to shop with other milk-white dolls who were her friends. He had gone around to the other side of the garage, made sure one of the servants wasn't cutting the hedge in the garden, and ran to the stables. The thoroughbred was grazing in the adjoining enclosure when he heard a noise from the barn. Maria. He approached softly, imagining her back bent over the broom, her very individual smell, and the shock hit him full in the face. Maria was leaning over the rail of one of the stalls with her dress up while a big man pleasured her. His father. He was breathing as heavily as an ox, his feet in horseshit. All Brian could see was his huge ass contracting as he thrust into her, his crumpled pants hanging over his boots, and Maria clinging on in order not to fall.

"I'll kill him. I'll kill him," he kept repeating, his eyes misting over with tears.

But it was too late. Brian hadn't dared to grab the pitchfork hanging at the entrance to the stable, he hadn't had the guts to nail his father like a moth to the barn door, to plunge the pitchfork into his back until it came out through his throat.

He was afraid of him.

"I'll kill him."

Maria didn't reply. She was crying in the wood where they had made love. She was ashamed. In vain, she hid her face in her pitiful hands. Brian didn't ask her how long it had been going on, if he had forced her the first time, if she had had a choice. Her laughter wouldn't hide with them in the bracken anymore. From now on her shoulders, her legs, her cunt wouldn't smell of anything but his father's loathsome smell.

In the months that followed, Maria had continued coming to the house to work, but Brian had carefully avoided her. He felt betrayed, humiliated, still in love in a confused way. And then one day, Maria hadn't showed up. He had watched out for her all weekend, then the following weekend, but in vain. He had questioned his mother, one morning, in the kitchen, as casually as he could.

"Maria?" she said, her hands in the dough. "Your father fired her last week."

"Really?"

"The stables were in a terrible state!" she stated, even though she herself never set foot in them.

Brian had brooded for a few days, then had searched his

father's office. He had found Maria's address in a filing cabinet, with her pay slips and the papers she had needed to come and work in the city. Maria lived in the township. Six miles away—the ends of the earth.

No white ever ventured into the townships. Brian had asked the black taxi driver to wait for him outside the house, a plywood hut painted yellow, a luxury in the neighborhood. Maria's mother made a frightened gesture when she saw the white boy at her door. Three little children were clinging to her apron, torn between curiosity and shyness. The woman didn't want to talk at first, but Brian insisted until she gave in. Maria had left for work one day, and hadn't come back. There were rumors that she'd been picked up by a police car on the way out of the township, but her mother didn't believe that. Maria was four months pregnant—she must have run away with the baby's father, probably one of those good-for-nothings who promised the moon but brought only trouble.

Back home, Brian had checked the date of Maria's disappearance against the employees' rota. Maria should have been working in the stables that day.

Lying to the local cops, he had reported a theft, saying Maria was the culprit and giving them her description. He insisted they investigate, mentioned that his father was a prosecutor, and got what he wanted. An inspector made some inquiries, which proved fruitless. Maria didn't have a record. She'd never committed a crime, never been arrested. The cop was happy to take his complaint, but there was little chance it would get anywhere.

Maria's mother, whom Brian had kept informed of his search, steered him in the direction of an ANC militant. Underground activities, torture, disappearances, the arbitrary procedures of the special services, the murders of opponents—Brian discovered a reality he had been unaware of. But he made the connection. His father was a prosecutor, an immovable link in the chain of power.

A month had passed since Maria's disappearance. Brian had waited until his father was alone in the kitchen and then said, "By the way, did you know Maria was pregnant?"

His father had glared at him for a second, before gathering himself. "Pregnant?"

But his eyes had betrayed him. He knew, of course.

"It was you who made sure she disappeared, wasn't it?" Brian said defiantly. "You who sent the cops to pick her up outside the township?"

His father's massive body towered over him. "What on earth are you talking about?"

His veins were swollen with anger, but Brian wasn't afraid of him anymore. He hated him.

"The child she was expecting wasn't yours," he said, "but mine. Stupid bastard."

Apartheid: separate development.

Brian had changed his home, his life, his name, his friends. He had toughened himself up away from his hated family, and had opened an office doing investigations. Looking for blacks his father had had eliminated became his specialty, a hard task but one he felt obliged to carry out, and one that had brought him into contact with underground ANC members and the police pursuing them. More than once, Ruby had picked him up from a ditch by the side of the highway, badly beaten. His life was spared on account of his father's position, but the hatred remained. Brian had dug up corpses—some that had lain buried just below the ground for months, skeletons with broken teeth, or with dislocated ribs when they'd been thrown off the roofs of police stations, corpses of opponents or mere sympathizers—but he had never found Maria's body.

His need for love was inconsolable. He kept Maria's memory alive, like a shameful secret. He did not know why he never talked about her. Why he stuck his head in places where other people never set foot. What he was punishing himself for. If taking refuge in the arms of women came from the same desire to sabotage everything. In the end, Ruby was right. His heart was made of ice—it melted easily.

Tracy, for example, magic trick number fifty-four, white dressing gown and russet tunic in the middle of the kitchen, a pencil cleverly keeping her hair in place, making scrambled eggs for breakfast with all the dexterity of a newborn baby.

"God, it's a mess here!" she laughed.

They had just woken up. The Young Gods were screaming from the living room—Swiss, according to the CD booklet— as she busied herself at the oven.

"Don't you like the music?" he cried, in a tone that fitted him like a glove.

"I have my ears full of it every evening!" Tracy said.

"You just have to keep them closed, darling."

"You're funny in the morning, you know."

"I'm feeling a bit groggy," he said. "I keep thinking it's still evening."

She murdered the frying pan with her fork. "Oh, yes? You were already half asleep when I got in."

"Sorry, darling."

Tracy had come over after her shift, but Brian had collapsed after the third joint of Durban Poison. It was the first time they had seen each other since that crazy Saturday night and the abortive Sunday at Jim's. Tracy was thirty-five. She knew that, working behind a bar, she could have as many men as she wanted, the problem was always the second time. Other drinks led them on to other girls, and the funny redhead behind the bar was part of the past. "You just have to find a proper job, girl," she would say to herself on the evenings when she felt depressed, "not one where everyone's eyeing your ass." But Tracy didn't believe much in other jobs—or men in general.

She stirred the mixture in the frying pan. "I hope I'm better in bed," she said.

"Like eggplant caviar."

"Is that good?"

"If you like garlic."

Tracy pushed what was left of the eggs onto the plates and threw the frying pan into the sink with a deafening clatter.

Brian grimaced—this girl certainly didn't smell of lavender.

"Can I ask you a personal question?" she said, sitting down opposite him.

"My shoe size is forty-three, if you must know."

"I'm serious."

"Go on, darling."

Tracy lowered her eyes. A lock had escaped from her pencil, and fell in red curls down her neck.

"You must tell me if I get on your nerves. I'm so unused to this, I keep thinking I'm overdoing it. I'm talking crap, aren't I?"

"A little, darling."

In spite of his show of stoicism, the magic trick kept going flat. You could see it escaping through the garden, conjured away. Brian looked at his watch. It wasn't that he was late, it was just that the world was running away from him.

*

When the ANC had refused to give their support to the system of Bantustans, the apartheid government had imprisoned Mandela and his associates on Robben Island, a small, verdant island off Cape Town that had the advantage of leaving the political opposition in total isolation—Mandela had had to wait twenty-one years before he even so much as touched his wife's hand again.

Sonny Ramphele did not have to suffer that cruel double sentence. Stanley's brother was serving two years in Pollsmoor prison, an insalubrious, overcrowded concrete building, where even the flies were in hell.

"Find what you're looking for?" the head guard said.

Dan Fletcher was peering down at the register, trying to get an idea of the visits and their frequency. Kriek, the red-neck everyone called Chief, was playing with his bunches of keys and waiting. Dan did not reply. Brian Epkeen was smoking, looking threateningly at Kriek. He didn't like prison—mankind should have come up with something better in eight thousand years—and he certainly didn't like a petty dictator like this one, a beneficiary of the sunset clause,[1] who had reenlisted because the prison population, when you came down to it, hadn't changed—you still had plenty of *kaffirs* and coloreds.

Sonny Ramphele had been on a suspended sentence when he was arrested at the wheel of a stolen car with a hundred ounces of marijuana crammed under the seat. He hadn't fingered anyone else, and had been given two years without remission. Sonny's story was a classic one. Parents—tenant farmers—who had died when he was young, the exodus with his brother to the city, overcrowding, unemployment, poverty, crime, prison. Sonny had just turned twenty-six, and if he didn't do anything stupid, he'd be out in a few months.

Forensics had searched the mobile home, but if the younger brother had taken over his business and had a stash of drugs hidden away somewhere, it seemed to have disappeared with him. They had found only a few prints, all of them Stanley's, and inquiries with the locals hadn't gotten them anywhere. The nearest shack was uninhabited, and the dropouts who lived on the coast didn't stick their noses in other people's affairs—as witness the fact that Stanley's body had been rotting for four days. Some had known Sonny—"Big guy, pleasant enough,

[1] In order to achieve a smooth transition, white officials who had worked under the apartheid system were kept in their posts for a period of five years.

looked after his little brother"—and Stan, who was really into fashion and motorbikes. No one had ever seen him with Nicole Wiese—a young blonde like that, they'd have remembered. The one clue that had confirmed the lead they were following was that there were several prints of Nicole's in the pickup, which had been used on the day of the murder.

Dan looked up from the register. "Stanley Ramphele has been visiting his brother regularly since he was incarcerated," he said. "But not for the past month."

Kriek was cleaning his nails with his teeth. "I didn't even know he had a brother," he said.

One of the guards chuckled behind him. For a moment, Brian forgot about the head guard's piggishness and that rancid odor of men in confined spaces that pervaded the air. "Can we have a quiet room to question Sonny?"

"Why? Planning to look up his ass?"

"You're a funny guy, Chief, you know that?"

"Ramphele's ass isn't up for grabs," Kriek insisted. "It's not me who says that, it's the other prisoners."

There was agreement from the other guards.

"What does that mean?" Dan said irritably. "That Ramphele's protected?"

"Apparently."

"There's no mention of it in his file."

"The animals eat each other, make no mistake."

"What do the informers say?"

"That his ass is out of bounds."

"You seem to be fascinated by his ass."

"Not me, them!"

Kriek laughed first, soon imitated by his cronies. Brian signaled to Dan that they needed a change of scenery. Kriek was exactly the kind of guy who used to beat him up and leave him for dead in the ditches.

Two hundred percent overcrowded, a ninety percent re-offending rate, TB, AIDS, lack of medical care, blocked pipes, people sleeping on the floor, rapes, assaults, humiliations—Pollsmoor epitomized the state of South Africa's prisons. As the prison population kept growing, the private sector had been given the task of building new detention centers, most of which dated from the apartheid period. There were few social workers, rehabilitation was a utopian dream, and corruption was endemic. The number of escapes had reached a record high, with the complicity of a poorly trained, underpaid, even criminal staff. Some prisoners had to pay a fee to attend classes or participate in activities, while others, even with life sentences, spent the weekend outside. New prisoners were occasionally sold by the guards to those who asked for them, the guards' first reflex being to put themselves under the protection of one of the bosses, who monopolized the *wifyes*, and distributed favors.

Prostitutes, drugs, alcohol—eight crime syndicates divided the prison system between them. In this jungle, Sonny Ramphele had coped pretty well. He had struck a deal, like everyone. He had caught scabies, and there were swellings between his fingers that made it look like his hands were turning into flippers—Sonny had never taken very good care of himself, not like his cute brother—but he had managed to preserve his integrity. He was waiting for the end of his sentence, listening to his fellow prisoners quarrelling about who would be next in the latrines, when a guard came and stirred him from his long apathy.

Sonny grumbled—why the fuck did he need to see a doctor?—but obeyed, assailed by sarcastic remarks from the others.

The prison corridors stank of cabbage and bodily fluids. Dragging an invisible ball and chain, Ramphele passed through two magnetic gates before being led into an isolated, windowless room. This wasn't the infirmary. There was a table, two plastic chairs, a short brown guy with piercing eyes sitting with a bunch of photographs in front of him, and a taller guy with his back against the wall, who looked as if he might once have been in good shape.

"Sit down," Dan Fletcher said, indicating the empty chair opposite him.

Like his brother, Sonny was a solid Xhosa, about six feet tall, with eyes that kept wandering to the sides. He walked forward sluggishly and sat down as if there were nails on the chair.

"Do you know why we're here?"

Sonny shook his head very slightly. He had the heavy-lidded look of a tough guy who had become a heavy smoker.

"You haven't seen your brother in a while," Dan went on. "A month, according to the register. Any news of him?"

He made a contemptuous gesture. This was all water off a duck's back. Hundreds of police officers had been indicted for assault, murder, rape. Sonny didn't want to talk to them, especially not about Stan.

"He's been running your business for you, hasn't he?" Dan said. "Too busy, I guess, to visit his big brother."

Sonny was keeping an eye on the other cop, who was prowling behind him.

"What was Stan dealing? *Dagga*? Or something else?"

Sonny made no reaction.

Brian leaned over his shoulder. "You were wrong to give your brother the keys to the truck, Sonny. Didn't you tell him he was going nowhere?"

Sonny did not react immediately. Fletcher turned over the photographs scattered on the table.

"Stan was found dead in your mobile home," he said, indicating the photographs. "Yesterday, in Noordhoek. He'd been dead for several days."

His bored gangster pose changed as he looked at the photographs: a livid Stan on the window seat in the mobile home, his face in close-up, eyes open, staring at a forever indeterminate object.

"Your brother died of an overdose," Fletcher went on. "A *tik*-based mixture. Did you know your brother was a user?"

Sonny was shrinking on his chair, his head bent over his unlaced sneakers. Stan as a boy, laughing, the slaps on the head he'd given him, their fights in the dust—their life flashed before him, fading to black.

"Stan didn't have any needle marks on his arms," Dan said. "What do you think of that?"

"Nothing."

It was the most he'd spoken so far.

"Your brother was involved in something big. We think he was dealing a new drug to young whites in the city. Did you know?"

Still in shock, Sonny shook his head.

"Your brother was going out with a girl named Nicole Wiese, the one who's been in all the papers. Did Stan ever mention her to you?"

"That's none of my business." He couldn't take his eyes off the photographs.

"Nicole was murdered, and everything points to Stan. We found drugs and the girl's purse in your mobile home, and we have proof they were together at the time of the murder. What is this drug?"

"Don't know." Sonny was nervously twisting his fingers.

"I don't believe you, Sonny. Try harder."

"Stan didn't say anything to me."

"Apart from the Chief, no one knows about our visit," Dan assured him. "No one will know you talked to us, your name won't appear anywhere. The appeals judge is lenient to people who turn State's evidence. Help us and we'll see what we can do."

Ramphele sat on his chair, brooding. Things were looking bad.

Brian tried again. "Stan took over your patch on the beaches. We're looking for his supplier. You must know him."

"I don't know anyone who deals *tik*. Neither did Stan."

"Your supplier may have changed direction."

"No. Too dangerous."

Brian sat down on the edge of the table. "Why do you think your brother stopped coming to see you? Why had he been playing dead for a month? He started selling the hard stuff, to earn money and live it up with little white girls by the sea. He even bought himself some nice clothes and a flashy motorbike. Stan stopped coming to see you because he knew you wouldn't appreciate the way he'd taken over your territory. Except that he hit a snag. They used your brother, Sonny. Don't expect to get any respect from these people. They treat you like beasts for the slaughter."

Ramphele shrugged. It was the same in here.

"We're offering you a way out," Dan said, more gently. "Tell us who was supplying your brother, and your sentence will be reviewed."

Sonny had stopped moving. His chin had fallen on his shabby T-shirt, as if his brother's death had broken his neck. There was only him left now—best to say nothing.

"*Dagga*, man," he said at last. "Only *dagga*."

A heavy silence fell over the interrogation room. Dan made a sign to Brian, who put out his cigarette. Either the brother knew nothing, or he had a good reason to lie. He was about to send Sonny back to his cell when Brian asked him point blank, "Stan was scared of spiders, wasn't he?"

Sonny's gloomy expression changed completely. He looked up questioningly at the cop in the black fatigues.

They'd found the flaw, a gaping one.

"Really scared," Brian insisted. "Like a phobia."

Sonny was disconcerted. Stan had fallen into a well when he was little, a dried-up well that hadn't been used for ages. They had searched for him for hours before they found him, trembling with fear, at the bottom of the well. There was no water there, but there were spiders, hundreds of them. Fifteen years later, Stan could barely stand to see those fucking spiders, let alone go anywhere near them.

"They used your brother to sell their dope for them," Brian went on, "and when Stan knew too much, they shot him up to make it look like an overdose. Or rather, they gave him the choice of shooting himself up or spending some time with one of those nice little animals. A trap-door spider was found in the toilet in your mobile home. A big one."

Sonny rubbed his face with his hands. The photographs on the table made sinister kaleidoscopes in his mind. The last pieces of his world were drifting away, and he had nothing to hang on to, only the moist eyes of the cop opposite him.

"Muizenberg," he said at last. "We were dealing on the beach at Muizenberg."

*

Used for five thousand years by the Pygmies for their medicinal qualities, the roots of the *iboga* contained a dozen alkaloids, including ibogaine, a substance similar to that present in various species of hallucinogenic mushrooms. By acting on the serotonin, ibogaine increased self-confidence and a sense of general well-being. While the plant and several of its derivatives had mind-stimulating properties, they could, in larger doses, also be responsible for auditory and visual hallucinations, sometimes very anxiety-provoking, which could even lead to suicide. Etymologically derived from a word meaning "to heal," *iboga* was an initiatory plant whose therapeutic properties and hallucinatory power made it possible for its user to connect with the sacred. *Iboga* was used during inner-directed ceremonies called *bwiti*, conducted under the aegis of a spiritual guide, a shaman known as an *inyanga*, who was thought of as a herbalist. Apart from these secret rituals, *iboga* root was used as an aphrodisiac or love potion.

True believers claimed that ibogaine provoked erections that could last six hours, in which the pleasure was indescribable. In Western medicine, ibogaine had been used in psychotherapy and the treatment of heroin addiction, but knowledge about its aphrodisiac qualities remained sketchy, due to the lack of scientific tests.

An African love potion.

Neuman was brooding like an old lion looking at its own reflection. Nicole Wiese had taken *iboga* a few days before the murder, a strong dose according to the medical examiner's analysis, probably in the form of an essential oil. What about the flasks found in Nicole's purse? Was her friend Stan also dealing *iboga*?

Neuman set off to see the medical examiner.

Tembo was the first black to run the Durham Road morgue. His short gray beard was reminiscent of that of a former secretary-general of the United Nations, and his glasses betrayed the fact that he was as short-sighted as a mole. A confirmed bachelor, Tembo loved anything old—baroque music, old-fashioned hats—and had a particular passion for Egyptian hieroglyphics. Dead bodies were for him parchments to be deciphered, puppets to which he was the expert ventriloquist. He only left them alone once he had exhausted their meaning. A man fiercely dedicated to his job—he and Neuman got on well.

The two men sat down in Tembo's laboratory.

Stan Ramphele's postmortem showed that he had died of an overdose following a methamphetamine-based injection. The exact hour of death was unclear, but it had happened four days earlier, in other words, not long after Nicole's murder. The sand on the flooring of the pickup matched the grains in Nicole's hair. Traces of salt had been found on Stan's skin, as well as pollen from the *Dietes grandiflora*, a flower better known under the name of Groot Wilde iris, confirming what they already knew—that Stan and Nicole had been together in the botanical gardens.

"But the most interesting findings were in the toxicological analysis," Tembo said. "First, the *iboga*. Ramphele also took some, but more recently, just a few hours before he died. In other words, around the same time as Nicole Wiese was murdered. We found the same essence in the flasks in her purse. A very concentrated formula, one I've never seen before."

"Homemade?"

"Yes. I wondered at first if this essence could change the behavior of its users, but the guinea pigs we tested the product on just fell asleep." Tembo fingered his beard. "So then I looked at the powder that caused Ramphele's overdose and noted that the same molecule was in the cocktail taken by Nicole. Thanks to the sample from the mobile home, I was able to dig a little deeper. Like all synthetic drugs, methamphetamine has intermediary components that are toxic to the brain, but however hard we looked among the usual substitutes, we just couldn't find it. We still don't know the name of the molecule."

"How do you explain that?" Neuman asked.

Tembo shrugged. "The Mafias are often ahead of State-funded research. They certainly have more resources than we do."

Tembo knew the subject well. Ever since LSD and BZ gas, innovations in the fields of neuroscience and pharmacology had widened the range of possibilities. It was now possible to reprogram molecules so that they targeted certain mechanisms affecting neuronal functions or cardiac rhythms. What had emerged from this extensive experimentation was increasingly computerized, and the most promising bio-active components could be identified and tested with amazing speed. After having experimented in Iraq with drugs that increased the vigilance of soldiers, the military hoped, in the near future, to see troops leaving for combat filled with medication that increased their aggressiveness and their resistance to fear, pain, and fatigue, while acting, through a selective erasure of memory, to suppress traumatic memories. Tembo, who followed these things with great interest, was not very optimistic. September 11th had ushered in a period when international norms had been infringed, especially in the US. Experiments on chemical weapons that were banned in theory continued, linked to the use of lethal injections in judicial executions and of tear gas to maintain order. But the real purpose of these experiments was "counter-terrorism," a sphere in which legal constraints were increasingly being ignored. There were research projects in progress everywhere. The Russians had not revealed the name of the chemical agent used to end the Moscow theatre siege in 2005. Since the first Gulf War, the US Air Force had been considering the development and dissemination of extremely powerful aphrodisiacs capable of provoking homosexual behavior in the enemy ranks. A Czech laboratory was working on the transformation of anesthetics combined with a series of ultra-rapid antidotes that could be used to induce a state of shock in crowds, after which special commandoes would be able to go in and carry out targeted assassinations.

Rejected because of undesirable side effects, thousands of molecules lay dormant on laboratory shelves. It was possible that some had been recycled by unscrupulous organizations.

Neuman listened without saying a word. There was no shortage of Mafias in the country—Colombian cartels, Russian, African Mafias. One of them might have perfected a new product.

Tembo's eyes lit up, as if he had just discovered the secret of the Pyramids. "I tested your samples on rats," he said, with a clinical smile. "Interesting. Come and take a look."

Neuman followed him into the next room.

The shelves were full of specimens in jars. Two female lab assistants were hard at work amid the tiled surfaces.

"Is the protocol ready?" Tembo asked.

"Yes, yes," one of the assistants replied, enigmatic behind her mask. "Start with number three."

They walked to the cages at the far end of the room. There were a dozen of them, hermetically sealed and carefully labeled.

"Here's the cage I was talking about earlier," Tembo said. "The one where we tested the *iboga*."

Neuman peered in. There were half a dozen rats, sleeping peacefully, one on top of the other.

"Cute, aren't they?" Tembo pointed to the next cage. "We filled this one with smoke from the powder found in the mobile home. The rats you see here are currently in phase two. In other words, they inhaled the product recently."

Neuman frowned. The occupants of this cage were extremely agitated. Half the specimens were going around in circles as fast as possible, others were copulating, and all of them seemed totally confused.

"Rape, deviant behavior, erotomania. After being high for two to three minutes, the existing couples and any sense of hierarchy just went to pieces, as you can see, as if it was the most natural thing in the world. Phase three is a little more unpleasant."

In the next cage, a dozen rats were roaming about frantically.

"Apathy, loss of sensory bearings, repetition of apparently illogical actions, breakup of the group, antisocial and even paranoid behavior. This phase can last several hours before the specimens sink into a deep sleep. The first ones still haven't woken up. But now," he said, with an icy glint in his eyes, "look at what happens when the dose is increased."

Neuman peered into the next cage and caught his breath. There were dozens of corpses behind the glass, in a terrible state: paws eaten away, muzzles torn off, fur flayed, heads half missing. The survivors, wandering in the middle of this charnel house, were not in much better condition.

"After a brief period of euphoria, all the specimens lost control, and not only of their inhibitions," Tembo explained. "Some started to eat each other. The dominant ones attacked the weakest, killing them and tearing them to pieces. Then they went on to the others. The carnage lasted for hours until they were exhausted."

Only the dominant ones remained. Two laboratory rats that must once have been white, each with its tail missing and part of its head scalped, eyeing each other from a distance.

"They're in a state of shock," Tembo said. "We did postmortems on several of the corpses and discovered serious aftereffects in the cortex. The drug seems to cause an acceleration in the chemical reactions, some of which give rise to a substance that acts as a catalyst, so that the speed of reaction starts from nothing and then gets out of control, setting off the catalysis and accelerating the process even more. Rather like a chain reaction in nuclear fission."

"In plain English?"

"Euphoria, stupor, withdrawal, anger, shock. The behavior varies depending on the dose."

"Any idea of the chemical reaction on humans?"

Tembo smoothed the tip of his beard. "The results could vary depending on the person's medical history, nervous system, and weight," he said. "But according to our comparative tests, we can state with some degree of confidence that with a dose of one cubic centimeter, you would get high. With two cubic centimeters, once past the initial rush, you would float in a kind of paranoid torpor—that was the state Nicole was in when she was murdered. With a dose of three cubic centimeters, you would enter a state of uncontrollable aggressiveness. With four, you would destroy everything in your path, usually ending with yourself. In short, you would go mad."

"What state was Stan in when he died?" Neuman asked.

"Completely off his head," Tembo replied. "He injected himself with more than ten doses."

Night was falling by the time Neuman left the Durham Road morgue.

He had seen Dan and Brian a little earlier on their return from Pollsmoor prison. Sonny Ramphele had been dealing grass to the surfers in Muizenberg, and his little brother had clearly taken over, but with a far more toxic product. Stan had used his looks to trap a white female clientele and spread his network among the gilded youth of Cape Town. Had he taken advantage of his ride to the beach at Muizenberg with his girlfriend Nicole to stock up on drugs? The *iboga* could explain the night visit to the botanical gardens—getting high under the stars and making love among the flowers—but the rest didn't fit. If the lovers had tripped out in the hope of a sex romp, then Stan had deceived Nicole about the nature of the merchandise. He had given her a sophisticated, highly dangerous product, buried in crystal meth.

The noise rumbling inside Neuman had a distant origin. That a young woman could have been killed while making love among the most beautiful flowers in the world, that you had to pay a price for pleasure, disgusted him.

*

Dan told the story of the unloved zebra and the magpie that stole his stripes. He got them back in the end, but all mixed up, with the result that no one in the herd recognized him—which was fine with the zebra.

"What about the magpie?" Tom asked.

"She waited for the rainy season, and when the rainbow arrived, she stole his colors."

The story was a big hit with the audience in the bunkbeds. He still had to say goodnight to the incredibly black panther, Baggera, negotiate with the collection of teddy bears laid out on Tom's bed, and after that was it Eve's turn to agree to be quiet, grab her security blanket, and stick her thumb in her mouth.

"Night night, my baby giraffe," he said, kissing her on the eyes.

Dan closed the door of the bedroom with a feeling like a knife in the stomach. Always the same fear. Fear of losing Claire, of not being strong enough. He had pulled off a magic trick to get the little angels to sleep.

By the time he joined Claire, who was downstairs reading, he had calmed down a little.

They had stopped watching TV since her illness. At first it had seemed strange—it never even crossed their minds to switch it on—and then they had realized that spending time together was more important than watching cookery shows.

Dan and Claire had met five years earlier in a bar on Long Street, an ordinary evening that had changed their lives. Dan Fletcher had grown up in an English-speaking lower-middle-class family in Durban, where his latent homosexuality had boiled down to a few semi-shameful episodes in the toilets of the sports club, where a few sexually adventurous young lads had masturbated him, but he hadn't dared go any farther—certainly not as far as penetration, the great male taboo. That night, Claire had been singing hits from the Seventies, accompanied by an aggressive black guitarist. "I Wanna Be Your Dog," even played acoustically, had led him on a leash to her supple hips swaying in a tight-fitting dress under the spotlights. Her charm, the blonde dreadlocks that fell over her bare shoulders, her grave, sad, almost masculine voice—Dan was electrified. He had approached her at the bar with his crippled eyes and Clare had said yes to everything, immediately—children, life.

Five years.

Today, Claire didn't sing anymore, her hair had fallen out in handfuls, even the miraculous curve of her hips had melted under the chemo. The shattered beauty, the dread beneath the flowers—Dan wouldn't be able to bear her death. The threat hanging over them had made them both as delicate as crystal and, beneath the reassuring male air he put on, he was the more fragile of the two.

"Everything all right?" Claire said, as he came into the room.

"Yes, yes."

She was reading on the couch in the living room, her feet folded under her. She had on a thigh-length white blouse, close-fitting cotton shorts and silver framed-glasses, which, together with her book, gave her quite an attractive student look. He peered at the cover.

"What's that?"

"Rian Malan."

The South African writer and journalist who had written the terrifying masterpiece *My Traitor's Heart*.

"It's his latest," Claire added.

But Dan wasn't especially interested in that. He watched her tuck a lock of blonde hair behind her ear—she was still not used to her wig—and kneeled on the floor. She had thin, soft ankles that moved him deeply. Claire forgot her book and, with a smile, closed her eyes. He kissed her feet, a host of little kisses, as if spreading love dust, then he started licking them, and his tongue weaving between her toes excited her. A lot. She loved his hands on her skin, his fingers ferreting under her cotton shorts. She could feel herself getting wet. Delighted, she let herself tip backwards.

They had just finished making love when the telephone rang at the foot of the couch. Fearing it would wake the children, Dan made a movement to pick up the receiver. Claire, still joined to him, clung on. He picked up at the fifth ring.

"Am I disturbing you?"

It was Neuman.

"No. No."

Dan had stars in his head and an archipelago of comets instead of a pillow.

"I'll come and pick you up tomorrow morning for a little trip to the seaside," Neuman announced. "Brian's also coming."

His wife's belly was still keeping him snug and warm. "O.K.," he said.

"Don't forget your gun this time."

"I won't."

Dan smiled as he hung up. Pure camouflage. He had never told Neuman, let alone Claire, but in reality he was scared stiff. His sick fairy, the children—he was just a little runt worried about the people he loved. Claire called him back to her with a subtle contraction of the perineum. Lovemaking had turned her pale cheeks pink. She was smiling for real now, brave, thin, confident.

Dan felt a lump in his throat at the sight of her slightly lopsided wig, but her pelvis was undulating slightly against his cock.

"Again," she whispered.

10

Gulethu couldn't remember when things had started to go off the rails. Ten years ago? Twelve? His troubled puberty, savage, white-hot acts—was it his sister, his cousin? Gulethu couldn't remember. Anything. He had repressed it so much, it had all been swallowed up. Now the iceberg was drifting with the current, without a destination or a pilot.

According to Zulu tradition, anyone who committed incest should rot while alive. *Sonamuzi*: the family sin, of which he had been guilty. "Not my fault," he would cry in the darkness. It was the curse that hung over him and those dirty little whores who had led him astray. It was *ufufuyane* that made them crazy. Sexually out of control. *Ufufuyane*, the illness that affected young girls and had struck him, too. The danger was everywhere, you just had to see the way they swayed their hips as they came back from fetching water, their heavy breasts in the sun, and their smiles that caught you as you passed like spider's webs. Gulethu had been their victim, their prey, not the opposite, as the chief of the village had said. *Ufufuyane* was the cause of everything, *ufufuyane* had been sent by the spirits to deceive him. But no one had listened to him. He had been banished from the village. "Let him rot alive!"

He could have had his throat cut like a sacrificed zebu, or been flayed to remind him of the power of the ancestral taboo, but the villagers had preferred to let him decay slowly, according to tradition. Gulethu had gone to the city, at least its townships, where others before him had lived amid the garbage.

Sonamuzi was powerful. The *umqolan*, the sorceress he had consulted, knew that perfectly well. Someone had told him about her, Tonkia, a toothless old woman who people said consorted with adverse spirits. The *umqolan* knew his curse. She had already treated others who had it. She would conjure away the family sin that hung over his nights. She would make a *muti* for him, a magic potion that would remove him from his destiny. He wouldn't rot. Not now. A young white girl would save him. Any white girl, provided she was a virgin. He just had to bring her back the sperm with which he had deflowered her.

Gulethu had carefully prepared the act. He had promised young Ramphele a lot, without telling him the whole truth. Things had happened as he had hoped until that damned whore had started screaming, like a bitch in heat. *Ufufuyane* had struck her, too—Zulus, coloreds or whites, the bitches were all possessed. A young virgin would never have opened her legs like that, or uttered all that crazy talk. The adverse spirits had intervened, before he had had the chance to make his *muti*.

He had tried to restrain her, but the bitch kept screaming, louder and louder.

The screams woke him with a start. Gulethu sat up, panting, his eyes wide open, his face covered in cold sweat. He was between two worlds, and could barely make out the shabby walls of the shed. After a while he saw the straw mattresses spread on the floor, heard the others snoring, and came back to reality. No, it wasn't the girl's screams that had wakened him. It was the *umqolan*, warning him of danger.

Stan was dead, but the cops could question his brother in prison. They could nose around the beach. The Cat must never know. *Never.*

11.

He felt uneasy as soon as he woke up. There was a weight on his heart, as if he had run in the rain for hours with his head thrown back. As if he had died for lack of breath. Brian Epkeen sat on the edge of the bed, searching in the chaos of his memories, and found only the tail end of a dream. A sense that he had an unpleasant chore to attend to hung in the air of the room. The morning would have done better to shut its big mouth. The fucking alarm clock hadn't gone off. Or he'd forgotten to set it. His head felt itchy. He'd slept badly. Standing up didn't help.

Brian was supposed to be meeting the others, the way things were going he wouldn't have time for breakfast, it was already hot, and this trip to the beach, with or without his friend "Jim," meant nothing to him.

"Hmm." Tracy whimpered, buried beneath the sheets. "Are you going?"

"Yes. I'm late."

Brian lifted the red hair from her cheek. Awkward in her love for him, Tracy caught his hand and pulled him toward her.

"Come here," she said, without opening her eyes. "Stay with me."

It was stupid, he'd just told her he was late.

"Please!" Tracy insisted.

"Let go of me, darling."

He wasn't in the mood for games. Her persistence got on his nerves. He wasn't in love—he should have told her last night that there was no point, their affair was hopeless, he was only the salt in an ocean of tears, but Tracy had rolled her big love-filled breasts over him, his heart had cracked like a log at the first skirmish, and he had admitted defeat. One more defeat.

"What's the matter?" Tracy asked, one eye venturing out from beneath the sheets.

Brian was coming out of the shower. "Nothing. Nothing at all."

He dressed with whatever he could find.

"The keys are on the kitchen table," he said. "Just throw them in the flower pot."

Tracy watching him, uncomprehendingly. He took his gun and left.

*

A strong wind was blowing over Muizenberg beach. Neuman buttoned his jacket over his Colt .45. Brian Epkeen and Dan Fletcher followed on, protecting their faces from the clouds of sand raised by the gusts of wind. Once past the picturesque old-fashioned beach huts, the beach stretched for miles, as far as the township.

They had questioned the parking attendants with their brightly numbered shirts, who also dealt a little *dagga*. One of them had recognized Stan Ramphele from his photo (he had a pickup) and the girl (a pretty young blonde). No other info, from either the local cops or the informers, who'd been grilled for days.

They left the wooden jetty that ran over the first dunes and started walking on the soft sand. On the weekends, people flocked here from the city, but now Muizenberg beach was almost empty. The few bathers were concentrated on the promenade, near the lifeguards' hut, where two blond guys with African necklaces were keeping a close watch on their muscles. Neuman had shown them the photo of Ramphele, but they saw dozens of young blacks wearing Gap and plastic Ray-Bans every day. Same with the young blonde who was supposed to have been with him.

The waves were breaking loudly, swallowing up a few surfers as they came in. The long-haired guys who got out alive, when questioned, gave them nothing but dirty looks. They walked. And walked. There were fewer and fewer houses. Soon there was only one windsurfer in the distance, and big waves crashing on the shore. Brian was sweating under his cotton blouson, he was starting to get sick of this walk, they had been plowing on for twenty minutes now. Beside him, Dan was saying nothing, an indolent figure in the sun and the wind lashing their faces. Neuman was walking upright, oblivious of the elements. Half a mile, a mile. Then they saw a group of men in the shelter of a dune. Blacks, half a dozen of them, drinking *tshwala*[1] beneath a tattered straw canopy. A girl was dancing in the shadows. It was only after a moment that the wind let them hear the music—a kind of reggae, being spat out by a ghetto blaster.

Neuman signaled to Brian to go take a look. They would carry on to the dunes—a little farther on, a thin gray wisp of smoke rose, borne on the wind. Brian walked straight toward the improvised bar, drawn by the girl's golden thighs.

The gusts of wind were raising clouds of sand. Dan kept grimly on behind Neuman and followed him to the white dunes.

A smell of grilled chicken floated in the air, and something else that was hard to define. They saw a worm-eaten beach hut, a *braai*[2] sheltered from the wind, and two men in canvas caps busy grilling meat. Neuman assessed the terrain, saw only the ridge of the dunes, and the two guys turning toward

[1] Bitter-tasting homemade beer.
[2] Barbecue.

them. Snatches of reggae from the straw canopy reached them, carried on the wind. Neuman approached. The half-open door of the hut was barely upright, holding on only by a whim. The two blacks, on the other hand, were stiff as ramrods.

"We're looking for this man," Neuman said. "Stan Ramphele."

The two men, both red-eyed, attempted smiles. One of them was a nervy-looking black of about thirty, teeth partly rotted by malnutrition and dope. The other one was younger, knocking back a beer and looking at the bottle as if the taste had changed with each swig.

"We don't know the guy," he said. His breath smelled.

"You look like one of his customers," Neuman replied. "Stan," he insisted. "He used to deal *dagga*, then he graduated to harder stuff."

"I don't know, man. We're just enjoying the beach, that's all!"

The ashes on the barbecue flew up in the wind. The two men had scars on their arms and necks.

"Where are you from?" Neuman asked.

"The township. Why, man?"

Dan was standing a few feet back, his hand on the grip of his gun.

"We found Stan in his mobile home with enough powder in him to burst his veins," Neuman said. "A *tik*-based mixture. What do you think of that, fellows?"

"We don't think anything," the nervy guy replied.

Neuman pushed open the door of the hut, saw a pair of binoculars on the dirty floor. A top-of-the-range model, which didn't seem like the kind of thing these losers would have. They had seen them coming. They had been waiting.

The nervy guy's smile froze, as if he had guessed what Neuman was thinking. His partner took a step toward the other side of the barbecue.

"Don't move," Dan said, taking his gun from his holster.

At the same moment, he felt a presence behind him. "No, don't *you* move!"

A revolver was jammed into his spinal cord. A third man had just emerged from behind the hut. Neuman had taken out his gun, but did not fire. The Beretta was trained on Dan's neck and the guy holding it had empty, lackluster eyes. A *tsotsi*, barely twenty years old—he'd seen him before, the other day, on the waste ground, the young guys who were kicking Simon. Dan scanned the surroundings out of the corner of his eye, but it was too late. The others had pulled revolvers from the sack of charcoal under the barbecue.

"Get your hands up, pig!" the nervy guy hissed, the barrel of his revolver pointed at Neuman. "Gatsha, take his gun—slowly!"

"One move, and your friend gets a bullet in the head!" the youngest of the three yelled.

Gatsha advanced toward Neuman as if he might bite, and tore the Colt out of his hands.

"Take it easy."

"Shut up, nigger!"

The nervy guy, holding his gun to the back of Dan's neck, had forced him to kneel with his hands on his head. The others, grinning triumphantly, hissed insults in Dashiki. Neuman did not move. Dan was sweating profusely beside the barbecue. He was white-faced, and his legs were shaking. Neuman swore through his teeth. Dan was losing his nerve. You could feel it by the way his pores were dilating, the aura of fear gripping him, his hands placed uselessly on his head.

"Over there, you!" the nervy guy shouted at Neuman. "Keep your hands still! You hear, asshole?"

Neuman moved back until his back and hands were against the cracked wood of the hut. Gatsha had followed him. He held his breath when the *tsotsi* pressed his revolver into his testicles.

"You move an inch, and I'll blow off your balls and all the shit that comes with them."

Joey, the young black he had seen on the construction site, took a knife from his belt, and waved it in front of his eyes. "We've met before, haven't we, cop?"

He laughed, and with one blow planted the knife in the worm-eaten wood. Neuman started—the *tsotsi* had just nailed his ear to the door.

"I said, don't move!" the boy cried, the veins in his eyes bursting.

The barrel of the gun was still tight against his testicles. His ear was burning, warm blood was running down his neck, his lobe and cartilage had been pierced by the blade that kept him fixed to the door. A few feet away, on his knees, the gun pressed to the back of his neck, Dan was shivering in the gusts of wind.

"So, cop, scared now?" The nervy guy pushed Dan down on the ground. "You know something? You look like a little fag. Has anyone ever told you that? A dirty little police fag."

The youngest of the three laughed. Gatsha was looking at his finger on the trigger.

"What would you say to a little grilled cop, boys?" their leader said. "This one looks good enough to eat!"

"Hey, man! Grilled cop! Better than grilled chicken! Yeah!"

"We could give him a try, couldn't we?"

"Yeah!"

"No!"

The two *tsotsis* were arguing for the fun of it, but Gatsha did not release the pressure on Neuman's testicles. There was a knot in his throat.

"Come on, Joey! Bring something to cut up the cop!"

Dan, now lying on the sand, could not stop shaking. Joey handed the older guy a *panga*.[3]

---

[3] Machete.

"Leave him alone," Neuman said.

"Go fuck yourself, nigger."

Neuman threw a furtive glance at the straw hut—as if Brian could see him from there.

"No point counting on your little white friend. We're taking care of him."

He thought he could make out the figure of Brian through the heat haze, bouncing up and down on the improvised dance floor beneath the straw canopy. What the fuck was he up to?

The nervy guy bent over the young cop on the ground and passed the machete over his back as if cleaning the blade.

"Now you're going to be a chicken. Do you hear?" He was whispering in his ear. "You're going to be a chicken or I'll kill you, you little fag. Do you hear? BE A CHICKEN!"

Fletcher looked at Neuman in panic.

"Leave him alone."

The gun barrel bored into his groin. Time stood still. There was only the wind scalping the dunes and the cruel eyes of the *tsotsi* oozing contempt all over Dan. He couldn't even hear the music anymore. The man was going to strike. Dan could feel it in his bones, it was only a matter of seconds. He looked around for Neuman, couldn't see him.

He let out a feeble splutter that did not cover the sound of his sobs.

"The slightest move and you're dead," Gatsha whispered in Neuman's bloody ear.

"You can do better than that!" the nervous guy bellowed, still holding the *panga*. "Come on!"

Dan emitted a feeble *cluck-cluck*, which was drowned by the noise of the rollers.

The man laughed, madness in his eyes. "Ha, ha! Look at this chicken! Oh, the pretty little chicken!"

Dan was trembling, his face buried in the sand next to the barbecue.

The *tsotsi* rose to his full height. "Look what I do to fags like you!"

With one stroke of the machete, he cut off Dan's right hand.

*

Brian looked at the small crowd gathered near the icebox. There were half a dozen people dancing under the straw canopy, including a colored girl in an impressively low-cut dress. She was strutting as she drank her beer, looking at him with an insistent air, lips playing with the neck of the bottle. The ghetto blaster was spluttering out reggae, Bob Marley and the Wailers. The girl wiggled her hips, the guys swarmed around her like bees—young guys, only the big black serving the *tshwala* was more than twenty. Tattoos on his arms, poor quality ones—probably done in prison.

"Hi!" the girl said, approaching Brian.

"Hi."

"Want to dance?"

Without waiting for a reply, she took his hand, wrapped her arms around him, and drew him onto the improvised dance floor. She smelled of licorice, with the unfortunate addition of hops. In spite of a missing tooth, she had a nice mouth.

"My name's Pamela!" she cried above the music. "But you can call me Pam!"

He bent over her cleavage and said in her ear, "Not so much a pompom girl, more a pampam girl!"

She smiled greedily. The others, bobbing up and down to the music of the Wailers, waved to them in a friendly manner. Caught up in the girl's movements, Brian wiggled around a little. Pamela snuggled up against him, playfully, provocatively.

He took out the picture of Ramphele. "Know this man?"

She twisted around to look at the photograph, shook her

head, and pressed herself against his back with a prolonged quiver—her peppery skin was on fire.

"Buy me a beer?"

She was looking at him with an expression of childlike supplication, as if the world was waiting for his answer. The others were watching them. Brian signaled to the tattooed man in charge of the beer. They grabbed their drinks with an acrobatic sensuousness and, still dancing, raised their bottles in the air in a toast. As the music was too loud to let them have a conversation, he pulled her toward the grass on the edge of the dunes.

Pam was smiling at him as if she found him very handsome.

"Stan Ramphele," he insisted, again shoving the photograph in front of her face. "A young guy who spent his days on the beach. A good-looking guy. You must have seen him around."

"You think?"

"Stan was dealing *dagga*, and more recently a kind of *tik*. Here, on the beach."

The girl was still wiggling her hips. "Are you a cop?" she said.

"Stan's dead. I'm trying to find out what happened to him. I'm not here to arrest you or your friends."

The wind made the charms in her hair jingle. She shrugged. "You know, I'm just a beach girl."

Her gap-toothed smile faded. The rest of her continued to sway. She drank her beer in one go, caught hold of him again, and started laughing.

"Don't tell me you brought me out here just to talk about this guy!"

"You looked like an honest girl," he lied.

"And now?" she said, putting her hand on his buttocks. "Am I honest or dishonest?"

The grass was bending in the wind, the sound of the waves

mingled with the reggae, and Pam was feeling the merchandise, like a connoisseur. She rubbed her groin against his, lin-
gered over his cock, kneeled and rubbed her breasts against it.
Brian felt the girl's hand moving over his back. Within a second, Pam had pulled the gun from his holster.

She stood up again, amazingly quickly given her position,
lifted the safety, and aimed the .38 at Brian, who had hardly
moved.

"Don't move," she said, cocking the hammer. "Hands on
head. Come on!"

Brian didn't bat an eyelid. A man appeared from behind the
dune, where he had been crouching. The tattooed man who'd
been serving beer.

"It's all right," she said to him, her gun still on Brian. "But
this idiot's refusing to put his hands up."

"Is that so?" the tattooed man said, coming closer. He had
a gun under his Rasta shirt.

"Get down on the ground!" Pam hissed.

Instead of obeying, Brian took a curious object from his
linen jacket. His forefathers' knout, with its copper loop.

"Too bad!" Pam cried, aiming at his head. "You had a nice
face!"

She pressed the trigger, twice, while Brian rushed at the
man. Pam continued to fire, until she realized that the . 38 was
not loaded. The tattooed man took out his gun, but the leather
thong struck his cheek and tore off a piece as large as a steak.
The man let out a muffled cry and staggered. His eyes filling
with tears, he did not see the second blow coming. The .32
leapt from his hand.

Pam had emptied the barrel between Brian's shoulder
blades. Now he turned to her. The knout broke her wrist, and
she dropped the .38 with a squeal. Behind her, the tattooed
man tried to pick up his gun. The knout stripped his fingers to
the bone. Brian's heart was pounding. They weren't dealing

with small-time beach dealers, but with *tsotsis* who killed cops. A sudden gust of wind made him screw up his eyes. Abandoning his gun, the tattooed man set off at a run toward the straw hut, holding his cheek. The girl had still made no move to run away. She was looking at her broken wrist as if it was about to fall off. Brian punched her on the chin, knocking her out. He looked up, saw the tattooed man running up the side of the dune.

That was when he heard a scream in the distance, above the rollers. A man's scream, coming from the other side of the dunes.

Dan.

*

"Go on," Gatsha breathed in Neuman's broken ear. "Give me the pleasure of cutting open your dirty nigger face. Go on, let me blow away your balls."

He was pressing so hard that Neuman wanted to vomit. One move and he was dead. That was what the guy was waiting for. Dan was weeping as he looked at his severed hand, wild-eyed, as if he didn't want to believe what was happening to him. The blood was spreading around the legs of the barbecue, the wind was swirling, and he was sobbing like a terrified child nobody would come and save. He was alone with his stump and his hand that lay there on the sand, detached from his body. He was living a nightmare.

Neuman closed his eyes when the *tsotsi* cut off his other hand.

Fletcher let out a terrible scream and passed out.

"Roast chicken! Roast cop!" the nervy guy bellowed, brandishing his machete.

Joey was smiling ecstatically. He picked up the severed hands and threw them on the barbecue. Neuman opened his eyes again, but things hadn't gotten any better—the blood spurting from the stumps, his friend lying unconscious on the ground, the wind stoking the charcoal, the smell of meat, the crackling of the hands on the burning griddle, the knife blade pinning him to the hut like an owl, the revolver in his guts, and Gatsha's bulging eyes and insane laugh.

"Ha ha! Roast cop!"

Sparks from the charcoal flew in the wind. The nervy guy planted his knee in Dan's back, but Dan had stopped reacting. He grabbed him by the roots of his hair and with a stroke of the machete cut his throat.

Neuman's heart was pounding as if it was going to burst. His brother's ghost passed behind his sweat-soaked back. They were going to cut Dan into pieces, they were going to grill him right here on the beach, and then it would be his turn. He clenched his teeth to chase away the fear that was making his legs turn to jelly. A warm liquid continued to run down his shirt, and Dan was dying before his horrified eyes.

The *tsotsi* with the machete turned to the younger man. "Joey! Go see what the others are up to while we deal with the nigger."

The nervy guy was dreaming of spectacular deaths when Gatsha's head exploded. Thrown by the impact, the boy didn't even have time to press the trigger. The others immediately turned toward the straw hut, where the shot had come from. A slender figure was running down the dune, a white with a revolver in his hand. They raised their guns and aimed at him.

In spite of the pieces of flesh and bone that had spattered his face, Neuman reacted in a flash. He pulled out the blade that was pinning him to the hut and rushed at them. Sensing danger, the nervy guy turned to him, but too late. Two hundred and twenty pounds of hate planted themselves in his abdomen. The *tsotsi* staggered back a few feet, and fell to his knees.

The first shot hit the sand at Brian's feet, the second went completely wide. When he got to the foot of the dune, he stopped and aimed his gun. With the sun in his eyes, the guy did not have a chance. Brian brought him down with a bullet to his gut.

The leader of the gang stood by the barbecue, looking down incredulously at his stomach, where the knife was plunged in up to the hilt. Neuman did not bother to pull it out. Instead, he grabbed the hands crackling on the griddle and threw them on the sand.

Brian was looking around, searching for another target, as if the whole world was his enemy. That was when he saw Dan's mutilated body lying at the foot of the dune. Neuman had rushed to his side. He took off his jacket, felt his pulse. Dan was still breathing.

At last, Brian ran up, pale as a sheet.

"Quick!" Neuman cried, pressing Dan's jugular. "Call an ambulance!"

PART TWO
ZAZIWE

1

"What's the matter, big brother?"

"I'm burning."

"What about your knees?"

"They're shaking."

"Your red shorts?"

"As you can see, they're soaking wet."

"And your cheeks, big brother, what about your cheeks?"

"Two trails of gasoline."

Andy had burned in front of his eyes, the black tears melting like rubber on his cheeks, petrified into filthy bubbles. The vigilantes[1] had let go of him, there was no point holding him, he could stand by himself, or rather, he was looking for a place where he could stand. Andy had tried to roll on the ground, but the rubber had already melted to him. He could still gesticulate, scream so loudly he might split the eardrums of the earth, he still couldn't find a place to disappear.

Time had condensed in Ali's mind. He was still too young to fully understand. Everything was vague, unreal, strangely distant. He could make out figures in the night, bloodshot eyes beneath the ski masks, the gallows tree in the middle of the garden, the cracked moon, the SAP's lights flashing at the end of the street, the vigilantes mounting guard around the house, the plainclothes cops turning away the neighbors, but everything was false, apart from those black tears tumbling down his brother's cheeks.

[1] Militiamen operating in the townships on behalf of local chiefs in the pay of the authorities.

Andy had become fire, a flaming torch, an upturned beacon. Ali didn't hear the screams or the noises from the street, he was deaf to the chaos, and the images continued to pile up, empty of meaning. His mother behind the window, her face pressed to the glass, being forced to watch, the cries of rage, the giants' fetid breath, even the smell of rubber passed over his head like a flight of arrows.

The men were holding him, making sure he missed nothing of the show. "Look, little Zulu! See what happens!" But the fear of dying had made him punch-drunk. Ali was ashamed, ashamed of being so weak he had almost forgotten about Andy burning. He was still alive, that was all that mattered.

He didn't see what happened next. The world had turned upside down, the moon had shattered into pieces.

When he opened his eyes again, the screams had stopped. Andy's huddled body lay on the ground, like a bird covered in oil, and that terrible smell of grilled meat was still there. Then Ali saw his father hanging there, and the reality of it came back to him like a boomerang.

No doubt about it. He was at home, which meant he was in hell.

A hand grabbed him by the roots of his hair and dragged him behind the house.

The wind blew across the grass and the quicksilver ocean glittered in the twilight. Neuman followed the stony path to the top of the cliff. Passing close to him, a hovering seagull gave him a stare before diving into the abyss.

The Cape Town lighthouse glowed, deserted. Neuman walked around the graffiti-covered wall and leaned on the parapet. Below, gray waves were tossing in the inlets. The fear had gone, but not the smell of burned flesh.

Dan had been transferred to the nearest hospital, in a critical state. The rescue team's helicopter had taken nearly twenty minutes to get to Muizenberg beach—to them, it had seemed like an hour.

They had done what they could, made tourniquets to stem the flow of blood from the arteries, sealed the open wounds with their jackets and shirts, but Dan's life was draining away like liquid through a sieve. They talked to him, told him his hands would be sewed back on, they knew a specialist, the best there was, he'd have new hands, better ones than before, more agile, hands like a surgeon's, they were talking nonsense just for the sake of talking. Claire and the children needed him, today and tomorrow and every day of their lives, they were talking to him even though Dan was lying unconscious, his cut throat open in a ghastly grin, his blood seeping into the sand. Neuman remembered the look of terror in his eyes when he saw the machete, his bright eyes imploring him, the way he had cried like a child when his first hand had been cut off. He was the one who had led Dan into that nightmare.

The medical team, the first aid given on the stretcher, the emergency transfusion, the helicopter that had carried him off into the sky, the assurance that everything would be done to save him—none of that made any difference. It wasn't that Brian had intervened too late, it was he himself who had failed.

But Dan was still clinging to life, and maybe he'd pull through—his heart was still beating weakly when they had transferred him.

Neuman stepped over the low wall surrounding the lighthouse and walked down to the mass of fallen rocks that hung on the precipice. A slice of moon yawned in the dead sky. He climbed over the rocks, closed his eyes, and let the wind buffet him. One more step, and the void would suck him in. One leap, and he would rest forever. But he could turn the skin of the earth inside out the way you skin a rabbit, merge with the silvery waves for a final embrace, at the end of the dizzy spell he was alone.

Neuman waited until night fell, then walked back down the path.

The moon guided him over the heath. In spite of the stitches, his ear had started bleeding again. A baboon approached, an old male, and Neuman gave him a fierce look to shoo him away. He was thinking about Claire and the children, and about all the things he hadn't done to save Dan. He was just leaving the reserve when his cell phone rang. It was Brian Epkeen, calling from the hospital.

A one-in-ten chance, the doctor had said.

Neuman held his breath, but it was no use.

"It's all over."

2.

For sixteen years, Joost Terreblanche had been a colonel in the 77th infantry battalion, the special unit given the task of keeping order in the Bantustan of KwaZulu.

The apartheid government had delegated authority within the enclaves to tribal chiefs, under the control of the ministry. These corrupt chiefs had the support of vigilante militias chosen from among the local beggars, who imposed the law with their blackjacks. The black population lived in terror, especially as the ANC and the UDF were ruthless in their reprisals against anyone breaking the boycott or collaborating with the oppressor. Politically isolated, apartheid had survived by dividing its enemies. So Chief Buthelezi's Zulu Inkatha movement had been left alone to battle with the ANC for leadership of the opposition, then criticize its possible participation in a coalition government, provoking ten years of virtual civil war and the worst violence in its history.[1] Demonstrations degenerated into bloodbaths. Whenever the rioting threatened to turn into an uprising, the Casspirs of the 77th battalion were sent in, those infamous armored vehicles that had traumatized a generation.

Joost Terreblanche had proved himself remarkably efficient at "cleaning up" the Bantustans, and his name was cited in military schools. Rewarding his exemplary service, the government had allocated him and his family a new home.

---

[1] In the 1980s, three times as many people were victims of interethnic violence as of police bullets.

Ross and François, the two strapping sons his wife had given him in spite of her shortcomings, had up until then grown up in the austere, confined atmosphere of a military barracks. Now, at the ages of sixteen and fourteen respectively, they would have the freedom of this delightful new property. Joost was proud of his position, and confident in the future. The one weak link was his wife, Ruth.

A woman of delicate constitution, Ruth claimed that she couldn't take care of such a big house alone—a residence in the purest Colonial style that Joost's Huguenot ancestors wouldn't have sniffed at. Cook, gardener, cleaning woman, houseboy—Ruth had soon surrounded herself with a host of servants. Naturally the house was protected by a security system. What Joost didn't know was that the enemy would come from within.

The black gardener, a Zulu named Jake. Always wearing his old, faded-red cotton sunhat, and holding his shears in his worn gloves, Jake's exterior concealed the soul of a traitor. Ruth should never have left François alone with him, let alone allow him to help the man plant his damned flowers. François was younger, more impulsive, more delicate than Ross, who was solid in every way—you just had to see him sawing wood. The gardener had put dark thoughts in the younger brother's head. He knew that François was vulnerable. He had manipulated him with his humble, sun-dazed *kaffir* smiles. After a mere two years, François repeated this nonsense to his father one day, in the middle of dinner, with all the conviction of a young fool discovering the world. Joost had been firm, but François had stood up to him. There had been arguments, threats, punishments, blows, and a lot of weeping from Ruth, but no one had given in. The gardener had been beaten and dismissed, and François sent to boarding school. Joost told himself it was only an adolescent tantrum—he had tamed people a whole lot tougher than this wet rag. The boy would thank him later.

The year he turned eighteen, François had come back from boarding school one day and announced that he was leaving home for good. His father threatened to disown him, his mother to kill herself, his elder brother to smash his face in. François had sneaked away to join his beatnik friends—as his father called them—a group high on human rights and marijuana, who had managed to indoctrinate him with their dreaming of egalitarian utopias—egalitarian my ass, the colonel fumed. As if the blacks were capable of equality! You just had to look at Africa, children's eyes crawling with flies, petty tyrants in their military caps appropriating their countries' riches for their own clans, pasteboard emperors, greedy, bloodthirsty warlords, window cleaners promoted to ministers, starving, ignorant populations displaced like cattle! Blacks in power were immature, violent, mendacious, incompetent, and uncultured. They had nothing to teach the whites, certainly not the spirit of liberty and equality. You didn't share the results of two hundred years of hard toil with people who still worked with machetes. You just had to look at their fine symbol Mandela and his wife, Winnie, participating in the torture of opponents of the ANC, those thousands of crimes committed in the name of "liberation"—Apazo, ANC, Inkatha, UDF, all killing each other for the sake of power! The so-called liberal whites who campaigned for the black cause were knee-jerk leftists, and François was quite crazy to defy his father. He was never to set foot in the house again, was that understood?

And in fact, he never had. For three years, they didn't hear anything about him, until the day Joost got a memo from the SAP to say that François Terreblanche had been arrested for the murder of his girlfriend, Kitty Brown, found dead in a seedy slum in the center of Jo'burg. In his shame, anger, and bitterness, the colonel had done nothing to defend his son. Five years in prison without remission.

They had visited François before he was transferred to prison. Crazy with grief, Ruth had predicted to her son that she would die before he was released, and that he would have her death on his conscience. More sober by nature, Joost had wished him good luck surrounded by all those niggers.

The time had passed. Three years during which Ruth had resorted to spiritualism and rest cures. She had never been a healthy woman, and now she had become obsessed with her own fate. She had died of an aneurismal rupture just before he was due to be released. François, who was not even allowed to attend the funeral, thanks to his father, had followed her within a month—suicide, according to the internal inquiry.

Ancient history.

Joost Terreblanche had not testified before the Truth and Reconciliation Commission.[2] He had obeyed orders in a country fighting the spread of Communism in Africa. The fall of the Berlin Wall had hastened the fall of apartheid, but the Western countries, although officially observing the boycott, had supported them in their fight against the Reds. That was the truth. As for reconciliation, well, they could always set up commissions.

Terreblanche was now sixty-seven, with an extremely lucrative new career, and anything related to that tragic period of his life left him as cold as ice. When brought to completion, the operation for which he was responsible would allow him to join his elder son Ross, who, after the expulsion of the white farmers from Zimbabwe, had taken refuge in Australia. They would have their revenge, and make a lot of money at the same time. They would enlarge the farm, make it the biggest in the whole of New South Wales.

He still had to deal with these fucking *kaffirs*. This one didn't seem to be in great form right now.

[2] In 1996, at the instigation of Desmond Tutu, those responsible for the excesses of apartheid were invited to testify as to the actions of the regime in return for amnesty.

"Where did you find her?" Terreblanche asked.

"Here, with the others."

The Cat was standing in the shadowy part of the shed, carefully filing his nails to sharp points. The sleeve of his shirt was red, his eyes misty beneath his deceptively sleepy eyelashes. The prey he had brought back to his master was an almost painful sight, her arms suspended on bicycle chains from the ceiling beam. Pam, the gang's whore, who had taken up residence in the shed.

Terreblanche approached the girl, who was grimacing in pain in the pale fluorescent light. Her toes barely touched the floor and the filthy steel was biting into her wrists. One was already broken, and she seemed to have exhausted her tears.

"Now," he said, "you're going to tell me what happened on the beach."

Blood was dripping from the whore's half torn-off scalp. A souvenir of the Cat.

Massive and compact, accustomed to combat sports and special operations, Joost Terreblanche was not a patient man. "Well?" his voice rang out in the silence of the shed.

Pam made a tremendous effort to look up. She stared at the riding crop with her bulging brown eyes.

"Gulethu. He was the one who told us to keep the cops away."

Gulethu was the leader of this pathetic gang. Someone you could trust, according to the Cat. But things always went wrong—one of the vehicles was missing from the shed, the Toyota, along with the five men who used it.

"What did the cops want?"

"They . . . they were trying to find out about this guy," the girl sniveled.

"What guy?"

"S . . . Stan."

"Stan who?"

"Ramphele," Pamela groaned.

"A small-time pusher," the Cat explained from the shadows. "Ramphele took over his brother's business on the coast. He was found dead two days ago. An overdose, apparently."

Terreblanche tightened his grip on his riding crop. At last he understood. "Gulethu unloaded his dope on Ramphele, is that it?" he growled.

The girl nodded, her eyes rolled upwards. He fumed in silence. Given the job of dealing in the squatter camps, Gulethu should have known how addictive the drug was. The idiot had tried to double-cross them by selling part of the stock to a small-time pusher on the coast, without even knowing what was in it.

"How long has this little game been going on?"

"Two . . . two months."

"How many dealers?"

"Ramphele. He was the only one."

He brandished his whip. "Who else?"

"No one!" the girl said, in a choked voice. "Ask Gulethu! He knows everything!"

She started crying. Terreblanche kept his composure. Gulethu had disappeared, but it wasn't too late. He must be hiding somewhere in the vicinity, they could still seal off the area, locate the Toyota.

"How many people took the drug?" he asked the girl.

"I don't know. There were about thirty customers. Only whites. They kept wanting more. As soon as they were hooked, the prices went up."

At most, they must have made a few thousand rand a day. A pitiful sum when you knew what was really going down. Terreblanche lifted the little whore's twitching head. "What happened with the cops?"

"We were supposed to sweet-talk them, keep them away from the house."

"What went wrong?"

No reply.

"Answer me!"

"Need any help?" the Cat called.

Pam was writhing at the end of the chain. Her ankles were giving way. Her strength was going. The pain of her broken wrist was boring into her skull.

"Joey," she moaned. "One of the cops had already seen him. They tried to hide him, but the cops must have suspected something."

There were twelve men in Gulethu's gang, divided into two groups. It was the day team the cops had run into. Three of them had died on the beach, three others were now in their hands—the girl hanging from the beam, and the two *kaffirs* counting their teeth in the dormitory next door. So there were still six black sheep at large.

"Where's Gulethu?" Terreblanche asked.

"I don't know. He left with the others, didn't say where he was going. He . . . he told us to stay here. Said he'd take care of everything."

Terreblanche grabbed her scalp. To judge by the scream she gave, she was telling the truth.

Gulethu would be sharing out the loot among six instead of twelve. They had searched the shed without finding any money, just those filthy things of theirs in their canvas bags and Gulethu's *grigris* under his mattress. The money from the side deal must be stashed somewhere, in a place where no one would think of looking for it. They had to find the rest of the gang, before the cops did.

Terreblanche peered at the trinkets, the short clubs and the other finery piled up in a corner of the shed. There was dried blood on one of the clubs.

"These are Gulethu's, aren't they?" he said to the girl. "What was he doing with these *grigris*?"

"He . . . he mentioned an *umqolan* who was casting out bad luck."

A sorceress, in the township jargon.

Terreblanche grinned contemptuously. He'd spent enough time in the Zulu Bantustans to know their beliefs, their rituals, all the old wives' tales they called their culture. "Do you know where we can find this sorceress?"

"No! No . . . I swear . . . Please . . ."

Overcome with nausea, Pamela drooped at the end of the chain. Terreblanche lifted one of her eyelids, but she had lost consciousness. She wouldn't hold out much longer in this state.

"What are we going to do with her?" the Cat asked. "Get rid of her, like the others?"

"No . . . No, we can still use them."

"To do what? Clean up the place?"

Pamela's blood had gathered in a dark pool on the dirt floor. Terreblanche looked up. The house had been evacuated, but there must still be traces . . .

3

Are you such a dreamer?
To put the world to rights?

Thom Yorke's voice was wailing from the car radio in the Mercedes. Concentrated despair. The asphalt was baking in the noon sun. Brian Epkeen was waiting outside the school of journalism. David wouldn't be much longer. A few boys with the same post-grunge look came out through the gates, as well as some neatly dressed blondes and colored girls who didn't do anything to brighten his mood. Dan Fletcher had died in their arms, more or less, and they hadn't been able to save him.

Brian was thinking about Claire, the scene at the hospital, and his heart contracted even more. It was the first time he had ever seen anyone collapse with grief. Her legs had given way, like a cripple whose spine has been struck. She collapsed on the plastic-coated hospital floor, tearing her hair and screaming, half crazy, that she wanted to be left alone, even though all she had for support was her blonde wig, which had fallen at her feet, and her bald head. He had helped her to her feet, and, frail as she was, she'd felt as heavy as an anvil. As heavy as a corpse.

Brian saw his son's gangling figure on the sidewalk, reminding him of himself a long, long time ago. There was a sexy blonde with him, presumably his girlfriend (he had forgotten her name—Marjorie, wasn't it?). He opened the windowless door and crossed the street.

The asphalt was white-hot, and his soles stuck to it. David saw his father and immediately froze.

"Hi!" Brian said.

"Hi. What do you want?"

The blonde was chewing gum as if it were leather. She gave Brian a long, impudent look.

"Nothing special," he said, with his hands in his pockets. "I just thought we could talk."

"What for?" His bluntness would have crucified a mountain.

Brian shrugged. "I don't know. To get to understand each other better."

"There's nothing to understand," David said, with a conclusive air.

The gum-chewing blonde with a diamond in her nostril and two chrome-plated nails in her eyelids seemed to agree.

"It's your exam soon, isn't it?"

"Tomorrow," David replied.

"We should celebrate. Why don't I buy you dinner?"

"Why not just give us some money? That'll save us all time."

"I know a Japanese chef who—"

"Don't knock yourself out," David cut in. "Mom told me how you harassed her on the phone. You're jealous of her happiness, is that it?"

"Sleeping with the king of the dentures, no thanks."

David shook his head as if it was hopeless. "You're really crazy."

"Yes. I was thinking of doing something dramatic, like slashing my wrists, but then I thought, why steal work from the young?"

"Reactionary old bastard."

The girl was smiling. She was his one hope.

"You're quite pretty when you stop chewing your gum, you

know that?" Brian said. "I hope David hasn't told you too much about me?"

"Not a lot."

"They can be sensitive at that age."

"I told you he was a sex maniac," David said. "Let's get out of here before he shows us his dick."

She laughed. "Cool."

"Have you found an apartment?" Brian asked.

"7 Wale Street," Marjorie replied.

Tamboerskloof, the old Malayan quarter, where the rents had doubled now that it had become bohemian.

"Come over sometime," the blonde said, with curly-haired innocence.

"Don't even think about it," David cut in.

"There's a bar just over there," Brian said. "We could have a drink."

"With a cop?" his son scoffed. "No thanks! If you want to do us a favor, go back to your fascists and your whores, and leave us alone, O.K.?"

"Aren't whores women? Maybe you think they're a sub-species of humanity? I thought you were the bleeding-heart liberal among us."

"Be that as it may, I don't mix with guys who used to throw blacks from the top floors of police stations."

"My best friend is a Zulu."

"Don't play Mother Teresa, dad. It suits you like a rainbow in the middle of your face."

With these words, David grabbed his girlfriend's hand and pulled her away, like it really had started raining. "Come on, let's get out of here."

Marjorie twisted slightly to wave him goodbye, then stamped off after the prodigal son. Brian stood there on the sidewalk, weary, hurt, and angry.

No common ground.

No future together.
You might as well run after a desert.

*

The New South Africa had to succeed where apartheid had failed. Violence wasn't just African, it was inherent in the human condition. In expanding, the world was becoming increasingly hard for the weak, the maladjusted, the pariahs of the big cities. The political immaturity of the blacks and their tendency to violence was merely an old saw of apartheid and the neo-conservative forces now in control. It would take generations before the black population would be well enough educated to take up key positions in the marketplace. The emerging black middle class might aspire to the same Western codes, but you had to know a system from the inside before you could criticize it, let alone reform it root and branch. Neuman lived with that hope, which had also been his father's. They hadn't left the Bantustans to end up in the townships.

But the figures told a different story. Eighteen thousand murders a year, twenty-six thousand serious assaults, sixty thousand rapes, officially (probably ten times as many), five million firearms for a population of forty-five million. The balance sheet was grim indeed.

Krüge and the government couldn't hide forever behind the excuse that he didn't have enough men and that those he did have were underpaid. The murder of the young officer made it look as if violence was the country's principal means of expression, as if the police were not only powerless but themselves victims of the situation.

The FNB's anti-crime campaign was in full swing. Everyone was demanding a clampdown, the prospect of the World Cup made the situation even more urgent, the challenge was a national one.

The spotlight was on Karl Krüge now. He had just been talking on the phone with the Attorney General, Marius Jonger. Murder in broad daylight, acts of barbarism—this time, a reassuring statement from the president wouldn't be enough. Worse still, the report he had just been handed by Neuman seemed to echo the criticisms of the media. The police had cordoned off the beach, but the killers had escaped over the dunes. They had found only an old tank half full of homemade beer beneath a rudimentary straw canopy, tracks on the sand that led toward the highway, a pair of binoculars and a walkie-talkie in a hut, and the bodies of three *tsotsis* near a smoking barbecue where a young sergeant lay dying.

"At least tell me you have a lead," Krüge said from behind his desk.

His left ear covered with a bandage, his shoulders stooped inside his dark suit, Neuman looked like a man who'd survived a shipwreck and could think only of those who hadn't. Sonny Ramphele had just been found in the latrines of Pollsmoor Prison, hanged with his own jeans. As usual, no one had seen or heard anything.

"We've identified one of the three men killed on the beach," Neuman said, in a hoarse voice. "Charlie Rutanga. A Xhosa, thirty-two years old. Prison terms for carjacking and grievous bodily harm. Probably a member of a township gang. I've sent his file and description to the police stations concerned. The other two are unknown to the police. We only know their nicknames, Gatsha and Joey. Almost certainly foreign. I met one of them in Khayelitsha last week, and he was speaking Dashiki to a friend of his."

Krüge crossed his arms over his belly, which was as large as a pregnant woman's. "What are you thinking? A Mafia-related gang?"

"The Nigerians control hard drugs," Neuman said. "And apparently a new product has been launched on the market. A drug with devastating effects, which Stan Ramphele was selling on the coast. He and Nicole Wiese went to Muizenberg the day of the murder. Sonny confirmed that, and probably signed his own death warrant in the process. Binoculars, a walkie-talkie, almost new guns—this isn't a bunch of *tsotsi* junkies we're dealing with, but an organized gang. The tracks we found on the dunes led to the highway. If they got through the road-blocks, there's a strong chance they took refuge in one of the townships."

There were half a dozen around Cape Town, in other words, a population of two or three million people, not to mention the squatter camps. Not much chance of laying their hands on them.

"What are you planning to do?" Krüge asked. "Send Casspirs into the townships, hoping they'll just fall into your lap?"

"No. I need you to trust me, that's all."

The two men looked at each other across the air-conditioning. A duel without a victor.

"The Wiese murder wasn't just any old crime," Neuman insisted. "They tried to get Stan Ramphele to take the fall. I'm sure the people who supplied him with the drugs are involved."

Krüge massaged his sinuses with his thick fingers and sighed. "You know how highly I think of you. But we're running out of time. The mob's after us, Neuman, and you're the first in the firing line."

Neuman did not flinch at this—he would shoot first.

*

Dan Fletcher lying mutilated on the ground, Dan Fletcher and his stumps covered in sand, Dan Fletcher and his pretty throat gaping open, Dan Fletcher and his blood-streaked smile,

Dan Fletcher and his burned hands, bearing the marks of the barbecue griddle. Janet Helms had looked at the photographs of the murder with a morbid fascination. They had killed her love, the one she had kept hidden for when his wife died, in that bed into which he would never climb. Two whole days she had cried, disorientated by tears, with rage in her heart and her heart in flames. She would avenge him. Whatever it took.

She looked up from her computer when Brian Epkeen passed the open door of the office. She smoothed her skirt, which had ridden up her thighs, and ran after him.

"Lieutenant!" she called down the corridor. "Please! Lieutenant Epkeen!"

Brian stopped by the watercooler. He had been trying to trace the girl he had met under the straw canopy, but none of the hundreds of faces he had looked at in the records at headquarters looked familiar. Ditto for the guy he had slashed with his knout. Too many javas. No memory left. Fletcher would have known. He'd been their hard drive. But Fletcher wasn't here anymore. Here was his colleague, though, running up to him, bursting out of her navy blue uniform.

Janet knew Epkeen by reputation (weird) and gossip (feminine), but she preferred to trust Dan's judgment: a man uninterested in power, although a stickler for the way it was exercised, an unreliable dandy who sought oblivion in the arms of pretty women. No chance of his replacing Dan.

"If you have a few minutes, Lieutenant," she said, breathless after her run, "I've got something that might interest you."

He looked at his watch—now wasn't the time to be late—and gave her five minutes.

Dan's things were still on the shelves, the photograph of Claire next to his computer. Janet Helms sat down at hers.

"The Simon's Town police have a body on their hands," she said. "A man named De Villiers, a surfer out on the peninsula. A patrol killed him two days ago after he tried to hold up an all-night drugstore. De Villiers was armed and started firing to cover his escape. He was shot down on the street."

A face appeared on the screen: a white Rasta of about twenty, his chin framed by a goatee with a pearl in it.

"According to the drugstore assistants," she went on, "De Villiers was unusually aggressive during the holdup. A real bundle of nerves. He'd been arrested before, for possession of narcotics—marijuana, cocaine, ecstasy—but never for assault or using firearms. Simon's Town isn't far from Muizenberg. I took the liberty of asking for a postmortem."

Janet had been fearing his reaction—she had exceeded her authority—but Brian merely looked at his watch. "Do we have the results?"

"They've just come in," she said, becoming emboldened. "De Villiers was under the influence of a drug during the hold-up. A *tik*-based product that seems to have driven him crazy."

"Methamphetamine and an unidentified molecule?"

"Exactly."

Brian lit a cigarette, even though the office was a non-smoking one. De Villiers was presumably not an isolated case. How many others had become hooked?

"There's another thing, lieutenant," she said, sensing how impatient he was to go. "I was checking out the area around the beach when I noticed there's an uninhabited house on the edge of Pelikan Park. It's about half a mile past the straw hut. I tried to contact the owners, but didn't have any luck."

"Maybe they're on vacation."

"No, I mean I can't get hold of the name. It seems obvious the purchase was made by a front man, or a bogus company, via a foreign bank."

"Is that possible?"

"And absolutely legal. A property-management company handled the transaction. I phoned them, but no one would tell me anything."

He grimaced—those assholes in the real-estate business.

"And no one lives in the house?"

"No. It's never been rented. It may, of course, have been acquired as a speculative venture. If the park is extended, the land may end up being a protected site, which would double or even triple its value. For the moment, it seems to have been abandoned, as if the owners are waiting for better days. I don't know if this gets us anywhere. But it is the only dwelling between the straw hut and Pelikan Park nature reserve."

"Carry on looking into this," Brian said. "You have full powers on this case."

Janet Helms was only an intelligence officer.

"You mean I'm joining the captain's team?"

Her brain was boiling over, filled with ambition and dead stars.

Brian shrugged. "If you don't mind a Zulu calling you at all hours of the night, trying to bring justice to our beautiful country."

"You mean he's a workaholic?"

"No, I mean he's an insomniac."

Janet smiled to herself as he left the office. With one machete stroke, she had taken Dan's place.

*

Brian found a place in the parking lot of the funeral home. Their friend's body was lying in a coffin for the wake, prior to being cremated. He left the Mercedes under an emaciated palm tree and walked toward the brick building. Neuman was waiting on the steps, lost in thought.

"Hello, Your Highness."

"You're on time."

"It does happen."

They tried to smile, but everything—the blue of the sky, the peaceful shade that lay over the steps, their friendship—seemed false. They had barely seen each other since the tragedy. Neuman hadn't come to the hospital. He had left Brian to deal with Claire, and had vanished until the following day, without a word of explanation.

"What happened to Ramphele's brother?" Brian asked.

He had just heard the news.

"He was depressed, according to Kriek."

"Do you believe that?"

"No."

"Kriek's a shit," Brian said. "If a prison gang was responsible, he won't lift his little finger."

"I'm sure you're right. They're conducting a postmortem, but it won't tell us anything."

Dying in prison was a natural occurrence in South Africa.

"And what's Krüge saying?"

"For the moment, he's covering our backs," Neuman replied. "It won't last."

"We couldn't have known what was going to happen."

"Men with guns, waiting for us, ready to kill us," he said through clenched teeth. "That was no accident. They saw us coming, and one of them knew me. They lit that barbecue to separate us, and were quite prepared to wipe us out if things got complicated. We fell into a trap, Brian. It's all my fault."

"Did you tell Krüge I was dirty dancing with a black girl while they were slicing you up?"

"What would be the point? Sonny Ramphele was killed because he told us about Muizenberg beach. The gang has contacts in prison and a bolt-hole in the townships. I met one of them in Khayelitsha. He was beating up a street kid named Simon Mceli, a kid my mother knows."

Brian sat down next to him on the steps. "We're in this together, my friend, whether you like it or not."

"I was in charge of the operation," Neuman said, stubbornly.

"Stop it with the big chief crap."

They weren't superior and subordinate, they were friends. They understood each other with a look.

"Right, what do our informants say?"

"Khayelitsha is outside our territory," Neuman replied. "And no one seems to know anything about the trafficking at Muizenberg. Either Stan was the only dealer, or there's something we don't know."

A sparrow was hopping on the marble flagstones. It stopped near them and gave them a sidelong look.

"There's an isolated house at the far end of the beach," Brian said, "about half a mile after the straw hut. It seems to be abandoned, but no one knows who the owner is. Some kind of property speculation. There's also a dead guy in Simon's Town, a surfer from the coast. The guy was killed while committing a robbery, but, according to the autopsy, he was high on a *tik*-based cocktail. The same as our young couple."

"So Nicole wasn't the dealers' only target. The network had widened."

"Seems like it. I've put Janet Helms on the case . . ."

Brian left the sentence unfinished. Claire had just appeared on the steps of the crematorium. She was wearing a black dress that made her look thinner, and carrying a small vinyl purse. The family members came out after her, their grief concealed behind dark glasses.

Claire saw the two men on the steps, whispered something to her sister, and walked toward them. They stood up together, saw how crushed she looked, and put their arms around her. For a brief moment, she let herself go, before regaining her balance. She hadn't been sleeping, in spite of the medication, but she wouldn't crack. Not now.

"I need to talk to the two of you," she said, freeing herself from their embrace.

Rain was falling in her Atlantic-blue eyes. They walked the

short distance to the parking lot, in silence. Claire stopped in the shade of a palm tree and turned to Neuman.

"What did they do to his hands?" she asked, in a toneless voice.

Brian remained impassive, but you could see the cracks getting bigger.

"Nothing," Neuman replied. "It all happened very quickly."

Claire bit the inside of her mouth. Her eyes were flickering now behind dark glasses.

"Dan didn't have time to suffer, if that's what's worrying you. I'm sorry."

He was lying, but what could he say to this bundle of grief? That he had had seen her husband being cut up alive, that Dan was weeping when he was put to death, and that he himself had not lifted a finger because he had a knife stuck through his ear and the barrel of a revolver pressed to his balls?

"It's all my fault," he said.

Claire was sounding him out, pale beneath the half-veil over her wig. At first she said nothing, searching for words. Ali and Brian had become her friends, that was why she was angry with them. Dan was afraid of physical violence. He didn't smell the same in bed the night before an operation. Claire had tried to talk to him, but Dan feigned indifference. He hadn't said much more to Neuman, because he knew that eventually Neuman planned to make him, and not the unconcerned Epkeen, his right-hand man. What angered Claire wasn't so much the fact that they hadn't been able to save him as the fact that they had been blind to how scared he was by this kind of operation. Neuman was right—it was all his fault.

"Dan wouldn't have liked us to be talking about him in the past tense," she said, in a toneless voice. "So I'm going to keep quiet, and look after the kids as if my life had never happened. Thank you for the support you gave us when I fell ill, and for all you did for him. But I don't want your help." She dug her small canines into her lips. "In any way, do you understand?" Only fragments were visible behind her dark glasses. "I'd prefer it if you didn't come to the cremation," she added. "Not you, not anyone from the force."

Claire lowered the black veil, which was flapping in the breeze, and turned to the crematorium. Brian made a gesture to hold her back.

"I know," she said, cutting him off. "You're sorry. Goodbye."

*

"You look tired," Tembo said.

"Not as tired as these guys," Neuman replied.

The *tsotsis* from the beach were lying on the aluminum table, their open entrails giving off a vivid, sickly-sweet smell. One of them had a nasty wound in the temple—Epkeen's bullet had taken off half his cranium. This was Joey, the crippled twenty-year-old he'd first met on the construction site in Khayelitsha. His features and morphology weren't Xhosa, and certainly not Zulu. Among his many tattoos and scarifications, there was a design at the top of his triceps, a scorpion about to attack. The one who'd been called Gatsha had exactly the same tattoo. The design, which was clearly several years old, had nothing original about it, except for the initials TB. Neuman took some photographs of the tattoos before turning to the medical officer.

Tembo was conducting his macabre dance around an open abdomen, that of Charlie Rutanga. Several scars on the arms and thorax, souvenirs of old knife fights, but no scorpion tattoo.

"I took some fluid and tissue samples," Tembo said, depositing some secretions on strips of glass. "There are the usual deficiencies associated with poor hygiene and deplorable living standards. I found a little homemade beer, maize porridge, bread, milk, dried beans, in other words, the staple diet of the townships. There are also a few insect bites, a broken humerus that had been badly patched up, some corns on the feet. The two younger ones are riddled with bullet holes. Half a dozen each, on different parts of the body. Old wounds."

Ex-soldiers? Militiamen? Deserters? Africa was spewing out its killers on a production-line basis, like rivers of skeletons in the dry season.

"What about drugs?" Neuman asked.

"All three of them had consumed marijuana recently," Tembo said. "I also found traces of crystals, less recent, but not our famous cocktail."

The point of the business was to get the customer hooked, not to kill him. The *tsotsis* hadn't acted in a sudden fit of madness.

"How about *iboga*?"

Tembo shook his graying head. "None at all."

*

With the end of South Africa's apartheid-era isolation, criminal activity had become transnational (drugs, diamonds), and the country a place of transit to which criminals flocked from all over. Neuman had pursued his research in the impersonal office on the top floor of headquarters where he spent half his nights.

He began with the tattoos on the upper arms of the two *tsotsis* killed on the beach: a scorpion about to attack, and those initials, TB. He checked the available data on the gangs for which the SAP had records, but couldn't find anything similar. Widening his search, he found the information he was looking for on an army site. TB stood for ThunderBird, the name given to a militia of child soldiers that had fought in Chad but had originated in Nigeria. The Dashiki, the violence, the total absence of compassion . . . Gatsha and Joey had ended up in South Africa, like thousands of other rejects of history, and they had quite naturally mingled with the dropouts and known criminals waiting for them in the area. What was the connection with Nicole Wiese? Were they working with Ramphele? One detail continued to bother him: the *iboga* that Stan and Nicole had taken, those little flasks she'd had with her on the night of the murder, and the drug she had tried a few days earlier. Neuman hesitated, staring at the screen. Anxiety crept up his legs, pinning him for a moment to the desk. The same feeling of suffocation as always, eating away at his heart.

Beyond the tinted window of the office, night was falling. It would be a beautiful suicide.

He typed two words on the keyboard: Zina Dukobe.

The information soon appeared on the screen. The dancer who had been performing at the Sundance wasn't in any SAP file, but he found what he was looking for on the Internet. Born in 1969 in the Bantustan of KwaZulu, daughter of an *induna*[1] stripped of his position for refusing to collaborate with the Bantu authorities, the former Inkatha militant Zina Duboke championed Zulu culture—in decline thanks to evangelization and political unrest—through her group Mkonyoza, founded six years earlier. *Mkonyoza* meant "to fight" in Zulu, in the sense of "to crush by force."

The group consisted of musicians and *amashinga*, fighters specializing in the Zulu martial art of *izinduku*, the traditional fighting stick, the names of which varied depending on the size and shape. According to Zina's statements, *izinduku* was a way of preserving Zulu identity. Taking it out of context and exploiting it for political ends, she argued, had given a false image of this art. She referred to Zulu protest marches during apartheid, when the members of Inkatha and their chief

[1] Chief minister of a tribe, the guardian and interpreter of the *Mthetwa*, the tribal laws.

Buthelezi had claimed and obtained the right to carry the traditional sticks, previously forbidden by the regime—thereby provoking violent clashes with the ANC, most of whose members were Xhosa. With Mandela in prison, the Zulu opposition was legitimized. Divide and rule—a technique that had provoked a bloodbath.

For many, *izinduku* had become synonymous with violence, not with art, even martial art. *Umgangela*, those interethnic competitions that had once been so prized, were now only held in regions where there was little political tension. In fact, *izinduku* was intended to prepare the young for society and pass on the rules of the community, as well as being a way of mastering the body and the mind. The aim of the group's performances was to revive this lost aspect of Zulu culture while at the same time modernizing it, with video, electronic instruments, and sound effects. It was a question of building bridges between the traditional art and current trends in order to nourish a living culture.

Zina's character was starting to come into focus. Mkonyoza had been performing in Cape Town since the beginning of the festival, and was finishing its tour in city center clubs. He went back to the videos from the Sundance, and took another look at the tape from Wednesday, the night Nicole had not come back to Judith's. Eleven o'clock, midnight, five after midnight, six. Twelve minutes after midnight: there was Nicole, coming out of the club, alone, as he and Dan had seen the other day. Neuman let the tape run on.

The doorman was swaying from side to side, with his back to the camera, gray figures were going in and coming out. Four minutes had passed when a figure crossed the field of vision.

Neuman rewound the tape. He felt a tingling under his skin. It was a fleeting glimpse, but the figure was agile, and easily recognizable. Zina.

4.

"*hen I kill a white, my mother is happy!*"

To get out of the Bantustan into which the apartheid government had herded them, the South African blacks had had to have a pass, which regulated their travel to and from white areas. Taking advantage of interethnic and family rivalries, the powers that be had left the authority of the Bantustans to local chiefs, who were forced to cooperate if they did not want to be deposed. Some of them had not hesitated to use militias, vigilantes armed with clubs, who, where necessary, replaced the police within the enclave or the township. With the ANC banned, Chief Buthelezi had founded the Zulu Inkatha movement, a party that, while declaring itself to be against apartheid, had agreed to take control of the Bantustan of KwaZulu. Considering this collaboration a double game, Neuman's father, Oscar, had turned to the Black Consciousness movement led by Steve Biko, whose fiercely anti-apartheid speeches had revived a resistance movement seriously shaken by fifteen years of police repression.

"*When I kill a white, my mother is happy!*"

Biko had come out of the student environment, Oscar was a professor of economics at the University of Zululand. Biko's tone was radical. Contempt for blacks would be met with hatred for whites, it was time to forget the slave mentality. Biko proposed a union of students, boycotts to protest against cut-price education,[1]

---

[1] South Africa spent five times as much money on a white student as on a colored, and ten times as much as on a black.

an active resistance movement. Oscar tried to make his students realize that their destinies belonged to them, that no one would help them. He had organized a forum for Biko at the university, despite the hostility of Inkatha. Because of its geographical situation inside the territorial borders of KwaZulu, it was from the university that the government of the Bantustan recruited its civil servants, its experts, its ideologues. Inkatha didn't need a hotheaded student leader calling for murder, what it needed was technocrats to lay the foundations for its own resistance movement. Oscar's meeting had been disrupted by fights, and the riot police had dispersed the crowd with purple rain.[2]

Three months later, Biko died at the hands of those same police.

"When I kill a white, my mother is happy!"

Ali was five when the radio had announced the news. His father had been so shocked that his skin had partly lost its pigmentation. From that point on, Oscar would carry the mask of death, a portion of Steve Biko's corpse, the deathly complexion of the whites.

"When I kill a white, my mother is happy!"

Ali had never seen his father cry. Oscar was a kind of benevolent demigod who knew everything, in several languages, a calm-looking, bespectacled man with the air of an intellectual, a man who understood his enemy but never forgave him, a man who kissed his wife in front of everyone, and had already spent time in prison. What Neuman remembered most of all was when he took them with his hot, gentle hands, him and his brother, to see the stars from the roof of their house, and told them stories of Zulu kings, old monkeys, leopards, and lions.

"When I kill a white, my mother is happy!"

---

[2] Name given to the purple dye used in water cannons in Africa, in contrast with the green dye used in the West.

Neuman knew that Zulu chant. Biko and his activists had made it their war cry, a way of saying to the defenders of apartheid that they had no weapons but that they would still be dangerous even after they died. After Biko was killed, the banned ANC had adopted the same chant.

"When I kill a white, my mother is happy!"

The voices echoed beneath the brick vaults of the Armchair. Neuman was standing in the middle of the audience, staring spellbound at his totem. Those grimacing old monkeys were coming back to the surface.

"When I kill a white, my mother is happy!"

On the smoke-filled stage, Zina and her Zulus were dancing the *toi*, the war dance of the townships. Their feet hit the ground, raising clouds of dust just as they had in the enclaves into which they had been herded, the drums grew ever more intense, the spotlights flashed, images of bloodstained demonstrators appeared on a screen at the back of the stage, and the members of the group stamped on the spot, cradling imaginary AK-47s in their arms, just like in the old days, and still chanting:

"When I kill a white, my mother is happy! Drrrrrr!"

Zina was the first in the group to fire a burst at the packed crowd. The dust whirled on the stage, the drums thundered. It was now that she spotted Neuman's face in the crowd, a head taller than the others. With a smile, she decapitated him.

*

"What are you doing here?"

"You missed me just now," Neuman said, his eyes twinkling in the corridor leading to the dressing rooms.

"You moved," she said. "Otherwise, you wouldn't be here."

Zina was barefoot, covered in dust and sweat. The cop had been waiting for her to come offstage, she felt electric, confused, vulnerable.

"You didn't tell me everything the other day," he said.

His air of knowing a lot put her on the defensive. "Maybe you didn't ask the right questions."

"How about this one? There's a camera at the entrance to the club, did you know that?"

"I'm not especially interested in electronic surveillance," she replied.

"Neither am I, but it can sometimes come in useful. Is there somewhere quiet we can talk?"

The musicians were just coming offstage, clapping their hands. Zina opened the door to her dressing room.

"What happened to your ear?" she asked as they went in.

"Nothing."

Neuman was staring at her, gripped by contradictory feelings. Zina took a colored shawl from the dressing table and wrapped it around her, then looked him up and down, all six feet of him.

"You have those snake eyes of yours," she said. "What's up?"

"We don't know where Nicole Wiese slept three days before she was murdered," he said. "According to the club's security tapes, she left here that night at twelve minutes after midnight. Four minutes later, you came out. We don't know where Nicole spent the night, or who with. Four minutes— enough time for you to pick up your things from the dressing room and join her. What do you have to say to that?"

"I prefer up-and-coming politicians, without children, but I don't say no to a little candy from time to time. What is this crap?"

The dust had made gray craters on her skin, which was starting to crack.

"Nicole was a girl who'd led a sheltered life and was so eager to become liberated that she was skipping the stages, collecting sex toys and erotic experiences. Nicole took *iboga* that Wednesday, and I think you spent the night together."

Their eyes met, two wild animals. He was bluffing.

"Bring me a warrant," she retorted, "and I'll open my nest."

Neuman removed a hair from the sweat on her shoulder. "Will you talk now, or do you prefer to wait for the lab report?"

Zina's black eyes flashed. "I didn't smash Nicole's head in," she said through clenched teeth.

"No, you're much too smart. But you did lie to me."

"Just because I don't tell you what you want to hear doesn't mean I'm a liar."

"Then I suggest you tell me the truth."

Zina pulled her shawl tighter around her shoulders. "Nicole came up to me at the bar after the show on Wednesday," she said. "She said she'd liked the show. It didn't take me long to see that she liked me, too. She wanted to see life through rose-tinted spectacles, so I initiated her into *iboga*."

Neuman nodded—it was as he had feared.

"Were you alone?"

"Why not? We were both adults."

"Where did you spend the night?"

"In the room I've been renting during the tour, not far from here."

"Why didn't you tell me this before?"

"I'm not an *impimpi*," she said.

An *impimpi* was someone who passed on secrets to the whites.

"What secret are we talking about?"

"My grandmother was a herbalist," she said with a touch of pride. "She passed on some of her talents. Preparing *iboga* is part of them. We're not in the habit of divulging our little formulas."

"A simple love potion," he said. "Hardly worth making such a mystery over."

"I wasn't born yesterday. I'm one of the last people to have seen Nicole alive, and we spent the night together three days before she was killed. I didn't want the police prying into my private life."

"Have you done so many things you regret?"

"Apart from meeting you, no."

Silence fell in the dressing room.

"Well?" he insisted.

Zina grinned provocatively. "Well, Nicole was a pretty little blonde doll who, as it happens, was delighted at the prospect of spending the night with me. She liked the experience, but I'm too old to play nanny, so we left it at that. That was Wednesday. On Saturday evening, Nicole dropped by my dressing room to say hello and pick up the flasks I'd made for her. She'd asked for them—and what better farewell gift could there be than a love potion?" Her eyes gleamed, but not with joy.

"Did she pay you?"

"I'm not a charity."

"So you do this to supplement your income?"

"It's vulgar to talk about money, Mr. Neuman, and vulgarity doesn't suit you."

"Did Nicole tell you who she was planning to share her precious flasks with?"

"We didn't talk much, to tell the truth."

"Not even pillow talk?"

"We girls don't need words."

"The silence must have been deafening." He took his hand from his pocket. "Stan Ramphele. Mean anything to you?"

Zina peered at the photograph he showed her—a black, about twenty, quite good-looking.

"No," she said.

"Nicole and Stan were both high when they died, on a highly toxic *tik*-based substance that modifies behavior."

"I only use natural ingredients, my friend. *Iboga* has a subtler effect. Want to try it?"

"Maybe in another life."

"You're making a mistake," she assured him. "My secrets are quite harmless."

"I'm not so sure of that."

"I'm a dancer," she said, looking him straight in the face, "not a serial killer."

He noticed the little scar just above her lips. "Who said anything about other killings?"

"I can see it in your eyes. Or am I wrong?" She was looking at him as if she knew him well.

Neuman changed tack. "Why haven't you cooperated with the police?"

"I'm getting pissed off with your questions."

"I'm getting pissed off with your answers."

Zina's face, close to his now, grew sharper. An abrupt change of direction. "Listen to what I'm going to tell you, Ali Neuman, and listen carefully. I saw policemen stamp on my mother's stomach when she was pregnant, I can still hear her screaming, and my father saying nothing. Yes, I can still hear him saying nothing! Because that was the only thing those poor niggers were entitled to do! The child she was expecting didn't live, and that killed my mother. And when my father tried to report it, they laughed in his face—my father, the *induna*! One day, the police came and told him he'd been stripped of his position, because of insubordination to the Bantu authorities. Then more police came and threw us out and bulldozed our house. And it was the police who fired into the unarmed crowd during the Soweto uprising, killing hundreds of us. So just because times have changed and you can fuck a white girl without getting a *kaffirpack*[3] doesn't mean I'm going to throw myself into your arms."

"That's not what I'm asking you to do."

[3] A thrashing for blacks, in Afrikaans.

"Oh, but it is," she hissed. "The reason I haven't cooperated with the police is because I don't trust them. None of them. Nothing personal, as you may have noticed, unless you're as blind as you're stubborn. Now I'd like to be alone, so I can take a shower. That doesn't mean I don't feel sick about what happened to Nicole. And stop looking at me with those snake eyes of yours, I have the impression you think of me as a fucking guinea pig!"

She was nothing like Tembo's rats. But there was murder in her eyes.

"You were a member of Inkatha," he said.

"A long time ago."

"To fight the whites?"

"No," she said, angrily. "To fight apartheid."

"There were less violent ways."

"Did you come here to talk about my past or about Nicole's killer?"

"Have I touched a raw nerve?"

"It killed my mother. Don't you think that's reason enough?" Her aristocratic manner returned, but he sensed that he had hurt her.

"I'm sorry," he said, more gently. "I'm not very used to pestering women."

"You must feel alone."

"Like a dead man."

Zina smiled, her face covered in powder. "My Zulu name is Zaziwe," she said.

It meant "hope."

But her eyes were as black as night.

*

Ukuphanda: the word meant, literally, scratching the ground for food, like chickens in a farmyard.

In the context of the townships, phanding—the English word that derived from it—meant, if you were a woman, looking for a boyfriend for the purpose of obtaining money, food or accommodation. It wasn't just a question of getting material security in exchange for sex. It was also a matter of finding someone to look after you, someone who'd make it possible for you to escape the brutality of everyday life. A quest embarked on by many young women, which led in most cases to their being exposed to violence or contaminated by AIDS.

Maia had been no exception to the rule. She had been competed over by men who considered her, at best, as their property. Her last boyfriend, believing the gossip a drunken neighbor had fed him, had taken Maia to the river bank, stripped her, smeared her with dish soap, and ordered her to wash in the brackish water, to teach her not to whore with other men. After which, he had taken a leather strap and beaten her for hours, six, eight, ten, Maia couldn't remember. Then he had raped her.

She had been found by the riverside early in the morning, almost dead.

It was while visiting his mother at the dispensary that Neuman had seen her for the first time, lying in bed, surrounded by other patients. Her eyes were so swollen from the beating that she could barely blink. Was it the terrible marks on her body that had reminded him of his father's agony, her smile when he had squeezed her hand, her beautiful, helpless brown eyes that had drunk him in like a false elixir? That day, he had promised her that no one would ever hurt her again.

He had installed her in the largely colored township of Manenberg, in a small permanent house with real windows and a solid door, a door he'd knock at from time to time.

At first, Maia had wondered if this big cop with eyes like stone wasn't another one of those crazy men who were both fascinated and horrified by women's bodies—he could caress her for hours, and his hand on her body was like an ointment or a blade—but she had known a lot worse. Her new boyfriend could fondle her as much he liked, he could ask her to lift her ass like a lighthouse in order to rub ice cubes over it (code number three), or explore her anus with his fingertip (code number five), he could stuff her with whatever he wanted and she sometimes didn't want, Maia was not very particular. She survived in Manenberg as best she could—bartering, doing odd jobs, painting, occasionally sleeping with guys. Two years had passed since the beginning of their relationship, two years during which everything had changed. Today Maia waited for his footsteps, his knock at the door, his face, his hands on her body, as if she was his pet. Over time, it had stopped being a chore for her and become the sweetest of tortures. She had never been caressed like that before.

She had never been caressed at all.

It was after midnight when Ali knocked at the door that night. Maia woke with a start—he hadn't told her he was coming. She put on the short nightdress he had bought her the previous month, fought with sleep as far as the front door, lifted the latch, and saw him standing there, looking haggard.

Ali had a bandage over his ear, and in the moonlight his eyes looked sad. Something had happened, she knew that immediately. She lifted her hand to his cheek to comfort him, but he stopped her.

"I have to talk to you," he said.

"Of course. Come in."

She didn't know what to say, how to behave. They had never talked about love. Love had never come into the equation. It was enough of a miracle that he condescended to touch her. Deep down, Maia felt impure, soiled, dishonored, he came from an educated family, probably an important clan. Maia imagined all kinds of things—Ali didn't make love to her because he was afraid of lowering himself, compromising himself with a girl from the country, a colored girl who'd had lots of men and who he'd found in the gutter. She didn't know anything about his feelings, or understand his strange pleasures, but, in spite of everything, she still hoped, because that was her nature.

The man she loved didn't even bother to sit down. The look he gave her made her retreat to the couch.

"I won't be coming again," he said abruptly.

"What?"

"We had an agreement. I'm releasing you from it."

His voice wasn't the same. It came from the darkness, from a place where Maia had never set foot, a place she would never go.

"But. Ali. I don't want to be released. I want to stay with you."

He said nothing. He was looking at the paintings proudly displayed on the living room wall, naive paintings scrawled on pieces of board, colorful images depicting scenes of township life—so brave, so pathetic, so bad.

"I'll still help you out," he said, "if that's what's worrying you."

Sitting on the couch to which he had driven her, Maia gritted her teeth. It wasn't about money anymore, he knew that perfectly well. Anger was welling up inside her. Even a good man like him was casting her out as if she was unclean. She really was nothing but a pet to him.

"You mean you don't want me anymore?"

"That's right."

His harshness hurt her. Something had happened since last week. He couldn't just abandon her like this, without a word of explanation.

"Have you found another girl? Is that it? Have you found another poor tramp who thinks you're going to save her? Or do you have a few?" She was angry now. "A harem, that's what they call it, right?"

There was a sound in the distance, in the night, a gunshot, or a door being slammed.

"Shut up," he said in a low voice.

"Do you fuck her?"

"Shut up!"

"Tell me!" she cried, with venom. "Do you fuck *her*?"

Ali raised his hand, and she instinctively shielded her face. The blow was so rapid that Maia felt the breath of it on her disheveled hair. His fist grazed her temple and crashed into the wall, which cracked under the impact. Maia let out a cry of astonishment. Ali kept raining down blows, with all his strength, destroying her paintings one by one, shattering the plywood wall with his bare hands. Wood flew across the room, splinters falling on her hair. She screamed for him to stop, but the blows kept coming endlessly. He was going to smash everything to pieces, her, the house, their life, with his fists.

The storm stopped suddenly.

Maia was huddled on the couch, moaning softly, not daring to move. She risked a glance through her terrified fingers. Ali was standing over her, his fist clenched, full of scratches and splinters, his eyes sparkling with anger.

A growl rose from deep within him, a sound that froze her blood.

"Shut up."

5

A red dress crossed his field of vision. With one hand, the woman was holding down the straw hat that was threatening to blow away to the ends of the earth, with the other she balanced gracefully on the immaculate beach. Brian Epkeen was just passing the apparition when a gust of wind blew sand in his face.

He had walked past the colored wooden huts along the promenade, the first-aid post, the scattered beach umbrellas, and the few toothless men selling trinkets from the nearby township. The farther he walked along the ocean, the more deserted Muizenberg beach became. Dust and sand stirred by the wind rose and vanished in the shimmer of noon. He turned, but the girl was now just a red spot in the heat haze. The resort was almost out of sight. He continued walking, struggling in the soft sand, spitting up cigarettes and alcohol.

Last night, Brian had gone to the bar on Long Street where Tracy worked. He had wanted to have a serious talk with her, but she kept going into raptures over her young colleague juggling three cocktail shakers behind the bar. If something like that got her so excited, then they might as well call it a day, O.K.? Tracy was taken aback. Brian's words had hit home, but she hadn't really grasped what he was trying to say. He was no good at breaking up. He didn't know how to go about it. His heart wasn't in it. Dan's death had made him lazy. Disappointment, bitterness, sadness—they had parted without hope of a relapse.

Brian saw the site of the straw hut, then the barbecue in the hollow of the dunes, the worm-eaten hut. There were still traces of burned sand, a few spilled lumps of charcoal. A shiver went down his spine. When the colored girl had come on to him, wiggled her hips at him, she was already planning to kill him. She and the guy he had slashed would have done to him what they had done to Dan. They might have cut him in pieces and grilled him. He licked his lips, tasted the salt of the nearby ocean, and dismissed the fear that was preventing him from thinking.

The beach stretched all the way to Pelikan Park. The house he was looking for couldn't be far. He adjusted his dark glasses, climbed to the top of a dune, swayed in the wind. Hovering in the sky, the seagulls stared at him with their mad eyes. He saw the railroad line in the distance, then the start of a wire fence running behind bushes that bent in the sea wind. The M3 was barely a mile away, along a bumpy track. Brian went down the slope to the main gate, which had a big padlock on it. A sign on the fence, half eroded by salt, said that this was private property and that there was no entry—hardly a threat to anyone except the butterflies. He clambered over the fence, cursed as he scratched his wrist on the wire, and fell to the sandy front yard. Seagulls rose, squawking. It was then that he saw a woman trotting along the path toward him on horseback.

He was still by the fence when the woman hailed him. She was riding a black Friesian glistening with sweat.

"Hello!"

She was a brunette, about thirty-five, a tall woman with incredible laughing blue eyes. "Lost something?" she asked.

"Let's say, looking for something."

"Oh, yes?" she said, feigning surprise. "What exactly?"

"That's what I'm trying to find out."

She tugged at the horse's bridle. The horse was clearly desperate to gallop straight to the ocean.

"Do you often ride this way?" he asked.

"Sometimes. I keep my horse stabled at the riding club next to the park."

Pelikan Park, the nature reserve situated a few hundred yards away. Brian forgot the ocean glittering like pearls on the other side of the fence and turned toward the house. "Do you know who lives here?"

The woman shook her head, imitated—curiously—by her horse. "No."

"Ever seen anyone around?"

She shook her head again.

"Any vehicles?" he insisted.

The Friesian pulled on the bridle. She made him do an elegant little pas de deux, then her face slowly lit up, as if the memories were coming back to her in flashes of blue sky.

"Yes, I saw a four-by-four here once, very early in the morning, going through the gate. I sometimes cut across the dunes, but usually I follow the beach. Why do you ask?"

"What kind of four-by-four?"

The woman leaned forward in the saddle to relax her posterior. "Let's see, it was big, dark, a recent model, the kind that'd really tear up the dunes. To be honest, I barely saw it. Not like you. You did notice this is private property?"

"You said early in the morning. About what time?"

"Six o'clock. I like to ride in the morning, when the beach is deserted."

Right then and there, so did he. He'd just have to find a depressive horse that liked to drink.

"When was this?"

"I don't know." She shrugged her shoulders beneath her tight-fitting T-shirt. "About ten days ago."

"Anyone since then?"

"Only you." Her blue eyes went through him like he was antimatter.

"If you were shown a list of similar vehicles, do you think you'd be able to identify the four-by-four?"

"Are you a policeman?"

"Sometimes."

The Friesian was chewing at his bit and stamping his hooves. The woman turned him right around to face the other way.

"Do you work at the riding club?" Brian asked, when the maneuver was over.

"No, I just ride. He's three years old," she said, patting the horse's neck, "and still mettlesome. Do you like horses?"

"I prefer ponies," he said.

She burst out laughing, which made the animal even more nervous. "I told myself you didn't look like someone with a feel for horses."

"Really?"

"You're looking at me—he can sense that you're afraid of him. Someone with a feel for horses would have done the opposite."

"Can I at least have your cell-phone number?"

She nodded. He took out his notebook, and she gave him her number. The Friesian was still stamping irritably, his big eyes turned toward the sea.

"My name is Tara," she said, and held out her hand over the fence. "Can I give you a ride?"

"Another time, maybe. We could go somewhere."

She gave a devilish smile. "Never mind!"

She turned the animal's bridle and, with her heel, set his trapped energy free. They soon vanished, swallowed by the sky and the sea spray. Brian stood there by the fence, looking after them skeptically, before coming back to reality.

The wind blew through the front yard. The sun was high and overpowering, the seagulls like lookouts. Brian turned toward the building, which stood isolated among the pines.

With its closed shutters and rusted antenna, the house Janet Helms had discovered looked like a disused weather station. He walked up to the reinforced door, checked the front of the building. No upper floor, no security protection, just a sloping roof and a barred basement window covered with cardboard. Everything seemed padlocked, abandoned. But the woman's sighting of a four-by-four was strange. He went around to the other side.

Brian didn't have a warrant. What he did have was a small crowbar in his revolver pocket. He was expecting to have to force open the back door of the house, but it wasn't closed. A squat? He grabbed his .38 and pressed himself against the wall. He loaded his gun, gently opened the door, and peered inside. Air rushed in through the open door, disturbing the flies. He aimed his gun into the semi-darkness. There was a musty smell in the house, and something else, something strange, stirred by the wind from outside. He went into the next room, which was empty. He found the meter—the electricity was working—and a third room that looked out on the front yard, with boarded-up windows and a concrete floor. There was a paint-smeared wooden table, brushes with hardened hairs, bits of wallpaper torn from the wall, and flies zigzagging madly around him. That unpleasant smell was still hovering.

A door led to the cellar. Brian peered down the steps, and immediately lifted his hand to his face. This was where the smell came from. A smell of shit. A deadly smell of human shit. He switched on the light and held his breath. The cellar was alive with flies, thousands of flies. He walked down the steps, finger tensed on the trigger. The cellar stretched the whole length of the building, a room with every opening blocked, the scene of an apocalypse. Shuddering, he made out three corpses beneath the swarm of flies: two males, one female. Their state recalled that of Tembo's rats. Scalped, limbs torn off, they lay in a lake of congealed blood, lost beneath a sea of flies. The bodies were shapeless, eviscerated, the faces lacerated, tooth-less, unrecognizable. A battlefield in an enclosed space. A cage. He looked up, and saw that the walls were covered in excrement. Shit had been smeared all over the room, at the height of a man.

Brian breathed through his mouth, but it didn't help. He walked through the cloud of insects, protecting himself with his hands. There was a wash basin at the far end of the room, and a tiled work surface onto which guts had been emptied. Two knives lay on the ground, the handles still sticky. The strident buzzing and the smell of shit and blood made him nauseous. He bent over the corpses, and with the flat of his hand brushed away the flies swarming over their faces. One of the blacks had a big cut on his left cheek, and tattoos on his arms. Even disfigured, he recognized the guy from the straw hut, the one who had followed him behind the dunes, the one he had whipped with his knout. The maimed girl beside him must be Pam. Half her scalp was missing. Unable to breathe, Brian went back upstairs, slammed the cellar door behind him, and stood there for a moment with his back to the wall.

He had dug up the bodies of militants killed by the special services, zombies rotting in dungeons, bodies burned by Inkatha vigilantes or ANC comrades,[1] people without skin, their faces grinning as if in gratitude, and he had never felt pity—that wasn't his job. Today, all he felt was disgust. He ran to the door and threw up everything he had inside him.

*

The Harare police station was a red brick building sur-rounded by barbed wire, with a view of the new law courts. A

[1] Self-defense units in the Bantustans.

constable stood at the gate, sweating under his cap. Neuman left him to the flies, avoided the drunks being shoved into cells, and announced his name to the girl at the desk.

Walter Sanogo was waiting for him in his office, mopping himself beneath the sluggish fan. He was drowning under the number of cases in progress, and Neuman's request had led nowhere. The three blacks killed on Muizenberg beach didn't have records. The photographs had done the rounds of Khayelitsha, without success. They hadn't established any links to a gang, old or new. Most of the homicides he dealt with were due to rivalries between gangs, many people had no papers, there were thousands of illegals. For his own sake and that of his men, Sanogo was quite happy to let them kill each other, to keep it in the family, so to speak.

"I met one of these guys ten days ago, near the gymnasium site," Neuman said, pointing to the photograph of the youngest man. "He called himself Joey."

Sanogo made a face like an iguana. "These guys usually invent stupid nicknames for themselves: Machine Gun, Devil Man."

"There was another young guy with him, who limped."

"What makes you think he's still in the area?"

Neuman changed tack. "These tattoos," he said, indicating the photographs he himself had taken. "Mean anything to you?"

Scorpions about to attack, and the two letters TB, with faded ink. Sanogo shook his head.

"Thunderbird," Neuman said. "A militia that used to operate in Chad, but had its origins in Nigeria. They killed one of my men, and they're dealing drugs on the peninsula. Something new, like *tik* but worse."

"Listen," Sanogo said, in a fatherly tone. "I'm sorry about your officer, but I have only two hundred men here, for tens of thousands of people. I rarely have enough men to deal with clashes between the taxi collectives, and sometimes they turn on us. I also lost an officer last month—shot down like a rabbit, on the street, for his service pistol."

"Keep the gangs under control, and your men will be safer."

"We're not in the city," Sanogo replied. "It's a jungle out here."

"Then let's try to do something about it."

"Oh, yes? And what are you planning to do—find every gang leader and ask him if he can tell you who killed your man?"

"Oh, I'm not going alone," Neuman said, icily. "You're coming with me."

Sanogo shifted on his plastic chair. "Don't count on it," he said, as if there was no room for discussion. "I have more than enough work with the current cases." His eyes wandered over the heaps of files.

"Joey had an almost new Beretta M92," Neuman said. "The serial numbers had been scratched out, but it was definitely police issue. Would you prefer us to take a close look at your stocks?"

The number of weapons declared lost went beyond acceptable limits, as Neuman had already ascertained. Weapons here had a tendency to get up and walk.

Sanogo was silent for a moment—he knew which of his constables was involved in the traffic, and he himself regularly got his "Christmas box."

Neuman looked him up and down, contemptuously. "Call your men together."

*

The establishment of whites-only areas had caused massive population shifts, scattered communities, and destroyed the social fabric. Cape Flats, where the blacks and coloreds had been herded, was divided into territories, each controlled by a different gang with its own activities. It was an old tradition, and had even been unionized—using the argument that gangsterism was a product of apartheid, one thousand five hundred *tsotsis* had demonstrated outside Parliament, demanding the same amnesty as the police. Some gangs were employed by the owners of *shebeens*—illegal drinking joints—or by the drug barons, to protect their territory. Others formed pirate groups, stealing from other gangs to keep themselves supplied with drugs, alcohol, and money. There were gangs of pickpockets who operated on the buses, collective taxis, and trains, the Mafias who specialized in protection, and last but not least the prison gangs, who ran life inside (smuggling, rapes, executions, escapes), and to which every prisoner belonged, voluntarily or involuntarily.

Khayelitsha had been controlled for years by the gang known as the Americans. Their leader, Mzala, was feared and respected. Mzala had been a thief as a child, a killer as a teenager, and had spent three years in prison before carving out a place for himself among the township *tsotsis*. They were his only family, as they were for so many others—a family which, at the first sign of weakness, wouldn't hesitate to kill him. The Americans ran drugs, prostitution, and gambling. They also owned the Marabi,[2] the most lucrative *shebeen* in the township, where Mzala and his personal bodyguards had established their HQ.

As three-quarters of the population was excluded from the labor market, this was where the parallel economy was concentrated. An essential part of popular culture, the *shebeens* had been created by women from the countryside, making use of their traditional brewing skills. The *shebeens* were tolerated in spite of the dubious characters who hung out in them and the armed gangs who used them to sell drugs and alcohol.

The Marabi was a dirty, crowded place where poor blacks got drunk, applying themselves to this activity with the zeal of people who had no other way out: brandy, gin, beer, *skokiaan*,

[2] The word denotes both a musical style and a lifestyle. It is also an insult.

hops, *hoenene*, Barberton, and even more powerful concoctions—the place sold everything, without authorization and without qualms. The *shebeen* queen who ran the establishment was named Dina, a massive, witch-like woman who kept order with her equally massive voice. Neuman found her behind the bar, with her huge cleavage in a pink dress, pestering an old drunk to drink up more quickly.

"Where's Mzala?" he asked.

Dina looked at his badge, and then at his not very friendly face. The half-stupefied drinkers on the straw mattresses fell silent. The township police had overpowered the two heavies who were meant to be guarding the entrance. Sanogo was following in the shadow of the big cop.

"Who's this?" she asked Sanogo. "We haven't—"

Neuman grabbed her wrist and pulled her forward across the bar counter. "Shut up."

"Let go of me!"

"Listen to me or I'll break your arm."

Unable to escape his grip, the *shebeen* queen was forced to lie flat on the wet counter.

"I want to talk to Mzala," Neuman said in a toneless voice. "Just a friendly chat for the moment."

"He isn't here!" she whined.

He put his mouth close to her ear with its big earrings. "Don't take me for any old nigger. Come on, hurry up."

The pain was spreading into her shoulder. Dina nodded so much it made her body shake. Neuman let go of her, and she sprang back. She cursed as she massaged her wrist—the animal had almost dislocated her arm—smoothed her dress with which she had just mopped the counter, and kicked one of the guys slumped on the floor. Neuman was still looking at her, threateningly. She ran behind the metal partition.

The customers began whispering among themselves. Sanogo signaled to his men to keep them at bay.

Mzala was sleeping it off in one of the back rooms, in the company of a girl, high on *dagga*, who had just given him a passionless blow job and was now snoring on her bed. Dina's sudden entrance drew him out of his torpor. He threw out the leech who had sucked him off, and put on the clothes that were lying on the floor. The two *tsotsis* guarding the entrance to the private room escorted him beyond the partition that marked off their territory.

Sanogo was there, with his army. There was a guy with him, a big, muscular black standing at the beer pumps, watching Mzala as he came in. He had a shaved head and eyes like paving stones. His suit must have cost him about five thousand rand. No comparison with the other cops.

"What are you doing here, Sanogo?" Mzala said.

"This gentleman is the head of the Cape Town Crime Unit," he replied, indicating Neuman. "He'd like to ask you a few questions."

It was the first time Neuman had seen Mzala—an angular black with faded eyes, a T-shirt with the logo of a cheap brand of whisky, and long nails tapered to a point and as thick as horn.

"Oh, yes?"

Two blacks flanked Mzala. Neuman kicked the first one between the legs. He was stunned for a second, then a grimace of pain spread across his face. His associate made the mistake of moving—Neuman aimed at his supporting leg with his heel, and dislocated his knee. The man let out a cry of pain and fell back against the metal partition.

"I'm not in a very peaceable mood," Neuman said, walking up to Mzala. "From now on I ask the questions, and you answer without making a fuss, O.K.?"

Mzala's sweat smelled rancid. He looked like the kind of man who'd happily stab you in the back. Dina kept by his side, like a pilot fish staying with a shark.

"You won't find anything here," he replied, without a

glance at his wounded men. "You'd do better to go back where you came from."

"And you'd do better to change your tone. Today I'm only here to ask a few questions, tomorrow I may come back with the Casspirs."

"What's the problem?" Mzala asked, in a softer voice.

"A new gang selling drugs on the coast," Neuman said. "They killed one of my men."

"I don't have any reason to take on the police. We have our little arrangements, like everywhere else. Ask the chief here," he said, indicating Sanogo. "The Americans are perfectly happy dealing *dagga*. Everything above board. Shit, I even pay my license for this place!"

That was rare indeed.

"Who's your competition?"

"The Nigerian Mafia," he said. "Sons of bitches, brother, real sons of bitches." He grinned scornfully in the direction of Dina's cleavage.

"Where can we find these sons of bitches?"

"Two in a common grave," Mzala replied, "another under lime. The others must have taken off. Anyway, we haven't seen them around here for a while. And I'd be surprised if those cocksuckers ever came back!"

The people around them chuckled. Neuman turned to Sanogo, who nodded—he didn't interfere too much when there was a showdown between gangs, just let them get on with it. Neuman showed Mzala the digital photographs of the killers on the beach. "Have you ever seen these men?"

Mzala's already inexpressive face became even more of a mask. "No. Just as well, they're not very pretty to look at."

His sarcasm fell flat.

"Curious," Neuman said ironically. "Because I saw one of these guys near the gym site about ten days ago. That's bang in the middle of your territory."

Mzala shrugged. "We can't be everywhere."

"They're dealing a new *tik*-based drug."

"I don't know anything about that. But if it's true, I'll find out soon enough."

"The Nigerian Mafia controls *tik*," Neuman went on.

"Maybe, but not here. I told you we haven't seen them for months, those sons of—"

"Bitches, yes, I know. What about the tattoos?"

"A scorpion, right?"

"You know your animals."

"All those TV shows, they stick in the mind."

"Like a bullet in the head. Well?"

Mzala's teeth were partly rotted, a tribute to youthful malnutrition, his arms covered in scars.

"I can't tell you anything," he grunted. "Never seen these guys. But if I see them around, you can be sure I'll kick their asses."

"They were beating up this boy," Neuman insisted, showing him the school photograph of Simon Mceli.

Mzala gave a twisted smile. "He doesn't look too bad."

"You know him?"

"No. I'm not interested in kids."

Mzala had had a younger brother, even more of a thief than him, who'd died stupidly, messing around with his gun.

"Stan Ramphele. Name mean anything to you? Or his brother Sonny, who was a dealer on Muizenberg beach?"

Mzala shook his head, as if Neuman was on the wrong track. "We deal *dagga*, and we defend our territory. These brothers and what they get up to on the coast has nothing to do with us."

Neuman was a whole head taller than Mzala. "That's strange," he breathed. "The guys I'm looking for are just the kind of ugly guys you go for."

A slight wind of panic blew through the *shebeen*. Sanogo shifted uneasily next to the pillar, the other officers tightened their hold on the grips of their guns, on the alert. They weren't at home here.

"We don't know anything about it," Mzala assured him. "Here we take things easy. No powder. Our customers can't afford it, and it brings nothing but trouble." He spat on the floor. "That's the truth, brother—easy."

But his yellow eyes were saying the opposite. Neuman hesitated. Either this guy was telling the truth, or they would have to haul him in to the police station for further interrogation, knowing that the rest of the gang had probably already surrounded the *shebeen* and were waiting, guns at the ready, to see how things developed. The ranks seemed to have closed around them. There were only nine of them, poorly armed—there was no way they were going to get out of here without a ruckus.

"We should go," Sanogo breathed behind him.

There was a growing murmur from the customers packed into the *shebeen*. Some were starting to eye the open windows. A scramble, and the whole thing would turn into a riot.

"I hope for your sake that you've told me the truth," Neuman said by way of farewell.

"So do I," Mzala replied.

But his words didn't mean anything.

*

Dust whirled across the construction site. Neuman walked amid the rubble. The workers had gone home, there were only the kids attracted by the police cars and the noise of the wind in the skeleton of the gymnasium. A few empty cans lay here and there on the ground, some litter, pieces of scrap iron. Neuman recognized the concrete pipe down which Simon had escaped a few days earlier. A water pipe, according to the plans he had managed to get hold of.

Sanogo and his men stood in the shade, watching. Neuman crouched and put his head into the opening of the pipe. It was barely wide enough to get his shoulders in. The beam of his torch danced for a moment over the walls of concrete, before vanishing into the darkness. Contorting himself a good deal, Neuman squeezed inside the pipe.

There was a strong smell of piss. He could barely move his elbows, but after a while he managed to start crawling forward, with the torch between his teeth. The pipe seemed to run on into darkness. Whenever he raised his head, it would scrape the concrete. The farther he went along the pipe, the cooler it got. Neuman crawled for another ten yards or so, then stopped. The smell of urine had gone, but there was another smell now, strong and unpleasant—the smell of decomposition.

Simon was there, in the beam of his torch, rolled up in a dirty blanket that was falling to pieces. It took Neuman a while to recognize him. His face was livid, necrotized. Beneath the blanket, his stomach was partly eaten away by animals. Neuman directed the beam at the objects beside him. One of them was Josephina's handbag. There was also a bottle of water, some burned-out candles, an empty cookie packet, and a photograph, spared by the rats and the damp, which the child was clutching in his hand. A photograph of his mother.

6.

Mzala's nickname was the Cat—they said he liked to play with his victims before he left them for dead. Mzala knew that his position as gang leader wouldn't last forever, and that fear was his best ally. With Gulethu and the rest of the gang at large, his money was no use. Cat or not, the others were going to lynch him.

Fortunately, they had managed to track down the old *umqolan* who was trying to cure that cretin Gulethu. A hut in the squatter camp, or rather a heap of planks with skins of long-dead animals nailed to the door. Mzala had gone in person to give the old madwoman a grilling and, as was usual with him, the process had been long and slow. Even his cronies, who weren't exactly the compassionate type, had to turn away their eyes. Weeping, the *umqolan* had told him what she knew: Gulethu had come two days earlier to her filthy hut, clearly in a hurry, had taken the money she had stashed for him, and had left again in the Toyota, with the handful of men who were with him. That had been at seven in the evening, on the day of the slaughter on Muizenberg beach. The Americans had been watching the approaches to the squatter camps well before the sun went down. Unless Gulethu and his gang had escaped on foot, they were still in the area—the Toyota hadn't been found, either intact or burned out. Mzala had tortured the *umqolan* to find out where the fugitives were hiding, and eventually she had passed out. She wouldn't open her eyes again. Not in the same state, anyway. It still gave him the shudders—the old witch.

The Americans had gone all over the squatter camp with their pockets full of rands, which had loosened a few tongues. They had found the Toyota hidden under a tarp behind a back-yard shack. A paint job, new hubcaps—they had started to disguise the four-by-four in preparation for their escape. Gulethu and his henchmen were hiding nearby in a hole in the ground, covered by a jute sack.

"So tell me, Saddam Hussein," Mzala said, mocking the ashen-faced figure hanging from the beam in the shed, "what were you waiting for? A sign from the spirits that it was time for you and those other three cretins to try your luck in your repainted car? Tut-tut."

What a loser.

Gulethu's guts were on fire. The Cat had celebrated their reunion in his fashion, but Terreblanche wanted him in one piece. The man had just arrived, the sleeves of his khaki shirt rolled up over his biceps. He had two of his henchmen with him, white through and through—he couldn't stand them.

"Is that him?" Terreblanche asked.

"Yes."

Gulethu's feet weren't touching the ground. He had been hanging there for two hours, twisting and grimacing. A coarse-featured, almost ape-like Zulu, with a jutting chin, a low forehead, a brow ridge like a congenital idiot's, and those dirty yellow eyes, quivering feverishly.

Terreblanche slapped the palm of his hand with his riding crop.

"Right, now," he said, "you're going to tell me everything, from the beginning. Do you understand me, ape-face?"

Gulethu was still writhing at the end of his chain. Mzala had stuffed red pepper up his rectum, which was gradually burning his insides. Terreblanche did not have to use his riding crop—Gulethu told him everything he knew. His high-pitched voice didn't match his story, which was quite incredible. Terreblanche listened stoically to the crap the Zulu was coming out with—this was the kind of specimen his youngest son wanted to save, a *kaffir* with a face like a chimpanzee, a pervert and a psychopath. He put his hand in his pocket and took out two sachets that had been found on Gulethu.

"What's this?"

There was a greenish powder inside the plastic.

"Plants," Gulethu said with a grimace. "Mixed plants. The *umqolan* gave it to me."

"What were you planning to do with it?"

"Perform a ritual. The *intelezi*. To cure me."

A Zulu pre-battle ritual. Terreblanche brooded beneath the overheated sheet metal of the shed. Mzala had just informed him that a cop from the city had come to the Marabi that morning, and not just any cop, but Neuman, the head of the Crime Unit. Ali Neuman. Terreblanche had known his father, Luyinda, a political agitator, who had been beaten to death. His wife and son had changed enclaves and names—Neuman, "new man" a combination of Afrikaans and English. He was also looking for the gang.

7

I s Daddy burning?"

"Yes, darling."

"Where's he going?"

"Daddy's going to make a pretty little cloud in the sky."

Tom sighed, visibly skeptical. Eve, too, was finding it all a bit boring. As their bereavement passed through the ordeal of fire, Claire hugged the two of them and stared at the furnace that had swallowed Dan's coffin. Unhappiness was contagious, Claire knew, but she needed their strength to blot out her nightmare visions. The children didn't know what had happened to their father, just that he had been killed by criminals. Claire was shaking, wondering why they had cut off his hands, she would have liked to hear their explanations, the reasons that had led them to commit such evil, if there were any.

"What Will You Say" was playing through the lousy sound system, a song by Jeff Buckley that she had covered with Chris, her black guitarist. Dan had loved it. A voice like a suspended wave turning tragic, Jeff and his ethereal smile—he'd drowned himself in the Mississippi, one night when he was drunk. In spite of the sedatives, Claire wasn't feeling exhausted, just violent. The cancer, the radiation, her hair falling out in handfuls—she had faced all that with a courage she didn't know she had, but no one had prepared her for this.

Even when she was a little child, she only had to smile and her halo grew. To the people around her, Claire was the one who sailed through everything, the one nothing bad would ever happen to—she was so pretty. Nonsense. Deceit every-where. No need to take a midnight swim in the Mississippi. The little blonde angel smiling in the photos didn't have a halo anymore, didn't even have any hair. Her husband was dead. Dead and gone.

Her sister Margo hadn't waited for the end of the cremation to take the children home. Collecting the ashes and attending to the final formalities would take hours and Claire needed to be alone with him, one last time.

She had waited for the family to go, then she had taken the urn and driven to their inlet, near Llandudno. It had been their place of pilgrimage as lovers, a place to meet from time to time, and now a place to say goodbye. The waves had rolled on the deserted beach, a twilit seascape on which to spread his human dust. Claire had hugged the urn to her heart and walked into the foam, as far as her legs would carry her. She had talked to him as she walked, her last words of love, before casting what was left of him on the waves. The ashes had floated for a moment on the surface, before the eddies carried them away. The urn had sunk, too, a terrified Titanic in the swirling water.

"Are you hungry?" Margo asked. "I made chicken with prunes."

Their favorite dish when they were little. Claire had just come in. "No, thanks."

Their eyes met. Compassion, distress. They would talk later, when the children were in bed.

"What happened to your dress?" Margo asked, trying to make conversation. "Didn't you notice?"

In drying, the salt had made rings on her black dress. Claire did not answer. At the kitchen table, the children were pushing shredded pieces of prune to the edges of their plates. Margo squeezed her younger sister's shoulder, even if it didn't help.

"Mummy," Zoe said sulkily, "I don't like prunes anymore."

Claire saw the box on the breakfast bar in the kitchen.

"Oh, yes!" Margo said. "A friend of yours dropped this package for you earlier. A tall brown-haired man, who looked as if he'd gotten out on the wrong side of the bed." She turned to the children. "But prunes are *very good!*"

It was a tin box, worth ten times its price in the shops on Long Street. Claire found photographs of herself inside—her and the children, her and Dan, her alone, surrounded by birds in Kruger Park. There was also a European travel brochure, Dan's case notes, which he had kept out of fear of computer viruses, two or three little things the kids had made at school, and some words on a folded white sheet of paper:

Dan kept almost nothing in his drawer—everything in his head. I thought you'd like to have these things. I don't know what to say, Claire. Best wishes? Kindest regards? Call when you can. Ali sends his love.

Brian

The words were like the man, beautiful and awkward.

*

Tara showed up in Brian's office and, for the brief time the mirage lasted, the world turned Klein blue. She had replaced her riding clothes with a tight-fitting pair of jeans and an equally sexy T-shirt. Tara strolled around the untidy room as if they were visiting their first apartment, peered through the large window looking out on the Greenmarket Square flea market, then turned back to Brian, who'd been following her little game and letting his mind wander.

"Nice view!"

"If you say so."

Tara was as beautiful from behind as she was from the front.

"Thanks for coming," he said, by way of preamble.

"If I can be of any help to the police," she said, not believing a word he was saying. "Where should I sit?"

"Wherever you like."

Tara pushed the files out of her way and parked her generous posterior on the edge of the desk. She sat there looking down at him, swaying in a playful way, clearly well aware of her charms. It made him feel slightly sick. He clicked on the icons.

"Will this take long?"

"That depends on what you remember."

"I can hardly remember today's date," Tara joked.

It was the eighth. The date of Dan's cremation.

"But I'll do the best I can," she added. "I promise."

"Right. I've prepared a selection of vehicles matching the description you gave me. Just say yes, no, or maybe."

"O.K.!"

Brian wondered where this disturbingly gorgeous woman had emerged from, reduced the voltage of the electric current drawing him to her, and soon fell back to earth when four-by-fours started appearing on the computer screen. Tara shook her long brown hair to indicate no. She concentrated all her attention on what was in front of her, her cobalt eyes flashing in the light from the screen. The vehicles passed one after the other, dozens of them, some muddy, some clean, four-by-fours, six-by-sixes, with bull bars, kangaroo bars, models of all makes, no, no, no, no, no, no, no.

"Have you noticed?" she said after a moment. "It's only men driving in these pictures."

"Women don't care for four-by-fours, do they?"

"They hate them."

"You're great." He turned to the screen. "Anything look familiar?"

Tara made a face at the next model that appeared. "No," she replied. "Mine was a big thing, with high wheels."

"Ugly?"

"Very." She made a grimace of disgust.

Brian went straight to the Pinzgauers.

It didn't take long.

"That one!" Tara cried. "The Steyr Puch 712K!"

She was suddenly five and a half years old, and he felt his brain breaking up into little blue blocks.

"Are you sure it's this model?"

"If it isn't, it's one of its cousins."

"But you were a hundred yards away."

"I have good eyes, lieutenant."

He impressed her, which was scary.

"A dark Pinzgauer Steyr Puch," he said, writing it in his notebook. "Any other details?"

"What would you like to know?" she said, ironically. "The color of the tires?"

"I was thinking more of a driver, or someone you might have seen near the house."

"Sorry. I didn't see anyone. I go by there early in the morning, maybe they were asleep."

Brian made a face. Isolated as it was at the far end of the beach, the house was a secure hideout, and the track gave access to the road leading to the townships. There couldn't be a hundred thousand of that model of Pinzgauer in the province.

"Thank you. You've been a great help."

"Don't mention it!"

Tara leaped down from the desk. She seemed to like bouncing up and down.

"Well, now," she said with a smile, "I have to go."

"Where?"

"None of your business, lieutenant!"

She grabbed her canvas bag from the desk, met his melting eyes, and thought for a couple of seconds.

"I have a few things to do before this evening," she said, mysteriously. "I assume you're free?"

"As the wind," he replied.

The adrenalin was pulsing in his veins. Tara smiled, then glanced at her watch.

"Hmm," she said, "it should be fine. Seven o'clock at the bar on the corner of Greenmarket, how does that suit you?"

*

The bodies found in the house at Muizenberg had been identified. Pamela Parker, twenty-eight, a drug addict well known to the police for her association with several of the township gangs. Arrested several times for soliciting on buses and in bus stations. No fixed abode. Suspended sentence for assault. Nothing on her for nearly a year. One sister, Sonia, current whereabouts unknown. Francis Mulumba, twenty-six, former Rwandan policeman wanted by the International Criminal Tribunal for a number of rapes and murders. Mujahid Dokuku, ex-member of the Movement for the Emancipation of the Niger Delta (MEND), a Nigerian rebel group specializing in the hijacking of petroleum belonging to the multinationals. Escaped two years earlier from prison, where he was serving twelve years for guerrilla activities. Suspected of having entered South Africa illegally, like thousands of other refugees, to swell the ranks of the gangs.

All the forensics team had found in the cellar was the shit on the walls, blood belonging to the victims, and two kitchen knives that had been used for the slaughter, with their prints on the handles. No firearms, or drugs, even though they had been pumped full of the same *tik*-based cocktail, in doses close to those that produce insanity, according to Tembo's protocol.

Had they taken shelter in the house to escape the police road-blocks? Had they killed each other while under the influence of the drug, or had they been helped the way Stan Ramphele had been helped? Was it their squat, a hideout from which they sold the drug? Neuman had seen Joey, the youngest of the gang, the other day on the construction site in Khayelitsha. Why was he attacking Simon? Where was his associate, the guy with the limp?

Neuman had been all over the area around the gymnasium site, but hadn't found out much. Street kids like Simon Mceli were two a penny in the township. He'd been sent from waste grounds to soccer fields. Some people had told him to fuck off back to the whites. Overcrowding, AIDS, violence—the fate of street kids from an endlessly overcrowded camp didn't interest anyone.

The postmortem report on Simon Mceli came in mid-afternoon. The animals living in the pipes on the construction site had eaten away much of the child's body, but the lesions on the proximal part of the third metacarpus were insect bites dating from a week earlier, the approximate date of death. There was no bullet hole, or any visible wound on the parts of the body that were still intact. The few objects found near him—candles, matches, water, food, blanket—indicated that Simon had taken a basic survival kit with him. No needle marks. The child had been suffering from severe nutritional deficiencies, calcium, iron, vitamins, proteins, he'd been lacking in everything, except toxic products: marijuana, methamphetamine, and that same molecule the lab couldn't identify.

So Simon had been on drugs, too. In fact, he'd been completely hooked. That might explain his scrawny state, the attack on his mother, but not the cause of death. Simon had died of blood poisoning, but it wasn't an overdose that had killed him. It was something much more devastating.

He had died of AIDS.

*

After violence, HIV was the second great scourge of South Africa. Twenty per cent of the population carried the virus, one woman in three in the townships, and the outlook was alarming. Two million children would lose their mothers in the coming years, and life expectancy, which had already decreased by five years, would go down another fifteen years, falling to only forty by 2020. Forty.

The government had taken the pharmaceutical industry to court for refusing to supply generic drugs to those infected. It was only with the help of the international community and after a virulent press campaign that access to antivirals had finally been conceded, but the subject remained controversial. To the South African government, a nation was like a united, stable, nourishing family, self-disciplined and only able to function if fully healthy. The president had ignored the statistics of HIV infection, deaths from AIDS, and sexual violence—all of which, according to him, were private matters. He had put the blame on the political opposition, AIDS activists, the multinationals and the whites, who were always ready to stigmatize the sexual practices of blacks—by speaking of a new "black peril," they were reviving apartheid. Because of this, AIDS had been proclaimed a simple disease linked to poverty, malnutrition, and hygiene, but not to sex. The consequences had been disastrous, especially as far as male behavior was concerned. Following the logic of this argument, the government had first attempted to contain the scourge by advocating garlic and lemon juice after sexual relations, the taking of showers, and the use of lubricating ointments. The rejection of condoms—in spite of free distribution—as being unmanly and an instrument of the whites had made an already desperate situation even grimmer.

Jacques Raymond, the Belgian doctor who worked at the dispensary in Khayelitsha for Mèdecins sans Frontières, was a seriously angry man. Vaccines, screening, home visits, an education center—Raymond had been active in the township for three years and had lost count of the dead. Neuman had asked to consult Simon Mceli's file and the doctor hadn't raised any objection. Violence, disease, drugs—the life of street kids wasn't worth anything on the open market, not even a Hippocratic oath.

Raymond had an impressive ginger moustache, thin nicotine-stained hands, and a strong French accent. He opened the metal filing cabinet in his office and took out the relevant file.

"Yes," he said after a moment, "I did treat the boy, twenty months ago. We took advantage of his coming here to do a check-up, but Simon wasn't carrying the virus at that time. The test was negative."

"According to the postmortem," Neuman said, "the virus he contracted mutated with unusual speed."

"That may happen, if the subject has a weak constitution."

"But Simon was in good health when you examined him, is that right?"

"Twenty months is a long time when you're living on the streets," the doctor replied. "Infected syringes, prostitution, rape. Street kids are drugging themselves earlier and earlier, and with the thousands of people who imagine they can beat AIDS by deflowering virgins, they're often the first victims."

Neuman knew the figures for child murders—the numbers were soaring. "Beliefs encouraged by the township *sangomas*," he said.

"Pooh," the doctor said without much conviction. "They're not all backward. There's good traditional medicine. The problem is that anyone can claim to be a healer, and then it's just a question of persuasion, credulity, and ignorance. As AIDS patients are viewed as pariahs, most are ready to believe anything for a cure. The microbicides haven't lived up to their promise." He paused, then added bitterly, "And as for our campaign to promote the wearing of condoms, we're preaching in the desert."

But Neuman was thinking of something else. "What's the incubation period—two weeks?"

"For AIDS? Yes, more or less. Why?"

Simon had contracted the virus in the past few months. He had become hooked on the same drug that was circulating on the coast. Nicole Wiese, Stan Ramphele, the *tsotsis* in the cellar—they had all succumbed to the cocktail as soon as they took it. All except De Villiers, the surfer shot down by the police. Neuman was suddenly gripped by doubt. He thanked the doctor without answering his question, walked past the line of patients waiting in the corridor, and left the dispensary.

Miriam was sitting on the steps, her hands folded over her knees, smoking and pretending that she wasn't waiting for him.

"Hello!" she said, with a gleam in her eye.

"Hello."

But he passed her by, almost without seeing her, and called Tembo.

*

Brian had left his cell phone switched on in his pants, which like the rest of his clothes lay on the wooden floor of the bedroom. It vibrated three times before it started ringing. The cracked alarm clock at the foot of the bed said 7:30 a.m. Brian groped in the darkness, found the phone, saw the name on the display, and took the call, whispering so as not to wake the Pegasus sleeping beside him.

"Did I wake you?" Janet Helms said.

"Pretend I'm listening."

"I carried on looking into the house on the beach," she announced. "Still no way of contacting the owner, but I did find out a few things. First of all, the land. Three and a half acres on the edge of Pelikan Park, bought just over a year ago. There don't seem to be any plans to renovate the house, but negotiations are under way for an extension of the neighboring reserve. If that goes ahead, the land could end up as part of a protected site, which would treble the price. Hard to say if it's insider dealing or just speculation. In any case, whoever bought the land did everything they could to cover their tracks. There's no way of finding out the name of the owner or the purchasing company. But, with a little bit of work, I did manage to trace a bank-account number in the Bahamas. Strictly confidential, as you can imagine. You can talk to the attorney but I don't think you'll get anywhere."

Brian cleared away the morning cobwebs from his head and started thinking. To open a case with so little to back it up would indeed lead nowhere, except to months of paperwork as complicated as it was useless—the account could be transferred to another tax haven with a single click.

"The banking world really makes you want to throw up," he said.

"If it's any consolation, so does the intelligence world."

"You reckon?"

The winged animal shifted beneath the sheets.

"I've drawn up a list of the Pinzgauer Steyr Puch four-by-fours registered in the province," Janet Helms went on. "There are thirty of them, but only a quarter, in other words, eight vehicles, are dark. I've also drawn up a list of people who rented a similar vehicle in the last few weeks. Maybe you want to take a look at it."

"O.K.," he sighed.

Brian threw his laptop on top of the untidy pile of books on his night table, and laid his head on the pillow.

"Hey," a voice beside him said, "the kind of things you talk about in the morning."

Tara must be feeling hot under the sheets, but, with her arm coiled around the quilt like a ribbon, she didn't seem eager to move.

Brian had kept the appointment at the bar on Greenmarket where they had arranged to meet. She had bewitched him with her outspokenness, her sense of humor, and the way her ass arched as if trying to take the air by storm. Tara was thirty-six, had a horse in stables that she rode whenever she got the chance, and worked as a freelance for a big architectural practice. She didn't tell him anything about her private life, her tastes, her loves, except that she liked Radiohead and men with sea-green eyes like him.

The dream had reached its climax in his house, in the upstairs bedroom, where they had made love with an abandon that made them feel quite relaxed with each other the morning after.

"Epkeen," she said, emerging from the sheets. "That's not an Afrikaner name."

"My father was a prosecutor during apartheid," he said. "When I came of age, I took my mother's name."

Tara came from a liberal British family that had fought the Boers during the war of the same name. She took hold of the end of his nose. "You're a crafty one, you."

He was crazy about her, in other words, completely done for. "Are you hungry?" he asked.

"Uh-huh."

Her sharp-cornered smile got him out of bed. He stood up, wondering how women managed to be so beautiful when they woke up. Tara ogled his buttocks as he wandered about the room, looking for his scattered clothes.

"You know something?" she said. "For an old horse, you're holding up pretty well."

"Actually, this isn't my real body."

"That's not the impression I got last night."

Brian dashed to the kitchen, seized with the kind of dizziness he'd been searching for ever since he was a teenager. He didn't know if he'd come up to scratch last night, if he ever would, or if he was still dreaming. He prepared a copious, varied breakfast, and took it into the bedroom piping hot. Tara was in the bathroom. He placed the overloaded tray on the bed, spilling tea on the scrambled eggs, and put on a T-shirt. Her scent hung in the room, a slight breeze ruffled the curtains. After a while, Tara came out of the bathroom, fully dressed and looking as spruce as she had the previous day.

She barely glanced at the breakfast. "I'm late," she said. "I have to run." Her isosceles smile seemed suddenly frozen.

"Now?" he said, ingratiatingly.

Tara looked at her watch. "Yes, I know, it's a bit rushed as a goodbye, but I completely forgot I'm the one who has to take the kids to the child minder this morning."

Goodbye.

Child minder.

Fairground fantasies.

"I didn't know you had children."

"I don't," she said, "but my boyfriend does."

Tara took out a little bottle of French perfume, sprayed two discreet bursts, and put it away just as swiftly in her overnight bag. "Do I smell O.K.?"

She stretched out her neck to him, slender and white—he felt like biting it.

"Like oats," he said.

Tara gave a little laugh that did not hide her embarrassment. "Right, I'm off."

"You'd better hurry if you want to be there on time," he said, barely concealing his bitterness.

"Hmm," she said, as if she understood. "Anyway, yesterday was great."

Great.

Brian wanted to tell her that half the pleasure had been his, but Tara planted a melancholy kiss on his lips, before disappearing like a city under bombardment.

A door slamming, then nothing.

That was it, no riding together, no races against the ocean. All that was left was the soft breeze in the curtains, the coffee steaming on the sheets, and the impression that he was just like those sheets, rumpled by life.

The cell phone vibrated from the pile of books. Brian would have liked to throw it to the other side of the Atlantic, but it was Neuman.

"Get over here," he said.

*

Brian passed through the line of journalists and onlookers who had gathered behind the two-colored police tape. Big waves were breaking on the beach of Llandudno, and moving out again, covering the sea with wild spray. The art of falling, that was what his life was all about.

Neuman watched him as he approached, looking glum and disheveled.

"Sorry to wake you," he said.

Brian was still thinking about Tara, plans that had led nowhere, all that love suddenly vanishing into thin air. He peered down at the sand.

The girl was lying a few feet away, arms outstretched, as if she had just fallen from the sky. A gruesome flight—Brian turned his head away from the girl's face. He hadn't had breakfast, and was still queasy from Tara's departure.

"A jogger found her this morning," Neuman said. "At about seven."

A disfigured girl, resting on her back. Her hands, too, were in a filthy state. Brian lit a cigarette, a mantle of depression over his shoulders.

"You couldn't introduce me to a living girl?" he said, to save face.

Neuman did not reply. The wind was lifting the ends of her skirt and throwing up sand. Tembo was bustling about the body, visibly concerned. The forensics team was combing the beach. A white girl, thirty at the most, sticky bleached-blonde hair, a face without a mouth, a nose, or anything. Black clouds were massing in the sky. Neuman stared at the seething sea. A seagull hopped toward the body and dipped its beak. Brian shooed it away with a nasty look.

"Do we know who she is?" he asked at last.

"Kate Montgomery. She lives in one of the houses above here, with her father Tony."

"The singer?"

"Uh-huh."

Tony Montgomery had had his hour of glory in the mid-nineties, a symbol of national reconciliation—that was why there were so many journalists here.

"We haven't been able to get hold of him yet," Neuman said. "Kate was working as a designer on a music video. We just had the crew on the phone, they were waiting for her. Her car was found about a mile from here, a little way up on the coast road. We haven't found her purse."

Tembo came toward them, trying to stop his felt hat from flying away. He looked gray. He gave them his first conclusions in a mechanical voice. All the blows had been to the face and head, the weapon a hammer, iron bar, or club. It hadn't been found yet, but the similarities with the Nicole Wiese murder were obvious. Same savagery, same kind of blunt weapon. Death had occurred about ten the previous evening. The absence of traces of blood on the sand suggested that the body had been moved to the beach. This time, there had definitely been a rape.

Brian put out his cigarette in the sand, but kept the butt.

"Any signs of a struggle?" Neuman asked.

"No," Tembo replied, "but there are cuts on the waist. The most recent date from a few days ago, the others are a few weeks old."

"Straight cuts?"

Neuman was thinking of the strange marks found on the body of the first victim.

Tembo shook his head slightly. "No. These cuts are deeper, probably done with a Stanley knife. Oh, and the nails have been removed. Clearly with a knife. Come and see."

They kneeled by the body. The fingertips had been crudely mutilated. Tembo pointed to the top of the skull.

"A lock of hair was also cut," he said.

Neuman cursed. A lock of hair, nail clippings—any *sangoma* could have gotten hold of these ingredients more cheaply. He saw the girl's torn blouse, where the blood had dried. The shoulder straps of the bra had been cut, the torso lacerated.

"Scarifications?"

"More like letters, I'd say," Tembo said. With a pencil, he lifted the blouse. "Or numbers, cut into the skin. Do you see the three 0's?"

The blood had congealed on her chest, but the cuts, being darker, were quite visible.

Neuman deciphered the marks. "O . . . lo . . . lo . . ."

"What is that?" Brian asked. "Xhosa?"

"No. Zulu."

We will kill you: the ancestral war cry, a cry taken up by the hardliners in Inkatha.

8.

A tropical storm broke over Klook Nef. Brian Epkeen set the windshield wipers of the Mercedes in motion. Tara bursting like a bubble in his hands, the murdered girl on the beach, the popular press baying for the killer, the crap they were going to print—he was having a shitty morning. The situation had a tendency to repeat itself lately. A consequence of Dan's death? He suddenly felt a great desire to take a vacation, a long one, to get far away from this country that was pissing blood, from a world under siege from bankers and shareholders and reactionaries, and die of love with the last woman he'd met, getting drunk in one of their stupid grand hotels, like characters in a book by F. Scott Fitzgerald. Instead of which, he climbed the winding road up Table Mountain to the cable car, and found a place in the line of cars parked along the road.

The rain was drumming on the asphalt at the foot of Table Mountain. It was so misty, you could barely see the summit. He cut off the Girls Against Boys song that was abusing the insides of the car radio, gave a coin to the boy with the numbered shirt in charge of parking, and ran to the souvenir shops, where the rain-drenched tourists were waiting for the cable car.

You could climb the steep slope all the way to the top, but the rain and the increasing number of attacks in the past few months had ended up deterring even the most foolhardy. The people who flocked here all seemed to be fat, red-faced, and dressed like farmers at a wedding. But then, everything looked black to Brian this morning, although a patch of blue sky was appearing through the murk. At last the cable car set off. The cabin grazed the sheer sides of the mountain as it climbed half a mile and the digital cameras clicked. The clouds that obscured the summit were still scurrying before the wind when they reached the top. Brian left the tourists to their unrestricted view of the city and, without a glance at the crashing ocean, took the trail leading to Gorge Views.

Tony Montgomery had sung about national reconciliation, and several of his records had been worldwide hits. "Loving Together," "A New World," "Rainbow of Tears," sung in several languages—like the new South African anthem—had made him a star. Brian found the lyrics of his songs incredibly syrupy, and the music pure crap, but his praiseworthy intentions had made him popular. Montgomery had an only daughter, Kate, whom he kept out of the public eye.

Kate Montgomery was twenty-two. She lived in Llandudno, on the east coast of the peninsula, and was working as a designer on a music video—for Motherfucker, a local death-metal group—being shot at the top of Table Mountain.

There was a stretch of flat, verdant heath land surrounded by rushes. Brian passed a gray squirrel as he walked along the path, surrounded by swarms of butterflies. The location for the shoot, marked off by metal barriers, was a mile or so after the rocks. Two black security men stood there with their hands over their crotches. They wore streamlined glasses and bored expressions, which barely changed when they saw his badge.

Contrary to what he had assumed, neither the storm nor the murder of their designer had stopped the shoot. A dozen people were bustling around the ruined tents and overturned sets—including a baroque zebu with devil's horns, made out of papier-mâché, lying upside down. Equipment and billycans were being hurriedly taken out from under tarps. He weaved his way between the puddles. Some yards away was a group of long-haired guys, looking like demented Batgirls in their Goth-metal makeup. One of them was grumbling that his guitar was full of water, that it would electrocute him. The others seemed to find that screamingly funny.

"Who's in charge here?" Brian asked the first person he met, a plump girl in a fluorescent yellow windbreaker.

"Mr. Hains? He must be in production, but his assistant should be around somewhere. Look, there she is," she said, pointing to an auburn blonde who was talking to the head grip.

Ruby.

Ruby in a tight-fitting dress, splashing about in the mud. She turned, sensing his presence, stood there in astonishment for a moment, then glared at him with her green eyes. "What are you doing here?"

"What about you?"

"I'm working, believe it or not!"

They hadn't seen each other for ten months. She had dyed her hair and let it grow, but nothing about her—her too-neat dress, her makeup, or her mud-caked pumps—would ever make her look anything other than a tomboy at war with the world.

"I already have four jerks stinking of beer to deal with," Ruby said impatiently. "What do you want?"

"To talk to you about Kate Montgomery," he said. "I've been put in charge of the investigation."

"Shit."

"I agree. No one told me you'd be involved in this, but just forget I'm the love of your life, think of me as a detective, and answer my questions, O.K.?"

The sun had returned, lighting up her sandy skin.

"O.K.?" he insisted, pulling her aside.

"O.K.! No need to shout!"

"Anyone would think you're doing this on purpose. Look, the quicker we start, we quicker we finish."

Ruby agreed.

"Are you in charge of this shoot?"

"Yes."

"Assistant director?"

"Production assistant."

"Same thing, isn't it?"

"Are you here to quibble about my job or to investigate a murder?"

"How well did you know Kate?"

"I knew her a bit."

"Had you worked together before?"

"No, this was the first time."

"But you knew her socially?"

"Kate sometimes came to dinner at the house, with other friends. That's all."

"What kind of friends?"

"Halfway between the opposite and the reverse of you."

"Showbiz people, I assume."

"Good people," she said.

"What time did you finish filming yesterday?"

"Around seven. The sun was going down."

"When did you last see Kate?"

"Around seven, as it happens. We went down together on the cable car."

"Was she meeting someone?"

Ruby pushed back her hair ruffled by the wind. "I have no idea. Kate didn't say." Then something occurred to her. "She did say she was going to have an early night. We had a heavy day's filming the next day."

"Was it your company that hired her as a designer?"

"Yes. Kate started on the shoot yesterday, like everyone."

Ruby, who had quit smoking, had been methodically crushing a match she had taken from a box.

"Did she have a close relationship with any members of the crew?" Brian asked.

"No."

"Did she take drugs?"

"How should I know?"

"People in showbiz are heavily into coke, don't tell me you don't know that."

"I don't work in showbiz," Ruby said, irritably.

"But you live with the dentist to the stars. You must have all kinds of fascinating guests to dinner, TV presenters, models, even PR people."

Ruby claimed to find money and most of the people who had it vulgar. "What are you getting at, Inspector Gadget?" Her eyes flashed wickedly.

"Had Kate seemed different lately?" he went on.

"No."

"Irritable? Impatient?"

"No."

"Do you know if she had a boyfriend?"

"No one special."

"What does that mean, that she often changed men?"

"Like any girl of twenty-two who doesn't fall in love with the first man that comes along."

Twenty-two. Ruby's age when he had met her at the Nine Inch Nails concert. Another life.

"Did Kate go for a particular type?"

"I don't know."

"Black men?"

"I told you I have no idea."

"Do you often have dinner with people you don't know?"

Ruby lifted a finely penciled eyebrow. That was her only reaction.

"Well?"

"Kate was twenty years younger than me," she said, becoming heated, "and she was a nervous girl who didn't give much away. Does everything have to be repeated ten times before you understand?"

"Eighteen times," he replied. "That's John Cage's theory."

"Are you taking an interest in conceptual art now?"

They exchanged caustic smiles.

"Did anyone phone Kate yesterday?" Brian resumed.

"Not as far as I know."

"Did she ever talk to you about an ex-boyfriend?"

"No."

"Or that she was meeting someone?"

"No," Ruby breathed. "I already told you, we had a hard day's filming coming up. We said goodbye in the parking lot, I left to get the halters from the riding club, and that was the last I saw of her."

Brian shivered, even though the sun had come out. "Halters?"

"You know, those big leads they put on horses to stop them from getting too excited," she said, ironically.

"Why?"

"It's in the script. 'The four demons of the night are attacked by furies, who put halters around their necks and whip them to make them pull the queen's carriage.' Don't you like death-metal imagery, lieutenant? But you like riding, don't you?"

A suspicion seized him. A huge one.

Tara.

Their unexpected encounter on the beach.

Their wild night.

Brian knew his devil well. That two-faced smile Ruby was wearing was too beautiful to be honest. She had hired Tara to seduce him, she'd bought a call girl to turn his head and then abandon him, like a sperm stain on the sheets.

"Something wrong, lieutenant?" Ruby was still smiling, with the criminal indifference of a cat playing with a mouse.

"Which riding club?"

"Noordhoek."

Brian dismissed his hot sweats. Noordhoek—a long way from Muizenberg beach, where he had met Tara. Good God, this business was making him paranoid.

"What car did Kate leave in?" he asked.

"A Porsche coupé."

They had found the car on the coast road, a mile from her house. Standing in the wind, Ruby was looking at him with a stubborn air.

"Is that all you can tell me?"

"I'm doing the best I can," she retorted.

"It's not very much, miss."

"Madam," she corrected.

"Really? Since when?"

"You didn't think I was going to invite you to my wedding, did you?" she said with relish.

"I'd have brought you flowers," he said, with an evasive look in his eyes. "Metal ones."

"You always did know how to treat a woman. Now, if you have an intelligent question to ask, ask it quickly, because I have four other specimens just like you to deal with, the rain has ruined the sets, and we're behind schedule."

"The show must go on."

"What do you mean, 'The show must go on?'" she repeated, imitating his voice badly.

"You don't seem all that upset about Kate's death."

"I've lost a lot of things in my life."

A pearl of tenderness ran aground amid the breakers.

"I'll probably be back to ask you some more questions," he said.

The crew was setting up. Ruby shrugged. "If that's what grabs you."

A gust of wind made them both sway. Brian shook his head. "Things still aren't working out, are they?"

*

Sixty thousand *sanghomas* plied their trade in South Africa, including several thousand in Cape Province alone. Sacrifices, emasculations, kidnappings, and torture of children and the most abominable murders were regularly committed under the pretext that they would provide miracle cures, and it was usually these ignorant, barbaric incense burners who were behind it.

The lock of hair and the nail clippings suggested that the killer had been trying to make a *muti*, a cure, or some kind of magic potion. A *muti*. To treat what? After the Minister of Health's unfortunate statements about AIDS, this kind of story gave the whole of Africa a bad reputation.

Neuman had searched in the Criminal Record Center, with a particular emphasis on ritual crimes. Several hundred officially, over the past ten years. In reality, thousands. Children mutilated, arms, sexual organs, heart torn out, sometimes when they were still alive to increase the effectiveness, testicles and vertebrae sold at exorbitant prices on the market for superstitions—the museum of horrors was in full swing, with a host of anonymous dupes as killers by proxy and the statistics constantly rising. He had found nothing.

The forensics team had searched the Montgomery mansion without finding any evidence of a break-in. The security system was working, and nothing had been stolen. So Kate hadn't had time to go home after the day's filming, or else she had brought the killer home with her, which was highly unlikely—they would have been caught on the surveillance camera at the entrance, and there was nothing on the tapes. Her Porsche coupé had been found at the side of the road, barely a mile from the house. As with Nicole, the killer had chosen an isolated spot, where nobody was likely to see anything. The coast road left Chapman's Peak and wound amid vegetation before reaching the trendy village of Llandudno. The only prints in the car were the victim's. The killer had stopped her on the road. Or Kate had stopped of her own free will and hadn't suspected anything, like Nicole Wiese. According to the information gathered by Brian, Kate should have reached Llandudno around seven-thirty in the evening. She had been killed about ten. What had she been doing for all that time? Had the killer drugged her, to stop her from resisting? Two hours during which he had imprisoned her, in order to prepare his *ololo*, his sacrifice, we will kill you, "we" meaning the Zulus.

Zaziwe: hope.

Association of ideas, chance, coincidence? Neuman sensed a trap. There it was, in front of his eyes. A divine temptation, a call, whose echo seemed to have been resonating forever. A trap into which he was falling.

Zina Dukobe had been an active member of Inkatha, and for the past ten years had been touring the continent with her group. She had not been involved with any political organization since the democratic elections but all her musicians were, or had been, in contact with Inkatha. Neuman drew up a list of the group's tours in South Africa, the places visited and the dates, and compared them with the many unsolved murders that had taken place during those periods. After cross-checking in the files of the Criminal Investigation Department and the various security forces, he noted that six homicides had taken place in Jo'Burg during their stay there in 2003. One of the victims had been Karl Woos, warden of a high-security prison during apartheid, found dead in his house, poisoned with curare, probably by a prostitute.

Neuman continued with his search and soon came across another unsolved murder: Karl Müller, a former police inspector from Durban, found in his car at the side of a minor road on January 14, 2005, with a bullet in his head—his revolver had been found beside him, but there was no suicide note. The group had been in Durban at the same time. They had played a week in the city's clubs before leaving the day after the murder.

Bamako, Yaoundé, Kinshasa, Harare, Luanda, Windhoek— Neuman widened his search to include all the cities where Zina's group had performed. The data was non-existent or difficult to find. The last suspicious death he noted down had taken place in Maputo, Mozambique: Neil Francis, a secret-service officer under apartheid who had switched to the diamond trade, found at the foot of a cliff, his skull smashed.

August 2007. Zina's company had spent ten days in Maputo.

Neuman was putting together all the little pieces lost deep inside himself when he received an e-mail from Tembo. The medical examiner had done a supplementary analysis on De Villiers, the junkie surfer killed in a holdup. According to the blood samples kept in stock, De Villiers had been HIV positive.

The virus had developed only recently, but, as with Simon, in a spectacular way. Life expectancy: less than six months.

Neuman's intuition had been right, which wasn't exactly comforting. What was in that drug—death? And what else?

*

As it had grown, the township had finally reached the sea.

So the boys played soccer on the beach, much to the delight of the tourists in their minibuses, who, thanks to the tour operators, bought themselves an easy conscience on the cheap with a lightning visit to the townships. You didn't see any of those tourists in Cape Town's black clubs—the only ones where you were frisked at the door—or any whites at all, a fact that was resented by the local youth.

It was here, on the edge of the dunes separating the beach from the squatter camps, that Winnie Got had seen Simon for the last time, with the other bums in his gang. Now that Simon

was dead, those kids were the last witnesses in the case. Neuman parked his car at the far end of the track and walked
toward the seething ocean. Boys' shouts could be heard in the
distance, carried on the wind. The sand on the beach was
blinding white in the sun. A pack of kids in shorts was running
after a partly devoured rubber ball. They didn't have time to
make passes, just general scrums at the four corners of the
field, with loud cheers every time the ball was cleared. Each of
the goalies moved from side to side between two sweaters
thrown on the ground, and waited.

Neuman's shadow fell on the featherweight guarding his
invisible goalposts.

"I'm looking for two boys," he said, showing him Simon's
photograph. "Local boys, about ten or twelve."

The little goalie took a step back.

"One of them's older, and wears green shorts. They were
both hanging out with this guy, Simon. I've been told they used
to play with you."

The boy was looking at Neuman as if afraid Neuman was
going to grab him by the throat. "I . . . I don't know, sir. You'll
have to ask the others," he said, pointing to the scrum.

There were thirty of them, happily thrashing each other in
the sun.

"Who does the ball belong to?"

"Nelson," the featherweight replied. "The one in the
Bafana Bafana shirt."

The national team, not in very good form apparently, even
though the World Cup was looming.

There was such noise and excitement around the ball that
Neuman had to grab it to make himself heard. He took Nelson
to one side, and the other players immediately surrounded
them. He explained what he was after, the boys crowding
around him as if he had candies for them. At first, they made
faces to indicate that they didn't know anything, but the pho-

tograph revived their memories. The gang had hung around the beach for a while, they had even tried to play soccer together, but those other guys liked to act tough, there was a risk they'd steal the ball.

"When were they last here?" Neuman asked.

"I don't know. Two or three weeks ago."

Nelson had his eyes firmly on the ball Neuman was holding under his arm—it was his, and they didn't have another one.

"How many kids were there with Simon?"

"Three or four."

"Can you describe them?"

"I remember a tall guy in green shorts. The others called him Teddy. There was another one, shorter, in an army shirt."

"You mean a khaki shirt?"

"Yes."

"What else?"

"Er . . ."

The kids were playing around behind his back, and passing remarks in slang.

"Did they have any unusual marks?" Neuman insisted. "Anything on their faces, a tattoo?"

Nelson thought hard about this. "The smaller one," he said, "the one in the army shirt, he had a scar on his neck. Here," he said, pointing to the top of his own skinny trapezius muscles. "It looked like he'd stitched it himself!"

The others laughed, slapping their thighs and jostling one another.

"Anything else?" Neuman asked.

"Hey!" Nelson laughed. "I'm not a Divix camera."

The only thing the kids were interested in was the rubber ball. Neuman kicked it as hard as he could, and it soared over their heads. The boys immediately ran off, screaming as if they had all scored goals.

*

Neuman walked all over the sandy, scrub-covered open spaces known to be the refuge of criminals. He came across a few spectral figures, rejects from the townships or the squatter camps, but didn't learn anything more about the boys. The wind sweeping the zone blotted out everything, even the memory of the dead.

Neuman walked toward the bare dunes. Nothing here but empty Coke cans, plastic wrappers, and bottle necks used as pipes for getting high on *tik* or Mandrax. The place was empty, disturbing, a lunar landscape where even the dogs didn't roam, afraid of being eaten. The rest of the gang must be around here somewhere. They had fled the squatters' camp and the beach three weeks earlier, and no one had seen them again. Simon had taken refuge in the nearby township, where he had lived before, but he'd been alone. The gang must have split up. They had fled to escape the dealers—Neuman had met two of them on the construction site. Brian had killed Joey, but his partner, the one who limped, hadn't been among the bodies found in the cellar.

Neuman returned to the path that led along the side of the no-man's land. His car was waiting for him on the hot stones, mirages shimmering on the hood. He opened it with the remote control.

At that moment, a boy emerged from the nearby ditch. A young black, about twelve years old, with a dirty T-shirt and rubber shoes. Causing a small landslide as he came up out of the ditch, he took a step toward Neuman, but kept his distance. His frizzy hair was gray with dust. He was twisting a length of barbed wire in his dirty hands, and brushing away the flies crawling around his eyes.

"Hello."

Sick eyes, with yellowish crusts around them where they had run.

"Hello."

The boy, strangely, did not ask for coins. He stood there close to the ditch, looking over at Neuman and fiddling with his barbed wire. Neuman had a vague feeling of unease. The boy reminded him of a rabbit suffering from myxomatosis, stuck there without moving, waiting for death.

"Do you live here?" Ali asked.

The boy nodded. The calves of his jogging pants were torn, and he wasn't wearing a cap. Neuman took out Simon's photograph. "Ever seen this kid?"

The boy moved the flies away from his eyes, and shook his head.

"He's part of a street gang. There's also a tall boy in green shorts, and a shorter boy in an army shirt, with a scar on his neck."

"No," he said. "Never seen them."

His voice hadn't changed, but the look he gave him wasn't a child's anymore.

"Twenty rand, sir." He put his hand on his pants. "Twenty rand for a blow job, how about it, sir?"

*

Josephina was one of the "mothers" of the Bantu Congregational Church, a congregation of the Churches of Zion established in the township. They didn't go in for the ready-made prayers of the Europeans, preferring lots of loud singing and constant dancing.

Neuman made his way through the crowd and found his mother in front of the platform with other singers transported with love. Josephina was shaking her huge paunch and praising the Lord fervently, as was the preacher performing this evening. The ecstatic audience repeated everything in chorus. Neuman stood for a moment watching his mother, her forehead bathed in sweat, smiling into the blue void. She seemed happy. He felt a sudden rush of tenderness, like a pang in the heart. He remembered April 27, the day of the first democratic elections, when they had gone together to the Khayelitsha polling station. He saw again the line of blacks and coloreds, all dressed up as if for a wedding, asking those coming out of the voting booth if they had had any problems—they were afraid of choosing the wrong candidate (there were ten on the list), not putting the cross in the right place, or letting it go outside the square, which would invalidate the vote, they were worried about the ink on their fingers[1], the fingerprints they might leave on the voting paper, which some people said could give them away—if they voted for the ANC, who was to say that the authorities wouldn't throw them in prison? He remembered Josephina entering the booth with the list of candidates, shaking all over, and her cry of horror when she realized she had made a mistake, she had ticked Makwthu's box, because he was the first on the list of candidates and with his gray hair he looked like Madiba[2]. They had calmed her cries of despair and given her another paper, which Josephina had been careful to fill in properly, without going outside the box, but she had gone over her cross so many times that she had made a hole in the paper. He remembered the faces, the people clutching their identity cards so tightly that their fingers turned white, the people who wept as they voted, those who seemed drunk as they emerged from the booths, and the indescribable party that had followed the election results, when even old women had come out onto the streets in their blankets to join in the dancing while car horns blared.

That stubborn old Josephina was right. Simon had died among the animals, clutching his mother's picture. Their des-

---

[1] Voters had to put their hands in an ink detector, to make sure that they had not already voted.
[2] Affectionate name for Nelson Mandela.

tiny was part of his own, that share of Africa for which his father and he had fought.

He waited for the service to finish, and drew her outside.

People in their Sunday best nodded to them with a slightly comical respect as they came out of the church on Gxabala Street, arm in arm.

"I heard the news on the radio earlier," Josephina said in a confidential tone. "About the new murder, and the marks on the body. Is it true what they're saying about that Zulu?"

"Yes—just like the death of Kennedy."

She laughed, but Neuman muttered to himself. The information had gotten into the media. How had they found out?

Hanging on his arm as if it was a hook, Josephina aired her long white dress. They talked about Simon, and the street became a lot darker. Neuman told her about the circumstances of his death, the AIDS, the powder that had poisoned him, the rest of the gang still at large, needing to be found. His mother listened and nodded, but she was thinking about something else.

"Yes," she said after a whole. "Simon must have been feeling very weak to attack someone like me. He knew I deal with the disadvantaged. It was a cry for help."

"A strange way to ask for help."

"He was dying, Ali." There were two big lines on her forehead.

"The kids who were with him were seen on the edge of the squatter camp," he said. "Probably immigrants. The older one has green shorts, his name's Teddy. The other one wears a khaki shirt and has a nasty scar on his neck. They've vanished, and I think they're hiding somewhere in the township. One of your friends may have seen them."

The congregation dealt with AIDS patients who were hidden—for fear that the news would get out and the family would be cursed—and just left to rot. Josephina and the other women had contacts all over Cape Flats, people would talk to them more easily than to the police.

"I'll spread the word," Josephina assured him. "Yes, I'm going to take care of this right away."

"I'm asking you to tell your friends," he said, "not to run all over the township. Have you got that?"

"Why don't you just say it?" she said, taking offense. "You think I'm sick!"

"You are sick, Ma. And old."

She laughed.

"I'm serious. Simon was hooked, and so are these kids. I'm sure they're sick, too, but they mustn't be approached, do you understand? I just want to locate them."

Josephina smiled and stroked his face, as she used to do when he was little, to soothe him. "Don't worry about your old mother, I'm in fine form!" she said, her cracked hands traveling over him. "You, on the other hand, should get more sleep. You look feverish and there are rings under your beautiful eyes."

"Let me remind you you're half blind."

"You can't fool a mother so easily!"

She stood up on tiptoe in her gilded pumps and kissed her Zulu king.

He left her as night fell, his heart at the bottom of a well.

*

The drapes were drawn, and a slightly sickening smell of incense hung in the cramped backroom. The only light was a red spot. He was lying on the padded table, his arms bent— arms as hard as a tank, which the young woman was massaging with scented ointments.

"Relax," she said.

She continued oiling his fine body, trying her damnedest to

defragment the turmoil trapped beneath his skin, but new blocks kept appearing, which she dealt with uncomplainingly—at least he had closed his eyes in the end. With expert circular motions, she kneaded the muscles of his shoulders, moved down to his lower back and buttocks, then came slowly up again, stretching his fleshy parts, tenderizing them in long lubricated caresses. At last, exhausted, the girl stopped her erotic game, contemplated her masterpiece, and disappeared behind the drapes.

He barely heard the steps approaching the table—light steps. A girl who couldn't weigh more than a hundred pounds. Had he seen her here before?

She set some metal objects down on the table and positioned herself over him.

"Feeling O.K.?"

No.

"Yes."

"Good."

The girl sorted through her instruments. The images followed one another behind his closed eyelids, images of death, of fire, of blows raining down on him as he lay spread-eagled, but his tears tonight were still on the wrong side—they were flowing inside him.

He wouldn't sleep. Or maybe he would. Either soon or never. With Maia, his last illusions had gone. He didn't want them anymore, except about Zina. She had bewitched him—her eyes like stars in the night, her animal grace, the powder and the coals beneath her feet, he loved everything, more than everything. He was stifling in his armor. His skin was worthless. He felt like an animal at the zoo. He was going around in circles, in his cage, like Tembo's rats.

The girl had picked up an object from the table, which she handled with almost clinical skill. On the edge of insomnia, he let himself be penetrated.

9.

Precious wood, colored concrete, aluminum bays, glass walls—the houses on the verdant hill of Llandudno were all the work of architects. Tony Montgomery had returned from Osaka by way of Tokyo and Dubai, cancelling the rest of his gala tour—Europe and the United States after Asia—and cutting short the promotional campaign for his latest album (*A Love Forever*—the record company hadn't overtaxed itself coming up with a name).

Montgomery was the kind of fifty-year-old you saw in men's magazines, led a VIP's life crisscrossing the global village, and had manicured hands that didn't know what to do with themselves this morning. Stevens, his bodyguard and chauffeur, had warned him that a police officer would be coming, a tall guy with unkempt hair the star barely listened to. Brian had found him by his swimming pool, draped in a silk kimono that went down as far as his tanned thighs. He seemed extremely confused. He had just come back from the morgue, where he had identified his daughter, and now, in a kind of macabre torpor, he was staring aimlessly at the ocean from the terrace of his villa. The fact that he hadn't seen Kate for four months was the finishing touch. Tony Montgomery didn't spend much time in South Africa, he was constantly away on world tours, which meant that they had hardly any acquaintances in common . . .

Brian dipped his hand into the pool to cool himself down a little, and got his notebook wet. He had questioned those closest to Kate: her aunt, a crazy woman in Prada, who was really out of it, Sylvia, an old junkie friend, the video crew, who knew nothing, neighbors who had seen nothing, other people who didn't give a damn.

"How come Kate's mother hasn't made an appearance?" he asked.

"She never did take any interest in her daughter."

"All the same."

"Helen's lived in London for years," Montgomery said. "We separated when Kate was born."

"And you kept custody?"

"Yes."

"With all your touring?" Brian said, feigning surprise.

"I wasn't well-known at the time."

"What you're saying is that Kate was abandoned by her mother?"

"You could put it that way."

He nodded. That explained a lot of things.

"Do you know if your daughter took drugs?"

"I assume Kate sometimes did a little coke for fun, like all these girls. Unfortunately, I'm not the best person to tell you anything about that."

"What did you talk about?"

"Mainly her work. The designing was going well."

He would have said the same thing about the banana trade.

"Did you introduce her to people?"

"No. Kate could get by without my help."

"Do you have any girlfriends she might have confided in?"

"It's common knowledge that I'm gay."

"Good for you. So you don't know anyone who can tell me anything about your daughter?"

"Unfortunately not."

"And did she ever talk to you about her boyfriends?"

"Kate was a bit shy about talking to me. I don't think she was very interested in boys."

Brian lit a cigarette. "We think your daughter was the victim of a serial killer," he said. "A Zulu who's probably part of a township gang. There are drugs involved. Someone must have served as a go-between, or an accomplice."

"My daughter wasn't a criminal," Montgomery said, "if that's what you're implying."

"That's what Stewart Wiese said about his daughter. Do you know him?"

"Stewart Wiese? I met him once, years ago, after his team won the World Cup."

The two young women didn't know each other, he'd already ascertained that.

"Any reason anyone might have had a grudge against you or Wiese?"

"Apart from the fact that we're well-known?"

"I want your opinion, not what the tabloids say."

"No." Montgomery shook his blow-dried hair. "They might resent my money, but not Kate. Kate's innocent. A completely normal young woman."

"Your daughter spent time in a convalescent home," Brian said. "Three months, according to her file. The first time at the age of sixteen, the second at eighteen."

Some of the color returned to Montgomery's face. "That's ancient history," he said.

"Detox?"

"No, a rest cure."

"Do you need that much rest when you're sixteen?"

"You know the kinds of things teenagers go through. But anyway, that's old news. And I don't see what all that has to do with my daughter's death."

Montgomery was starting to lose his temper. He wasn't used to being talked to like this. He was surrounded by people who spent all day telling him how wonderful he was.

"Listen, Montgomery, I wasn't born yesterday," Brian said.

"Your daughter was twice treated in a specialist clinic, and at that age there aren't that many reasons. Either she was on drugs, or she had tried to kill herself. Or both. I'm sorry to have to tell you this, but things weren't going so well for Kate. We found dozens of cuts on her body. She'd been regularly self-harming. Cutting, they call it. It's usually an attempt to reconnect with reality in order to avoid a complete mental breakdown." Brian blew cigarette smoke in Montgomery's face. "So talk or I'll drown you in your golden pool."

"Is there a problem, Mr. Montgomery?" Stevens asked.

"No, no." His sigh was covered by the gurgling of the pool.

"Kate's mother was a talented actress, but a bit . . . peculiar. I think she'd realized that starting a family wasn't quite my thing, but Helen got pregnant and decided she wanted to keep the child, thinking that it would help her hold on to me. But then my career started to take off, and Helen moved to England, leaving me with the baby. That was her revenge. Kate tried to see her mother again when she was a teenager, but it didn't work out well."

"So she started doing drugs," Brian said. "She may have started again."

"I don't know."

"You had her put away after a suicide attempt, right?"

"It happened once," Montgomery replied. "I didn't want it to happen again."

"Why hide it?"

"What?"

"That your daughter was a depressive ex-junkie."

"After the rest cure, and the follow-up treatment, Kate recovered," he said. "I don't see any point in making the whole thing public!"

"I'm trying to find out whether your daughter was easy prey," Brian replied. "Someone lured her into a trap. Kate was vulnerable, and drugs seem the most obvious avenue to explore."

Montgomery was nervously fingering his diamond signet ring. "Listen, lieutenant," he said at last. "I may not always have been there, but I do know a few things about my daughter. Kate had a difficult childhood and adolescence, I tried to give her the best schools, things didn't always work out, but Kate was a fighter, and she put her life together again all by herself. She wasn't interested in drugs anymore. She wanted to live her life, that's all. She wanted to live, do you understand?"

"Yes, by cutting herself."

*

Brian wasn't a great believer in chance, rather that different paths sometimes came together. He had just returned to headquarters after his interview with Montgomery when, emerging from her office like a mortar shell, Janet Helms literally fell into his arms.

"Did you get my message?"

He took a step back to get things straight. "No."

"I've tracked down a vehicle that might match what you're looking for," she said. "A Pinzgauer Steyr Puch four-by-four, the 712K model, filmed by the surveillance camera at a service station on the night of the murder."

Fletcher's murder. Janet's round eyes were red from lack of sleep, but her sadness had given way to a kind of excitement. He followed her into the nearby office.

"The service station in question is on Baden Powell, the road that goes along False Bay to Pelikan Park," she said, tapping on her computer keyboard. "At 3:12 in the morning. You can't see the driver's face behind the smoked windows, and the plates are illegible."

Brian peered at the gray stripes on the screen. The bodywork was dark. All you could see were the driver's hands—clearly a white, or a colored.

"I've done some research," Janet went on. "No Pinzgauer of that model has been reported stolen recently. I did find a similar four-by-four stolen in Natal province two months ago, and another in Jo'burg at the end of last year, but both were burned after being used in security van holdups. So I listed all the Pinzguaers in circulation."

Baden Powell was about a mile from the house, easily reached by the track.

"What direction was the four-by-four going in when it was filmed?" Brian asked.

"West. In other words, toward Cape Town."

And away from the townships.

"Are any of the owners Zulus?"

"No, I checked. If the color's correct, only three vehicles match the description. I called the rental companies concerned, but none of them rented out this model the day Dan was killed. As for private companies, only three use them. One is a travel company that organizes safaris, but the vehicle wasn't available during that week. The other two are a vineyard in the valley near Franschoek, which I can't get hold of, and ATD, a company providing security and private police. That might be worth taking a look at."

Brian nodded. Janet Helms smelled of lilac.

*

Neuman didn't know who had informed the media—according to Tembo, half the force would sell the date of his death to the first person who asked, and the other half to whoever put an extra zero on the check—but the revelations surrounding Kate Montgomery's death, coming as they did in the middle of the anti-crime campaign, had a disastrous effect. The savagery of the crime, the rape, the taking of hair and nails, the tribal slogan engraved in letters of blood on the body of a young white woman—the myth of "the Zulu" would be getting a lot of mileage in the editorial offices.

The largest ethnic group in sub-Saharan Africa, the Zulus had traumatized their era by massacring a British regiment[1]— before being killed themselves. Given the task of clearing the hostile territories, the Boer pioneers had fought the Zulus with equal ferocity before herding them into Bantustans during apartheid.

Ololo, we will kill you, was interpreted as a warning and a threat to the white population, a reminder of a kind of genocide, something coming from the sick mind of a killer.

The murders revived memories of a troubled past, which had been deliberately downplayed in the name of national reconciliation. The fall of the Berlin Wall, the relentless progress of globalization, and the exceptional personality of Mandela had prevailed over apartheid and internecine wars—everyone remembered the ANC leader's assumption of power, when the Xhosa Mandela had raised the arms of his worst enemies, the Afrikaner De Klerk and the Zulu Buthelezi, as a sign of victory. Nicole Wiese and Kate Montgomery were the children of two symbols, the world champion of the first multiracial team and the voice of the rainbow nation—attacking them was quite simply unacceptable. Between the lines of the most conservative news reports, there was a veiled allusion to a historic fear: the rape of a white woman by a black man, that old fear in which biology and politics came together. The allegations of rape and corruption hanging over Jacob Zuma, the ANC's most populist leader, didn't help matters.

Neuman had just emerged from a stormy interview with Krüge when he received Tembo's detailed report. The weapon that had killed Kate Montgomery could have been a pickax handle, a stick or a kind of club (splinters of wood were

[1] The British army had the reputation of being the best in the world.

embedded in the victim's skull). No traces of sperm had been found, but there were traces of the new drug, which had put the young woman in a state of advanced stupor. She had been bound and gagged with adhesive tape. Everything was similar to the Nicole Wiese murder, apart from the strange mixture of herbs found sticking to Kate's hair.

It wasn't *iboga*, as Tembo had thought at first, but two plants, *upindamshaye* and *uphind'umuva*, and one root, *mazwende*. Made into a powder, they formed the basis of *intelezi*, a Zulu pre-battle ritual narcotic.

Intelezi could be inserted under the skin in the form of powder, or ground in the mouth, in order to be spat in the opponent's face. That was what had happened to Kate.

Neuman's eyes burned with a wicked light. By spitting on his victim, the madman had provided them with his DNA.

*

The electric room, the wall of sound roaring on the smoke-filled stage, interference like a screaming siren, images of massacre projected on metal sheets, Soweto '76, the riots of '85, '86, faces of hanged and tortured people, Zina sent into a trance by the drums, her great body steaming, her mad eyes that had been pursuing him all these nights.

"Be careful," she said, seeing him waiting for her outside her dressing room, "or you're going to end up like poor Nicole."

The 366 was the club on Long Street where the group was performing tonight. Zina had known that Neuman would come back—they always came back.

"This isn't about Nicole anymore, it's about Kate," he said. "Kate Montgomery. Hear about that?"

She breathed out in exasperation, opened the door of the dressing room, and let him in.

"Why are you talking to me about her?"

Zina grabbed a towel from the dressing table and wiped her sweat-drenched arms.

Neuman took a folded paper from his pocket. "I'd like you to take a look at this," he said.

"What is it, a love letter?"

"No. A summary of the postmortem report."

"You always know the right thing to say to a woman."

"It's not every day I meet someone like you."

"How am I supposed to take that?"

"That depends a lot on what you think of this," he said, handing her the sheet of paper.

Nonchalantly, she looked over the document. "Nail clippings, locks of hair," she said. "The basic ingredients for a quack's remedy. He's trying to make a *muti*. Oh, and I see there are also some unusual plants, *upindamshaye*, *uphind'umuva*, *mazwende*. Don't you have any botanists in the police force?"

"What I don't have is a culprit."

"There's no lack of them in South Africa."

"You're an *inyanga*, aren't you? An herbalist."

"I thought I was just making potions for schoolgirls?"

"I was wrong about you."

"And I was wrong about you, if that's any consolation."

No.

"Do these plants form the basis of an *intelezi*?" he asked.

"Why are you asking me questions if you already know the answers?"

"That's my job, believe it or not. Well?"

"Yes," Zina replied. "A Zulu pre-battle ritual."

"Can you tell me anything more about that?"

She looked into his eyes, but they had become opaque. "The composition of an *intelezi* varies depending on whether you're trying to weaken your enemy or strengthen your own weapon," she said. "Judging by the composition of this one, I'd say it was used to weaken the enemy."

"Killing young girls with a club, I wouldn't exactly call that a battle."

"It may not be young girls he sees as his opponent," she said.

"Who then—the police?"

"You, the government, the whites who run the machine. If your guy believes he's a Zulu warrior, that means he feels strong enough to defy the whole world."

Neuman didn't know if it was the drug that gave the killer this feeling of invincibility, if he was planning to take his *muti* back to one of the township *sangomas*, if he was attacking these girls out of racism, cowardice, or pure insanity. His eyes wandered down to the orange patterns on the carpet.

"What are you afraid of?" she asked.

He looked up. "Not him, anyway."

"Your hands are shaking," she said.

"Maybe. Do you want to know why?"

"Yes."

Neuman's legs, although quite still, were giving way. "I have a list of murders committed in the cities where you and your group have performed," he said straight out. "At least three unsolved murders, all of men who were highly placed officials under apartheid."

She tightened her grip on the towel around her neck. She hadn't been expecting that. His eyes had lied to her. He did not love her. He was setting a trap for her. He had been hunting her down from the start.

"Did you use one of your love potions to poison Karl Woos?" he went on.

"I'm not a praying mantis."

"Woos, Müller, and Francis didn't testify before the Truth and Reconciliation Commission," he said. "Did you kill them because they'd gotten off scot-free? Are you still settling scores with the past?"

Zina again looked every inch the ex-militant. "You're talking to a ghost, Mr. Neuman."

"Did you kill in the name of Inkatha?"

"No."

"Could you kill in the name of Inkatha?"

"I'm a Zulu."

"So am I. I've never killed anyone as a Zulu."

"You would have done it for the ANC," she hissed. "You would have done it to avenge your father."

So she knew about that.

"You're still active in Inkatha," he said softly. "At least unofficially."

"No. I'm a dancer."

"Sugar to attract the wasps."

"I hate sugar."

"You're still lying."

"And you're crazy. I'm a dancer, whether you like it or not."

"Yes, you're a dancer." Neuman took a step toward the dressing table, where he had cornered her. "Is your next target here, in Cape Town? Have you already approached him?"

"You're crazy," she repeated.

"Really?"

For a brief moment, there was silence in the dressing room. Zina took hold of his hot, feverish hands and unflinchingly placed her lips on his. Neuman did not move when she slid her tongue into his mouth. He was the target.

Zina was kissing him, her eyes wide open, when the cell phone rang in his pocket.

It was Janet Helms.

"I've found the suspect's DNA in the records," she said.

*

Sam Gulethu, born December 10, 1966, in the Bantustan of KwaZulu. Mother a housewife, died in 1981, father died two years earlier in the mines. Leaves his native village as a teenager, wanders in search of a pass to work in the city. Convicted of the murder of a teenage girl in 1984, serves six years in Durban prison. Joins the ranks of the Inkatha vigilantes in 1986, during the state of emergency,[2] and remains with them until the end of apartheid. Suspected of several murders of opponents during the difficult period preceding the democratic elections, Gulethu is granted an amnesty in 1994. He is next heard of in 1997, when he is sentenced to six months' imprisonment without remission for drug trafficking, then to two years for armed robbery—again served in Durban prison. Moves to Cape Province, where he is associated with various gangs in the township of Manenberg. Involved in selling marijuana, extortion on buses and trains. Sentenced again in 2001, this time for six months for aggravated assault, kidnapping, and acts of torture—sentence served at Pollsmoor prison. Released September 14, 2006. Does not attend any of his appointments with social services in Manenberg, where he is supposed to be living. Unknown sangoma *activities. Has probably joined one of the township gangs. Distinguishing marks: pockmarked face, one upper incisor missing, tattoo of a spider on the right forearm.*

Neuman was staring at the screen of Janet Helms's computer, having quickly joined her at headquarters. Manenberg—the township where Maia lived—the tattoo, Pollsmoor. It was all coming together. There were shadowy areas, but the Gulethu lead seemed the right one. Most of the vigilantes who had maintained order in the Bantustans by force had stayed in the townships. Despised, unemployed, they ended up becom-

---

[2] Criminals serving long sentences were released with the promise that their sentence would be quashed if they killed members of Desmond Tutu's UDF in raids on the townships assisted by the police.

ing involved with the armed gangs and the Mafias. Gulethu may have set up a new gang on leaving prison, with whoever he found on the streets—former militiamen, child soldiers, whores, junkies. Gulethu and Sonny Ramphele had both spent time in Pollsmoor prison. Gulethu must have found out about Sonny's drug dealing on the coast, and when he got out had set up in business with Sonny's younger brother to sell his drug to a white clientele, which was more lucrative than the losers in the township. Stan must have said something to him about his tattoo, and mentioned his own fear of spiders. The young Xhosa may have pimped Nicole Wiese for him, for money, without knowing that he was going to kill her. But with Stan's "suicide," who had handed Kate Montgomery over to Gulethu?

Neuman couldn't take his eyes off the mug shot on the screen. Gulethu wasn't ugly—he was terrifying.

10

Hout Bay was the largest fishing port on the peninsula. The first boats were returning from the open sea, trailing a swarm of seagulls in their wake. Brian waved at the colony of sea lions nesting in the bay, walked past the picturesque Mariner's Wharf and the seafood restaurants on the edge of the beach, and parked his Mercedes near the market stalls.

Women in pretty dresses were setting out their wooden toys, in preparation for the arrival of the tourists. The ATD office was located a bit farther on, at the far end of the jetties. One of the biggest security companies in the country. Head of the Hout Bay branch was Frank Debeer.

Brian passed the refrigeration depots, where black workers were waiting for the day's haul, and headed for the office, a colonnaded building somewhat set apart from the bustle of the harbor. The forecourt was deserted apart from a Ford bearing the company colors, roasting in the sun. He walked to the nearby garage and pushed open the heavy sliding door. Another brightly colored Ford lurked in the shadows, and beyond it, partly hidden, the dark lines of a Pinzgauer four-by-four.

Swallows had nested under the metal beams. Brian approached the vehicle, and tried the door—locked. He peered in through the tinted windows—impossible to see inside. The bodywork looked almost new, without any traces of fresh paint. He was examining the few soil marks on the tires when a voice echoed behind him.

"Looking for something?"

A big white in blue fatigues had just come in from the fore-court: Debeer, a middle-aged Afrikaner with reflective sun-glasses and a huge beer belly.

Brian waved his badge in the direction of the swallows. "Are you Debeer?"

"Yes, why?"

"Is this toy yours?" he said, indicating the car.

The man wedged his thumbs under his pot belly. "It's the company's," he said. "Why?"

"Is it often used?"

"For patrols. I asked you why?"

"And I'm asking you to change your tune. What patrols?"

The looks they exchanged were like the current *pax americana*.

"For our work," Debeer grunted. "We're a security company, not an intelligence agency."

"Private police forces are supposed to cooperate with the SAP," Brian retorted, "not crap all over it. I'm investigating a homicide. You're the boss here, so you're going to answer me or I set this place on fire. What kind of patrols?"

Debeer lifted his belly as if it was a baby trying to get away from him. "We cover the whole peninsula. It depends on the calls we get. There are plenty of burglaries."

"Do you patrol at night?"

"Twenty-four hours a day," Debeer retorted. "Like it says on our sign."

The swallows started chirruping beneath the beams.

"Who used this vehicle on Thursday of last week?" Epkeen asked.

"No one."

"How do you know without checking your records?"

"Because I'm the one who uses it."

"This vehicle was filmed on Baden Powell at two in the morning last Thursday," Brian said.

He was bluffing.

Debeer pulled a face, which did nothing for his double chin. "It's possible. I was on night duty last week."

"I thought you said no one used the Pinzgauer."

"No one except me."

The guy was messing around.

"Did you get an emergency call?" Brian asked.

"We don't have to wait for people to be robbed to go out on patrol."

"So you were patrolling Baden Powell that night."

"If you say so."

Debeer was hiding behind a lot of bluster, hoping to pull the wool over his eyes. Brian caught his own reflection in the sunglasses—he wasn't looking too good.

"Do you patrol on your own?"

"I don't need anyone else to do my job."

"Don't you work in pairs?"

"Most of the time we check out break-ins. Sometimes, you only need one person for that."

Less manpower equals more profits, even if it meant doing a botched job. A standard procedure—Brian wasn't convinced. He took a photograph from his linen jacket.

"Do you recognize this house?"

Debeer looked at it blankly, as if he was reading Chinese. "Don't know it."

"A house in the dunes, near Pelikan Park. It doesn't have any security protection. Strange for an isolated house, don't you think?"

He shrugged. "If people want to be burglarized, that's their choice."

"This house is in your area. Didn't anyone try to canvass the owners?"

Debeer sniffed. "I'm the head of the branch, not a salesman."

"And yet you look like the kind of man who lies as easily as breathing."

"I don't breathe. That's why they gave me this job."

A billy club, a cell phone, and a service pistol hung on his broad hips.

"You're an ex-cop, right?" Brian said.

"That's none of your business."

"Can I take a look at the vehicle?"

"Do you have a warrant?"

"Do you have a reason not to show me what's inside?"

Debeer hesitated for a moment, emitted an unpleasant sound with his mouth, and took a key from his pocket. The lights of the Pinzgauer blinked.

The interior of the four-by-four smelled of detergent. To judge by the layout, the back had been used to transport goods. Brian inspected the passenger compartment. Everything was clean, no trace of ash in the ashtray, not a speck of dust on the dashboard.

"What do you carry in this car?"

"That depends on what we've been called in for," Debeer replied behind him.

There was room enough inside for eight people.

Brian emerged from the vehicle. "Have you cleaned it recently?"

"Nothing illegal about that, as far as I know."

"It's funny," he said, turning toward the Ford. "This other car's really dirty."

"So?"

Sweat was forming rings under his uniform.

Brian felt his cell phone vibrate in the pocket of his fatigues. Giving Debeer a dirty look, he left the garage to take the call. It was Neuman.

"Where are you?" Neuman asked at the other end of the line.

"In Hout Bay, with a jerk."

"Let it go. We've been sent a gift. Join me at Harare police station."

Brian grumbled as he put away his phone. Debeer was watching him scornfully behind his reflective glasses, in the shade of the garage, his thumbs stuck in his belt.

*

There was an unpleasant smell in Walter Sanogo's office, which the fan didn't do much to dispel. Ali Neuman and Brian Epkeen were standing in front of him, waiting in silence. Sanogo took the plastic bag from the icebox at his feet and placed it carefully on the desk. There was something round inside, a human head, its Negroid features visible through the blood-spattered plastic.

"Found this morning in a garbage pail outside the station," Sanogo said in a neutral voice.

He untied the handles of the bag and uncovered the decapitated head of a young black, his eyes and cheeks swollen, staring at them with a monstrous grin. The closed eyelids had been cut lengthwise, leaving only a bloody crack by way of eyes. Eyes like razors. The Cat had had a bit of fun, before sending his master the corpse.

"A gift from Mzala?"

"It bears his signature."

Neuman kneeled and looked at the head. He had met this boy on the construction site ten days earlier, with Joey. The one who'd limped.

"Do you know this man?"

"No," Sanogo replied. "He must be a foreigner, or from the squatter camps."

"I met him in Khayelitsha ten days ago," Neuman said. "He was beating up the boy who attacked my mother."

Sanogo shrugged. "I sent a patrol to the dunes on Cape Flats to look for the rest of the body," he said. "That's often where the wolves leave their prey."

Neuman looked at the decapitated head on the desk and its sliced eyelids. "In that case, let's go have a word with the leader of the pack."

*

Mzala was playing darts in the private room of the Marabi. The *shebeen* was already full of the kind of people who had suffered everything life could throw at them and so were ignoring the insults that Dina was flinging at them like bones at birds of prey.

"Buy drinks, you heap of vermin! This isn't a steam room!"

That was when she saw the big black cop in the entrance, with a whole bunch of Sanogo's cops following him, and released her pressure on the drinkers. Neuman walked though the alcohol-dazed crowd, with Brian covering his back.

"You—"

"I told you once before, shut up."

With a look, Neuman boxed her in behind the counter. He walked past the pillar and pulled open the metal partition that led to the Americans' private room. A noisy fan was stirring the smoke-laden air. Three guys were slumped on straw mattresses, waiting their turn to play. Mzala had his eyes fixed on the target, apparently contemplating his next throw.

"Did you like my gift?" he asked, and simultaneously launched the dart.

It landed a long way off target.

Two red-eyed *tsotsis* came from the corridor and took up position on either side of Mzala. Brian had them in his sights—they both had guns under their shirts. The other three seemed to be snoozing behind their eyelids. Sanogo was standing against the metal partition, next to Dina, who had come to the rescue.

"Where does the head come from?"

"Not far from here. Near Crossroads, on the edge of the township, where he was trying to sell his dope." Mzala gave an impassive smile. "Not a good idea."

He was about to throw another dart, but Neuman went and stood in front of the board. "So you cut his head off."

Mzala assumed a contrite air, which suited him about as well as a clown's nose. "I have nothing against cops," he said, "but I don't much like finding out from them what's happening on my own pitch. The story you told me almost kept me awake. It made me think the Americans' territory isn't watertight." He clicked his tongue. "You're an educated man, you know what private property means. We had to send a strong signal to those fucking foreigners."

"The Nigerian Mafia?"

"Apparently." He smiled enigmatically. "Dogs like that, you chase away ten, a hundred come back."

"How do you know they're Nigerians?"

"They talked Dashiki among themselves, and those gangs of theirs grow like weeds." He pointed his nose in Sanogo's direction. "Just ask the captain there."

Sanogo didn't bat an eyelid. There were two constables at the entrance of the *shebeen*, the others were keeping an eye on the drinkers in the main room.

"Who's their leader?" Neuman asked.

"One of those fucking niggers, I suppose."

"You cut his eyelids with a razor. That wasn't just for fun, was it?"

Mzala wiped the palm of his hand on his faded T-shirt. "I didn't ask their names, brother. They were just Nigerian dogs. A territory can't be shared. Especially not the Americans'."

For the moment, no one was making a hostile move. Brian

glanced through the barred window looking out on the street corner. Outside, boys in shorts were watching from a distance, held back by their elders.

"Where's the rest of the body?" Neuman asked.

"We sent the son of a bitch back where he came from!" Mzala said, swaggering in front of his court. "To the other side of the tracks."

The line separating Khayelitsha from the squatter camp.

"So the gang comes from the buffer zone?"

"Seems so, brother."

"What are they doing on your territory?"

"I told you—trying to sell their dope."

"What dope?"

"*Tik*. Anyway, that's what the guy told us. He didn't have any reason to lie," he added with a sly smile. "These hyenas were prospecting around here, for a while apparently. It's just not done, you agree. We're the Americans, we don't like sharing."

"You're a funny guy, you know that?" Neuman held out the photograph of Gulethu. "Know him?"

"Er . . ."

"Gulethu, a Zulu *tsotsi*. He was skimming off the gangs, then he disappeared. He's killed several people, two white girls in particular."

"Is he the Zulu the papers are talking about?"

"Don't tell me you can read."

"I have girls who've learned to read for me," he said, turning to a colored girl sprawled on the couch. "Isn't that right, girl, you know heaps about reading?"

"Yeah," the girl replied, her breasts bursting out of her red leotard. "I even have the Bible written on my ass!"

They all laughed coarsely. The girl's breasts shook rhythmically.

"Well?" Neuman said impatiently.

"No," Mzala replied. "Never seen the guy."

"What about the rest of the gang? Where's it hiding?"

"In Cape Flats. An old spaza shop according to the guy, down near the tracks. I didn't go see. It stinks over there."

Mzala was smiling with his yellow teeth when suddenly the windows exploded. Before the two cops at the entrance were able to raise their guns, they were riddled with bullets, and the sign and the door were both shot to pieces. A pickup truck with the tarp removed screeched to a halt outside the *shebeen*, and from the back of it three men sprayed bullets. Inside the *shebeen* the customers retreated from the entrance. A man fell to the floor face down, another collapsed in front of the bar counter, his neck broken. The strongest of them surged back, knocking over the stunned drunks, forcing their way through with their fists. A burst of fire took off the jaw of one of the constables who had been caught in the crush, and he let out a piercing scream. Neuman had thrown himself to the ground. Bodies were falling around him. People were taking refuge in the games room. The firing came from AK-47s. In a panic, some customers tried to escape through the windows, but the killers outside picked them off, and they dropped back inside, covered in blood. Neuman looked for Brian, saw him on the floor, his .38 in his hand. Crouching against the wall, Mzala was yelling orders into his cell phone. People were falling onto the metal partition, machine-gunned at close range. The bullets were still raining down in an explosion of plaster, glasses, bottles, billboards. Mzala and his men posted themselves at the window of the private room and opened fire in their turn.

Sanogo and his men had fallen back in confusion—seven uniformed officers, including the one who'd had his chin torn off and was being supported by a terrified young recruit. The bullets were coming thick and fast over the counter, behind which Dina was hiding, her hands over her head. There were more shots out on the streets, like an echo to the groans of the wounded.

Fully alert now, the Americans had launched a lightning counterattack, bombarding the pickup outside their HQ, until the rain of fire stopped.

Brian and Neuman ran out into the yard of the *shebeen*, a dead end heaped with crates and bowls of crushed corn. They looked up at the corrugated iron roofs, and climbed onto the gutter. The passersby had run away in panic. Cries could be heard from the neighboring alleys. The three blacks in the back of the Toyota had turned and were now responding to the Americans' fire. After a brief exchange, one of the blacks collapsed against the tarp, and the pickup set off at high speed. A fourth shooter covered their escape from the door of the truck. Brian and Neuman fired from the roofs, emptying their barrels at the *tsotsis* in the back.

They jumped off the roof in a cloud of dust.

The machine-gunned Toyota zigzagged on the street before crashing into a small brick house with a dull thud. The passenger who had been shooting from the door jumped out and ran off, screaming. Brian and Neuman ran to the truck, reloading their guns as they did so. The men in the back of the pickup had stopped moving, their bodies riddled with holes. Neuman covered Brian, who aimed his revolver at the smoking engine. The driver's face was resting on the wheel, his eyes open—the bullet had come out through his mouth. Brian looked up and saw people running in all directions. Neuman was already a hundred yards away, at the end of the alley.

The fugitive was holding an AK-47. He fired a burst blindly before turning the corner. He reappeared immediately, retreating, firing all over the place. The Americans had cut off the area, blocking off his retreat. A bullet-riddled car came charging at him in a cloud of dust, and stopped dead.

Cornered, the killer turned toward Neuman and, with his eyes bulging, aimed the AK-47. A black with a hideous face, who seemed to be defying him in his madness. Gulethu.

As he pressed the trigger, Neuman fired.

Mzala's men sprang out of the car, guns at the ready. Gulethu was lying on the beaten earth, a bullet in his hip. He blinked in the sun, saw the Americans at the end of the street, and tried to pick up the AK-47, but it was out of his reach. He smiled dementedly, squeezing the amulet around his neck. The *tsotsis* finished him off with a burst of fire at close range.

Neuman wanted to cry out, but he felt a sharp pain. Instinctively, he lifted his hand to his stomach. Removing it, he saw it was red. Hot blood was running down his shirt.

PART THREE
LET THE EARTH TREMBLE

1

Zina had been born without brothers. As the eldest child, she had learned the Zulu martial art of *izinduku*, usually reserved for boys, and had shown a skill and a determination uncommon in such a pretty girl. Her father had gone to the forest to cut her a stick that was the right size for her. She had fought with the boys, blow for blow, ignoring the sniggers.

Her father had been stripped of his position for refusing to kowtow to the Bantu authorities who had granted the tribal chiefs a relative autonomy in return for obeying the apartheid laws. He didn't want to be one of those little despots who'd sold out to the whites and would soon be imposing their power by force inside the homelands with the help of the militias. Their house had been bulldozed, their animals killed, and the clan driven out, its members scattered through the neighboring slums.

Zina had decided to fight back. The ANC was banned, and its leaders had been in prison for twenty years, so she had joined Chief Buthelezi's Inkatha movement.

There were few women fighters in Inkatha. From time to time, using a knitting club as a cover, they would help to organize political meetings or hide white sympathizers who were in danger of being arrested by the army or lynched by the comrades. Zina had demonstrated with the Zulu fighting sticks they were allowed to carry, she had challenged white power by parading with imaginary weapons, she had printed leaflets, and attacked and fled the militants of the ANC-UDF, which up until then had represented the opposition. Because she performed all these masculine activities and kept her femininity to herself, when her hidden side did eventually emerge it had been like an eruption: futile outbursts, cataclysmic love affairs and disappointments. It was as if Zina had thrown her heart off of a bridge a long time ago and was waiting for a little girl—herself—to appear and pick it up.

The years of apartheid had passed, her adult years, and the political struggle had made her as hard as the wood of the sticks her father had carved for her. By embracing his political enemies, President Mandela had put an end to the slaughter but the world, when you came down to it, had merely shifted. These days, apartheid wasn't political but social—and she was still up there on that bridge, looking down at her fallen heart.

But Zina didn't despair—not completely. She was an intelligent woman. She decided to work on her body.

Ali Neuman lay in his hospital bed, and smiled weakly in welcome.

She raised an ironic eyebrow. "I thought a Zulu king was indestructible."

"I'm not dead," he said. "Not yet."

Gulethu's bullet had entered his left side and passed along a rib, narrowly missing his heart. The cracked bone made him sigh from time to time. The hospital doctor had recommended complete rest—one or two weeks, until the cartilage had reset.

"How did you know I was here?"

"I read about your exploits in the newspaper," she said, mockingly. "Congratulations."

"Twelve people dead, I don't call that an exploit."

Birds were singing beyond the window. Zina wore a midnight-blue dress and a cobalt-blue stone hanging from a braid around her neck. She looked at the bouquet of irises standing imposingly on the night table.

"From an admirer?"

"Worse—my mother."

She picked up the book lying next to the flowers. "And this?"

"A present from Brian."

"A friend?"

"The only one I have left."

Zina read the title out loud. "*John Paul II: Essential Writings.*"

She gave him a questioning—and quite charming—look.

"I'm a bit of an insomniac," he said, euphemistically. "Brian hoped it would help me sleep."

"Does it work?"

"I usually drop right off as soon as I've read the cover."

Zina smiled, and a bead of sweat ran down into the hollow between her breasts. As if in a dream, the dew of her skin had disappeared beneath her dress.

"When are you getting out?" she asked.

"Right now. I have to attend a press conference."

"The doctor will be happy."

"I can walk."

"How far? The door?"

The tone was playful, but Neuman did not notice her smile. He was aware only of her bare feet on the plastic-coated floor, her legs shimmering in the daylight, and the desire that had grabbed him by the throat.

"I'm performing at Rhodes House on Saturday," she said. "It's the last date on the tour."

"Is that so?"

Neuman was playing his role badly, even though it was one he had at his fingertips. They hadn't said anything else the other night in the dressing room. He had escaped her lips to answer Janet Helms's call and then had left without a word. Zina did not know what he was thinking, if he still suspected her of killing people like in the old Inkatha days, or if she was still up there on the bridge, waiting for a day that would never come.

She leaned over the river flowing down there, a movement she couldn't resist. Part of her soul drowned when she placed her mouth on his lips. Too bad for the little girl hanging in the rain. Neuman was raising a hand toward her—even before she did—when there was a knock at the door.

The weight of the world immediately pushed them apart.

A big black woman entered the room, laden with food, groping at the air with her stick. Josephina sensed a female presence beside her son, and laughed. "Oh! I'm disturbing you! I'm sorry, I'm so sorry!"

"I was just leaving," Zina lied.

"Ah-ha!"

Josephina put down her energy-giving food at the foot of the bed and shifted her attention to Zina. Neuman introduced her but she was already exploring her with her fingertips.

"Ah-ha!"

"Yes, all right, that's enough."

But Josephina was in seventh heaven. The woman had a noble face, generous curves—a poplar tree gently leaning over her son's bed. "You're a Zulu, aren't you?" she asked.

"Yes. A bit too much for your son's taste, apparently."

Zina winked at Neuman, and hurried out.

Neuman turned a little paler.

Leaning on her cane, his mother was looking at him as if he was chasing clouds on Venus. "You seem on good form, son!"

He had the taste of her lips on his mouth and a black hole in his heart.

*

Brian had bought a yellow and red lion from a street vendor, and a zebra for Eve, wire figurines made in the townships. He rang the entry phone, his throat a little dry.

"Yes?" a woman's voice said.

"Claire? It's Brian."

"Who?"

Everything calm and white in the crushing sun.

The sidewalk felt like quicksand.

They'd spent enough alcohol-fueled evenings together to become firm friends. Dan wouldn't have liked his wife to be abandoned just because he wasn't around anymore.

"Let me in, Claire," he insisted. "Just for a few minutes."

First there was a heavy silence, then a barely audible sigh through the entry phone, and finally an electronic click that opened the gate.

The little garden was flooded with sunlight. Eve and Tom were splashing each other in a plastic swimming pool, watched over by their aunt Margo, who greeted him with a preoccupied smile.

"Uncle Brian! Uncle Brian!"

The kids threw their arms around him as if he was a pony, and enthused over his gifts.

"Where's Ali?" Tom asked.

"Polishing his nails. He'll come and see you when they're dry."

"Really?" Eve asked in surprise.

Claire was on the terrace, smoothing out the modeling dough the kids had been playing with. Margo suggested a new game to draw the children back to the pool. Brian went up to the table where Claire was silently applying herself.

"I told you I'd rather be alone," she said, without looking up.

He put his hands in his pockets, to stop himself smoking. "I just wanted to see how you were."

"What do you want to know?"

"How are the kids?"

"Have you ever seen orphans on top of the world?"

"You're alive, Claire," he said, in a friendly tone.

"I'm not dead. There's a difference."

She looked up at him. It was as if grief had eaten her up from inside. Even the blue of her eyes had faded.

"The situation is already difficult enough, don't you think?"

"Oh, sure, it could be worse," she retorted, with a harsh smile. "I could also lose my breast to cancer. But I'm lucky, my hair's growing back! Great, isn't it?" Her hands shook as they kneaded the dough.

"Did you get my package?" he asked.

"Dan's things? Yes. You should have put his hands in with them, as a souvenir."

Her own spitefulness was about to make her cry. Big tears were already welling in her swollen eyes. She had become unrecognizable to him. To herself, too, probably.

"Go away, Brian," she said. "Please."

The children's cries came from the pool. He kissed her fake hair, helplessly, while she massacred the figurines.

*

The buffer zones of Nyanga, Crossroads, and Philippi were where most of the squatter camps were situated. These buffer zones had their own laws, their own *shebeens*, brothels, music venues, and horse races. A few shack lords had short careers there. Sam Gulethu was one of them.

In the end, they'd found the shed, a former spaza shop, that they'd used as a hideout, on the edge of Khayelitsha. The fin-

gerprints and the traces of DNA left on the cigarette butts confirmed that the gang had stayed there. The shed was divided
into a dormitory and a kitchen, the windows covered with steel
sheets. As an HQ, it was easy to defend in case of attack, with
a lock-up garage and an alley that led to the dunes on the nearby open space. A four-by-four could get to the highway in a
few minutes, Muizenberg in less than half an hour. The police
hadn't located the stock of powder, but they had discovered
unused syringes and traces of marijuana all over the rooms.
Two of the *tsotsis* killed during the attack on the Marabi were
known to the police: Etho Mumgembe, a former *witdoeke*, one
of those militiamen tolerated during apartheid who clashed
with the young progressives in the Bantustans, and Patrice
"Tyson" Sango, a former recruiting sergeant for a rebel militia
in the Congo, wanted for war crimes. No one knew what had
led the *tsotsis* to kill each other in the cellars, or if Gulethu had
eliminated them because the police were after them. They had
found sixty-five thousand rand in Gulethu's pockets. The
money from the drug dealing, presumably. That didn't tell
them where the stock of dope was, if it still existed, or if the
gang was being supplied by one of the Mafias, but toxicological tests had provided an explanation for the suicide attack on
the Americans' HQ. Gulethu and his killers had been high
during the shootout, on that same *tik*-based drug, with the
same level of toxicity as the mutilated *tsotsis* in the cellar. Had
they become hooked, too? Had Gulethu manipulated them in
order to carry out his criminal rituals? The shed was packed
with weapons: police revolvers with their numbers erased,
offensive grenades, two assault rifles, and Zulu fighting sticks,
including a shorter one, an *umsila*, still stained with Kate
Montgomery's blood and covered in Gulethu's prints. The
young woman's hair and nail clippings were hidden in an iron
box under a makeshift mattress, along with *grigris* and
amulets.

Gulethu hadn't had time to put together his *muti*, and his "battle" with the Americans had come to an abrupt end. War, genocide, suicide—whatever crazy ancestral idea he'd had in his head, his secrets had died with him.

Anyway, now wasn't the time for psychological speculations. The auditorium of the courthouse in Cape Town was packed for the chief of police's press conference, and the atmosphere was electric. Photographers and journalists squeezed up against the platform where Superintendent Krüge, in his dress uniform, was delivering the preliminary conclusions of the investigation.

Twelve dead, including two policemen, six people in hospital in a critical condition—the operation in the township of Khayelitsha had ended in carnage. What with the FNB's anticrime campaign, the presidential elections looming, and all the things the damned World Cup meant to the economy and the media, Karl Krüge was facing early retirement if he didn't pull this off.

The first part of his speech was a paean of praise for the Crime Unit, which had gotten rid of the Mafia-related gang and the killer of the two young women, but the rest of it evaded the issue. There was no resurgence of Zulu identity, no disappointed Inkatha members ready to take on the rest of the country, demanding secession or independence. There were no extremist political factions, no resentful ethnic groups, just a gang of mercenaries with Mafia links selling a new drug on the peninsula, and their leader, Sam Gulethu, a *tsotsi* stupefied by years of extreme violence, who saw himself as some kind of exterminating angel, led by some kind of indigenous vision, a jumble of vague beliefs, homemade witchcraft, revenge, and chronic degeneration, a coward who had taken advantage of the innocence of white youth to settle scores with his old demons.

The Wiese/Montgomery case was closed. The country wasn't facing social breakdown, just a lot of economic problems.

Ignored by the flashlights, Ali Neuman watched the scene with a vague sense of embarrassment.

He had just been speaking to Maia on the telephone. They had arranged to meet in Manenberg, where Gulethu had lived. Every step he took was like a knife to the heart, but he could still move. The journalists were jostling one another in front of the platform, where Krüge was sweating in his impeccable uniform. Neuman left the courthouse before the press conference was over.

Brian Epkeen hadn't even bothered to show up.

2.

The Cape wine road was one of the loveliest routes in the country. The vineyards at the foot of the mountain, the architecture of the French and Dutch mansions, the wildness of the rock against the blue of the sky, the dense, pervasive vegetation, the restaurant menus—a paradise on earth, for those who could afford it.

For Sunday lunch, Brian and Ruby used to come to La Colombe, a gourmet restaurant owned by a French chef, where they would blow a week's money on one meal. They may have maintained their anti-establishment credentials in the few underground venues of a city condemned to the pastoral boredom of "separate development," and lived from hand to mouth more often than they should have, but when the weekend came he and Ruby didn't make do with fish and chips—no, they deserved an à la carte lunch washed down with Chardonnay and Shiraz from the valley, come what may. They would spend hours drinking in the shade of the amorous cypresses, relaxing in the restaurant's pool talking about her famous record label, the indie groups she was going to produce to get up the nose of this regime of sexual retards, before working off their own frustrations in the bushes. The good old days. Those boozy Sunday lunches hadn't lasted. David had come along, and it had gotten harder to make ends meet—most of Brian's black clients couldn't pay for his services, and it was Ruby who provided for the household. Then there were the frayed nerves whenever the police or the intelligence services came down on him, making their lives hell with petty little bureaucratic or legal obstacles, not to mention all the times he'd been left beaten up in a ditch, the fear of a phone call announcing that this time he wasn't going to make it, his attempts to reassure her, her pathological mistrust, and then the day she had caught him in town with a black woman, in a position that left no room for misunderstanding.

The breeze stirred the ashes in the driver's compartment of the Mercedes. Brian turned off the sun-drenched road and drove between the vines.

Ruby had come back into his life just when everything seemed to be going wrong, and there had to be a reason for that. Unable to understand, Brian drove on through the countryside.

The Broschendal estate was two hundred years old, and was one of the most famous vineyards in the country—like all migrants, the French Huguenots had come here with their own expertise and the means to develop it. Brian drove past the fields of vines to the next property, a former farm that could be glimpsed at the end of the trail.

A chorus of cicadas greeted him in the sun-drenched yard. A bull mastiff with glistening jowls advanced toward him, baring its teeth. It was the property's guard dog, stocky, powerful, weighing more than a hundred and thirty pounds, and capable of knocking a man to the ground and pinning him there.

"So, big man, getting enough to eat?"

The dog was suspicious. It was right to be—Brian wasn't afraid of dogs.

The dentist's house stood on the side of a hill, a tastefully refurbished former farmhouse. Snapdragons, cosmos, azaleas, petunias—the garden that bordered the vineyard filled the air with fragrance from beyond the left wing of the building. Brian walked past the ceramic swimming pool, and found his ex-wife half-naked on a deckchair in the shade of a Belle Portugaise climbing rosebush.

"Hi, Ruby."

Dozing behind her sunglasses, she had not heard him coming, and she gave a start. "What are you doing here?" she cried, as if her eyes were playing tricks on her.

"Obviously, I've come to see you."

Ruby was wearing a yellow bikini and nothing else. She covered herself with a pareo, then glared at the bull mastiff trotting on the lawn.

"And you, asshole," she said to the dog, "would it hurt you to do your job?"

The animal passed close to them, slavering, and swerved to avoid the gestapo chief who had it in her sights.

Brian put his hands in his pockets. "Has David had the results of his exam yet?"

"Since when have you taken an interest in your son?"

"Since I saw his girlfriend. Can we talk seriously?"

"What about?"

"Kate Montgomery, for instance."

"Do you have a warrant to enter people's houses like this?" She held her pareo tight over her breasts, as if he stank.

"I need to fill in the details," he said, trying to focus. "Kate didn't have any friends, I haven't been able to find out anything about her, and you were the last person to see her alive."

"Why don't they send a real cop?" she said, with disarming frankness.

"Because I'm the craziest of them all."

A mocking little smile played on Ruby's lips. At least he made her laugh.

"I don't think there's anything else I can tell you," she said, softening.

"All the same, I'd like your help. Kate was high when she was killed. Did you know she used to do drugs?"

She sighed. "No. But you didn't need to be Sigmund Freud to see she wasn't quite right in the head."

"Kate was into cutting. You know what that involves?"

"Cutting your skin and watching the blood flow to feel alive, yes. I never saw her do that, if that's what's on your mind, or organize orgies with the local butchers."

"The killer butchered his victims. Maybe he promised to relieve her, or something like that."

"I told you, I didn't know anything about her."

"He knew when Kate would be driving along the coast road," Brian went on. "He was waiting for her near her house to flag her down, pull a gun on her, whatever. It's also possible they'd arranged to meet, and she was lured into a trap. Either way, the murder was premeditated. That means the killer knew her schedule."

"What difference does it make, now he's dead? The case is over, isn't it? They said so on the radio."

"You're responsible for the schedules. One of the crew may have told Gulethu, and made sure Kate fell into the trap, just like the Nicole Wiese case."

"I thought you'd questioned them?"

"I didn't get much from them," he admitted. "But I checked out this death-metal band of yours, all this satanic bullshit, cutting the throats of chickens, crap like that. Is that just to impress teenagers, or are they really interested in the occult?"

"They're all vegetarians," she said.

The tires of a car crunched in the yard, soon followed by the sound of a door opening and closing. A tall, long-haired, unshaven young man appeared at the other end of the garden, baggy jeans hanging down over his calves. David saw his parents by the pool, stopped for a moment in surprise, then came striding toward them.

"What's he doing here?" he asked his mother.

"I already asked him that," she replied.

"How did your exam go?"

"Go back to your girlfriends."

Brian sighed—what a family. "What's wrong with wanting to know?"

"Nobody asked you," David retorted. "Ma, tell him to go."

"Go," she said.

Never far from tears, Brian almost felt like laughing. "Isn't Marjorie with you?" he asked.

"Yes, she's hiding in the vines taking photos of you to sell to porn magazines."

"I love you, too, son."

"Listen, Brian," Ruby intervened. "I've told you everything I know about this business, in other words, nothing. Now, be good, and leave us alone."

The tension rose a notch.

"Would it hurt you to talk to me differently?" Brian said, though clenched teeth.

At that moment, a slim man with graying hair appeared on the shady terrace. He saw Ruby's son with his unkempt hair, Ruby half naked under her pareo, an untidy-looking guy in fatigues, and the guard dog circling around them.

"What's going on? Who are you?"

"Hi, Ricky."

"I haven't introduced you," Ruby cut in, still in her deckchair. "Rick, this is Lieutenant Epkeen, David's father."

Rick frowned. "I thought he was a traffic cop."

Brian gave his ex-wife a look of fake surprise, and she blushed slightly. Apparently, he'd gotten a promotion.

"Not that it makes much difference," she said.

She got up from the deckchair, pulling her pareo around her and lifting her five and a half feet with catlike suppleness. She had always been one hell of a cockteaser. Rick welcomed her into his arms in a protective gesture.

"What are you doing in my house?" he asked.

"Investigating a murder. Nothing to do with our private lives."

"First I heard of it," David said.

"Stay out of this, O.K.?"

"I'm sorry, but she's my mother."

"I said shut up."

"Don't talk to your son like that," Rick intervened. "We're not at the police station here."

"I don't have to take lessons from a specialist in molars," Brian growled.

Rick van der Verskuizen wasn't going to let Brian scare him. "Get out of my house," he hissed. "Get out of my house, or I'll lodge a complaint with your superiors for harassment."

"Rick's right," Ruby said, huddled by his side. "You're jealous of our happiness, that's all."

"Yeah!" David said.

"Is that so?" Brian said, sharply. "And what's the price of your new happiness? What does a girl like you have to do to get all this?"

Ruby's expression changed abruptly.

Ricky took a step toward Brian. "Do you have a warrant to come and insult us in our own home?"

"Would you rather be summoned to headquarters? I've been looking through Kate Montgomery's papers. Seems she had several appointments at your clinic."

"So what? I'm a dentist, I look after teeth."

"Six appointments in a month. That must have been one hell of a toothache!"

"Kate Montgomery had an abscess," Rick said. "I took her on as a priority case, to please Ruby. My patients are very demanding, I don't like to keep them waiting. Which is more than can be said for the police."

Brian's gave a nasty smile. "I know Ruby by heart," he said. "She hates men so much, she always chooses old skirt chasers."

"You're repugnant," Rick bellowed.

"Oh, *I'm* repugnant? Like tooth decay is really pretty."

Ruby had had enough. She threw herself at Brian but he knew her moves by heart. He caught her by the elbow, twisted, and sent her sprawling. She slid over the ceramics, narrowly missed the edge of the diving board, and fell into the turquoise water of the pool. Rick rushed forward, yelling insults that Brian didn't hear. He grabbed the man by the collar of his silk shirt and, with all his strength, flung him in after her.

David, who had not moved, threw his father a dirty look.

"Well?" Brian yelled. "You want to take a dip, too?"

For a moment, David stood there speechless. He saw his mother in the pool, the pareo floating, Rick coming up spitting water, and his father on the terrace, his eyes shiny with tears.

"Fuck this," the prodigal son said. "You're completely sick, you know that?"

Completely.

They were all starting to piss him off.

*

There wasn't much mixing in the townships, where racism and xenophobia were as prevalent as they were anywhere else. The black population was concentrated in Khayelitsha, the coloreds in Manenberg. Maia had lived there for years, and had had her share of "boyfriends" to help her survive. Neuman had hesitated before phoning her—they hadn't spoken since breaking up—but she had immediately agreed to help him.

Gulethu, although a Zulu, had lived in Manenberg, and one of her companions in misfortune may have had dealings with him. And in the end, one of them had in fact agreed to testify for a small sum of money—Ntombi, a country girl now living in a hostel.

The absence of street lighting and the drug trafficking kept most people indoors. Neuman drove slowly, peering at the occasional figures that loomed up in front of the car headlights then vanished again.

"Are you sure you don't want a soda?"

Maia had bought two cans at the local spaza shop, thinking he'd be pleased.

"No. Thanks."

She was wearing a new dress, and her talent for acting as if nothing had happened made him uncomfortable. They had been driving for half an hour around the cracked streets of Manenberg, the cortisone had knocked him out, he felt wary, irritable, impatient.

"So where is this hostel?"

"Next right, I think," Maia replied. "There's an all-night drinks shop, from what Ntombi told me."

Maia wanted to talk to him, to tell him it was okay about the other night, a neighbor had patched up the living-room wall, she'd do other paintings, better ones, she might even have found someone who'd sell them in the city for her. She'd stop relying on boyfriends as a way of making ends meet, if that was what bothered him. He could come more often, stay as long as he liked, they just had to carry on as they'd done before, his codes, his caresses, they just had to carry on as if he had never said anything to her.

Maia caressed the back of his neck. "Are you sure you're O.K.? You look very pale."

A dog ran in front of the wheels of the car. Neuman turned right.

In spite of the prohibitive prices, the local hoboes were gathered outside the reinforced door of the drinks shop, asking through the grille for something that would freeze the smile on their lips. The hostel where Ntombi lived was a little farther on, a cinder-block building with a corrugated-iron roof. They parked the car outside the reinforced door.

Non-existent privacy, terrible hygiene, humiliating living

conditions, TB, AIDS—the hostels were dangerous places, typical products of apartheid-era social planning. They housed migrant workers, unmarried people, ex-convicts, even the occasional poor family with no connections who'd latched onto the "owner" of a bed.

Maia's friend had been *phanding* since she'd arrived in Manenberg five years earlier, and had shared the bed of a local dealer, a permanent resident. Thanks to him, Ntombi didn't have a cement bunk bed in an overcrowded dormitory but a real room, with a mattress, a door with a lock, and a modicum of privacy.

Ntombi's hostel was run by a heavy-lidded colored who was as friendly as an oil tanker. Neuman left him looking at the school exercise book that served as a register. They stepped over the people sleeping in the corridor and made their way to Room 12.

Ntombi was waiting for them by the light of a candle, dressed in a close-fitting bright red dress. She was a round, well-built colored woman, with tired skin. Once the introductions were over, she sat Maia and Neuman down on the bed and offered them an orange-colored drink from her icebox, before tackling the subject that had brought them.

Ntombi had met Sam Gulethu five years earlier, when her destiny had led her to Manenberg. Ntombi was young at the time, not yet twenty, a country girl who couldn't tell the difference between a "boyfriend" and a habitual rapist. Gulethu had taken her under his wing, and they'd slept in different places, depending on what he was dealing. He boasted of belonging to a gang, but she didn't want to know about that, all she wanted was to survive. Gulethu was weird. He liked to be called Mta-gaat, the Sorcerer, as if he had gifts, but mainly he came across as sick.

"He hated everyone," Ntombi said. "Especially women. He beat me all the time. For no reason at all. Or at least . . ."

Ntombi left the sentence unfinished.

"Why did he beat you?" Neuman asked.

"He was crazy. He would say all kinds of things. He said I was possessed by the *ufufuyane*."

The endemic disease that affected young Zulu girls and, in the terminology used, caused them to be "out of control" sexually. A paranoid delusion that seemed to fit what they knew of Gulethu's character.

"You're not Zulu," he said.

"No, but I'm a woman. That was enough for him."

Her eyes wandered over the skirting board, as if the wolf was prowling in the room.

"Was he jealous? Was that why he beat you?"

"No." She shook her head. "No. I could tell him anything, he didn't care. But he'd made up his mind I had the young girls' disease, and that was what he punished me for. He'd get these tempers, really bad tempers, and he'd beat me with whatever he could find. Bicycle chains, sticks, iron bars."

Nicole. Kate. Whites or coloreds, he didn't care.

"Did he make you do drugs?"

"No."

"Did he do drugs himself?"

"He smoked *dagga*," Ntombi replied. "He also drank, with the others. I preferred to keep out of their way when they drank."

"The other members of the gang?"

"Yes."

"Where were they from? Abroad?"

"Mostly they were from the local *shebeen*."

Neuman nodded. Maia, sitting next to him, hadn't batted an eyelid.

"Did Gulethu have a ritual?" he asked. "Particular things he did when he beat you? Things to do with *sangomas*, or Zulu customs?"

Ntombi turned to her friend, who gave her an encouraging look. She stood up and, by the light of the candle, took off her dress.

She was wearing white undergarments, and there were nasty scars on her stomach, waist, buttocks, and thighs. The scars were purple and raised, and ran, strangely, in straight lines.

Neuman's face clouded over. "How did you get those marks?"

"Barbed wire. He'd tie it around me."

"Gulethu?"

He remembered Nicole, the scratches on her arms—rusted iron, according to Tembo.

"Yes," she said. "He'd tell me to strip, and he'd tie me up with barbed wire. The *ufufuyane*." She shuddered. "He said I was possessed. That if I screamed, he'd kill me. He'd leave me like that, on the ground, and he'd call me names—whore, bitch. Then he'd beat me."

Maia sat impassively on the bed—she'd also met a few crazy men in her time.

Ntombi shivered in the middle of the room, but Neuman had stopped looking at her. Gulethu had tried to tie up Nicole with barbed wire, but she wasn't as far gone as he'd anticipated. She'd defended herself, so he'd beaten her to death.

Ntombi put her dress back on, looking anxiously toward the door as if any minute now her boyfriend was going to come in.

"Did he often lose his temper like that?"

"Every time he got aroused," Ntombi replied. "And he always used barbed wire. That was his thing, the filthy pervert. The others didn't know. He said that if I told them, he'd tie me to a car and drag me through the township. I believed him."

"Did he rape you?"

Ntombi laughed. "Oh, no! There was no risk of that."

"Why?" Neuman asked, frowning.

"Gulethu was a mule," she said, scornfully.

A mule, in township slang, was someone who refused all contact with the opposite sex. Neuman felt a pang in his heart. Gulethu beat women, but he didn't touch them. He was afraid of them. He would never have raped Kate. Her death had been stage-managed.

*

Janet Helms had followed up on Brian's lead.

Frank Debeer, the ATD branch manager, was a former *kitskonstable*, one of those policemen trained in three weeks during apartheid to swell the ranks of the vigilantes. After the regime had come to an end, Debeer had been involved with various private police forces, and for the last three years had been running the Hout Bay branch of ATD, one of the most successful security companies—property surveillance, personal protection—with branches throughout the country. The Pinzgauer parked in the garage in Hout Bay matched the description of the suspect vehicle, and Debeer, caught unawares, had admitted being out on patrol that night.

Janet was as good as any hacker around at getting past security systems. What she was doing was illegal, but Epkeen had given her a free hand. She hacked into ATD's computer system and, after a labyrinthine journey through the technological jungle, managed to obtain a list of ATD's shareholders and examine their bank accounts.

The dividends were distributed among half a dozen banks, in other words, the same number as the accounts whose numbers she had acquired. Here, too, the operation was illegal, the results uncertain, but she'd been right. One of the Hout Bay numbers corresponded to the offshore account that had rented the house at Muizenberg.

Tax evasion? Secret funds in a tax haven to finance covert

operations? The ATD dividends were transferred via a South African bank, First National—the very same one that had started the anti-crime campaign. A name appeared: Joost Terreblanche.

Janet continued her research, but there wasn't much information available. Terreblanche was a former colonel in the army, who had taken early retirement when Mandela was elected, and didn't even seem to be living in South Africa anymore. There was an address in Johannesburg, but that was four years old, and after that the trail petered out. It was all a question of method, though. Janet switched her attention to the intelligence services and, once again illicitly, gained access to the army records.

These were more specific. Joost Terreblanche had served in the province of KwaZulu during the apartheid era, as a colonel in the 77th battalion, a unit that recruited and trained men for operations in the Bantustans. Frank Debeer had been a *kit-skonstable* in the same battalion.

She searched through the registers, the files, the commissions. After a while, a name came up on the screen. A sinister name. Wouter Basson.

3.

Wouter Basson (born July 6, 1950). Cardiologist and chemist. Brigadier general and private doctor to President Pieter Botha. Begins his career in 1984, when, fearing a Communist biochemical attack, General Viljoen, head of South African defense, develops a special unit for Chemical and Biological Warfare (CBW). Code name: Project Coast.

Wouter Basson is asked to set up a military laboratory at Roodeplast, in the suburbs of Pretoria. With the threat of Mandela and his program (one man, one vote), the authorities realize that the demographics are against them. Basson recruits two hundred scientists, given the task by the CCB (Civil Cooperation Bureau) of developing chemical weapons—sugar containing salmonella, cigarettes containing anthracene, beer containing thallium, chocolate containing cyanide, whisky containing colchicine, and deodorant containing S. typhimurium—with the aim of eliminating anti-apartheid militants, not only in South Africa but also in Mozambique, Swaziland, and Namibia. (Number of victims still unknown.) Basson pursues his secret research and comes up with a deadly molecule, sensitive to the melanin in black people's skin pigmentation. Carries out studies on the spreading of epidemics in the African population, mass sterilization of black women through the water supply, etc. Despite signing treaties on the non-proliferation of biological and chemical weapons, and despite the anti-apartheid embargo, the United Kingdom, the United States, Israel, Switzerland, France, Iraq, and Libya cooperate in the laboratory's programs *until 1990, when the new president, De Klerk, calls a halt to the production of chemical agents and orders them to be destroyed.*

Project Coast is dismantled in 1993, and an internal inquiry is held into Basson's activities, but in 1995 he is hired by the Mandela government to work with Transnet, a company specializing in transportation and infrastructure, before joining the armed forces medical unit as a surgeon.

In 1996, the Truth and Reconciliation Commission under Desmond Tutu investigates the activities of the security forces in the field of biological and chemical weapons. Basson tries to leave South Africa, and is arrested in Pretoria, carrying large quantities of ecstasy and a number of confidential documents. He is charged not only with tax fraud and drug production on a massive scale but also with some sixty murders and attempted murders, the intended victims including such high-profile figures as Nelson Mandela, and Rev. Frank Chikane, adviser to the future President Mbeki.

1998: Basson, dubbed Doctor Death, appears before the Commission. Refuses to ask for amnesty. Sixty-seven of the charges against him are accepted, including possession of drugs, drug trafficking, fraud, 229 murders and attempted murders, and theft. The prosecution presents 153 witnesses, including ex-officers from the special forces, who tell stories of opponents anaesthetized or poisoned and thrown out of planes into the sea. The trial drags on.

1999: Presiding Judge Hartzenberg, brother of the president of the South African Conservative Party that was in office during the apartheid regime, reduces the number of charges to 46.

2001: Basson presents his defense, claiming that his actions were on the level. Several military figures from the apartheid era speak in support of him, including General Viljoen, former head of the high command, now an Afrikaner nationalist politician, and Magnus Malan, Minister of Defense during the events in question. Three CD-roms listing Basson's experiments suddenly disappear.

2002: Basson, who has pleaded guilty throughout the longest trial in the country's legal history, is acquitted by Judge Hartzenberg.

The South African State appeals to the Supreme Court, which refuses a new trial. Wouter Basson is safe from further prosecution. "A dark day for South Africa," Desmond Tutu declares.

Today, Basson lives in a well-to-do suburb of Pretoria and is again working as a cardiologist, with a position at the Academic Hospital.

NOTE: Joost Terreblanche, colonel in the 77th battalion, took part in Project Coast until 1993, when it was dismantled. He was in charge of equipment delivery, and the maintenance and security of the research sites.

Neuman put Janet Helms's report down on the table and looked at Brian. The three of them had arranged to meet in a bar in the Waterfront, the shopping complex in the city's harbor area. Close by the terrace, a group of "ethnic" con artists were joylessly playing a selection of tunes tailor-made for the sandal-clad tourists. Neuman hadn't said why they were meeting here rather than at headquarters. Janet had showed up without asking any questions, in her uniform that was too tight for her, files under her arm.

"What do you think?"

"Same as you, Big Chief," Brian replied. "We've been led down the garden path." He blew out cigarette smoke, one eye on the document supplied by Janet. "The Muizenberg house, the Pinzgauer at the ADT branch, the offshore account. Sounds like Terreblanche is back on duty."

"Yes. Apparently the aim of the operation isn't to get young people on drugs, as it was in the apartheid days, but quite simply to eliminate them. The *tik* base to hook the user, the virus to kill him."

"Basson's done all this before," Brian said. "Do you think the old bastard's still involved?"

On the other side of the table, her nose in a milkshake that wasn't going to make things any better for her, Janet Helms was asking herself the same question.

"No," Neuman said. "Basson knows he's too closely watched. But Terreblanche is in on it. He and his accomplices."

"Debeer?"

"Among others."

The seal that had been basking on the edge of the jetty for the last half hour finally dived into the harbor, to the delight of the crowds. The waiter asked Brian to put out his cigarette—the terrace was a non-smoking area—but Brian sent him packing.

"O.K.," he said. "Let's assume Terreblanche and his cronies produced a fatal drug, and were using Gulethu's gang to sell it on the peninsula. Let's assume the Muizenberg house was their hideout, that the gang was given the job of providing security, and that the premises were cleaned out when we got too close, leaving a few bodies in the cellar to put us off the scent. Let's also assume that Simon and his gang were minions in the operation. *Tik* or Mandrax would have been enough to keep them on a leash. What was the point in giving them this new crap, too?"

"To limit their life expectancy," Neuman said. "The incubation period is too long for it to have been detected in Nicole or Kate, but the surfer in False Bay and Simon contracted the same virus several weeks ago. A strain of AIDS, which was added to the drug. That means all the people who took it are now infected. Unless they're treated soon, they have only a few months to live."

"Which also means it's not the young whites on the coast who were the targets, but the kids in the township."

"So it seems."

Janet Helms was taking notes in her notebook, her lips sugary from the milkshake.

Brian swore into his espresso. "And where the hell's Terreblanche?"

"For the moment," Neuman said, "nowhere."

"I didn't find anything in the SAP files," Janet said, "or in social security or the health service. Just a note in the army records."

"How can that be?"

"No idea," she said. "Terreblanche part-owns a number of South African companies, but hasn't lived here for years. At the same time, it's impossible to track him down abroad. I've looked in the army records but there's practically nothing about him. Just his service record and the fact that he was part of Doctor Death's Project Coast."

"We could at least try talking to the Attorney General, get him to authorize an investigation," Brian suggested.

"He'd send us packing," Neuman said. "We don't have anything, Brian. Just information obtained illegally and twenty-year-old data on a case that's completely closed. Purchasing a house via an offshore account and patrolling in a Pinzgauer on the night of a murder aren't indictable crimes. We need evidence."

Through loudspeakers, a recorded voice advised tourists not to venture beyond the gates of the complex, as if a horde of gangsters were waiting to rob them.

Brian lit another cigarette. "I can try leaning on Debeer," he said.

"That would risk alerting Terreblanche," Neuman objected. "I don't want him to get away. Janet," he said, turning to the milkshake addict, "I need a list of everyone who collaborated with Basson on Project Coast, with their addresses and phone numbers, all the info you can find. Terreblanche may have recruited some of his former chemists into this business. Look in the special services files, the army records. I don't care how you do it."

Janet nodded over the creamy leftovers. She would hack into the Pentagon's computers if he asked her.

"Can you get into computer networks without leaving a trace?" he asked.

"Er . . . yes. As long as you have the codes and a secure computer, it can be done. But it's risky, captain."

All the same, she was putting her career on the line.

"There've been too many leaks in this case," Neuman said. "If Kate Montgomery was killed in such a way as to make it look like Gulethu's work and get the case declared closed, that means Terreblanche and his accomplices had access to the postmortem reports. Or even our own files."

"I thought they were secure?" Brian said.

"So were the army records Janet looked at."

Brian made an exasperated gesture. There was corruption at all levels of society, from the individual buying stolen equipment on a street corner to the ruling elite. Tax evasion, fraud, financial irregularities, fiddling of accounts—two-thirds of the leaders were implicated.

"Janet, do you feel up to it?"

She nodded with almost military stiffness. "Yes, captain."

Playing at being a soldier.

"O.K. I want you to concentrate on Project Coast. Brian, take a look at the ADT office in Hout Bay. See if you can find something, papers, anything. The four-by-four wasn't in the vicinity of the Muizenberg house for no reason, and they took the risk of leaving those bodies in the cellar because they were trying to hide something else."

Brian followed his reasoning. "Their traces."

"Presumably. Covered up by all the blood and shit."

Janet abandoned what was left of her milkshake.

"What do you think was in the house?" Brian asked. "A drug factory?"

"That's for you to find out." He gave Brian a knowing look. "Be discreet. I'll take care of the rest. Let's meet again tomorrow morning, same place. Shall we say eight o'clock? Until then, let's keep communication to a minimum."

Neuman needed Krüge's authorization for a large-scale raid in the township. If, as he believed, Gulethu had been sacrificed during the suicide attack on the *shebeen*, then Mzala and the Americans were accomplices. They couldn't be arrested without a ruckus.

The last ferry from Robben Island was returning on the evening breeze by the time they finished working out the final details of their plan. Janet Helms was the first to leave, school exercise book under her arm, heels clicking on the floor, off to look for her precious codes. Brian went to the bar to pay, and Neuman took advantage of his absence to make a call.

Zina picked up at the first ring. "So," she laughed, "left your sarcophagus, did you?"

"Let's say I'm fond of my bandages. Am I disturbing you?"

"I'm going onstage in three minutes."

"I won't be long."

"We have time."

"Not sure of that."

"Why? Do you still think I'm a terrorist?"

"Yes—that's why you're going to help me."

"So nicely put. Help you with what?"

"I'm looking for a man," he said. "Joost Terreblanche, a former army colonel who's gone into the security business, with numbered accounts in tax havens and a fog of mystery surrounding his activities."

Zina blew into the phone. "You're pissing me off, Ali."

"Terreblanche has disappeared from our records, but I'm sure he's still in yours."

"What are you talking about?"

"Inkatha's records."

"I don't give a fuck about Inkatha."

"That wasn't always the case."

"I've given up politics! All I do now is dance and put together stupid powders for idiots like you, or hadn't you noticed?"

Dead kisses were raining on the deserted terrace.

"I need you," he said.

"Not as much as I do, *Ali*."

He kept glancing toward the entrance, where Brian might appear at any moment. He didn't want to be seen talking to her.

"Terreblanche worked with Doctor Basson," Neuman resumed in a low voice, "but never testified before the Truth and Reconciliation Commission. Someone's protecting him. His name has virtually disappeared from our records. Inkatha must surely have kept a file on him, with information we don't have access to."

"I don't belong to Inkatha anymore," Zina said.

"But you still have contacts. One of your musicians is the brother of Joe Ntsabula, who's close to Chief Buthelezi, and Joe is an old friend of yours, isn't he?"

She said nothing.

"Terreblanche has a base somewhere," he insisted. "Either abroad, or here in South Africa."

"Is that all you could find to trap me?"

"You said the word 'trap,' not me. It's Terreblanche's skin I want, not yours."

"Really?"

He sensed her hesitation. "This'll be strictly between the two of us," he assured her.

She brooded at the other end of the phone. The stage manager was making panic-stricken signs in the doorway of the dressing room—it was time.

"I have to go," she said.

"This is urgent."

"I'll call you."

"*Ngiyabonga.*"[1]

Neuman hung up just as Brian came out of the bar. Brian threw the check in the garbage, and saw his friend standing there in the middle of the terrace, looking distraught.

"Did you talk to the Inkatha girl?"

"Yes," he said. "She's having a look on her side."

The walkways of the Waterfront had emptied.

Brian went closer to Neuman. "What's going on?"

"Nothing."

But for a moment Brian thought Neuman was going to cry.

"Send me a message when you get back from Hout Bay," Neuman said, cutting things short. "We'll meet tomorrow morning."

Brian nodded, his heart in a vise. "Bye, Cassandra."

"Yeah, bye."

A horrible feeling. As if they were seeing each other for the last time.

*

The stuff had all been collected, the samples, the tests, the hard disk. Terreblanche closed the second trunk and looked up at Debeer, who'd just entered the room.

"Someone's gotten into our files," Debeer announced.

"What do you mean, someone's gotten into our files?"

"A hacker."

Terreblanche's face went red. "What was in the files?"

"The company's accounts. The cop who came here the other day was looking for a Pinzgauer. Maybe they've made a connection with the house."

[1] Thanks.

The police hadn't risen to the bait. They knew the vehicle existed. Terreblanche hesitated a few seconds, connected the working circuits in his brain, and soon felt reassured. There was no way they could trace things back to him, unless they caught him red-handed, and it was too late for that. Everything was ready, finalized, the lab had been destroyed, the research team was already abroad. They just had to get the stuff out—the plane was ready—and wipe out the last traces.

"How many men are left?"

"Four, including me," Debeer replied. "Plus the two workers."

They didn't know a thing. They could leave a security guard at the office, the others would come with him. Terreblanche picked up his cell phone and dialed Mzala's number.

The rooms situated in back of the *shebeen* had been spared during the shootout. The sticks of incense burning near the knife couldn't hide the smell of feet, but Mzala didn't care. He was in the middle of getting a blow job on the straw mattress he used as a bed when his cell phone rang—the ringtone was a burst of machine-gun fire downloaded from the Internet, which always made people laugh. He pushed away the fat girl in a bra slobbering over his cock, saw the number on the display—what did that asshole want now?—and stuck the girl's head back again.

"Yeah?"

Terreblanche wasn't in a playful mood. "I want you to throw a big party tonight in honor of the Americans," he announced in a voice that didn't match the event. "Tell all your friends to be there with flowers in their buttonholes."

"That won't get them excited!" Mzala laughed. "What are we celebrating?"

"Victory over a rival gang, the money that'll be coming in soon, whatever you like. Drinks on the house."

Mzala screwed up his eyes, while making sure the girl was still doing her job.

"That's nice, boss. What's this all about?"

"You just have to keep an eye on what they drink," Terreblanche said. "I'll supply the sleeping powder and the after-sales service. The important thing is that everyone involved should be there tonight. We have to be out of here by dawn."

Mzala abruptly forgot all about the girl, her large breasts crushing his balls. This was the Big Night.

"A clean sweep before we leave, is that it?"

"A clean sweep, right. I'll be at the church around seven-thirty to hand over the material."

"O.K.."

"One more thing. I don't want a single witness left. Not one."

"You can trust me," Mzala assured him.

"No way I'd risk that," Terreblanche said. "I need you to bring me proof. Do whatever you have to. No evidence, no money, is that clear?"

Mzala's mind wandered over a carpet of blood. "Very clear," he said, hanging up.

The girl sucking him off was moaning, her fat ass in the air, as if being mounted by a thousand bulls. Mzala smiled as she sucked him rhythmically. He thought of her big breasts dangling over his balls, her round throat that would soon receive his sperm, the knife lying next to the straw mattress, and came very quickly.

*

"Do you still need me, Mr. Van der Verskuizen?"

It was seven in the evening and Martha had finished for the day.

"No, no, Martha," he said. "You can go home!"

The secretary smiled back, grabbed her pink purse from behind the counter, and opened the door.

"See you tomorrow, Mr. Van der Verskuizen."

"See you tomorrow, Martha."

Rick watched her as she left the clinic. He had only just hired her, she was still on probation. Martha, a blonde fresh from the employment agency, who must have the tightest pussy in the southern hemisphere—ha ha! He had just gotten rid of his last patient, a tiresome architect who was suffering from an abscess caused by a stray wisdom tooth. He had managed to land him with six appointments. If you have money, you might as well spend it, right?

There was a knock at the door of the clinic. Martha must have forgotten something. Her knickers maybe—ho ho ho. He opened the reinforced door, and his oily smile froze as if he'd just been given an anesthetic.

Ruby.

"You look surprised. Were you expecting someone else?"

"No, of course not!" he cried, taking her by the arm. "It's just that you never come to the clinic. Everything O.K., darling?"

Rick had regained his George Clooney smile, the one he used on local celebrities, to show them they were equals. He drew Ruby into his office, with its huge plate-glass window looking out on Table Mountain.

"I just have to find a few papers, and then I'm all yours."

"I was talking to your old secretary on the phone earlier," Ruby said, her voice sounding exaggeratedly calm. "She told me you were quite intimate with your younger patients."

"What?"

"No need to look so scared."

He'd seen Ruby in this state before. It wasn't how he liked her. He liked her wild ass, her solar energy, her passion, the hope that had driven her into his arms, but her uncontrollable side completely put him off the idea of marriage.

"Well?" she insisted.

"Fay's a little tramp," Rick hissed. "A tramp who lies as easily as drawing breath!"

"For a liar, she has quite a memory," Ruby said. "She's particularly good on names and times of appointments."

"What are you talking about?"

"Kate Montgomery was always your last patient of the day," she said. "She always arrived just as your secretary was leaving. What do you think of that?"

"My God, Ruby," he said, imploringly. "We chose times that were convenient for her! What on earth will you think up next?"

Ruby wouldn't let go. "Admit you slept with Kate," she spat.

"You're crazy!"

"At least admit you tried to sleep with her!" Her eyes were glittering with rage. A madwoman. He was living with a madwoman.

"Ruby, I'm telling you the truth! I never had relations with Kate Montgomery. Jesus! *I was looking after her teeth!*"

"With your dick."

Rick closed his eyes and put his face in his hands. He had never slept with Kate. She wouldn't have wanted it. Unless it was the one thing she had wanted. In any case, she was a sensitive girl, a girl with problems. He cared for his patients, in every sense of the term—the main thing was to keep them. Rick sighed, suddenly weary. He was hemmed in on all sides, and now Ruby showing up here like a fury.

"It was that bloody cop," he said at last. "That bloody cop put all these stupid ideas in your head, didn't he?"

Through the window, a plane passed in the sky. Ruby lowered her head.

She didn't want to admit it. She felt ashamed of her desperation. Suspicion and resentment were playing dirty tricks on her. She always expected the worst—worse still, she provoked it. She was eating her own tail, like a fucking scorpion, stinging herself with her own poison. Her need to be loved and protected was too strong. The world had abandoned her before, when she was thirteen. Ruby felt confused, torn between two realities. She didn't believe either of them. Rick was standing there, a few feet away, waiting for a gesture from her, a gesture of love. But something still told her that she was right, that she was going to be betrayed yet again. Ruby gritted her teeth, but her lips were quivering by themselves. Her lips were going to move without her. Her lips were moving without her.

"Take me," she whispered. "Take me in your arms."

*

Josephina had passed the information around the clubs and associations in the township. They were mostly run by women, charitably minded women who fought hard so that the rats could survive the sinking ship. The kids her son was looking for were lost children. Ali could have been in the same situation if he hadn't fled the militias that had killed his father. And all these children who were going to lose their mothers to AIDS, the orphans who would soon be swelling the ranks of the unfortunate—if they didn't take care of them, who else would? The government had quite enough on its hands already, what with urban violence, unemployment, the mistrust of investors, and this World Cup everyone was talking about.

But she was in luck. Mahimbo, a friend from the Churches of Zion, had contacted her. She had seen two boys matching the description ten days earlier, near Lengezi—a slender boy in green shorts and a younger one in a khaki shirt, with a scar on his neck. There was a church in Lengezi, on the edge of an open space, where they tried to provide food for the most disadvantaged. The priest had a young maid, Sonia Parker, who ran a soup kitchen at least once a week—she may have seen them often. Sonia Parker didn't have a telephone, but she finished work at seven, after the evening service.

It was now ten after seven.

The bus had dropped her half a mile from the church. But Josephina was getting over her pains. She walked up the street, trusting the shadows, and made out the church in the gathering darkness. The area was deserted. People preferred to stay in and watch TV in their own houses or at a neighbor's house if he had one, rather than wander aimlessly and risk running into some crazy person coming out of a *shebeen*. A dog without a tail walked alongside her, intrigued by her stick. She stopped on the steps of the church to catch her breath, big beads of sweat on her forehead. A few stars hovered in the petroleum-blue sky. Josephina felt the plywood planks under her feet with her stick, and hoisted her weight to the wooden door.

She didn't have to knock, it was open.

"Is anyone there?" she called into the shadows.

The chairs seemed empty. The altar was in darkness.

"Sonia?"

Josephina couldn't see any light, and smelled a familiar smell as she approached the great hanging Christ. A sooty smell. The candles had not long been blown out.

"Sonia?"

She waddled to the altar, which was covered in a white cloth, and looked up at the cross. The martyred Son of God looked down at her passively.

It suddenly felt cooler under the vaults of the church, as if there was a draft, chilling her. Josephina sensed a presence behind her, a still indistinct shape that had emerged from behind a pillar.

"Well, well. What are you doing here, Big Mama?"

She froze. The Cat was lurking in the shadows.

4

The night wind coming in through the window covered the distorted sound of Cop Shoot Cop on the car radio. It was two in the morning on the M63, which ran toward the south coast of the peninsula. Brian Epkeen was driving fast, his equipment strewn over the seat. According to what Janet Helms had found out during her hacking session, the ADT building had a security camera on the outside, which covered the entrance and most of the forecourt, but not the garage. A security guard in an ATD uniform patrolled on the outside, linked by radio to a colleague inside watching the TV monitors. There was a switchboard operator in reception to take calls and contact the night teams crisscrossing the area.

When Brian reached the outskirts of Hout Bay, he slowed down. The town was empty at this time of night. He drove past the harbor restaurants and the deserted parking lot, and parked the Mercedes at the far end of the jetties. The cry of a seagull echoed from the direction of the sea. He grabbed the equipment from the seat. It was years since he'd last done this kind of thing. He took a deep breath to relieve the stress creeping up his legs. There wasn't a soul near the landing stages. He put on a black ski mask, checked he had all his gear, and set off into the night.

The fish warehouses were padlocked, the nets piled up. He wormed his way between the pallets, reached the sheds, and stood waiting in their shadows. The ADT building stood out beneath the mouse-gray clouds. The only sounds were the wavelets lapping the hulls of the trawlers and the wind in the wooden buildings. A beam of light soon appeared from around the east wing of the former mansion—the security guard, his cap pulled down on his head. He didn't have a dog, but there was a holster and a club hanging from his leather belt. Brian calculated the length of his round: he had exactly three minutes and sixteen seconds before the man's alter ego sitting at the monitor got worried. He let the guard turn the corner and then, avoiding the eye of the camera, ran to the garage.

Three clouds passed beneath the intermittent moon. Brian was starting to sweat inside his ski mask, which stank of mothballs. The security guard finally reappeared at the corner of the building. Brian tightened his grip on his baton, his back up against the wall of the garage. The beam of the torch passed in front of him. The man didn't have time to make a move before the baton hit him on the back of his head, at the top of the spinal cord. Brian held him as he fell and pulled him under cover. The security guard, a white with a crew cut, looked as if he had fallen asleep. Brian took a handkerchief from his pocket, soaked it in chloroform, and pressed it over the man's nose— that'd leave him feeling woozy for several hours. Two minutes forty seconds—avoiding the camera, he ran to the south wing.

The windows on the first floor were barred, but not those on the second floor. He tightened the straps of his small backpack and, supporting himself on the rim of the gutter, hoisted himself onto the balcony. Then he took out a crowbar, and wedged the end of it under the wooden window frame. The wood yielded in a terrible splintering noise. He grimaced, and climbed in.

The second-floor room was obviously used as a junk room. There were two padlocked trunks against the wall, piles of crates. No noise. Brian softly opened the door. At the end of the corridor, there was light coming up from the first floor. One minute. He walked softly to the stairs, forgetting about the seconds. He could hear voices from downstairs, a man and a woman, laughing in front of the TV monitors. He walked down the stairs, gripping his baton.

"How about the blonde who sees a boat in the desert, know that one?"

"No."

"Well, this blonde and this brunette are in a car, and they see a boat in the middle of the desert, and the brunette says . . ."

The security guard was sitting on a swivel chair, with his back to the door. Standing by the monitors, the switchboard operator was drinking in his words, smiling in advance. She suddenly opened her eyes wide in surprise, cried out with her hands raised to her mouth, but too late—the baton hit the back of her colleague's neck. The man swiveled in the chair and collapsed at her feet, small feet squeezed into moccasins with pompons, which didn't dare move.

"No." She tried to struggle. "No!!!"

Easily controlling her feeble writhing, Brian grabbed her by the neck and pressed the soaked handkerchief to her face. She twitched for a moment, then fell like some bold princess into his arms. He laid her out on the floor, administered a dose of chloroform to the security guard, and at last took off his stinking, sweat-soaked ski mask. He felt a little dizzy, but he had no time to waste—if they couldn't make radio contact, one of the patrols would come straight back.

The central computer was in an office on the first floor. Janet Helms had already visited it. He searched in the files stored on the shelves, came across figures, reports, client lists. It would take hours to go through them carefully. There was a ringing from the switchboard in the adjoining office. He went upstairs. The metal crates he had glimpsed earlier were lined up against the wall, two big trunks without names or destinations. With the crowbar, Brian forced the padlock on one of them. Inside were rows of tubes neatly laid out and protected by foam rubber, hundreds of samples with incomprehensible labels. He extracted one of them and took a good look at the liquid. Blood.

He put the sample in his pocket, glanced unnecessarily at the window, and forced open the second trunk, which immediately yielded. In it was a hard disk, packed in polystyrene. Brian lifted it out and placed it on the wooden floor. Then he aimed his torch at the other contents of the trunk. Sachets of powder, hundreds of doses wrapped in plastic. Same texture, same color as the drug found in the mobile home. He thought he heard the sound of a car in the yard. At the same moment, the telephone rang downstairs.

Brian looked feverishly at his watch. The quarter of an hour he had given himself had passed. He put his stinking ski mask back on, stuffed the hard disk in his backpack, took two of the sachets of powder, and left.

*

(1) Persons suffering from a deficiency of neurotransmitters (NTs) are especially susceptible to many of the conditions peculiar to Western man: obesity, depression, anxiety, insomnia, menopausal problems, etc. In depressives, several areas of the brain, relating to mood, appetite, sleep, sexual desire, and memory, are disturbed. Apart from the hypophysis, all these areas are part of the limbic system and usually receive signals from the neurons that secrete serotonin and noradrenalin. A decrease in the activity of the serotonergic and noradrenergic circuits contributes to the establishment of a depressive state. According to our studies, many depressions seem to be the result of disturbances of the cerebral circuits that use monoamines as neuromediators. The most common antidepressants on sale in Europe and the United States, such as Prozac, work by artificially increasing the level of serotonin in the synapses of the neurons affected by

these conditions. Find the gene that makes it possible to achieve a sufficient regulated level of this NT and you will have "supermen": no more obesity, no more anxiety, depression, insomnia. In the same way, we could be subjected to the most extreme stress without the mind being affected. This is a potential goldmine, with customers numbering in the hundreds of millions.

2) In our research, we focused on the intracellular enzyme MAO (monoamine oxide), which modulates synaptic concentration and degrades the monoamines (serotonin and noradrenalin). Its gene was cloned, as were the prior areas that allow its regulation. The pieces of the DNA corresponding to this enzyme were therefore successfully introduced into an AAV. This viral vector was successfully tested on monkeys. We used gene therapy in vivo, *which consists of injecting the vector carrying the gene of therapeutic interest directly into the bloodstream in such a way as to specifically reach the target cells.*

As the side effects of this kind of substance can only be seen on human subjects, we prepared and tested these recombinants on specified persons.

After much trial and error, linked to the problems of hypertension and, above all, of increasingly violent suicidal reactions, we can now state confidently that these tests were positive.

3) In addition, we selected a strain of HIV-1-4 before proceeding to the obtaining of viruses mutated into the gene of gp41. This glycoprotein possesses the peptide corresponding to an area responsible for the interaction with caveolin, a protein of the cellular membrane which, in association with other constituent parts of the membrane, is involved in the internalization of external elements, such as viruses. This area of gp41, known as CBD1, plays a major role during the infection of cells by HIV. The mutation, unlike the research developed by our colleagues, allows a larger and more effective penetration of the T4s. The virus thus becomes capable of infecting and destroying 80% of the T4s in a matter of weeks. Persons infected by this "super-

virus" die from opportunistic diseases before they have even been
found to be HIV positive.
The virus was successfully introduced into 100% of the sub-
jects treated.

Brian read the document for the third time.

His adrenalin had dropped since his nocturnal excursion to
Hout Bay. The computer was purring in the bedroom at the
back, David's room, which had been empty for ages—there
was still a Nirvana poster on the wall, in the upper-left-hand
corner hanging at half-mast, as a sign of mourning.

It was 5:43 by the alarm clock. He was starting to feel
sleepy. He was supposed to be meeting Ali and Janet in a couple of hours and he wasn't sure he had grasped all the ins and
outs of the case, let alone the technical gibberish written by the
director of research. Charles Rossow, his name was. A specialist in molecular biology. Brian had clicked the icons on the
hard disk he'd stolen from the trunk at Hout Bay, and found
files with cryptic names, containing series of charts, details of
experiments, and various analyses, in a jargon that was almost
incomprehensible to a layman. But he had understood the gist.
Goldmine, virus. This file was dynamite.

He made two copies of the hard disk, and stuffed the memory sticks in the pocket of his black fatigues. 5:52 now by the
old alarm clock. Brian still stank from his earlier stress. As he
contemplated taking a shower, his eyes wandered over the
posters in this room that he had transformed into an office.
David. The prodigal son. Top of his class. He was jolted out of
his lethargy by a strident beep from the fax machine next to
the printer. Yawning, Brian peered at the machine. There was
no sender's name, not even a number. A list of names soon
appeared on the glazed paper. A message from Janet Helms—
three pages detailing the structure and membership of Project
Coast.

He tore off the roll and looked through the document. There were two hundred names in all, with the skills and specialties of Wouter Basson's various colleagues. Brian went straight to the letter *R* and found what he was looking for. Rossow. Charles Rossow, specialist in molecular biology.

Neuman had been right. Terreblanche had recruited the scientist to develop a revolutionary new kind of chemistry. They had conducted secret experiments, enjoying protection and collusion from all sides. He sent a text to Janet Helms's cell phone by way of reply, confirming the Rossow lead—she still had two hours before she met them at the Waterfront. Epkeen reread the fax in detail, from the top. Burger, Du Plessis, Donk . . . Terreblanche, Van Haas, Van der Linden . . . He was just lighting another cigarette when his eye fell on a name at the bottom of the list. Van der Verskuizen. First name Rick.

"Shit."

Rick van der Verskuizen was on the Project Coast roster.

That toupéed fashion plate had worked with Basson and Terreblanche . . . Kate Montgomery. The dentist. It was him, he was the accomplice, the man who had been waiting for Kate on the coast road.

A slight noise made him prick up his ears. A creaking in the rafters, his imagination, exhaustion? The wind was blowing outside. He held his breath. Silence. Brian was about to take a shower when he heard another noise, this one much nearer. His heart started pounding. This time he was sure of it: someone was coming up the stairs. David? The floorboards creaked, somewhere very close. He flattened himself against the wall of the bedroom. The steps had come closer, they were in the corridor—at least two people. He saw the hard disk connected to his computer, the holster on the Red Indian bedspread, contemplated diving for his .38, thought better of it as the door burst open and thudded against the wall. Two figures rushed into the room, Debeer and another man, and began spraying the room with bullets. They were using Walther 7.65s with silencers. The feathers from the pillow on David's bed went flying, while Debeer demolished the computer. The killers looked for their prey through the shower of plaster, saw the figure climbing through the window, and opened fire at the very moment it threw itself into the void.

A bullet whistled past Brian's ear and hit the wall of the house next door. He landed in the flowerbed and ran across the lawn. Four more bullets decapitated a few innocent stalks and pursued him toward the garden. He felt a pain, and took refuge behind the corner of the wall. He heard muffled voices cursing above his head, then the sound of boots rushing to the stairs. He ran toward the gate.

Debeer jumped from the second floor but, not being very agile, twisted his ankle as he landed and yelped with pain. He waved his gun in the darkness. All he could see at the end of the silencer was flowers.

Brian dashed into the empty street and ran to the Mercedes, parked ten yards away. He had the keys in his pocket and fear in his belly. Feverishly, he opened the door, switched on the ignition, and put the car in first gear. A stocky figure came running out through the open gate. The tires of the Mercedes screeched on the asphalt. The killer stood still and fired from twenty yards. The rear windshield shattered as he was pressing his foot on the accelerator. The other shots were smothered by the clatter of the firing pin.

Brian turned right at the first corner. He didn't have his gun, or his cell phone. Cold sweat was trickling between his shoulder blades. Shards of glass from the rear windshield had flown as far as the dashboard.

It was 6:01 by the clock. That was when he saw bloodstains on the seat.

*

Ruby couldn't sleep. After endless talking and torrents of tears snatched from the nothingness surrounding her, she and Rick had ended up fucking. He had convinced her that she was the only woman in his life, and in his bed. It wasn't that she had believed him, not *completely*, but she felt guilty. She was going to spoil everything again with her impetuousness. Just like when she'd had her label and dropped her top group because in her opinion they'd stopped playing rock and were producing popcorn, and they'd switched to one of the majors and had a big hit. That was it—she had to calm down. To concentrate on her happiness. Rick was a good guy. He loved her. He had told her that tonight. Several times. Rick wasn't her father.

The sky was still pale above the garden. Ruby was drinking her coffee on the stool in the kitchen, staring in front of her, when she froze—Brian had just appeared on the other side of the plate-glass window.

She got down off the stool like a sparrow going to pick up a crumb of bread and pulled open the sliding door that led out onto the terrace.

"Is Rick up?" he breathed.

"Fuck off."

"This isn't a game, Ruby," he said in a low voice. "Your Rick worked with the intelligence services in the apartheid days on a top secret project called Project Coast."

"Blah blah blah."

"Shit!" Brian whispered. "Two guys just came to my house and tried to kill me."

Ruby saw the sweat on his forehead, and the handkerchief he was pressing to his left side. Was that blood?

"What's the catch this time?" she asked, intrigued.

"There's no catch. I want you to leave. *Now.* Rick is mixed up in Kate's murder. I know I'm the wrong person to tell you this, but you have to believe me."

Ruby's head was buzzing with all this information. "Do you have proof?"

"It's only a matter of time."

Ruby tried to close the door, but he put a foot on the sliding rail and grabbed her by the arm. "Shit, Ruby, don't argue!"

"You're hurting me!"

Their eyes met.

"You're hurting me," she said softly.

Brian released his grip. The handkerchief he held pressed to his side was dripping—the bullet had left a deep gash.

"Rick knew your schedule, which means he also knew Kate's, and—"

"Rick didn't kill Kate," she cut him off. "He was home with me that night."

"He was with you at the time of the murder, yes. You took your band of metalheads back to their hotel, you dropped by the riding club, and you got home around nine. Rick's clinic closes at seven. That left him two hours to get to Llandudno, intercept Kate on the coast road, and hand her over to the killers before going home to establish an alibi. Damn it, why don't you just open your eyes?"

A man appeared in the doorway of the kitchen. "What's going on here?"

Rick was wearing shorts and a beige sweatshirt. He must have heard them arguing, or maybe he was another one who couldn't sleep.

"Don't try to fuck with me," Brian growled. "You're going to come quietly down to headquarters, or I'll tear you to pieces."

"You have no right to be here," Rick retorted. "I warn you right now I'm going to call my lawyer."

"Wouter Basson, Joost Terreblanche, Project Coast. Mean anything to you?"

Rick kept his cool. "Ruby's right," he said. "You're crazy."

"Really? '86-'91, Johannesburg military hospital. What were you treating? The few teeth the political prisoners still had left? Or were you trying out Basson's new products, testing them on human guinea pigs?"

"Jesus!" he said, heated now. "I'm a dentist, not a torturer!"

"And I'm a cop, not an idiot. You're sweating like a pig, Ricky, and I know that smell. It's the smell of fear."

Rick went red beneath his sweatshirt. He was lying. Not only to Ruby.

"You don't even have a warr—"

Brian grabbed him by the neck and threw him to the tiled floor of the kitchen. "I've heard enough from you," he breathed, hands tightening on his tendon.

Rick squealed with pain. Ruby was looking at them, too stunned to move, when a man in a ski mask suddenly appeared on the terrace. A powerful hand grabbed her before she could even lift a finger. Letting out a cry of surprise, she took a step back and felt the cold steel of an automatic weapon against her temple.

"Don't move, cop!"

Brian saw Ruby's face, paralyzed with fear, and the Walter 7.65 pressed to her head. He let go of Rick, who was moaning at his feet. There were two men on the terrace now, armed to the teeth.

"Hands on your head!" the man in the ski mask screamed, his gun still trained on Ruby.

Feeling nauseous, Brian obeyed. Rick stood up, massaging his neck, his head down, and retreated to the breakfast bar in the kitchen. Another man now came into the room. He had a thinning gray crew cut, and a firm body that belied his sixty years. Joost Terreblanche wasn't wearing a ski mask, but he was carrying a gun under his beige military jacket. Brian, his hands raised, was looking for an unlikely way out when a blow in the small of his back with the grip of a gun sent him sprawling.

He stifled a cry. The kitchen floor was soon stained with blood—his wound had reopened.

Terreblanche gave Rick a piercing look with his metallic eyes: "You've done well for yourself, V.D.V."

Rick met Ruby's eyes. She was looking at him in utter dismay. This was no time for explanations. Terreblanche looked down at Brian, who was lying at his feet, unable to get up. He lifted his foot, and brought his boot down on Brian's liver.

A long moan escaped his throat as he rolled toward the breakfast bar. Terreblanche took a step toward him.

"No!" Ruby cried.

Brian was crawling on all fours now, not sure he was still alive. The heel of the boot broke his back.

5.

Janet Helms corresponded with other hackers via lines they themselves had set up, whose access codes changed every month, but never on the same dates. It was as good a way as any other to compensate for her loneliness and to become even better at hacking. What had they thought in intelligence—that she had become a hacker by paying for intensive courses in high-tech institutes that cost two hundred rand an hour?

Chester Murphy lived in Woodstock, two blocks from the two-room apartment she rented. Chester was a real vampire; he avoided sunlight and, like her, lived mainly on junk food and computers. Janet spent the night at his place once or twice a week, depending on what the club was currently up to. Chester wasn't good-looking, with his fat face and tapir-like nose, but Janet liked him—he had never come on to her.

Chester had put together a network of hackers, twelve members whose identities were secret, and who sent each other individual or collective challenges: to be the first to hack into the computer system of an institution or company suspected of fraud, or to join together and hack into one of the army's radar systems. The network he had set up had so far proved undetectable, independent, and undeniably effective.

Chester hadn't asked any questions when Janet had showed up at his place at about ten in the evening—he was busy on the computer in his bedroom. Janet had settled down in front of the screen in the living room, with her fizzy drinks, her exercise books, and her mints. She had picked up her precious codes from her office at headquarters and felt up to hacking half the universe. After a few hours spent testing the enemy's defenses, she finally managed to get into certain classified army files. Many dated from the apartheid period. By five in the morning, she had the whole organizational structure of Project Coast—two hundred names in all. She had immediately faxed the list to Brian Epkeen, who had gone night fishing in Hout Bay. His reply had come quickly, in a text: *Rossow*.

Dawn was breaking when Chester told her he was going to bed—she barely heard him climb the stairs. She continued her research and found some interesting information. Unlike Joost Terreblanche, Charles Rossow's name was mentioned on several websites, and his activities as a chemist were displayed for all to see. He had worked for several major national and, more recently, international pharmaceutical companies. There was nothing, though, about his collaboration with Basson—only his successes were recalled. Now fifty-eight, Charles Rossow was currently a researcher in molecular biology for Couvence, an organization that worked under contract for a number of large pharmaceutical companies and specialized in setting up clinical trials abroad. Rossow had also published several articles in prestigious reviews, focusing in particular on genome sequencing, which he described as "a major advance in the molecular knowledge of the human body."

Digging a little deeper, Janet collated the content of the articles.

The composition of most genes was not yet known, nor the place and time when they were expressed in the form of proteins, but the genome provided an extremely useful toolbox. The next stage would involve the discovery and localization of most genes, understanding their significance and, above all, analyzing their control mechanisms. Thanks to molecular biology, a precise knowledge of the human genome and the genomes of infectious and parasitical agents would gradually lead to a description of all the mechanisms of living things and their disorders. Once that had been achieved, it would become possible to take specific action to correct anomalies, alleviate or eradicate illnesses, even to act beforehand to prevent them: a fundamental advance in regard to the human condition, and the future of mankind as a whole. Quoting Fichte—"What man must be, he must become"—Rossow stated that whereas other animals were finished, man was only sketched. Recent discoveries were a step on the infinite road to perfection. The power of current research lay in its capacity to modify human nature itself. It would distinguish itself from traditional medicine by its ability to act on the very genotype of man, affecting not only the person concerned but also all his descendants. Biotechnology would then be able to achieve what a century of ideology hadn't: a new kind of human being. It would be possible to give birth to individuals who were less violent, free of criminal tendencies. Man could be remodeled like a faulty product that is sent back to the factory, biotechnology would allow us to modify his faults, his very nature.

Staring at the computer screen with burning eyes, Janet Helms was starting to understand what was going on. It was he, Rossow, who had invented the unknown molecule found in the drug.

By leaving industrialists to finance clinical research, the political authorities had made a serious mistake. Whenever a pharmaceutical company applied for a license to put a new product on the market, it alone was in a position to supply the elements by which that product could be evaluated—with the result that expensive medications falsely claiming to be innovative had become the rule. The same company also kept exclusive rights, opening the way to human life itself being patented. Rossow and his sponsors had seen that opening and had moved in.

Janet found an address for Rossow in a well-to-do and highly protected suburb of Johannesburg, but nothing in Cape Province. Next, she took a closer look at Rossow's employer, Couvence, an organization specializing in clinical trials. Activities listed in India, Thailand, Mexico, South Africa.

"This is it," she said under her breath.

Seven-fifteen. Janet Helms went home to take a shower before dashing to the harbor.

The Waterfront was almost deserted at this time of day. The shops were just opening, stalls being set up. Janet was the first to arrive at the bar where they had arranged to meet. She was five minutes early, and she was starving. She sat down on the terrace and put down the exercise book in which she had made notes on the information gathered during the night. As Neuman had asked, it couldn't be traced back to her computer.

The air was cool, the young waiter indifferent to her presence. She managed to catch his eye and ordered a tea with milk and some sweet cakes.

In spite of her sleepless night, Janet was excited. Quite apart from the chance to avenge her lost love, this was the biggest case she'd ever worked on. If they brought it off, it would establish her as an essential part of the captain's team. She would be promoted, and work directly under Neuman. She would make herself indispensable. Irreplaceable. As she had with Dan Fletcher. He would find he couldn't do without her. She would end up ousting his current right-hand man, Brian Epkeen, who wasn't exactly in Superintendent Krüge's good books. Time was on her side. Her capacity for work was unequaled. She would take the place Neuman had intended for Dan.

Janet looked at her watch again. Eight-eleven. The lanyards of the sailboats flapped in the breeze, the shipping company shuttles gleamed in the sun, waiting for the tourists to arrive; the Waterfront was gradually waking up. The waiter passed her table, all smiles, drawn to the young blonde who had just sat down at the next table.

The light climbed up the verdant mountain. Eight-thirty. Janet Helms was waiting on the terrace of the cafe where they had arranged to meet, but no one came.

No one ever came.

*

The heel of a boot breaking his back—that was the last thing Brian Epkeen remembered before he had sunk into limbo. Reality came back, little by little, green daughter of the sunlight filtering in through the drawn blinds—Ruby's eyes, just above him, swaying in the post-boreal atmosphere.

"I was starting to think you were dead," she said in a low voice.

He was. Only it wasn't visible. His eyes finally came into focus. The world was still here, half-nocturnal, painful—a searing pain in his lower back, boring into his spine. He could hardly move. He wondered if he would ever walk again. He was thinking in fragments, pieces of thought that, when he put them in order, didn't make any sense. It wasn't only his back that hurt—his skull did, too. He realized he was lying on the wooden floor of a dark room, with Ruby's large emerald eyes all he could see.

"What happened to my head?" he asked.

"They hit you."

"Ah."

He felt like a drowning man who had come back to the surface. They had tied his hands behind his back with tape. He turned on his side to relieve the pain in the small of his back. His head would have to wait.

"Where are we?" he asked.

"In the house."

The blinds were drawn, the window handle had been removed. Brian was seeing stars.

"How long have I been out?"

"Half an hour," she replied, sitting down on the bed. "Shit, who are these guys?"

"Rick's pals. He worked on a top-secret project with an ex-soldier named Terreblanche. That's the old guy with the shaved head who beat me up."

Ruby said nothing, but she was sick with rage. This bastard Brian was right. The world was populated with bastards—the world was full of Rick van der Verskuizens who whispered sweet nothings in her ear and sniffed her ass and then dumped her in the end for his faggot friend in the boots.

Brian tried to stand, thought better of it. "Do you know where David is?" he asked.

"In Port Elisabeth, celebrating his diploma with Marjorie and his friends. Don't worry, he won't be back before next week."

Steps squeaked in the corridor. They fell silent, waiting. The door opened wide. Brian saw a pair of boots on the polished floor, then Joost Terreblanche's athletic physique above him, a military jacket, weasel eyes staring at him.

"So, cop, woken up?" The voice matched his boot studs.

"I liked it better when I was asleep."

"A wiseguy, I see. Who knows you're here?"

"No one."

"Coming out of a shootout? What do you take me for—an idiot?"

"No, just a son of a b—"

Terreblanche placed his boot on Brian's head, and pressed down with all his weight. He wasn't very tall, but he was as thick as an anvil.

"What did you do when you left your house?"

"I came straight here," Brian replied, his mouth twisted by the boot.

"Why didn't you go to your police friends?"

"I wanted to get Ruby out of here. You might have used her . . . for blackmail."

"Did you suspect the dentist?"

"Yes."

He squashed Brian's face under his boot. "And you didn't tell anyone on your way here?"

"I left my cell phone behind," Brian managed to say. "With your friends after me."

Debeer had found the fax with the Project Coast list, the samples, and the hard disk stolen from Hout Bay. But this shit stirrer had had the time to look at it. Terreblanche took his boot away, leaving stud marks on Brian's cheek. His story seemed to match Debeer's.

He took an object from his jacket. "Look what we found in your pocket."

Brian looked up and saw the memory stick. The leather heel smashed into his stomach. He may have been expecting it, but he still writhed on the floor.

"Leave him alone!" Ruby cried, from the bed.

Terreblanche didn't even look at her. "Shut up, bitch, unless you want a pickax handle up your ass. Who did you show the contents of the hard disk to?"

Brian was snatching at the air like a flying fish. "Nobody."

"Is that right?"

"I didn't."

"Didn't what?"

"Didn't have time."

Terreblanche kneeled and grabbed Brian by his shirt collar. "Did you send a copy to headquarters?"

"No."

"Why?"

"The lines . . ." he spluttered, hardly able to breathe. "The lines weren't secure. Too many names erased from the records."

Terreblanche hesitated. His men had destroyed the computer in the bedroom during the attack, so there was no way of knowing what he might have done with the files.

"Did you send a copy of the hard disk to anyone else?" Terreblanche was getting impatient. "Well, did you? Talk or I'll kill her!"

He took out his gun and aimed it at Ruby's head. She shrank back toward the bed in fright.

"That won't make any difference," Brian breathed. "I was trying to make sense of the files when your guys jumped me."

The hand that held the gun was covered in brown spots. At the end of the barrel, Ruby was shaking for the two of them.

"So nobody knows these files exist?"

Brian shook his head—this asshole reminded him of his father. "No," he said. "Only me."

Silence bounced off the walls of the room. Terreblanche lowered his gun and glanced at his Rolex. "O.K. We'll see."

*

The cellar was a cold, gloomy room that smelled of casks. Brian was trying to loosen the ropes binding him, but without much hope. He had been tied to a chair, and with the lamp shining on his face all he could see was a black dot.

A corpulent man was preparing something on the nearby table. He thought he made out Debeer, and a machine that didn't look very encouraging.

"I see we haven't kicked our old habits," he said to the soldiers.

Terreblanche did not reply. He had tortured people before. Blacks, mostly. Some who didn't even belong to the ANC or the UDF. Usually losers who'd let themselves be manipulated by Communist agitators. Thatcher and the others had dumped them after the fall of the Berlin Wall, but he still felt the same hatred for Communists, *kaffirs*, liberals, all that riffraff now in power.

"You'd do better to save your saliva," he said, supervising the setting up.

He looked at his watch. They still had a little time before dashing to the airfield. Rick's house was isolated, nobody would disturb them. It was when they returned to Hout Bay for the loading that they had found the guards and the switch-board operator out cold. Someone had broken into the build-ing and stolen the hard disk. They'd guessed it was the cop who'd been nosing around, and they'd been proved right, but the bastard had escaped. Luckily, Debeer had seen the fax he had received, the Project Coast list, with V.D.V.'s name on it. The cop was sure to have made the connection.

Brian's one thought was to play for time.

"You're the one who dreamed up this Zulu business, aren't you?" he said. "You kept Gulethu alive so that his DNA would implicate him in Kate's murder and make it seem like a racist killing. Gulethu was supplying dope to the street kids in Cape Flats, except that he tried to double-cross you by selling to the young whites on the coast. He and his gang were guarding the house while Rossow was putting together his little potions. Were they the same kinds of experiments you used to do with Doctor Basson?"

Terreblanche, his big hairy forearms folded over his beige jacket, pricked up his ears.

"Was the Muizenberg house a mobile research unit that could be packed up quickly and put in the back of a Pinz-gauer? You knew we were going to ferret around the area, so you dreamed up this story of the place being a squat and a base for the *tsotsis*. Who were you testing your miracle product on—street kids?"

Terreblanche was watching Debeer struggling impassively with his equipment.

"You should have used the mentally handicapped," Brian went on. "They talk less than kids, and anyway, between you and me, what use are they to anybody? Don't you think?"

Terreblanche looked him up and down with a sardonic grin—the cop had regained his strength, it seemed. The machine was almost ready.

"Whites couldn't deal drugs in the townships, that was why you subcontracted the work to gangs. Except that with Gulethu, you came across someone who was really out to lunch. He was the one who killed Nicole Wiese, wasn't he? He wanted Ramphele to take the rap, without even knowing what was in the dope—a miracle product mixed with the crystals to test on guinea pigs, and a strain of AIDS to guarantee their silence. What was their life expectancy—a few weeks?"

Debeer made a sign that everything was ready.

"I'm asking the questions now," Terreblanche said, approaching the chair. He passed the tip of his riding crop over Brian's eyes to irritate him. "For the last time, who else knows about the stolen files?"

"I told you, nobody. Too many leaks in our computer networks."

"What did you do when you left Hout Bay?"

Brian tried to push the riding crop away from his eyes. "I went straight home to see what was on the hard disk. Your hit men arrived just as I was trying to make sense of it."

"You might have tried to get a copy to your chief."

"I don't have a chief."

"Does Neuman have a copy?"

"No."

"Why not?"

"I didn't have time to give him one."

The riding crop caressed his nose. "Why didn't you send it?"

"I was still trying to make sense of what was on the hard disk," Brian retorted. "Do I have to say it in Afrikaans?"

"You're lying."

"I wish I was."

"You could have e-mailed the file in a couple of minutes. Why didn't you?"

"Our lines aren't secure."

"That didn't stop you getting a fax."

"If I'd sent a copy to headquarters, I wouldn't have taken the memory stick with me."

"Is there another copy?"

"No."

Brian was starting to sweat on his chair. Terreblanche lowered his riding crop. A veil fell over his clouded eyes, and he signaled to Debeer, who had just connected electrodes to the machine on the table. Debeer sniffed and pulled up his belt, then placed himself behind Brian, grabbed him by the scalp and pulled his head back. Brian tried to break free, but the ex-cop had a grip like iron. Terreblanche applied one clip to one lower eyelid, then the other clip to the other.

Brian's eyes were already damp with tears. The clips bit into his eyelids. This was quite painful in itself—but nothing compared with how it felt when the current went through them.

6.

Mzala hadn't met up with the others in Hout Bay, as originally planned, but in Constantia, an area of vineyards and mansions where he'd never set foot before. He'd soon have his place in the country, too, with plenty of wine and lots of whores. A million dollars. That was worth making a few sacrifices for. Mzala placed a small bag on the living room table.

"It's all here," he said.

Terreblanche, informed of his arrival, had just come up from the cellar. He opened the bag, and hardly batted an eyelid at the sight of all those pieces of bleeding flesh. Severed tongues. There were about twenty of them in the jute bag, a viscous mass that he emptied onto the polished wood. They looked disgusting, but they were definitely human tongues. Twenty-four in all.

"Are they all here?"

Mzala smiled blissfully, like an animal that had eaten its fill.

"Good. There's gasoline in the garage. Burn them in the garden."

Mazala started collecting his tongues from the table. "Who's the girl in the bedroom?" he asked, casually.

"Who let you in there?"

"I saw her through the blinds as I came across the garden. Nice chick." He was still smiling.

"Keep your hands off her," Terreblanche said, threateningly. "I still need her . . . in one piece."

"For what?"

"Just get on with your barbecue."

Rick appeared at the door of the living room. He didn't know the black with the scarred face who was talking to Terreblanche. He saw his tapered nails and the movements of his reddened fingers, and only then the bits of bleeding flesh on the table. "When . . . when are we leaving?" he stammered.

"Soon," Terreblanche said. "Are your things ready?"

"Yes. Well, almost."

Mzala was taking his time collecting his booty.

Rick screwed up his courage. "Can we do something about Ruby? I mean—"

"It's too late, old buddy," Terreblanche cut in. "She knows too much now. You played with fire, V.D.V. Your girlfriend's ex-husband was investigating the case, that really wasn't very clever."

"Ruby told me he was a traffic cop," Rick said apologetically.

"Tut-tut."

"It's the truth."

"Is this the old friend?" Mzala said, amused.

A cry rang out from the cellar. Someone was obviously having a bad time down there.

Mzala forgot his tongues for a moment. "Need a hand, chief?"

Terreblanche made a negative sign, then turned back to Rick. "We'll talk about it later. Now get your things together. The plane leaves in an hour."

"Yes. Yes."

Rick hadn't had the courage to say goodbye to Ruby. His past had caught up with him, youthful errors that needed to be seen in the context of the time. They had bought his silence. (What did Ruby imagine, that you became a friend to the stars with a seedy clinic on Victoria? That he had acquired this property with his army pension?) Terreblanche had kept reports with his signature on them, reports of experiments conducted on the fringes of Project Coast, including the names of political prisoners. A leak to the tabloids, and the "dentist of the stars" could swallow his own molars. Rick had obeyed orders, as he always had done. Kate Montgomery had been easy prey—a quick glance at Ruby's schedule and the thing was done. But her ex-husband had fucked it all up. Rick was sorry for her, for him. His life was draining away before his eyes and he knew nothing could stop the hemorrhage. He had to abandon everything he had built up over the last twenty years, leave the country, start again from scratch.

The sun was licking the first rows of vines beyond the garden. Rick turned to go upstairs to the bedroom. He would take what was in the safe, the cash, a few jewels.

Terreblanche let him take a few steps before pulling out the .38 he had taken from the cop. He aimed at Rick as he reached the glass door and shot him down like a nigger, with a bullet in the back of the head.

*

A well-built white with a cowlick was standing guard outside the bedroom door.

"I need to talk to the girl," Mzala said.

"Does the boss know?"

"Sure," he said, smiling with his yellow teeth. "He sent me."

The idiot opened the door.

The room was in semi-darkness. The girl was on the bed, her hands tied behind her back. Ruby threw a venomous look at the slender black who closed the door behind him.

"What do you want?"

"Calm down, sweetheart."

The man was holding a small jute bag in his hand. His nails were filthy, tapered to points. He was wearing wide pants and a shirt with bloodstained sleeves.

"Who are you?" Ruby said.

"There . . . there."

But his face reeked of vice and death. He was looking at her as if she were a trophy. Prey. Ruby's heart was pounding.

"Don't be afraid," he whispered. "I'm not going to hurt you."

He was stroking his bag as if it were a pet. In one piece, Terreblanche had said.

"I won't hurt you if you keep quiet," Mzala said.

Ruby wanted to tear his eyes out but they were empty of humanity. Fear crept up her legs, and she pressed them tightly together and moved back against the wall.

"One word from you," he said in a honeyed voice, "one word, and I'll slit you open."

"Fuck off."

"In your mouth, how would you like that? Hmm?" He smiled. "Yes, of course you'd like that. With a mouth like yours, you need them big. You're going to love it, darling, oh yes, you're going to love my big—"

"Come on, then," Ruby cut in, threateningly. "I have good teeth."

Mzala was still smiling, as if thinking of something else. Terreblanche had gone back down to the cellar, leaving him with the body of his "old friend" on the living room floor. The plane wasn't leaving for another hour. There was time for a bit of fun. The *tsotsi* plunged his hand into his little bag and chose a tongue at random. Ruby went white. She tried to retreat, but she already had her back against the wall. Mzala placed the piece of flesh on her hair.

"Scream," he said, "and I'll make you eat it."

The Cat wasn't smiling anymore.

She fell silent, paralyzed with fear.

Clearly pleased with himself, he put another of the tongues on her ear. The girl was shaking all over, like a sparrow in a storm. She would soon be eating out of his hands—or rather, she'd be eating his cock, ha ha ha. Ruby pursed her lips while he was decorating her, a cruel smile on his irregular features. Now she had tongues on her hair, her shoulders. When he adorned her cleavage, a tear slid down her cheek.

Mzala contemplated his work. She was perfect now. He had a hard-on that was almost painful. He was just taking out his powerful member when footsteps echoed rhythmically in the corridor.

Debeer was the first to come in, supporting a man who was in a pitiful state. Terreblanche followed them in. He saw Ruby, silently weeping, then Mzala, smiling nervously on the bed.

*

The world wasn't formatted anymore, the data had been erased. Time, too, had become porous, gravity was turning in a loop. Brian let the cells dance around in the uncertain chemistry of his brain. With matter sent flying to the other side of the universe, he clung to the particles of thought that whizzed over his head like meteorites. At the end of his mad race with himself, he saw flecks of dust on the wooden floor, then Ruby, close to him. The blurred images drew burning tears from him.

"What have they done to me?" he murmured.

"I don't know," she replied in a neutral voice. "But you pissed in your pants."

Brian was content just to breathe. His eyes stung horribly, his muscles hurt, his bones, his whole body was nothing but one long moan, and the lioness he could see through the burned grass didn't look very happy, as if the hunting hadn't gone well. He examined the damage to his pants.

"Fuck."

"Yes."

His shirt, too, was soaking wet.

He remembered Terreblanche, the electric generator, his brain reduced to a transformer, his lashes burning, words coming involuntarily from his mouth, snakes he had spat out in the middle of his pain. A terrible doubt grabbed him by the throat. Had he talked? Incandescent sparks throbbed behind his eyelids, he could barely see Ruby on the bed, the shadows on the wall. He tried to stand, but couldn't, it hurt too much.

"Help me, please."

"Help you to do what? A fucking madman came in here earlier and stuck tongues on my face! Men's tongues! Shit! Can't you see these guys are crazy? Can't you see they're going to kill us?"

Ruby was an inch away from a nervous breakdown.

"They would have done it already," he replied.

"If anyone had told me we'd die together . . ."

"Stop daydreaming and help me up."

Ruby grabbed one of his arms. "What are you planning to do, Superman—blow down the walls?"

Brian's tears were flowing by themselves over the floor. Getting to his feet made him feel like a lighthouse cast out to sea, but he could make out shapes better now. The lowered blinds, the window without a handle, the desk, the rickety wooden chair, and Ruby, her jaws clenched in order not to scream. She was a tough cookie, she wouldn't give up. He stuck his face between the drawn blinds. You could make out the fruit trees in the garden, then the vines stretching over the gray sides of Table Mountain. Even if they managed to escape, they wouldn't get far in their condition.

"We have to get out of here," he said.

"Go on, I'll watch."

Brian evaluated the situation—not great. "The reason Terreblanche hasn't killed us yet is because he's planning to use us."

"As what, hostages? You're not worth much on the second-hand market, Brian. Me even less."

She wasn't wrong about that.

He indicated his hands, held tightly together with adhesive tape. "You have good teeth, try to bite into this."

"I've already tried, smart-ass. While you were out cold. It's too hard."

"I wasn't exerting any pressure. Try again."

Taking a deep breath, Ruby kneeled behind him and tried to find a way in.

"Go on!"

"That's what I'm doing," she growled.

But the tape was solid, too tightly wound to offer the slightest grip for her teeth.

"I can't do it," she said, giving up.

Birds were singing in the garden. However hard Brian tried, he could see only one solution. Something political prisoners used to do. The prospect, given his condition, made him sigh agonizingly.

"How far's the nearest house from here?" he asked.

"About half a mile. Why?"

"We don't have much choice, Ruby. I don't see any guard in the garden. With a bit of luck, you can reach the vines before they jump us. Run under cover without turning around, and when you get to your neighbor's house call the police."

"Oh, yes?" she said, feigning surprise. "And how do I get to those vines? In my dreams?"

"There's only one pane in the window," he said in a low voice. "If I can break it, you have a chance to escape. In ten seconds, you're in the vines. By the time the others react, you'll be a long way away."

She frowned. "And you?"

"I'll follow you."

"And what if there's a guard outside?"

"At worst he'll kill you."

"And that's your plan?"

"At least you'll save time."

Ruby shook her head, unconvinced by his two-faced smile. "You're forgetting one thing, Brian. How do we break the window?"

"I have a hard head," he said.

She screwed up her pretty little face. "Smashing the window with your head—this plan of yours is completely pathetic."

"It's rock 'n' roll."

Ruby looked at him as if he were a half-wit. "Still as crazy as ever."

"Isn't that what you love about me? Now come on, let's not waste any time." He pushed the chair from the desk to just under the window. "Climb on that to get out. Are you ready?"

Ruby nodded, and focused on the objective. Their eyes met for a moment—fear, tenderness, a mixture of memories. He kissed her on the mouth and it didn't even occur to her to bite him. He moved back to the door, and evaluated the ideal trajectory. Finally, he wiped all thoughts from his mind and ran forward, head first.

According to his calculations, there was a fifty-fifty chance of knocking himself unconscious. His skull struck the glass, which shattered on impact. Ruby stifled a scream. Brian's head got caught in the blinds, stopping him from getting through the window. For a second, he stood there, tangled in the slats, then collapsed, surrounded by fragments of glass.

The light from the garden dazzled Ruby. The window was partly broken, the trees only a few yards away. She rushed forward, forgetting all about the remaining strips of glass, climbed on the chair he'd pushed up against the wall, and went through the window with her eyes closed. With one leap, she was outside. Her legs felt shaky on the cracked earth, warm blood dripped on her eyelids, but her one thought was to run. She cut a path through the trees, weaving between the low branches. The vines were only ten yards away now.

"Don't kill her!" a voice cried, somewhere to the right of her.

Ruby reached the first vines. She bent low, ran down one of the rows for twenty yards, then abruptly turned left. The bushes scratched her skin, her bound hands slowed her down in her headlong run, she went down another row, panting, and headed due north. About half a mile to the neighbor's house. Ruby was running through the vines when she ran straight into something and fell, face down. A huge weight immediately pinned her to the ground. A cry of pain escaped her lips—the man was holding her down firmly, his knee digging into the small of her back. People were running from the house, figures emerged from the rows of vines.

"Where were you planning to go, bitch?" Terreblanche growled.

Ruby's mouth was full of earth. Brian's plan was a washout. No surprise there, then.

*

Brian was standing groggily against the wall of the room, waiting. The impact had almost killed him, but by some miracle he was still conscious. The guards had found him on the ground surrounded by fragments of glass and torn blinds. Anxious to retrieve the girl who had escaped through the window, they had left him with his open wounds and set off in search of her. Ruby wouldn't get far, he knew.

And in fact, here she came, with nasty gashes on her forehead, her pretty dress in shreds, her arms grazed, her face and shoulders covered in blood. Terreblanche threw her on the bed like a toy that had outlasted its purpose.

"Tie their ankles," he ordered Debeer. "And clear up these pieces of glass. We wouldn't want them cutting themselves."

Military humor. Ruby looked at Brian, distraught. Part of his scalp was torn away. Debeer started with him.

"You can untie them when they're dead," Terreblanche said.

That was the second part of his plan. The first was lying in the middle of the living room, with the cop's bullet in the back of his neck. Terreblanche had planned to eliminate Van der Verskuizen and his whore before getting to the airfield—making it look like a burglary that had gone wrong—but the latest developments had modified his plans.

"Give them a first injection of 4cc. Wait for half an hour until it's taken effect, then give them the second one. They'll both be groggy and won't offer any resistance."

Debeer nodded.

Terreblanche wiped his prints from the .38. "After that, kill the girl with this gun," he said, placing the revolver on the desk. "Don't forget to wear gloves, or to put the cop's prints on the gun. It has to look like a murder during a fit of madness, followed by an overdose. Understood?"

"Affirmative."

Debeer was in charge of the dirty work. He didn't particularly like it. The main thing was not to think. Terreblanche placed a small leather case on the ground. Inside was a tourniquet, syringes, powder, and a pickax handle.

"Rape the girl before you kill her," he said. "It'll be important for the postmortem. We meet up as planned."

Ruby huddled on the bed, her eyes bulging.

"No one will believe I killed her," Brian cried. "Everyone knows we love each other."

"That's right!" Ruby said.

Terreblanche did not even look at her. "Do it."

The first injection was like a thunderbolt in an already dark sky. Brian felt the heat rise to his cheeks, spread in a spasm to his muscles, and run along his fingers. The burning was intense, although in a subtler way than the electrical generator. He went from pain to insensibility, and came to a halt between indifference and dynamite, almost imploding. Finally, once past the first shock, the miracle—after the flow of lava carrying away his veins, the shards of glass in his head, his back, he stopped feeling anything at all. With the Earth atomized beneath his feet, the smells of skin and the flames of the fire ravaged him from floor to ceiling. A long crack soon laid him flat like a plain in the moonlight.

"Don't touch me!"

The voice had emerged from nowhere. He opened his protruding eyes.

"Shit! Don't touch me!" the voice repeated.

Brian shuddered. Ruby was there, very close. He felt her breath on his mouth.

"But . . . I'm not touching you," he cried.

He looked around him, saw only a nightmare. Good God, yes, he *was* touching her. But it wasn't him. Those hands, those fingers. Ruby was there, a few inches away. The blood was dripping from her wounds, spattering her face, and he was lying over her, somewhere else. Desire had fled from love, infinity had disappeared. He saw things that didn't exist, without believing them, Ruby lying beneath him with her thighs open, her eyes rolling with the effects of the drug, the convulsions, the patterns on the striped blanket, and that female breath constantly on his neck. Everything came back to him at the same time: the cellar, their attempt at escape, the first injection.

Brian rolled over on the bed and let himself fall to the wooden floor.

The guards had appeared as soon as the window had broken, but he had had time to send a shard of glass under the bed. He looked in the corners, saw only blackness surrounded by stars. At last he saw a pale glimmer against the skirting board. The piece of glass. He twisted on the ground, and with his foot managed to move it toward him.

Heavy footsteps approached in the corridor. The key turned in the lock. Brian writhed about, closing his eyes as the door opened.

Debeer came in. It was half an hour since the first injection. He went to the bed and put the small case down next to the girl. The cop was also in a lethargic state, lying on the floor. Debeer put on a pair of latex gloves, and prepared his instruments. The sooner it was over, the sooner he'd get to the airfield. He began by tearing off what was left of the dress, then snapped the elastic on her panties and sent them spinning to the floor. After which he put a condom on the end of the pickax handle and parted the girl's legs. The main thing was not to think.

"Show me your ass, bitch."

Brian, on the floor, saw Debeer on the bed, with his back to him. Ruby had stopped reacting. He got to work on the tape, but the drug had turned him to wood, and his hands were almost completely numb—he might have been cutting his own veins for all he knew. A torn pair of panties flew to the ground. Brian had cramps from sawing through the tape, his fingers were gashed with a thousand cuts, but nothing came. Debeer was muttering insults in Afrikaans when all at once Brian's hands came free. He hesitated a moment, realized he could barely move. His brain sent his body orders, without effect. He saw Ruby on the bed. Debeer had put one of her legs over his shoulder, the better to part them. The heaviness that had kept Brian riveted to the floor disappeared in a flash. He threw himself on the man, foaming at the mouth with love and anger. A fatal mixture—the piece of glass sank into Debeer's throat, severing the carotid artery.

7

The moon was slowly fading in the sky. Neuman was finalizing the plan of attack he would soon be presenting to Karl Krüge when he got the call from Miriam. The young nurse had passed Josephina's house early this morning on her way to work and had been surprised to see the shutters open. She had knocked at the door, but there had been no answer. Worried, she had woken the old woman's friends. One of them told her that Josephina had had an appointment the previous evening at the church in Lengezi, on the edge of Khayelitsha, with the priest's maid, Sonia Parker, to talk about a gang of street kids.

Neuman turned pale.

Parker.

Pamela, the colored girl found dead in the cellar, was named Parker.

He had thanked his mother's guardian angel, then checked the SAP records. He soon found what he was looking for. *Pamela Parker, born November 28, 1978. Parents deceased. One sister, Sonia, whereabouts unknown.*

Neuman filled his pockets with bullets and left the deserted station.

The sandy area bordering Lengezi stretched as far as the sea. Old newspapers, pieces of plastic, sacking, sheets of corrugated iron—the shelters on the edge of the open space were among the most wretched in the township. Neuman slammed the car door shut and walked down the unpaved street.

A subdued wind was knocking at the closed doors. Everything seemed deserted, abandoned. He advanced, chasing away the shadows, saw only a rat scampering beneath his feet. The front of the church was turning red in the light of dawn. He climbed the steps to the half-open door and slipped inside without a sound.

He aimed the barrel of his gun into the shadows. The chairs were empty, the silence like a locked trunk deep in his head. Nobody. He walked down the cold aisle, the handle of the gun now warm in the hollow of his hand. He made out the pillar near the altar, the white cloth, the extinguished candles. He stopped halfway along the aisle. There was a black shape behind the altar, a very distinct shape, which seemed to be hanging from the cross. Josephina. Her wrists had been tied to the big wooden crucifix with a rope. Her head was drooping on her chest, slumped, inert, her eyes closed. Neuman went close to her face and stroked her eyelids. Her makeup had run, blue makeup still sticky with tears. Mechanically, he stroked her cheek, for a long time, as if to reassure her. It would soon be over, yes, it would soon be over. The images became confused. His jaws were quivering. He didn't know how long it had lasted, but his mother wouldn't suffer anymore. The Cat had planted the spoke of a bicycle wheel in her heart.

Neuman took a step back and let go of his gun. His mother was dead. Blood had come from her mouth, staining her white dress, her beautiful black skin, congealed blood that stuck to her chin, her neck, her half-open mouth. He saw the cuts on her lips. Gashes. Left by a knife. He opened his mother's mouth and shuddered. She didn't have a tongue. It had been cut out.

The cry drilled into his temples. *Zwelithini*. The war cry of the last Zulu king, before his nation was massacred.

Zwelithini. Let the earth tremble.

*

Like all township cops, Constable Beth Zumala lived in fear—fear of someone breaking down her door during the night and raping her, fear of being killed for her service pistol, fear of a random murder in broad daylight, fear of reprisals if a big-time *tsotsi* was arrested—but she loved her job.

"Any good at shooting?" Neuman asked.

"I was one of the best in my year at hitting moving targets," she replied.

"These targets fire back."

"I won't give them time."

Stein, her partner on the night team, was a sturdy albino in an impeccably ironed uniform. He, too, had never imagined he'd ever be working with the head of the Cape Town Crime Unit, let alone on an operation of this kind. He adjusted his bulletproof vest and checked his gear.

The first rays of sunlight were touching the bullet-riddled facade of the Marabi. The Americans' lair was all closed up, the door protected by a metal grille, the windows barricaded with wooden planks and sheets of steel. No sign of life. The street, too, was strangely calm.

"Let's go," Neuman said.

"Maybe we should wait for backup," Stein suggested.

"Just cover me."

Neuman wouldn't wait for Krüge's Casspirs or Sanogo's no-hopers. He cocked the pump-action shotgun he'd found in the trunk of the patrol car and moved forward. Stein and Xumala hesitated—they were paid two thousand rand a month to uphold the law, not to die in a suicide mission against the top gang in the township—but Neuman had already gone around to the other side of the building.

At his signal, the two officers climbed the adjoining roof. Neuman stifled a groan as he fell into the backyard of the *she-*

been. He weaved his way between the overturned garbage pails and scattered bottles, and was the first to reach the iron door leading to the games room.

"If there's any suspicious movement, fire," he said in a low voice.

The officers were nervous. This man didn't care. The armor-plating dated from apartheid, the lock from the Great Trek. Neuman tilted the pump-action shotgun and fired two salvos one after the other, smashing the lock to pieces. Stein kicked the door open. Neuman ran into the private room. On the right was the storeroom and the *tsotsis*' rooms, on the left Mzala's room. He aimed straight for his target, rushing through the half-open door and aiming the shotgun at the gang leader's straw mattress.

A naked woman lay there in the half-light, a plump colored woman he had seen the other day with Mzala. She was staring up at the yellowed ceiling, her eyes bulging, her throat cut. Her clothes lay strewn on the tiled floor, but the closet was almost empty. Neuman slowly kneeled and parted the girl's jaws. She'd lost her tongue, too.

"Captain!" Beth called from the dormitories. "Captain!"

Neuman stood up, not even feeling the pain in his ribs anymore. Officer Stein was in the corridor, radioing for backup. His partner was just coming back from the bedrooms, ashen-faced.

"They're all dead," she said.

Neuman found posters of naked women on the cracked walls, a portable stove for heating canned food, empty beer bottles, and a corpse on each of the bunk beds. All members of the Americans. Others lay on the floor, their heads tilted, their noses in puddles of alcohol. Twenty-two bodies, all executed with a bullet in the head. Even Dina, the *shebeen* queen, had been liquidated—her body lay behind the bar counter, surrounded by empty bottles and half-smoked joints. The American gang had been wiped off the map. They had been killed in their alcohol-induced sleep, and then their tongues had been cut out.

Mzala wasn't among them.

Neuman ground his teeth. Everything was being stolen from him, even death.

He left the officers to call the emergency services and went out without a word.

A small, silent crowd had gathered outside the Marabi. Neuman didn't want to think—not yet. He got in his car, deaf to the screaming police sirens, and set off for Lengezi. A few women were walking along the street, carrying baskets or plastic bowls. Khayelitsha was slowly waking up. He slowed down outside his mother's house, and stopped without even realizing it. The hedge was trimmed, the shutters were open. Neuman closed his eyes, and took a deep breath, felt the anger rumbling. The monster inside him was stirring. *Zwelithini.* He wouldn't sleep. He'd never sleep again.

At that moment, absurdly, there was a signal from the cell phone in his pocket. Neuman saw Zina's text, and it made his anguish even sharper. *Meet you at 8 a.m. Boulder National Park. XXX.*

His eyes misted over. He looked up and saw his mother's house through the windshield, the sun on the shutters. Kids were playing on the street, with their cars made of wire. Neuman opened the door and vomited the breakfast he hadn't eaten into the hedge.

*

The revolving lights outside the church, the ambulance, the police officers dispersing the last onlookers, Miriam sobbing at the foot of the steps with her head in her hands—Neuman walked through the desolate reality of it all with another man's eyes.

Two constables were guarding the front door of the church. Neuman walked past them without seeing them. The Methodist minister stood in the doorway. He had a graying crew cut, and eyes like flickering candles. With a gesture, Neuman ordered him to be quiet. He wanted to see the medical examiner first.

Rajan worked at the Red Cross Hospital in Khayelitsha, a sickly-looking man of Indian descent he had met once or twice. Rajan greeted him with a mixture of sympathy and embarrassment. His initial conclusion was that the murder had taken place in the church, around nine the previous evening. The tongue had been severed, probably with a knife, but death seemed to have been caused by a sharpened wheel spoke plunged straight into the heart.

That had been the preferred style of execution in Soweto, in the days when the vigilantes and the comrades settled their scores at the expense of history. The horror of it was trying to make him lose his footing, but Neuman was already a long way off the ground, in Zulu country, where he would bury his mother beside her husband, when all this was over.

There was a glacial silence in the church, barely disturbed by the murmurs of the crowd outside. The stretcher bearers were waiting near the altar.

"Can we take the body away?"

Rajan was waiting for the word from Neuman.

"Yes. Yes." He looked at his mother for the last time, before she disappeared beneath the zipper of a plastic body bag.

"I know it's no consolation," Rajan said in a low voice, "but if it's any help, it seems the tongue was cut out after death."

He didn't flinch. Too many vipers in his mouth. History didn't repeat itself, it stammered. Neuman walked over to the minister, who was waiting by the pillar.

"My mother had an appointment with your maid," he said, looming over him. "Where is she?"

"Sonia? At home, I assume. There's a little house next to the church. That's where she sleeps."

"Show me."

The minister was sweating despite the coolness of the morning. They went out through a concealed door.

The little plot of earth behind the building belonged to the congregation. There were a few rows of sweet potatoes, carrots, and lettuce, which his maid used to make soup for the poor. Neuman opened the door of the shack. It was already hot beneath the corrugated iron. There was a smell of sweat in the main room, and a heady odor of blood. A young black woman was lying on the mattress in the bedroom. Blackish blood had flowed from her severed throat.

"Sonia?"

The priest nodded wordlessly. Neuman examined the body. The girl had clearly tried to defend herself—there were red marks on her wrists and one nail was broken. The blade had severed the throat, then her tongue. The time of death must have been about twelve hours ago. He looked around at the furniture, the shelves, the soup she had been making in the adjoining kitchen.

"How long had Sonia been working for you?" Neuman asked the timid little minister.

"Since last year. She came to see me. A lost girl, who wanted to expiate her sins by helping her neighbors and answering the call of the L—"

Neuman grabbed the minister's tunic and pinned him to the wall. "The Lord has been silent for a while now," he said between his teeth. "Your maid's sister was killed because of her involvement in the selling of drugs to street kids, and Sonia was in contact with the kids hanging about the zone. Well?"

"I don't know . . ."

"A kid in green shorts called Teddy, and another one with a scar on his neck. Mean anything to you?"

The minister trembled in Neuman's grip. "Sonia!" he said in a strangled voice. "It was Sonia who made soup for them."

Neuman thought of the garden, the huts. "Do you have animals?"

"Hens. A few pigs, too, and rabbits."

He dragged the little man out to the vegetable garden. The rabbits were in their hutches, sniffing at the grilles. A small distance from them, the hens were pecking at the straw as if it were boiling water. A cinderblock shack at the far end of the garden served as a pigsty, with an iron roof and a trough filled with brackish water. Neuman pulled out his Colt .45 and shot off the padlock.

A foul odor greeted him inside the shack. The three pigs wallowing in the mud came up to the barrier and grunted. A larger male and two females, their pink snouts smeared with shit.

"What do you give them to eat?"

The priest was standing in the doorway. "Whatever . . . whatever's available."

Neuman opened the barrier and freed the animals. The little man tried to make a gesture to hold them in—the pigs were going to trample his precious vegetable garden—but then changed his mind. Neuman leaned over the trough. He opened his penknife and stirred the revolting swill until he found bones in it—human bones. Most had been ground down by the pigs. Children's bones, to judge by their size. Dozens of bones.

*

Boulder National Park was home to a colony of Cape penguins, which frisked about freely on the sandy beach, using the thundering waves as diving boards. Neuman strode across the wet sand.

Zina was waiting for him on the rocks, the wind blowing sea spray onto her dress. She saw him coming from a distance, an incongruous giant amid the waddling penguins, and drew her arms tightly around her bent knees. He walked up to her, and immediately killed all thoughts of love.

"Do you have the document?"

A plastic wallet lay beside her, on the rock. Zina wanted to talk to him about the two of them, but this didn't seem like the time or the place.

"This is all I could find," she said.

Neuman forgot the black rockets exploding in his head and grabbed the wallet. The document had no heading or anything to identify it, but it contained a complete report on the man he was looking for.

Joost Terreblanche had worked for the secret service during the apartheid regime and was a member of the Broederbond, the "League of Brothers," a secret society bringing together the Afrikaner pseudo-elite, few of whose activities ever came to light. In spite of his involvement in Project Coast and the disappearance of several black activists, Terreblanche had never had any run-ins with the law. Most of the trials had come to nothing, which was why few former members of the army had cooperated with Desmond Tutu's Truth and Reconciliation Commission. As a result, some branches of the former security services had benefited from almost total immunity, despite serious human-rights violations. When the regime had fallen, Terreblanche had left the army with the rank of colonel and had gone into the private security business, working with a number of South African companies, including ATD, of which he was one of the principal shareholders. According to the source, Terreblanche enjoyed protection at all levels, both in South Africa and in Namibia, where the conflict between the two countries had allowed for a great deal of infiltration. He was suspected of conducting paramilitary operations in several countries of the Great Lakes, supplying arms and hiring mercenaries. The report mentioned, among other things, a base in the Namib Desert, a former farm in the middle of a protected area, where Terreblanche went about his business undisturbed.

Namibia.

The waves crashed on the shore, spewing out penguins. Zina was watching Neuman as he read the document, looking strangely pale. Their encounter had been something fleeting, an unexpected gust of wind that shouldn't have happened but had flung them together. This wasn't the moment, but it would never be the moment.

"Shall we stop playing games?" she said.

He looked up, a black totem planted in the sand.

"Do you think I'm shortsighted?" she went on, gallantly. "Do you think I don't see how you look at me?"

His face fell a little more, but he said nothing. Corpses were floating to the surface, dozens of them, drained of blood.

"The tour finishes tomorrow night," she said. "After that, I don't know. I'm leaving town, Ali, unless you stop me."

He had stopped hearing the roar of the waves or the cries of the penguins. The world had been turned upside down. He was in free fall.

"I'm sorry," he said, halfheartedly.

Zina clenched her pretty teeth. "Say that again!" she hissed. "Go on, say that again!"

Tears were streaming down her cheeks. She had been waking up every morning with the smell of his skin, it resisted water, wind, the fire beneath her feet, his smell waited for her in her bed, in her dressing room, it followed her in the corridors, the streets, the warm air of evening, it was even in the sea spray, his smell, his smell was everywhere.

Neuman lowered his eyes. He saw her bare feet on the jagged rock, her shapely ankles, her legs, her dress blowing in the wind.

"I'm sorry . . ."

And he died there, surrounded by penguins.

8.

The animals came out at night. A couple of oryx passed on the plain, in search of tender leaves that had grown since the last rain.

"What are those fucking things doing here?" Mzala cursed from the terrace of the farmhouse.

He was nervous. He didn't give a fuck about animals, sand, desert. He was thinking dollars. Mozambique. Early retirement. Luxury hotels and bitches in heat.

"How long are we going to stay here?"

"As long as it takes," Terreblanche replied. "Why don't you get some sleep?"

The ex-soldier was drinking rooibos tea, comfortably installed in one of the armchairs on the terrace.

Mzala peered out at the desert. All this vastness depressed him. He didn't want to sleep. The amphetamines kept him awake—or better still, the fear of waking up with a knife between his shoulder blades. Terreblanche hated anyone who didn't go red in the sun. The Cat had taken certain precautions to stop the other man killing him on the spot, but he would only close his eyes once he was a long way from here, with his money. This wait was getting on his nerves—Mzala hated waiting. As a gang leader, he'd had privileges within the township, but that was all over now. The American gang was gone, God save their damned souls. Mzala had respected his side of the contract. He had collected the sleeping drugs from the Lengezi church, taking the opportunity to eliminate the little whore who fed the pigs and the big mama who had showed up unexpectedly, and finally doused the tongues in gasoline and set fire to them before following the others to the airfield.

"What's stopping you giving me the rest of the money here and now?" he grunted.

"We've already talked about that," Terreblanche declaimed from his wicker throne. "They must be watching the borders, and I'm not crazy about you falling into the hands of the police. You'll go abroad when the coast is clear."

It wasn't true—he could move from one country to another without the danger of coming up against an overzealous official. But the man was an idiot and, as soon as the money was pocketed, he would blow his fortune on luxury cars, gold jewelry, and flashy bimbos. The hard disk was in a safe place, with his sponsors; his fortune and his son's fortune were assured, but the cops were still on the alert. Joost would play dead until things settled down. Only then would he join Ross in Australia. Money bought everything. Money redeemed everything.

"This isn't the way we planned it," Mzala said stubbornly. "We agreed that once the operation was over I'd take my cut and go."

"No one's going anywhere without my approval."

"Meaning what?"

"Meaning I have to agree."

"We already agree, about the money. A million dollars. In cash. Where are my dollars?"

"You'll wait, like the others," Terreblanche concluded. "Period."

Mzala grimaced in the darkness. He was wondering if this moonface had the money here, in a safe somewhere, or some pathetic hiding place. The Cessna that had landed them here this morning had left again with the stuff, and now they were alone in the middle of this desert he didn't know.

A leaden silence fell over the terrace, barely disturbed by the night breeze. The night birds had fallen silent. The oryx, too, had fled. Mzala was about to lock himself in his room, his gun within easy reach, when a cry rang out from the direction of the garage.

*

Neuman had parked the four-by-four on the edge of the trail, and done the last miles on foot. Holding the case in his hand sent shooting pains to his aching rib. According to his map of the region, the farm was located behind the Sossusvlei dunes, west of here, a long way from the tourist sites.

The moon guided him over the barren plain. He walked half a mile following the Southern Cross, the pockets of his dusty suit weighed down with the cartridge clips. The dunes stood out in the darkness. At last, he glimpsed a light in the distance, then a fence that marked the boundary of the farm.

An ostrich fled as he approached, a panic-stricken sentinel. Neuman threw the case over the fence, then climbed over himself, gritting his teeth. He was in private property—about fifty acres, according to Zina's information, stretching as far as the foothills of the Sesriem dunes. He made for the flickering light, stopping halfway to get an idea of the layout of the place. He wedged his case on his shoulder and, after a few minutes' difficult climb, reached the top of the highest dune. He could see Terreblanche's farmhouse in the moonlight, and the prefabricated building below it, near the pens.

Neuman put the metal case down on the sand. The rifle was a Steyr, equipped with a laser-zoom-x6 sight, a silencer, and three cartridge clips of thirty 7.62 caliber bullets each. A sniper's weapon. He assembled it carefully, and made sure it was in working order.

He wiped the sweat from his forehead and lay down on the

smooth ridge. The sand was soft, almost cool. He swept the expanse with the infrared sight, checked out the farmhouse, the extension—a warehouse, presumably. There were two men on the terrace, who seemed to be arguing, and two four-by-fours in the yard. The prefabricated building was about fifty yards farther on. A guard was patrolling, with a light machine gun slung across his shoulder. Another was smoking on the path leading to the main track. Neuman put him in the center of his sight and shot him with one bullet in the back. The man fell face down. He aimed his rifle toward the yard and found the second man. The target danced for a moment in the sight before swiveling abruptly under the impact.

Neuman let out his breath. Nobody had stirred near the buildings. He made sure the guards had died immediately and aimed the sight at the terrace. He thought he recognized the figure of Mzala near the pillar. Just then, two men emerged from the nearby warehouse, both with shaved heads, carrying crates. Neuman followed their movement—they were heading for the four-by-fours—and pressed the trigger. He killed the first with a bullet in the throat, the second as he was turning to his partner.

A third man emerged from the farmhouse. He saw the bodies on the ground and took his revolver from his belt. Neuman hit him in the left shoulder, before a second bullet threw him back against the door. He cursed from the top of the dune—the guy had had time to sound the alarm.

Neuman aimed toward the terrace, but the two figures had taken shelter in the house. A man in an undershirt emerged from the prefab, a weapon in his hand. His head exploded. The building must be a dormitory. They were going to wake up, organize a counterattack. Neuman aimed at the window frames and methodically emptied his magazine, firing at random and sowing panic as the bullets went through the walls. He heard cries and the first clatter of returning fire. He took the second cartridge clip from where it lay on the sand, jammed it into the magazine, and fired thirty more bullets, one after the other. The dormitory was soon riddled with bullets. One man had attempted to come out, but Neuman had nailed him with a shot to the solar plexus. The survivors ducked inside the building.

Bullets whistled a few yards from him, punching holes in the sand. They had finally located his position. Neuman loaded the last cartridge clip and peered into the darkness. He spotted a man hiding just inside the door of the dormitory, carrying a light machine gun and signaling frantically to his invisible companions. Neuman fired twelve 7.62-caliber bullets, which shattered the door and the wall round it. Hit in the leg, the man dragged himself along the ground to escape the sniper. Neuman finished him off with a bullet in the cheek.

Neuman, focused on his objective, had stopped breathing. A figure crossed the infrared field—a man dashing out of the dormitory and running in a zigzag toward the farmhouse. Neuman followed him in a macabre dance, then squeezed the trigger and sent him sprawling onto the ground, face down.

His fingers were stiff, his breath coming from deep in his guts. At last, he relaxed. No movement in the moonlight. He abandoned the rifle case to its shroud of sand, walked along the ridge, and groaned in pain as he descended the dune. He heard doors slamming in the darkness. Neuman stopped, panting, and directed the sight of his rifle toward the farmhouse. One of the four-by-fours was escaping westward, raising a cloud of dust.

He fired six bullets, blindly. They vanished in the murk.

A deathly silence fell over the barren expanse. Neuman was not thinking of anything. All that was left was the night wind whistling through the bullet-riddled planks of the dormitory, the rifle he held in a madman's grip, and the Toyota parked in the yard.

*

The tracks ran toward the sea—sixty miles of dunes and pebbly plains in one of the largest national parks in the world. Neuman was following the parallel lines that ran ahead of his headlights, clinging to the wheel to ease the pain in his ribs.

He had found seven bodies in the dormitory, including a coarse-looking young white who was still alive, holding his stomach and shaking. He had left him to die. Apart from the bodies in the yard, the farm was empty. He had found weapons and ammunition in the warehouse, but Mzala and Terre-blanche had fled. They were planning to join the Walvis Bay road by cutting across the desert, but Neuman wouldn't let go of them. He had cast from his mind any thoughts that might interfere with the job at hand. He peered at the dunes through the windshield, increasingly high the farther he got into the Namib. The Toyota jolted and swerved over the loose sand, sending shooting pains through his body. He clung even more tightly to the wheel.

A jackal flashed across his headlights. He was driving along, burning with fever, when, rounding a slope, he saw them. Two phosphorescent red dots, in the hollow of the dunes. Neuman stopped three hundred yards from them, at the top of a dune, and cut the lights. He opened the door and looked at them through the infrared sight of the Steyr. The four-by-four seemed to have gotten stuck in the sand. Alerted by the lights of the Toyota, Mzala had abandoned his money and taken refuge behind the bodywork. Terreblanche had joined him, a light machine gun in his hand. They were both hiding behind the four-by-four, waiting for an invisible enemy.

Neuman wedged the barrel of the Steyr against the door and aimed for the water tank. He fired five bullets, to no avail. They were using an armored vehicle.

Neuman thought hard, his shirt soaked in sweat. Finally he

put the rifle down on the passenger seat, opened his pocket knife, and sat down behind the wheel. The fugitives' four-by-four was armored, but not the Toyota. The plan was simple, and suicidal.

The tires skated on the soft sand before getting a grip. He started driving down the slope. Two hundred and fifty yards . . . two hundred. He switched on the headlights, jammed the accelerator with the tip of the pocket knife, and headed straight for his target. Two gun barrels had emerged from behind the hood of the four-by-four. Neuman grabbed the rifle from the seat and threw himself through the door.

The windshield, the hood, the seats, the radiator grill, everything was demolished by the fire from the guns, but none of that stopped the vehicle from continuing to come straight toward them. The Toyota smashed into the rear of the other four-by-four, which was stuck so fast in the sand that it barely moved in spite of the impact. Terreblanche and Mzala had retreated toward the dune to escape the collision. Now they emerged from the darkness and aimed their weapons at the damaged Toyota. The front was smashed in, the windshield shattered, the door riddled with bullets, but there was nobody inside.

Neuman had rolled on the sand for about a hundred yards, recovered the rifle, and taken up position. His elbows on the ground, he aimed at the gas tank of the Toyota, which exploded with the third bullet. For a moment, the valley of sand was lit up by a jet of flame. Neuman couldn't see his targets, who were hidden by the screen of smoke. The flames quickly spread to the armored vehicle. Mzala and Terreblanche, who had been sheltering behind the bodywork, moved back. They fired a new volley, blindly, then another, which fell short. Overwhelmed by the inferno, the gas tank of the four-by-four now also exploded. The conflagration took Mzala by surprise, and the breath of the fire engulfed him.

Neuman heard his screams before he saw him. He was a human torch, turning around in circles, trying to flee the flames consuming him. He took a few clumsy steps over the sand, beating his arms to get out of the fire's fatal embrace, but it pursued him. He rolled on the ground, screaming ever louder. Neuman looked through his sight and searched the darkness for his other target, but all he could see was dense smoke. Terreblanche seemed to have vanished. A few yards away, Mzala was still screaming in agony. The smell of burning flesh reached Neuman. Mzala was gesticulating wildly and hitting the ground, all to no avail. Neuman finished him off with a bullet to the chest.

Beads of feverish sweat forming on his face, Neuman crawled about twenty yards, increased the angle of the zoom, and finally spotted Terreblanche, who had climbed to the top of the dune. He had a revolver in his belt, but no rifle. Neuman hit him in the shoulder as he was tumbling to the other side.

The flames were crackling, spreading black smoke. Neuman inspected the ridge behind which Terreblanche had disappeared, and slowly stood up. The earlier fall had rekindled the pain in his ribs. He went around the roaring inferno and followed the ridge that wound on in the moonlight. The tracks led to the top, which he reached after a laborious climb. The wind up here didn't exactly cool him. In front of him, the waves of sand stretched as far as the eye could see. There were footprints on the smooth side of the dune, running westward. Neuman cursed. He would never catch up with him on foot—not with this pain in his ribs.

He checked the magazine of his rifle, and gave a start when he saw the cartridge clip. He had only one bullet left.

A warm wind was blowing over the dunes. Neuman lay down and looked through his sight. A field of humps, their outlines indistinct, stretching away monotonously. Before long, he noticed a straight line of tracks. He followed them until he spotted the fugitive. He was walking with rhythmic steps, a revolver in his hand. Three hundred yards, as the crow flies. Neuman held his breath, forgot even the emptiness in his head, and pressed the trigger.

The explosion shattered the silence.

The figure collapsed on the sand.

*

Neuman aimed his Colt as he approached, but Terreblanche had stopped moving. He was lying on the ground, his automatic within reach of his hand, half unconscious. Neuman threw the gun as far as he could and kneeled by the wounded man. Sweat was pouring off him. He felt his pulse, saw that he was breathing. Neuman lifted the khaki T-shirt, which was sticky with blood. The bullet had hit a kidney, narrowly missing the liver.

Terreblanche opened his eyes while Neuman was examining the wound.

"I have money," he muttered. "Lots of—"

"Shut up or I'll leave you to die here."

Eaten by jackals—a happy ending. But Neuman wanted him alive. The documents relating to the experiments had disappeared, along with all trace of the lab, all the witnesses. He hadn't found anything on the farm. With Mzala dead, bringing this son of a bitch back alive was his last chance.

Terreblanche was pale in the starlight. Neuman saw an unpleasant-looking bite on his forearm—clearly a spider bite. He squeezed the skin, and a thin thread of yellow pus came out. A sand spider. Their bite could be fatal.

"Fucking thing bit me," Terreblanche cursed.

The night was still dark, the dunes vague outlines beneath the stars. Neuman lifted Terreblanche from where he lay on the sand and, without a word, helped him walk.

It took them nearly an hour to get back to the smoking car-
casses of the vehicles.

Neuman was sweating blood and water, and Terreblanche
had moaned all the way. Exhausted, he collapsed near the
burned-out four-by-fours. There was still an acrid smell coming
from the vehicles, stinking out the valley. What remained of
Mzala lay a few yards away, a black, shriveled shape that
reminded Neuman of his brother Andy. Busy pressing a handkerchief to his wound, Terreblanche did not even glance at his
accomplice. His complexion was waxen in the first light of
dawn. The poison was starting to take effect. Neuman again
checked his cell phone, but it was no use. There was no network.

Anxiety fell over his face like a veil. "How far is it from
here to the road?" he asked Terreblanche.

The ex-soldier barely raised his head. "Walvis Bay," he said.
"About thirty miles."

"And the nearest house?"

Terreblanche made an evasive gesture. "There's nothing but
sand around here."

Neuman grimaced. The farm was more than fifteen miles
away. He looked at the blue sky over the ridge of the dunes. The
vehicles were out of service and the emergency services weren't
coming—it was more than an hour since they had caught fire.

Terreblanche tore a piece of his undershirt to replace his
soaked handkerchief. The blood was starting to congeal, but
the wound hurt like hell. His arm was beginning to swell. He
threw a glance at the black cop, who was looking anxiously for
a sign in the sky. Terreblanche understood why when he asked,
"Does anyone else know we're here?"

"No."

The Namib Desert was one of the hottest places in the
world. By noon, the temperature would reach 120 in the shade,
160 in the sun. Without water, they wouldn't last a day.

9

Scientists had known for a long time that genes weren't simple things. The relationship between genotype and phenotype was so complex that it left no room for an elementary description of a person's genome or the pathological phenomena from which that person suffered. Human life became even more complex if you took into account each person's social background, his way of life and his environment, all of which contributed to the often unpredictable incidence of diseases—an Indian from the Amazon jungle did not always suffer the same ills as a European. Not that this mattered, since the research carried out by pharmaceutical companies were not intended for the Third World, which was incapable of paying the going rate. Moral and legal constraints having proved too restrictive in the rich countries (especially the Nuremberg Code, adopted as a result of the trials of Nazi doctors), the companies had outsourced their clinical trials to "low-cost" countries like India, Brazil, Bulgaria, Zambia, and South Africa, where guinea pigs, mostly poor and without access to medical care, could enjoy the best treatment and state-of-the-art equipment in exchange for their cooperation. As thousands of patients had to be tested before a medicine could be validated, the labs had subcontracted the clinical trials to research organizations. Couvence was one of these.

After years of research, Rossow's team had perfected a new molecule capable of curing conditions suffered by millions of

people in the West—anxiety, depression, obesity, and so on—
a product that would generate a staggering income.

They still had to test the product.

With its increasingly overcrowded townships, South Africa
and the Cape region in particular were a perfect testing
ground. Not only was there an endless supply of untreated
patients, but after certain tragic results linked to problems of
degeneration and other undesirable side effects, it had become
impossible to continue the research in a transparent manner.
Faced with determined competition from other companies,
speed was of the essence, so they had opted for a mobile unit
on the edge of the townships where they would do their tests
on docile and unattached guinea pigs, street kids that no one
would worry about.

To limit the risks, they would inoculate them with the AIDS
virus, which was extremely effective. There were two advan-
tages: the subjects' life expectancy was limited anyway, and, as
the disease was endemic in South Africa, a few more deaths
wouldn't arouse suspicion in case anything went wrong.

Placed in charge of the operation, Terreblanche had taken
advantage of the no-go areas to come to an agreement with
Mzala, whose gang controlled Khayelitsha. Mzala had subcontracted the actual dealing to Gulethu and his band of mercenaries who hung around the buffer zones. Gulethu and his
bunch of misfits had distributed the cocktail in the squatter
camps without arousing suspicion. The *tik* hooked the local
kids, and they were taken at night to the Muizenberg lab, on
the edge of the township, in order to evaluate the development
of the molecule. Those who survived would die of AIDS and
end up as pig swill. But then Gulethu had tried to double-cross
them, and had fucked the whole thing up.

Brian Epkeen was dying from the heat in spite of the air-
conditioning in the hospital room. He'd been beaten up,
scalped, put in an electric chair. Sitting beside the bed,

Suprintendent Krüge was listening to his report in silence. The police had collected about twenty dead bodies in the township, including Ali Neuman's mother, and human bones behind the Lengezi church. For the moment, the press didn't know anything.

"Do you know where Neuman is?" Krüge asked.

"No."

Brian had only just resurfaced when Krüge had arrived to question him.

The superintendent wedged his double chin on the collar of his shirt and sighed. "If there's any evidence for what you're saying, then show it to me. You don't have anything, lieutenant."

A flight of crows passed across his clouded eyes. "What do you mean, I don't have anything?"

"Where's your evidence?"

"Being held prisoner at Van der Verskuizen's house, Debeer dead, Terreblanche at large. What more do you need?"

"We don't have any witnesses in this case," Krüge replied. "Not one."

"Obviously, they're all dead."

"That's the problem. No one knows where the bones found behind the church came from, or who put them there. With Neuman nowhere to be found, we don't have any explanation. As for what happened at the dentist's house, we haven't found any prints. Or rather, yes, we found yours."

"Everything was wiped, you know that perfectly well," Brian retorted from his heaped-up pillows. "Just like in the Muizenberg house. The offshore account is—"

"Information obtained illegally," Krüge cut in. "Officer Helms has told us all about how you got hold of it."

Brian's face turned a little paler in the artificial light. Janet Helms had betrayed them. She had dropped them just as they were reaching their goal. They had let themselves be fooled by those fucking seal eyes of hers.

"Terreblanche and Rossow took part in Dr. Basson's Project Coast," Brian said, recovering his composure. "Terreblanche had the expertise and the logistical backup to organize an operation on this scale. Couvence provides a legal cover. You just have to question Rossow."

"What do you think, lieutenant? That you're going to attack a multinational pharmaceutical company with that? Terreblanche, Rossow, and Debeer don't have criminal records. There's nothing to corroborate your story." Krüge looked at him as if he were a rabbit caught in the headlights. "You know what's going to happen, Epkeen? *They're* going to attack *you*, with an army of lawyers. They're going to find out things about you, your loose morals, your son who refuses to see you, your quarrels with your ex-wife, the divorce you still haven't come to terms with. They're going to accuse you of murdering Rick van der Verskuizen."

"*What?*"

"It would have been interesting to hear the dentist's statement," Krüge conceded. "Unfortunately, he was found dead in his living room, shot in the back of the neck with a bullet from your service pistol."

"What are you implying? We were held prisoner, I was tortured to reveal what I'd found out in Hout Bay, and then we were injected with enough drugs to make a buffalo high. The crap I have in my blood, Debeer's body, the stuff in the small case—doesn't any of that count?"

Krüge didn't give an inch. "The gun used to kill the dentist was found in the bedroom with your prints on it. They're going to pin it on you, which will discredit your testimony and your ex-wife's. She'll be depicted as some kind of vixen with violent mood swings, willing to do anything to punish a man who cheated on her, even getting together with her biggest enemy. They're going to say you were hooked on that famous drug, that you were trying to make up for your losses by getting rid of your rival, and that you killed the dealer, Debeer, in a violent fit of anger."

"It was a setup!" Brian said, angrily. "You know that!"

"Prove it!"

"But it's just ridiculous!"

"No more so than your story of an industrial plot," Krüge retorted. "After what happened during apartheid, you ought to know that South Africa is the country where medical research is most closely monitored, especially when it comes to tests on humans. You'll have to convince a jury of your allegations. You really caused carnage in that house. And the photographs we took in the bedroom where we found you don't look good for you either."

"What photos?" A flash of suspicion appeared in his dulled eyes.

"You didn't see the state you put your ex-wife in," he said. "Hands tied behind her back, your blood all over her body, her torn clothes, the scratches, the blows, the sexual violence. That's not love, Epkeen, that's rage. When we found you, you were frantically circling the bed."

A shiver ran down his spine. A lion. A lion defending his territory.

"I didn't rape my wife," he said—a slip of the tongue.

"But it was her skin we found under your nails. That will have quite an effect on a jury."

For a moment, Brian's head spun, and he clutched at the air. The drugs, the rats in Tembo's laboratory, the final phase—extreme aggression.

"They drugged us," he growled. "You know that as well as I do."

"Your prints are on the syringe."

"They were trying to frame me. Shit, Debeer had plastic gloves on when you found him, didn't he?"

"That doesn't explain anything. At least that's what they'll say in court. Whatever happens, anything you say about collusion between your phantom pharmaceutical company and a paramilitary group led by an ex-colonel can be turned against you. Your night visit to the ADT office in Hout Bay—quite apart from the fact that none of the documents you claim you found are still around—will in any case be declared inadmissible."

"It's all on the memory stick."

Krüge opened his hands in a gesture of good faith. "Then show it to me."

There was a foul taste in Brian's mouth, and he felt dizzy. Ruby, Terreblanche, Debeer, the injections, Ali's disappearance, everything was going around in his head, he was going to fall, a long way down. He looked closely at the superintendent's flabby, impassive face beside the bed.

"Are you in on this, Krüge?"

"I put that comment down to a confused mind," Krüge muttered angrily. "But take care what you say, lieutenant. I'm just trying to warn you. The pharmaceutical industry is one of the most powerful lobbies on the fucking planet."

"And one of the most corrupt."

"Listen," Krüge said, softening, "believe it or not, I'm on your side. But we're going to need really solid arguments to convince the prosecutor to authorize an investigation, searches. You'll also have to demolish whatever accusations they throw at you, and we have only your word."

Brian was listening, in a daze. "What about my eyes?" he said. "Did I burn them to make myself look nice?"

"They'll ask for a psychiatric examination and . . ."

Brian raised his hand, as if throwing in the towel. He was coming back to life, too late. The situation was absurd—they hadn't gone through all this shit to end up here, in a hospital room.

"I'm not taking any action against you," Krüge announced by way of conclusion. "Not for the moment, anyway. But I advise you to watch your step, until we get this cleared up.

Whatever happens, you're off the case. Gulethu killed the two girls—that's the official version. There's no industrial-criminal network, there's only a terrible fiasco and my head on the block. The case is closed," he insisted. "And that's how I want you to consider it. Apart from anything else, there was another murder last night. Van Vost, one of the principal donors of the National Party, apparently killed by a black prostitute—"

"Where's Ruby?" Brian cut in.

"Next door," Krüge said, with a movement of the head. "But don't count on her testimony."

"Why, did you cut her tongue out, too?"

"I don't think much of your sense of humor, Lieutenant Epkeen."

"You're wrong, life's one big laugh after you've been tortured."

"You exceeded your instructions and acted in a reckless manner," Krüge said, becoming heated again. "I'll talk to Neuman as soon as he shows up and take whatever action I deem necessary."

"Cover the whole thing up, you mean? Are you afraid for your fucking World Cup?"

"Go home," Krüge growled. "And stay there until further orders. Understood?"

Brian nodded. Message received. Destination nowhere.

Krüge left the room, leaving the door open, muttered something inaudible in the corridor and walked away. After a moment, Janet Helms came in. She was wearing her tight uniform and carrying a plastic bag.

"I brought you some clean clothes," she said.

"Do you want a medal?"

She advanced timidly, met Brian's accusing look, and placed the things on the chair next to the bed.

"Krüge give you the third degree, is that it?" he said, haughtily.

Janet lowered her head like a little girl caught doing something naughty and fidgeted nervously. "None of the information we gathered is admissible in court," she said, in an attempt to clear her name. "I had no choice. My career's on the line." She lifted her big, wet eyes. "I hadn't heard from you since yesterday morning. I thought they'd killed you."

Her little ploy wasn't working.

"Do you have any information on Rossow?" he asked.

Janet Helms pursed her brown lips.

"Have you located him? Do you know his whereabouts?"

"I'm not allowed to tell you," she said at last.

"Krüge's orders?"

"The case is closed," she pleaded.

"You're forgetting Neuman. Did Krüge ask you to grill me, is that it?"

Janet Helms did not reply immediately. "Do you know where he is?"

"If I did," Brian said, peremptorily, "I'd have gotten out of here before now."

Janet sighed. She was clearly hesitating. Brian let her stew in her own juice. The girl disgusted him—and she knew it.

"There's something I didn't tell Krüge's men," she said at last. "There's a Steyr rifle missing from the armory. Captain Neuman signed it out—yesterday morning."

A sniper's weapon.

Brian's heart started racing. Ali was going to kill them.

All of them.

With or without Krüge's consent.

*

Brian was walking on an invisible wire along the corridor of the Park Avenue hospital. The duty doctor had refused to let him leave in that condition, so he had discharged himself—

why didn't they just leave him alone?—and asked to see Ruby. Request denied—she had just come out of her coma and was resting after the emergency tritherapy they had been given. He phoned Neuman from the hospital switchboard, just in case, but there was no network.

The asphalt was melting in the afternoon sun when Brian left the hospital. All he could see was a blurred filter behind his burning eyes, the rest was a complete mess. He felt nauseous, wanted to vomit. He bought a ten-rand pair of Ray-Bans from a stall in Greenmarket, and picked up a cell phone and his car from the basement of headquarters. The rear windshield was shattered, the front one was cracked from left to right, but the car started up at the first attempt.

And then, she . . . closed.
Her baby blue . . .
Her baby blue . . .
Oh . . . her baby blue . . . EYES!!!

The ash flew about in the passenger compartment of the Mercedes. Brian threw his cigarette out the window and climbed toward Somerset. His head still hurt terribly, and the conversation he'd had earlier had driven him over the edge. Krüge was covering up the case for reasons that escaped him, or rather, that were beyond him. But Brian wasn't fooled. Faced with competition from world markets, sovereign states could do very little to withstand the pressures of finance and globalized trade, unless they wanted to alienate investors and threaten their own gross national product. The role of states was now limited to maintaining order and security in the midst of a new world disorder controlled by centrifugal, supranational and elusive forces. No one genuinely believed in progress anymore, the world had become an uncertain, precarious place, but most decision makers were happy to let the pirates of this phantom system continue with their plunder and to take advantage of it themselves while hoping it would all blow over. The excluded were pushed farther out onto the periphery of huge cities reserved for the winners of a cannibalistic game in which, with no prospect of collective action, people's widespread frustration was channeled into television, sports, and celebrity culture.

Whether or not someone was exerting pressure on him, Krüge was a pragmatist. He wasn't going to risk frightening investors away from the country that was getting ready to organize a great sporting carnival, just for the sake of a few street kids, whose prospects boiled down to a bottleneck filled with *tik* or a stray bullet. Neuman was Brian's one hope—a hope that had vanished nearly two days earlier.

Brian coasted home and lay down wearily on the couch in the living room. Debeer's injection had sent him into a terrifying state, and the night he had spent delirious in a hospital bed had left him exhausted. Like a horse that had died in the mud. He lay there for a while, putting back the scattered pieces of himself. The atmosphere in the house suddenly felt sinister. As if it wasn't his anymore, as if the walls wanted to throw him out. The ghost of Ruby, a specter contaminated by the virus, coming to take her revenge on him? He dismissed his junkie visions, took two painkillers, and put on the latest Scrape. All the way—the crows will pick you clean. And indeed, a black veil soon fell over him as he lay on the couch. The music howled in the living room, loud enough to tear the skin from the sky. His thoughts gradually organized themselves. What did Janet Helms's betrayal matter? Ali had cut off contact with them in order to have a free hand. And the fact that he had chosen a sniper's weapon from the armory meant that he knew where the killers were.

Mzala—escaped.

Terreblanche—untraceable.

The American gang—wiped out.

The kids—a heap of bones.

Brian turned the mystery over a thousand times in his messed-up head, and at last understood. Zina.

*

Rhodes House was the hip club in the City Bowl, where models and advertising personalities met between shoots—a lucrative activity due to the region's exceptional light.

A self-satisfied male clientele was pouring in that evening, selected by the well-dressed, muscular young bouncer—anyone without a tan and an open white shirt had few chances of getting in. With his bandaged head, his walk—like a rusty robot—and his red watery eyes, Brian Epkeen looked like someone at the end of his tether. He showed his badge to the bouncer and found a place at the bar, which overlooked the stage.

The show was just finishing. To the accompaniment of Zulu drums, a wall of electronic sound, and wildly flashing lights, Zina was tearing the strings from an incandescent guitar. Brian screwed up his eyes to calm his dizziness, his nerves in meltdown. A brief moment of harmony. When the earthquake was over, Zina went up in smoke, beneath a flood of sound and feedback.

After a moment or two, the lights went up, and they started playing elevator music to cover the voices. Brian tried to order a drink but the barman with his hair full of gel ignored him. Now that the evening's show was over, the models resumed their commercial break on the dance floor, where Casanovas in Versace flirted with their sulky shadows. Brian watched the stage door, in agony—the tritherapy was turning his stomach. Zina finally came out of her dressing room. Brian introduced himself, with all the noise around them, and drew her toward the bar. She was wearing a dress cut low at the back, but no shoes. A real beauty.

"Ali told me you were a former Inkatha militant," he said, as they reached the bar. "Not an electronic maniac."

"Ali told me you were a friend," she retorted, "not a mummy."

"Do you like my bandage?"

Zina looked at his scabs and pulled a face. "Is it for decoration?"

"Actually, I'm in terrible pain."

She raised an eyebrow, her face bright in the spotlights. "You're quite funny for a white," she said.

"Can I buy you a drink?"

"No."

In any case, the barman with the slicked-back hair was literally under siege.

She leaned on the damp counter. "You wanted to talk to me?"

"No one's heard from Ali since yesterday," Brian said. "I'm looking for him. It's really urgent, if you must know."

The room was throbbing with bass. Zina's face did not betray the least emotion.

"You don't seem surprised," he said. "He came to see you, didn't he?"

She forgot about his bandages and looked into his sea-green eyes. "Yes, we talked."

"About Terreblanche?"

She nodded.

"This is important," he said, his pulse beating faster. "Do you have any information?"

A veil of melancholy fell over her face. "I know Terreblanche bought a farm in Namibia," she said at last. "Two years ago, through a bogus company. A former training camp in the middle of the Namib Desert. Your friend seemed interested. I wasn't."

Brian didn't see the tears well in her eyes. Namibia. By cutting off all contact, Ali had cut himself off from the law. The adrenalin came flooding back. He noted down the information on his cigarette pack and turned back to Zina, who was still leaning on the bar.

"Any chance we can see each other again?" he asked.

Surrounded by the clubbers, Zina smiled. "Sorry, Prince Charming. It was the Zulu king I loved."

A lovely smile, as lovely as she was, and just as fractured.

10.

Acattle truck screamed past the windows of the Mercedes. A mechanic had put on some insulating tape to mend the rear windshield, but the sun beat down on the driver's side. Brian Epkeen had been driving for hours on the N7, which ran due north to the Namibian border. He had crossed the Veld, Afrikaner country, three hundred miles of yellow hills and barren plains where nothing grew except vines, and there were just a few scattered farms flung down here like men thrown overboard into the sea. The image of a contaminated Ruby returned as the dotted lines on the asphalt sped past. What if the tritherapy didn't work, what if the mutant virus resisted shock treatment? He saw himself back in the bedroom, trembling for her when Terreblanche had aimed his gun at her face, and then groggy, lying on top of her bloodstained body.

He reached Springbok in the early hours of the morning, exhausted.

Springbok was the last stopping-off point before the Namibian border. The golden age of mining had passed, all you saw now were gaudy Wimpy restaurants, churches, a few businesses supplying deer hunters, and a collection of semi-precious stones displayed in the window with pride by Joppie, the owner of the Café Lounge. Brian parked the Mercedes outside the café, the only place open on the deserted main street at this hour.

A *boeremusierk*[1] tune was playing softly. Wedged behind a

---

[1] Traditional Boer music.

counter overloaded with badges and empty cigarette lighters used purely for decoration, Joppie was talking in Afrikaans to another redneck, weighing about three hundred pounds, who was as graceful as a cow shitting itself. Heads of springboks and oryx adorned the walls, frozen forever in an expression of supreme indifference.

"What can I do for you?" the boss asked, in a surly tone.

Even his voice wore a check shirt. Brian asked him, in English, for a coffee, and went and sat down on the terrace that looked out on the main street. He drank the coffee— more like hot water colored black—and waited for the gun shop to open its doors so that he could buy a hunting rifle and a box of cartridges.

When the assistant saw his police badge, there were no problems. "Was it a springbok that did that to you?" the man joked, winking at his scabs.

"Yes, a female."

"Ha ha!"

A group of blondes encased in flounce dresses was coming out of church as Brian put the rifle in the trunk of his car. The coffee was still in his stomach, like the atmosphere of this god-forsaken city. He set off again, bidding farewell to the fat majorettes with a cloud of dust.

After another forty miles, he reached the Namibian border. He parked his car by the huts that served as a border post and stretched his body shaken by the road.

There weren't many tourists here in summer, when the sun burned everything. He left the elderly German couple in safari suits by the immigration desk, presented his request to the constable in charge of stamping documents, and consulted the register of arrivals. Neuman had crossed the border two days earlier, at seven in the evening.

Bits of punctured tires, a smashed car, a truck across the

road, a body under a blanket—the B1 that crossed Namibia was particularly dangerous, despite all the work done on it in the past few years. Brian filled up with water and gas at the service station in Grünau, ate a sandwich in the noon shade and shared a cigarette with the mango vendors dozing under their cotton sunhats. The temperature climbed the farther he got into the red desert. The sheep had taken shelter under the few trees, the truck drivers were napping in the shade of the axles. He called Neuman for the first time that morning. Still no network.

"What the fuck are you doing?"

Brian was talking to himself. Men on their own always talk too much, or keep silent like carp. That was a line from a film. Or a book. He couldn't remember. He left behind the vendors from the village of cinderblock huts that bordered the highway and continued on his way to Mariental, two hundred and fifty miles in a straight line across plateaus and mesas scalped by the wind.

Not many people lived in the Namibian furnace—descendants of Germans who had massacred the Herero tribes at the beginning of the previous century, and were now shopkeepers or hoteliers, and a few nomadic tribes, like the Khoikhoi. All the rest belonged to nature. The Mercedes crossed the arid plain beneath a fiery sun.

According to Zina's information, Terreblanche had established his base in a reserve near the Sesriem dunes. He would be there before nightfall. An old locomotive dragging dismembered wagons belched black smoke on the way out of Keepmanshoop, and disappeared into the stony terrain. The miles flew past, a permanent mirage in the heat haze above the asphalt. Brian's throat was dry in spite of the gallons of water he had drunk, and his eyes felt as if they were under an electric dryer. The border police had his description, which meant he could get a reprimand from Krüge for acting without authorization, but he didn't give a damn. For the moment, the Mercedes, although running at full throttle, was holding up. After miles of this furnace, Brian turned off the potholed highway onto the road to Sesriem.

The only things he passed were tame-looking springboks in the shade of scrawny trees, a big kudu that bolted at his approach, and a boy on a bicycle carrying a bottle of boiled water on his rack. He reached the gates of the Namib in the first glimmer of twilight.

The Sesriem post was ghostlike at this time of year. After stretching his legs in the yard, he talked to the affable official who was distributing entry tickets to the reserve, but there was no record of any Neuman having passed through here.

"I've only seen the odd tourist," he said, consulting his register. "All of them white."

Brian again filled up with water and gas before plunging into the desert. Terreblanche's farm was some thirty miles, somewhere in Namib Naukluft Park. He threw the rest of his sandwich on the floor of the car and smoked a cigarette to calm down.

A magpie was disemboweling a jackal that had been run over when the Mercedes left the tarred section of the road. The Sossusvlei dunes were among the highest in the world. Red, orange, pink, and mauve—the colors varied depending on the angle of vision and the position of the sun. A Dantesque landscape he barely noticed, with his nose in the map. He followed the main trail for about eight miles, turned west, and after a while came to a metal fence and slowed down.

A sign in several languages forbade access to the site, and the fence clearly ran for miles. Brian smashed through it, and continued driving along the bumpy trail.

There was a sudden storm, like a storm at sea, and lightning streaked across the sky. Ali had a head start of almost two days. What had he been doing all this time?

Angry clouds threw veils of rain over the thirsty plain. At last, Brian saw a building in the shade of the dunes, a farmhouse with a prefabricated hut as an extension.

The handful of oryx lazing on the plain fled when he stopped his vehicle on the side of the trail. In the distance, the farm seemed empty. He took the binoculars from the glove compartment and inspected the site. The farm swayed for a moment in his sights—the wind had burned his eyes. He couldn't see any movement. Falcons were whirling in the orange sky. Then he saw a patch on the trail. A man. Lying motionless. A corpse. There were others close to the prefabs, at least six, being fought over by the magpies. And another one in the yard.

*

Neuman and Terreblanche had waited in the shade of the burned-out vehicles, but nobody had come. The carnage at the farm, the shots, the exploding gas tanks, the burning vehicles, had all passed unnoticed. The giant dunes must have hidden the flames, and the darkness the trail of smoke. The sun had climbed, a sun that stung the skin and baked sheet metal, making it impossible to stay in one place for too long, and still they were waiting and nothing came. No reconnaissance plane crossing the sky, no cloud of dust raised by a ranger's patrol car. The horizon remained a pure, hopelessly empty cobalt blue.

A yellow lizard took shelter beneath the burning sand.

"We're going to fry here," Terreblanche predicted, his back against the blackened side of the Toyota.

The blood had stopped flowing from his wound, but long ravines had appeared in his crimson face. The poison from the spider bite had spread through his body and was starting to paralyze his limbs. The heat showed no sign of abating. His cracked lips were encrusted with sand, and a sickly light hovered at the back of his eyes—thirst.

"Save your saliva for your trial," Neuman said.

"There won't be a trial. You have no evidence."

"Except you. Now shut up."

Terreblanche fell silent. His forearm had swollen to almost twice its size. The hole had necrotized, the skin around the bite had first turned yellow and was now blue. Neuman had handcuffed him to the bodywork, but he was in no state to escape. The shadows of the clouds passed over the ridges of the unreal dunes.

There was nothing to hear, only the immortal silence over the motionless desert.

They waited some more, under their makeshift shelter, without exchanging a single word.

They were steaming.

Nobody would come.

Their existence, even inside the reserve, was a secret. No one would report them missing. Joost Terreblanche didn't even exist, he had melted into the chaos of the world. He had set up his Namibian base with the complicity of people who took great care to keep their noses out of his affairs, a retreat where he could play dead until things sorted themselves out. No one cared about their fate. They had been left in this valley of sand, this ocean of fire, to die of thirst.

Evening fell.

Neuman had razor blades in his throat. He lifted his aching carcass and took a few steps. In the shade of the Toyota, Terreblanche barely reacted. His mouth was like a wrinkled apple, his features those of a recumbent statue. He had lost too much blood on the road. He had no more saliva left. His arm was misshapen.

Neuman shook him with his foot. "Stand up."

Terreblanche opened one eye, as misty as the other. The sun had disappeared behind the ridge. He tried to speak but emitted only a barely audible wheeze. Neuman took off the handcuffs and helped him to his feet. Terreblanche could hardly stand. He looked at Neuman wild-eyed, as if he was no longer of this world.

Neuman turned toward the east. "We're going to take a little walk," he announced.

Eighteen miles across the dunes. They had a chance to get to the farm before dawn—a chance in a thousand.

*

Brian had searched the buildings and the corpses that littered the ground. Nine around the farmhouse, four more in the dormitory. All paramilitaries, killed by high-caliber bullets. 7.62s, to judge by the piece of steel extracted from a wound. From a Steyr rifle. He was on the right track, but neither Terreblanche nor Mzala was among the victims. Had they escaped? Brian had checked the surroundings, but the wind and the storm had wiped out any tracks.

He gave up his search at dusk.

He informed the local authorities of the carnage at the farm and found shelter in Desert Camp, a lodge on the edge of the reserve.

As it was summer, the place was almost empty. He parked his heap of dust in front of the vast plain and negotiated his keys from the young Namibian girl at reception. From the tiny ceramic swimming pool there was a view of the red desert. The tents were top of the range, cleverly made, with outside kitchens, Moroccan bathrooms, and lots of windows with views of the surroundings. Brian took a cold shower and drank a beer as he watched night fall. The savannah was an unreal expanse stretching all the way to the jagged mountains of the Namib. Ali was out there, somewhere.

Brian left the terrace and took a few steps into the desert. An ostrich passed in the distance. Exhausted, he stretched out at the foot of a dead tree. The sand was soft to the touch, the silence so total it swallowed the vastness. He thought of his son, David, who had gone to have a wild time in Port Elizabeth, then of Ruby, who must be languishing in her hospital bed. He didn't know if they were saved, if the virus would mutate, if she bore him a grudge. Ali's face took up all the space. Why hadn't he informed him? Why hadn't he said anything?

A hundred, a thousand stars appeared in the sky. With much flapping of wings, an owl came to rest on the branch of the dead tree beneath which he lay. A night bird with carefully folded white feathers, staring at him with intermittent eyes. The night was black now. Swarms of stars jostled one another along the Milky Way, shooting stars crisscrossing the sky.

Brian lay there, arms outstretched on the warm orange sand, counting the dead—a procession floating, like him, in the nebula.

"Where are you?"

Up on his scraggy perch, the owl did not know. He was looking down stoically at the human being.

A brief moment of fraternity. At the far end of despair, Brian fell asleep by the light from a stick of Durban Poison that sent him down to the bottom.

*

The moon had guided them toward the sleepy horizon, a mute witness to their stations of the cross. Terreblanche had been wandering for a while in a semi-coma, his complexion ever paler under the white moon. The wound on his arm was now covered in a yellow crust. He was walking like a lame puppet, his eyes lost in the mists of time. Finally, after four hours of this forced march across the dunes, he collapsed.

He wouldn't get up again. After the blood he had lost, the spider poison, the day he had spent in this sauna, and the walk, he was completely dehydrated. They had only covered a few miles. It was still a long way to the farm, somewhere at the other end of the night. Neuman made hardly any attempt to talk to him. His throat was so dry that all that came from his mouth was a thin wheeze. Terreblanche, at his feet, was like a little old man now. He tried to revive him, in vain. There was no reaction. But his lips, cracked by the heat, were moving.

Neuman attached one handcuff to Terreblanche's wrist, the other to his own, and started pulling him across the sand.

Every step bent his broken rib, every step cost him two lives, but he held fast to his prey—his prey was all that mattered.

A hundred yards, two hundred, five hundred. He talked to him to encourage him, he talked to this lifeless piece of shit in order not to think, of his mother or anyone. He had dragged him like that for two whole hours, as far as his legs could carry him, without wondering if Terreblanche was still breathing. He was walking on an imaginary line. But his strength was going. His shirt, previously soaked, was now as dry as his skin. He couldn't stay on his feet. Or bend. The effort had completely devoured him. His thighs were like brittle wood. Worst of all, his throat was burning horribly. He staggered, still holding on to his prey, tumbled down the slopes, pulled it back up to the top, fell down the other side, raving. His prey was dead. Done for. He dragged it a few more yards, but his strength had finally gone: He was seeing double, triple, he couldn't see anything. The farm was too far. His mind was shot to pieces. No more saliva in his thoughts. No more oil in his fine body.

He collapsed against the side of a dune.

A deafening silence hovered over the desert. Neuman could barely make out the little chrome eyes observing him from the celestial vault. A black night.

"Are you afraid, little Zulu? Are you afraid?"

Nobody knew. Not even his mother. There was his father's

body to take down, strips of flesh falling off in the clear water, Andy reduced to something twisted and black, the funeral, the dead to be mourned, the ignorant *sangoma* who had sounded his chest, their escape to be organized. No one knew what the vigilantes had done to him behind the house. His father's torn body, Andy's black tears, his shorts full of piss, the smell of burned rubber, it had all happened too quickly. The vigilantes tearing him apart behind the house, his terrified screams, the three masked men slaughtering his testicles with their kicks, the dogs of war determined to make him impotent—the film replayed one last time on the black screen of the cosmos.

Neuman opened his eyes. His lids were heavy, but a strange feeling of lightness was slowly taking over his mind. The end of his insomnia? He thought of the mother he had loved, and had an image of her happily laughing her big, blind woman's laugh, but another face soon took up all the space. Zina, *Zaziwe*, that dream he had had a thousand times when, at night, her countryside smell enveloped him and drew him far from the world, with her. A warm wind smoothed the sand in the hollow of the dune.

Neuman closed his eyes, the better to caress her. It was done.

11

Have you seen my baby? Tell me, sir. Have you seen my baby?"

An old woman in rags had approached the gas pumps. Brian Epkeen, frying inside the car, barely paid her any attention. This Khoikhoi woman was from the village next to the service station—no more than about twenty wretched huts without water or electricity. She spoke with the clicks characteristic of her language, a woman of no clear age, her face covered in sand.

"Have you seen my baby?" she repeated.

Brian emerged from his lethargy. The woman was holding a dirty old cloth against her chest and was looking at him, imploring him. The Namibian attendant tried to shoo her away, but she returned to the attack, as if she hadn't heard. She wandered like this all day. She had been cradling her piece of cloth, repeating the same sentence, always the same one, for years, to every motorist who came to fill up here.

"Sir . . . please . . . Have you seen my baby?"

She had gone crazy.

It was said that she had left him sleeping in the hut while she went to fetch water from the well, and when she came back she saw baboons carrying him away. The men of the village had immediately set off in pursuit, they had searched everywhere in the desert but the child had never been found, only a torn piece of cloth from his baby clothes among the rocks. It was this piece of cloth she had been carrying with her ever since, cradling it to assuage her sadness.

All just gossip.

"Have you seen my baby?"

Brian shivered in spite of the heat. The old Khoikhoi was begging him, with those crazy eyes of hers.

That was when he received a call from the post at Sesriem. A ranger had found the burned-out remains of two vehicles, and an unidentified human body.

*

Four-by-fours.

Two heaps of metal embedded in the burning sand of Namib Naukluft Park. The bodywork had turned black in the flames, but Brian counted several bullet holes—large-caliber bullets, one of which had pierced the Toyota's gas tank. The body lay a few yards away, burned to cinders. A man, to judge by his size. The material of his clothes had melted to his swollen skin, which, in cracking with the heat, had revived wounds that vultures and ants were fighting over. A bullet had pierced his chest. A man of medium height. You had to take off his boots to see that he was black. Mzala?

Brian peered down at the AK-47 on the ground, near the sheets of metal, checked the cartridge case. Empty. A whistle made him look up. The ranger who was with him—Roy, a talkative Namibian with an enigmatic smile—was signaling to him from the top of the dune. He had found something.

The noon sun crushed everything. Brian adjusted his water-soaked cap and climbed the dune with small methodical steps. He stopped halfway up, his legs shaking. Roy was waiting for him at the top, crouching, impassive beneath his visor. Brian reached him at last, his eyes full of stars after the ascent. A weapon lay there, half covered by the sand, a Steyr rifle with a precision sight.

The Namibian said nothing, his eyes creased by the bright

light of the desert. From up here, the burned-out vehicles seemed tiny. Brian looked at the empty expanse. A valley of red sand, white-hot. Caught in the trap, with no means of communication or transportation, Neuman and Terreblanche must have set off on foot, cutting across the dunes to get back to the road. The wind had wiped out their tracks, but they had kept walking due east, toward the farm.

They drove for nearly an hour through the furnace without seeing a single animal. Roy navigated with a sure hand, in silence. Brian didn't feel like talking either. Through his binoculars, he looked at the ridges and the few trees lost in the ocean of sand. Royal-blue sky, scarlet earth, and still not a soul to be seen in this desolate land. 117 degrees, according to the dial in the car. The heat blurred the outlines, danced in misty waves in the sight of the binoculars. Hovering mirages.

"The road isn't far," Roy announced in a neutral voice.

The Jeep jolted over the soft sand. Brian saw a black patch, on his right, about two hundred yards away, against the side of a dune. He informed Roy, who immediately veered right. The tires skidded on the slope. Rather than risk getting stuck in the sand, Roy stopped at the foot of the dune.

A cloud of acrid dust blew past the windshield. Brian slammed the car door shut, his eyes riveted on his target—a shape, a little higher up, half covered by sand. He climbed the ridge, protecting himself from the dry, burning wind that stung his face, and soon slowed down, out of breath. There wasn't one man lying against the dune, but two, side by side, facing the sky. Brian climbed the last few yards like an automaton. Ali and Terreblanche were lying on the sand, clothes partly torn, unrecognizable. The sun had reduced their bodies to two shriveled stumps, two scrawny skeletons eaten by the desert. The sun had drunk them dry. Emptied them. Brian swallowed the saliva he didn't have. They had already been dead for several days. The bones stuck out on their dried-up faces—Terre-blanche's face had turned black, skin like dead leaves that crumble when you touch them—with a hideous smile on his wrinkled lips. They had baked. Even their bones seemed to have shrunk.

Brian bent over his friend, and swayed a moment in the sauna. Ali was handcuffed to his prey. They were barely a mile from the road.

12.

Not many people would be there to meet what remained of Ali.

Brian didn't have Maia's number—he didn't even know her surname—Zina had left the city without leaving an address, and Ali didn't have any remaining family. His body was arriving from Windhoek, by special plane. Brian would see that it was transferred to Zulu country, to be with his parents and ancestors who were, perhaps, waiting for him somewhere.

The Namibian manhunt had been a fiasco. Neuman had left nothing but corpses in his wake, and no evidence that the pharmaceutical industry and the country's Mafias were in league. Krüge had avoided a diplomatic incident, and nobody wanted any publicity about the case. The bodies of Terreblanche and his men were still in the hands of the Namibian authorities. It wasn't in their interest, either, to start an investigation. Out of guilt and disgust, Brian had handed in his badge and everything that went with it. He had spent the whole of his adult life chasing corpses. Ali's was one too many.

He'd had enough. He was making way for others. He'd concentrate on the living now. Beginning with David—returning from his trip, the prodigal son had opened his mail, and subsequently phoned.

Corruption, complicity—Terreblanche and his sponsors had enjoyed protection at all levels, including their own unsecured lines. Brian had posted one of the two memory sticks before going to Rick's that other night, with his name on the back of the envelope by way of explanation. He hadn't talked under torture. No one knew the existence of those files. David would have time to go back over the trail, supplement his investigation and, above all, choose his allies. A baptism of fire, which might reconcile them.

Claire came out of the house before Brian had had time to cross the garden. She ran to him and threw herself in his arms.

"I'm sorry . . . I'm sorry . . ."

Claire clung to him as if he might escape her. She wanted to tell him that she had been unfair to them, she had been thinking about it for days, she ought to have talked to them, but Dan's death had left her without a voice, her heart sewn up. Now it was too late. Too late. Brian stroked the back of her neck as she sobbed. He felt the blonde down growing back under her wig, and now he also held her tight. He was shaking—they were the only two left now . . .

He lifted her face and dried her tears with his finger. "There, now."

The sun was falling gently over the Veld bordering the runway of the little airfield. Like him, Claire wasn't saying anything. Like him, she was waiting on the tarmac for a sign from the sky. The grass, bent by the wind, was turning emerald, a few pink clouds swelled on the horizon, but still nothing came. Brian was thinking about their friendship, Ali's shyness with women, the sadness in his eyes when he didn't know anyone was looking. Whatever might have happened, Ali's secrets had died with him.

Brian pricked up his ears. The slender wings of a light aircraft appeared, a quicksilver dot in the twilight. Claire pushed back the lock of hair that was blowing about on her cheek.

"There he is," she said in a low voice.

The noise of the propellers came closer, muffled now. They were waiting near the runway when a voice rang out.

"Brian!"

He turned and saw Ruby on the tarmac. She was wearing tight-fitting black jeans, her hair was cut short, and there was a long gash on her forearm. They hadn't seen each other since the hospital. She nodded to Claire and walked toward Brian, shyly.

"David told me. About Ali."

Her eyes were the color of the Veld, but something had broken inside her. Brian didn't ask what. They looked up at the sky, which, like Ali, kept disappearing. The twin-engine plane had begun its descent, its nose aimed for landing. Ruby slid her hand into Brian's and kept it there. Her short hair suited her. So did her black jeans. An intense burst of tenderness gripped him, and soon overwhelmed him. Ruby was shaking as he held her, but the nightmare was over. She wasn't going to die. Not now. He would protect her from the virus, from other people, from time. He would tell her about Maria. He would explain. Everything. He . . .

"Help me, Brian."

ACKNOWLEDGEMENTS

The author would like to thank his scouts, Alice, Aurel, and Zouf, as well as Corinne, for the scientific elements of the book.

Thanks also to Christiane, for the gymnastics in southern Africa.

ABOUT THE AUTHOR

Caryl Férey's novel *Utu* won the Sang d'Encre, Michael Lebrun, and SNCF Crime Fiction Prizes. *Zulu*, his first novel to be published in English, was the winner of the Nouvel Obs Crime Fiction Prize, the Critics' Prize for Mystery, the *Elle* Readers Grand Prix, and the Quais du Polar Readers Prize. In 2008, it was awarded the French Grand Prix for Best Crime Novel.

Férey lives in France.

www.europaeditions.com

Carmine Abate
Between Two Seas
"A moving portrayal of generational continuity."
—*Kirkus*
224 pp • $14.95 • 978-1-933372-40-2

Salwa Al Neimi
The Proof of the Honey
"Al Neimi announces the end of a taboo in the Arab world:
that of *sex!*"
—*Reuters*
144 pp • $15.00 • 978-1-933372-68-6

Alberto Angela
A Day in the Life of Ancient Rome
"Fascinating and accessible."
—*Il Giornale*
392 pp • $16.00 • 978-1-933372-71-6

Muriel Barbery
The Elegance of the Hedgehog
"Gently satirical, exceptionally winning and inevitably bittersweet."
—Michael Dirda, *The Washington Post*
336 pp • $15.00 • 978-1-933372-60-0

Gourmet Rhapsody
"In the pages of this book, Barbery shows off her finest gift: lightness."
—*La Repubblica*
176 pp • $15.00 • 978-1-933372-95-2

www.europaeditions.com

Stefano Benni
Margherita Dolce Vita
"A modern fable...hilarious social commentary."—*People*
240 pp • $14.95 • 978-1-933372-20-4

Timeskipper
"Benni again unveils his Italian brand of magical realism."
—*Library Journal*
400 pp • $16.95 • 978-1-933372-44-0

Romano Bilenchi
The Chill
120 pp • $15.00 • 978-1-933372-90-7

Massimo Carlotto
The Goodbye Kiss
"A masterpiece of Italian noir."
—*Globe and Mail*
160 pp • $14.95 • 978-1-933372-05-1

Death's Dark Abyss
"A remarkable study of corruption and redemption."
—*Kirkus* (starred review)
160 pp • $14.95 • 978-1-933372-18-1

The Fugitive
"[Carlotto is] the reigning king of Mediterranean noir."
—*The Boston Phoenix*
176 pp • $14.95 • 978-1-933372-25-9

www.europaeditions.com

(with Marco Videtta)
Poisonville
"The business world as described by Carlotto and Videtta
in *Poisonville* is frightening as hell."
—*La Repubblica*
224 pp • $15.00 • 978-1-933372-91-4

Francisco Coloane
Tierra del Fuego
"Coloane is the Jack London of our times."—Alvaro Mutis
192 pp • $14.95 • 978-1-933372-63-1

Giancarlo De Cataldo
The Father and the Foreigner
"A slim but touching noir novel from one of Italy's best writers
in the genre."—*Quaderni Noir*
144 pp • $15.00 • 978-1-933372-72-3

Shashi Deshpande
The Dark Holds No Terrors
"[Deshpande is] an extremely talented storyteller."—*Hindustan Times*
272 pp • $15.00 • 978-1-933372-67-9

Helmut Dubiel
Deep In the Brain: Living with Parkinson's Disease
"A book that begs reflection."—*Die Zeit*
144 pp • $15.00 • 978-1-933372-70-9

www.europaeditions.com

Steve Erickson
Zeroville
"A funny, disturbing, daring and demanding novel—Erickson's best."
—*The New York Times Book Review*
352 pp • $14.95 • 978-1-933372-39-6

Elena Ferrante
The Days of Abandonment
"The raging, torrential voice of [this] author is something rare."
—*The New York Times*
192 pp • $14.95 • 978-1-933372-00-6

Troubling Love
"Ferrante's polished language belies the rawness of her imagery."
—*The New Yorker*
144 pp • $14.95 • 978-1-933372-16-7

The Lost Daughter
"So refined, almost translucent."—*The Boston Globe*
144 pp • $14.95 • 978-1-933372-42-6

Jane Gardam
Old Filth
"Old Filth belongs in the Dickensian pantheon of memorable characters."
—*The New York Times Book Review*
304 pp • $14.95 • 978-1-933372-13-6

The Queen of the Tambourine
"A truly superb and moving novel."—*The Boston Globe*
272 pp • $14.95 • 978-1-933372-36-5

www.europaeditions.com

The People on Privilege Hill
"Engrossing stories of hilarity and heartbreak."—*Seattle Times*
208 pp • $15.95 • 978-1-933372-56-3

The Man in the Wooden Hat
"Here is a writer who delivers the world we live in…with memorable and moving skill."—*The Boston Globe*
240 pp • $15.00 • 978-1-933372-89-1

Alicia Giménez-Bartlett
Dog Day
"Delicado and Garzón prove to be one of the more engaging sleuth teams to debut in a long time."—*The Washington Post*
320 pp • $14.95 • 978-1-933372-14-3

Prime Time Suspect
"A gripping police procedural."—*The Washington Post*
320 pp • $14.95 • 978-1-933372-31-0

Death Rites
"Petra is developing into a good cop, and her earnest efforts to assert her authority…are worth cheering."—*The New York Times*
304 pp • $16.95 • 978-1-933372-54-9

Katharina Hacker
The Have-Nots
"Hacker's prose soars."—*Publishers Weekly*
352 pp • $14.95 • 978-1-933372-41-9

www.europaeditions.com

Patrick Hamilton
Hangover Square
"Patrick Hamilton's novels are dark tunnels of misery, loneliness, deceit, and sexual obsession."—*New York Review of Books*
336 pp • $14.95 • 978-1-933372-06-

James Hamilton-Paterson
Cooking with Fernet Branca
"Irresistible!"—*The Washington Post*
288 pp • $14.95 • 978-1-933372-01-3

Amazing Disgrace
"It's loads of fun, light and dazzling as a peacock feather."
—*New York Magazine*
352 pp • $14.95 • 978-1-933372-19-8

Rancid Pansies
"Campy comic saga about hack writer and self-styled 'culinary genius' Gerald Samper."—*Seattle Times*
288 pp • $15.95 • 978-1-933372-62-4

Seven-Tenths: The Sea and Its Thresholds
"The kind of book that, were he alive now, Shelley might have written."
—*Charles Spawson*
416 pp • $16.00 • 978-1-933372-69-3

Alfred Hayes
The Girl on the Via Flaminia
"Immensely readable."—*The New York Times*
164 pp • $14.95 • 978-1-933372-24-2

www.europaeditions.com

Jean-Claude Izzo
Total Chaos
"Izzo's Marseilles is ravishing."—*Globe and Mail*
256 pp • $14.95 • 978-1-933372-04-4

Chourmo
"A bitter, sad and tender salute to a place equally impossible to love
or leave."—*Kirkus* (starred review)
256 pp • $14.95 • 978-1-933372-17-4

Solea
"[Izzo is] a talented writer who draws from the deep, dark well of noir."
—*The Washington Post*
208 pp • $14.95 • 978-1-933372-30-3

The Lost Sailors
"Izzo digs deep into what makes men weep."—*Time Out New York*
272 pp • $14.95 • 978-1-933372-35-8

A Sun for the Dying
"Beautiful, like a black sun, tragic and desperate."—*Le Point*
224 pp • $15.00 • 978-1-933372-59-4

Gail Jones
Sorry
"Jones's gift for conjuring place and mood rarely falters."
—*Times Literary Supplement*
240 pp • $15.95 • 978-1-933372-55-6

Matthew F. Jones
Boot Tracks
"A gritty action tale."—*The Philadelphia Inquirer*
208 pp • $14.95 • 978-1-933372-11-2

www.europaeditions.com

Ioanna Karystiani
The Jasmine Isle
"A modern Greek tragedy about love foredoomed and family life."
—Kirkus
288 pp • $14.95 • 978-1-933372-10-5

Swell
"Karystiani movingly pays homage to the sea and those who live from it."
—La Repubblica
256 pp • $15.00 • 978-1-933372-98-3

Gene Kerrigan
The Midnight Choir
"The lethal precision of his closing punches leave quite a lasting mark."
—Entertainment Weekly
368 pp • $14.95 • 978-1-933372-26-6

Little Criminals
"A great story…relentless and brilliant."*—Roddy Doyle*
352 pp • $16.95 • 978-1-933372-43-3

Peter Kocan
Fresh Fields
"A stark, harrowing, yet deeply courageous work of immense power and magnitude."*—Quadrant*
304 pp • $14.95 • 978-1-933372-29-7

The Treatment and the Cure
"Kocan tells this story with grace and humor."*—Publishers Weekly*
256 pp • $15.95 • 978-1-933372-45-7

www.europaeditions.com

Helmut Krausser
Eros
"Helmut Krausser has succeeded in writing a great German epochal novel."—*Focus*
352 pp • $16.95 • 978-1-933372-58-7

Amara Lakhous
Clash of Civilizations Over an Elevator in Piazza Vittorio
"Do we have an Italian Camus on our hands? Just possibly."
—*The Philadelphia Inquirer*
144 pp • $14.95 • 978-1-933372-61-7

Lia Levi
The Jewish Husband
"An exemplary tale of small lives engulfed in the vortex of history."
—*Il Messaggero*
224 pp • $15.00 • 978-1-933372-93-8

Carlo Lucarelli
Carte Blanche
"Lucarelli proves that the dark and sinister are better evoked when one opts for unadulterated grit and grime."—*The San Diego Union-Tribune*
128 pp • $14.95 • 978-1-933372-15-0

The Damned Season
"De Luca…is a man both pursuing and pursued. And that makes him one of the more interesting figures in crime fiction."
—*The Philadelphia Inquirer*
128 pp • $14.95 • 978-1-933372-27-3

Via delle Oche
"Delivers a resolution true to the series' moral relativism."—*Publishers Weekly*
160 pp • $14.95 • 978-1-933372-53-2

www.europaeditions.com

Edna Mazya
Love Burns
"Combines the suspense of a murder mystery with
the absurdity of a Woody Allen movie."—*Kirkus*
224 pp • $14.95 • 978-1-933372-08-2

Sélim Nassib
I Loved You for Your Voice
"Nassib spins a rhapsodic narrative out of the indissoluble
connection between two creative souls."—*Kirkus*
272 pp • $14.95 • 978-1-933372-07-5

The Palestinian Lover
"A delicate, passionate novel in which history and life
are inextricably entwined."
—*RAI Books*
192 pp • $14.95 • 978-1-933372-23-5

Amélie Nothomb
Tokyo Fiancée
"Intimate and honest…depicts perfectly a nontraditional romance."
—*Publishers Weekly*
160 pp • $15.00 • 978-1-933372-64-8

Valeria Parrella
For Grace Received
"A voice that is new, original, and decidedly unique."—*Rolling Stone* (Italy)
144 pp • $15.00 • 978-1-933372-94-5

www.europaeditions.com

Alessandro Piperno
The Worst Intentions
"A coruscating mixture of satire, family epic, Proustian meditation, and erotomaniacal farce."—*The New Yorker*
320 pp • $14.95 • 978-1-933372-33-4

Boualem Sansal
The German Mujahid
"Terror, doubt, revolt, guilt, and despair—a surprising range of emotions is admirably and convincingly depicted in this incredible novel."
—*L'Express* (France)
240 pp • $15.00 • 978-1-933372-92-1

Eric-Emmanuel Schmitt
The Most Beautiful Book in the World
"Eight novellas, parables on the idea of a future, filled with redeeming optimism."—*Lire Magazine*
192 pp • $15.00 • 978-1-933372-74-7

Domenico Starnone
First Execution
"Starnone's books are small theatres of action, both physical and psychological."—*L'Espresso* (Italy)
176 pp • $15.00 • 978-1-933372-66-2

Joel Stone
The Jerusalem File
"Joel Stone is a major new talent."—*Cleveland Plain Dealer*
160 pp • $15.00 • 978-1-933372-65-5

www.europaeditions.com

Benjamin Tammuz
Minotaur
"A novel about the expectations and compromises that humans create for themselves."—*The New York Times*
192 pp • $14.95 • 978-1-933372-02-0

Chad Taylor
Departure Lounge
"There's so much pleasure and bafflement to be derived from this thriller."
—*The Chicago Tribune*
176 pp • $14.95 • 978-1-933372-09-9

Roma Tearne
Mosquito
"Vividly rendered...Wholly satisfying."—*Kirkus*
304 pp • $16.95 • 978-1-933372-57-0

Bone China
"Tearne deftly reveals the corrosive effects of civil strife on private lives and the redemptiveness of art."—*The Guardian*
400 pp • $16.00 • 978-1-933372-75-4

Christa Wolf
One Day a Year: 1960-2000
"Remarkable!"—*The New Yorker*
640 pp • $16.95 • 978-1-933372-22-8

www.europaeditions.com

Edwin M. Yoder Jr.
Lions at Lamb House
"Yoder writes with such wonderful manners, learning, and detachment."
—*William F. Buckley, Jr.*
256 pp • $14.95 • 978-1-933372-34-1

Michele Zackheim
Broken Colors
"A beautiful novel."—*Library Journa*
320 pp • $14.95 • 978-1-933372-37-